An Elegant Façade

Books by Kristi Ann Hunter

HAWTHORNE HOUSE

A Lady of Esteem *
A Noble Masquerade
An Elegant Façade

*e-novella only

HAWTHORNE HOUSE

AN ELEGANT FAÇADE

KRISTI ANN HUNTER

BETHANYHOUSE

a division of Baker Publishing Group
Minneapolis, Minnesota

© 2016 by Kristi Ann Hunter

Published by Bethany House Publishers
11400 Hampshire Avenue South
Bloomington, Minnesota 55438
www.bethanyhouse.com

Bethany House Publishers is a division of
Baker Publishing Group, Grand Rapids, Michigan

Printed in the United States of America

Library of Congress Control Number: 2016930774

ISBN 978-0-7642-1825-5

Scripture quotations are from the King James Version of the Bible.

Cover design by Kathleen Lynch/Black Kat Design
Cover photography by Lee Avison/Trevillion Images

Author represented by Natasha Kern Literary Agency

16 17 18 19 20 21 22   7 6 5 4 3 2 1

To the Giver of Perfect Gifts,
even those we don't understand at the time.

James 1:17

And to Jacob,
for being the voice in my head
when I needed it,
even when I didn't want it.

Author's Note

To readers of *A Noble Masquerade*, I first want to thank you for choosing to continue to visit the Hawthorne family and share their journeys. This book is Georgina's tale and, in true Georgina fashion, she refused to wait patiently for her turn. At the opening of this book, you will find that things are not exactly as you left them at the close of *A Noble Masquerade*. That is because Georgina's story begins before Miranda's ends. I hope you will enjoy this rare opportunity to see a few of the events from a different perspective and know that it won't take long before you'll be venturing into new territory.

If this is your first visit to Hawthorne House, rest assured that you will be able to thoroughly enjoy your time here without any prior knowledge. If what little you see of Miranda's story intrigues you, I invite you to read *A Noble Masquerade* and learn more of her adventure.

And now, *An Elegant Façade*. . . .

Prologue

There was something fascinating about the rhythm of writing, at least when someone else was doing it. Dip the quill, write a line, dip the quill, write a line. The quiet *scritch* of quill against paper broke the silence of the night, accompanied only by Lady Georgina Hawthorne's steady breathing ruffling the yellow curls on the head of the doll clutched against her chest.

She hugged her doll tighter and leaned her head against the doorframe. Mother probably knew she was there. Mother always knew everything that happened in the house, including the fact that Georgina often slipped away from the nursery after Nanny was asleep.

There was nothing nefarious about her midnight wanderings. It was simply that the only time her mother wasn't surrounded by people was in the evening when she sat at her desk, encircled by books, papers, and flickering candlelight.

She was beautiful, peaceful, and everything Georgina wanted to be when she grew up. One day she would be a lady with her own desk and quill, writing important letters deep into the night. Of course, first she had to master holding chalk and writing the letter

A. It wasn't at all the same as holding a watercolor brush. Nanny assured her that it was only a matter of time before Georgina would be writing as smoothly as her mother and sister. Everyone had some difficulty in the beginning.

"You'll be able to see better if you sit in the chair." Mother turned her head and smiled at Georgina, beckoning her forward.

Georgina's bare feet made little noise on the cold wooden floor as she crept closer to the desk, the paint-splattered doll held snuggly under her arm. She clambered into the blue upholstered chair beside the desk and peeked over the edge, eyes glued to the writing rhythm her mother had already returned to.

"What are you doing?"

Mother stopped and set the quill aside before blowing lightly across the page filled with even lines of black scrawl. "I am writing a letter to your aunt. She wrote me this morning about a particularly fine foal, and I am telling her of the new fan you painted yesterday."

Georgina glanced at the paper but couldn't see how all of that black ink could tell Aunt Elizabeth about the green fan covered in purple and gold flowers. "Why?"

Mother laughed and leaned over to kiss Georgina on the head. "Because, my dear, a lady always responds promptly to correspondence. Especially when it is from family. It is one way for a lady to show her esteem for the other person. As to why I'm telling her about your fan, it is because it is such a splendid effort for a girl only five years old."

"Oh." Georgina thought about the many times she'd seen her mother sit at this desk, dipping her quill and writing for what seemed like hours. "You know a lot of people."

Mother smiled as she folded the letter, being careful to smooth the edges evenly. "When one is a duchess, my dear, it seems that everyone wants your opinion about something. Some I hold in higher esteem than others and enjoy trading letters with them, but a lady must always be polite, even in correspondence."

Georgina looked across the desk at the neat pile of papers that had already been folded in a similar manner. To the left of the folded letters sat a large leather-bound book. "Who is getting that one, Mother? You must regard that person most highly."

A laugh bounced around the room as Mother slid the book onto the empty desk in front of her, but the laugh was sad. "These are the estate accounts."

Georgina tucked her doll under her chin, the scraggly yellow hair sticking up and making her cheek itch. "Did you write about my fan in there too?"

"No, dear." This time Mother's laugh was light and joyful, and she reached over to pull Georgina into her lap.

With one arm wrapped around her young daughter, Mother flipped back the cover of the book, revealing more dancing black lines as well as boxes with numbers.

"That's nine." Georgina proudly pointed to a number on the right side of the page.

"Yes, it is. That is how much we paid young Charles to load all the coal bins this week." Mother ran her finger from the number to a word on the left side of the page. "See? I put his name here along with what I paid him for."

Georgina frowned. "But Timothy filled my coal bin last week. Doesn't he still work for us?"

"Yes, but you see Charles has a sick sister, or was it his brother?" Mother frowned and reached for another leather-bound book from the shelf by the desk. The cover was light brown leather, but the edges and spine had darkened, leaving the book with a well-used appearance. She laid it on the desk and flipped through the pages covered with neat, handwritten lines. After turning several pages, Mother ran a finger along the last line written halfway down the page. "Ah, yes, sister. His sister is ill, and his mother is having a difficult time both taking her dolls to the market and taking care of young Clara. So we hired Charles to help them out for a while."

Georgina's eyes widened. "You learned about that from a book? Is it a magic book? Nanny read me a story with magic boots in it, but a magic book would be much more exciting."

"No, darling, the book isn't magic, but it is my little secret. One day when you are running your own household and helping your husband oversee tenants and such, you will need a book like this." Mother slid the book over so Georgina could see better. "Whenever I learn something about one of our people I write it in here. A lady should always know what is going on in her home. If she falters, the entire family will suffer. That is why I write everything down."

"Everything?" Georgina ran her fingers down one page, covered edge to edge with writing.

Mother nodded. "Everything. Every tenant, servant, friend, and peddler. That way your brother . . ." She cleared her throat. "When your brother comes home from school, his people will feel like he still knows them, that he cares, that he is ready to be the duke."

"And one day I'll have a book like this."

Mother nodded. "I would recommend that, yes."

Georgina patted the still-opened estate book. "And I'll have one of these too?"

Mother's eyes grew wet as she wrapped her arm a little tighter around Georgina's shoulders. "God willing, you will never have to do estate accounts. Your father—"

Her voice cracked and it took a few moments for Mother to start speaking again. "Your father always took care of these. One day your brother will take them over from me, but until he finishes school it is up to me to keep things running smoothly. There is a smaller book for the household accounts. I'll teach you about those one day."

Georgina looked up into her mother's blue eyes, still glistening from earlier emotion but strong and steady as they looked at her youngest child. "I want to be a duchess just like you when I grow up, Mother."

With a wide smile, Mother hugged Georgina to her chest. "There aren't that many dukes around, so you might have to settle for an earl. But don't you worry. When you keep your own secret book, everyone will think you the most attentive of ladies. You shall be the envy of the aristocracy. Now, where is Nanny? Did she fall asleep reading to you again?"

Georgina nodded. "Poor little Margery only has one shoe, but Tommy has two and he got to go to London. Margery didn't and she's very sad, but at least the man who took Tommy to London gave Margery two shoes to console herself with."

Mother smiled. "At least you will be able to tell her where you left off when she picks the book up tomorrow. Speaking of shoes, you seem to have left yours behind. Let me finish here and I'll walk you back upstairs."

Georgina waited as Mother sealed the last letter with a dollop of wax and extinguished the candles. In the glow of the remaining lantern, the study looked magical, like something from the stories Nanny fell asleep reading every night. All it needed was a fairy doll like the ones Charles' mother made and sold at the street fairs. One day Georgina would have a study of her own and she would be just like her mother.

Only her study would have fairies.

Chapter 1

LONDON, ENGLAND
SPRING 1813

Perfection, even the fabricated appearance of it, was a nearly impossible feat. Lady Georgina Hawthorne should know. She'd spent the past three years carefully preparing and planning, determined to make her debut Season perfect or, at the very least, convince everyone else it was.

Exuding anything less than complete excellence could lead someone to the truth: that she wasn't just imperfect—she was elementally flawed.

If the sparkling creation nestled in the tissue paper before her was a sign of things to come, her hard work was about to reap handsome rewards. The custom-designed mask was everything she'd hoped it would be.

"It looks even prettier than I imagined." Harriette, Georgina's lady's maid and companion, released the reverent whisper as she extended a hand to brush the cluster of feathers bursting from the top left edge of the mask. "You are remarkable."

Georgina smiled, unable to resist the urge to touch the mask herself. While acknowledgment of the craftsman who constructed the mask should certainly be made, Georgina felt comfortable taking some of the credit for herself. She had given the man very detailed drawings of exactly what she wanted.

"If everything else follows the plan this well, I'll be married and settled by the end of the Season." With a sigh, Georgina slid the lid onto the box, blocking the delicate creation from view. As much as she would enjoy looking at the mask for the next three days, she couldn't risk marring the white silk or bright white feathers before the ball. "Has the dress arrived?"

"It came this morning." Harriette took the box containing the mask and disappeared into Georgina's dressing room. Moments later she reappeared with a large bundle of white in her arms. "It's quite splendid as well."

Georgina fought past her initial excitement over the dress to look at it with a critical eye. If anything needed to be changed they needed to do it now. The ball was only three days away. Even though it was a masked event, it would be Georgina's societal debut. It needed to be more than simply perfect. It had to be exceptional.

It would take a fairly spectacular appearance to make everyone forget what a fool she'd made of herself chasing the Marquis of Raebourne last year before she'd even been officially out of the schoolroom. That was what happened when she let emotion cause her to stray from her plan. The marquis would have suited her needs perfectly, but his absurd interest in a woman of little significance put her prime marital target out of reach.

Even so, she should never have allowed the ensuing panic to convince her to share family gossip with Lady Helena Bell. She should have known Lady Helena wouldn't be able to use the information to successfully break the couple's attachment. It had all been horribly embarrassing, but Georgina had learned a very important lesson: No one else could be counted on to carry out any part of her plans.

This year she would rely only on herself. She looked at her maid, inspecting the skirt for loose threads. And Harriette. Dependable, loyal Harriette could always be relied upon. In fact, Georgina would be lost without her. "Your brother is due to start school soon, isn't he?"

The maid looked up from the dress, plain brown eyes narrowing in her commonly rounded face. She straightened herself the full length of her average height and scolded Georgina with a voice laced with an extraordinary amount of intelligence and tenacity. "You've already taken care of it. I won't take any more of your pin money."

Georgina tried to hide her smile as her friend gave a decisive nod and turned back to the dress.

Though no one else in London would likely believe it, the two were friends. No one on earth knew Georgina as well as Harriette did. Without the other woman's friendship as a child, Georgina would never have been able to keep her shortcomings hidden from her perfect, noble family. As it was, they all thought her a hopelessly spoiled brat, a condition she tried to use in her favor as often as possible. "I could tell Griffith to give you a higher wage. He wouldn't doubt me. Probably thinks you deserve one."

Harriette draped the dress over the bed and crossed the room to grasp Georgina's hands. "Don't fret. I've been with you since you were seven. I'm not going anywhere."

It was hard to believe that Harriette was only two years older than Georgina's eighteen years. Sometimes she seemed too settled and mature for one so young.

Georgina pulled her lip between her teeth. "This is going to work, isn't it?"

"Stop that." Harriette shook a finger at Georgina. "You'll make your lips all cracked and wrinkly if you bite them."

Georgina smoothed a finger along her bottom lip.

The maid nodded before continuing. "Of course it's going to work. We've been through *Debrett's Peerage* three times since last Season, making a list of all the options. We know every unmarried man who fits your requirements. One will come up to snuff. Four of them are even dukes."

"I can hardly marry my brother, so we can consider there to be only three." Georgina held the masquerade dress up to herself and spun around the room, enjoying the novelty of the Elizabethan-styled gown. "Spindlewood is most likely going to be escorting his granddaughter around this Season, though he's been out of mourning long enough to consider remarrying."

"You don't consider him too old?" Harriette's eyes widened as she sank into the chair at Georgina's dressing table.

"I do, as a matter of fact. Were he to die, I would be a very young dowager with no firm ties to the next duke. There's not nearly enough power in that position." Georgina slipped her feet into her slippers and did a final inspection in the mirror. "It's too bad that his grandson is so young. He's not even out of school yet."

Harriette tilted her head to the side. "You could wait for him. He's sure to enter society within the year."

As if Georgina could afford to wait an entire year in the hopes that the duke's grandson would prove as socially proficient as the rest of the family.

Georgina shook her head before carrying the dress into the dressing room for storage. Harriette's light footsteps followed her.

"What I need, Harriette, is for the Duke of Marshington to make a reappearance, seeking the most advantageous bride for his reentry into society. That would set me up for life. I might actually believe God was looking out for me if that were to happen." Which meant she had little to no hope of it happening. She was certain God was up there somewhere, but she was just as certain that He'd tossed her aside long ago.

"There's still one other duke, a marquis, and two earls on your list, though I do wish you would reconsider removing the Earl of Ashcombe. Your sister—"

"My sister should have married him when she had the chance." Georgina checked the reticule she'd had made for the upcoming ball, ensuring it was packed with everything from a spare pair of slippers to a needle and thread for urgent dress repairs. Nothing could be allowed to ruin her night. "Ashcombe is popular, wealthy, and conscious of the importance of reputation. He stays on the list."

Harriette said nothing as she laid a white velvet cloak on the shelf beside the white ball gown.

A pang of guilt nudged the back of Georgina's thoughts. Ashcombe had courted her sister during her first Season, but Miranda was embarking on her fourth turn through the ballrooms this year. She'd had plenty of chances to win the man's hand. Now it was Georgina's turn.

The fact that she thought the man a supreme bore placed him a bit lower on her list, but she'd rather be bored than ruined.

Not for the first time, Georgina wished Miranda had gotten married last year. The threat of Miranda's impending spinsterhood might make Georgina's quest to be the Season's Incomparable a little more difficult. Association carried its own form of guilt, after all.

She pressed her hand to her chest, as if she could reach through and force the nerves into submission.

"Everything is ready, my lady." Harriette fluffed the skirt on the dress until the white-on-white embroidery was shown to perfection.

Georgina's heart calmed as she looked over the ensemble she would wear as she took her first turn in society as an adult. It was the epitome of everything she'd been working to build. Entering on the arm of her brother, the powerful Duke of Riverton, would seal her as one the most popular girls of the evening.

The masquerade was going to be the best event of her life.

This was one the ugliest places he'd ever been in his life.

Colin McCrae glanced over his shoulder at the rickety stairs he'd carefully picked his way up. They looked even worse from the top than they had from the bottom, which meant he'd be holding his breath when it came time to travel back down them.

Assuming he lived that long. Calling on his friend Ryland without warning wasn't the safest thing to do. Spies for the Crown tended to be a little wary of things like that. Fortunately, the man was inclined to look first and shoot second, a politeness that could probably be attributed to the fact that the man was also the Duke of Marshington. He may have dropped out of society for the past nine years, but he'd had eighteen years before that to learn gentlemanly behavior.

The passage at the top of the stairs looked as if someone had at least considered doing some maintenance in the past decade. In truth, it wasn't the worst place Colin had visited Ryland in the five years they'd known each other, but it was close.

He took care to keep his greatcoat away from some of the grimier-looking shadows. Just because Ryland chose to eschew the finer things in life to pursue English justice didn't mean Colin had to.

After three strong knocks on the grey wooden door, Colin stepped back, positioning himself so that whoever cracked open the door would be able to see him.

The door opened enough to reveal the face and shoulder of Jeffreys. The man was Ryland's valet, though his duties included far more clandestine activities than simply shining the duke's shoes. This was probably the only set of rooms in the entire building that could boast a manservant of any kind.

Colin grinned at the thin man. "Please don't shoot me, Jeffreys. I'm quite fond of this coat."

Jeffreys laughed as he opened the door wider and allowed Colin in. Sure enough, Jeffreys had been hiding a pistol behind his back as he answered the door.

Another, deeper, laugh came from the next room, and Colin followed it to find Ryland sprawled in a chair that could be called upholstered if one was feeling charitable. There were a series of threads covering whatever remained of the chair's cushioning.

Ryland waved an arm toward the only other chair in the room, a plain wooden chair that looked old but sturdy. "What brings you by?"

Colin sat, crossed his booted feet at the ankles, and placed his hat in his lap. "Other than the joy of welcoming you back to Town, you mean?"

A single dark eyebrow lifted in an expression of condescension, the aristocratic arrogance of the duke showing through, despite the fact that Ryland looked considerably more like a dockside worker. "I haven't officially returned."

"And I'm not officially here." Ryland worked for the War Office. Colin didn't. At least not in any capacity that anyone would recognize as official. He had been known, on occasion, to use his business contacts and observation skills to assist them in one project or another. Though he made sure to say no often enough to keep the War Office from taking advantage, he never turned down a request from Ryland.

It was the developments from just such a request that had brought him to this decrepit building.

Ryland sat up a little straighter. "You have news?"

Colin nodded. Ryland had recently disguised himself as a valet on the Duke of Riverton's estate. As the two were old school friends, Riverton was, of course, in on the plan and had agreed to engage in false correspondence in order to trap the group of Napoleonic spies operating on the estate. Colin's contribution had been business letters about a doomed mining venture.

The decoy information, originally intended to be little more than fluff to fill out the fake correspondence, was actually being used. As only the people selling secrets to France had access to that information, the interest in the mine was certainly suspect.

While Colin filled Ryland in on the details, Jeffreys went about his business, moving quietly around the room.

A glaze of deep thought covered Ryland's grey eyes. Colin settled into his wooden chair as best he could, knowing the other man could contemplate the ramifications of Colin's news for five minutes or five hours, and he would expect Colin to be there when he was done.

"All the more reason to come out of hiding, Your Grace." Jeffreys hauled a small trunk from under the bed and began folding clothes into it.

Colin sat up a bit, mild curiosity replaced with genuine surprise.

Was Ryland truly planning to come out of hiding? It would be a good time for it, with the social Season prepared to start within the week.

Instead of berating the other man for interrupting his thought process, Ryland turned his intense gaze to the valet. Clearly there was a hidden meaning to Jeffreys' proclamation. "And have you also planned where I shall make my debut?"

Only years of practice at remaining outwardly calm kept Colin in his seat. Ryland was not only returning to London but to society as well? Was this a new project? A new case that required he come out of hiding? Or was he truly following through on his intentions to stop spying?

Jeffreys extracted a small white card from his pocket and flipped it across the bed. Ryland snatched it out of midair, crumpling the corner a bit.

Colin strained to get a look at the card. It looked like an invitation. Who would have sent Ryland an invitation? Half of London thought he was dead.

"She's going to be there?" Ryland ran a thumb along the edge of the card.

Jeffreys nodded. "The servants have been speaking constantly of the various costumes their lords and ladies have procured. That invitation was meant for your aunt. Price said it was a shame she never received it."

Ryland looked over the card and grinned. Grinned. The jaded, world-weary spy grinned.

Colin rose and leaned over Ryland's shoulder, his thoughts ticking through everything that had been said or done since he arrived. The invitation was for a masquerade ball, but that fact paled as the importance of Jeffreys' statement became evident. There was a girl involved, and by the look on Ryland's face, she wasn't related to his work.

And since it was personal, Ryland wasn't about to volunteer information. Colin turned instead to the valet. "There's a she?"

"What is her costume going to be?" Ryland tapped the invitation against his palm, probably hoping he could learn what he wanted without letting Colin ask any questions of his own. Which made Colin all the more determined to know who the *she* was.

Jeffreys continued packing as he spoke. "We aren't sure, though we know it's blue. She and her sister and mother were all seen at the modiste ordering dresses for that event. The sister was quite excited. The mother was less so."

"Not surprising." Ryland's face turned thoughtful once more. He seemed to have forgotten Colin was in the room. "Masquerades are not known for keeping the faint blush of youth in a young lady's cheeks. I wonder at Lady Blackstone letting that be Lady Georgina's first society appearance."

Colin had never met the Ladies Hawthorne or their recently remarried mother, Lady Blackstone, but he had done business with their eldest brother, the Duke of Riverton—whose estate Ryland had recently been spying on in the guise of the duke's valet.

This was going to end badly.

Colin coughed. "Lady Georgina Hawthorne?"

Even though Colin hadn't met the young lady, he'd certainly heard of her. And what he'd heard would have made her the last lady he'd have expected Ryland to become interested in.

"The hostess, Lady Yensworth, is a particular friend of Lady Blackstone's—otherwise I'm sure they would be skipping the event." Jeffreys pulled a pair of ruined-looking boots from the bottom of the closet. "Are we keeping these?"

Ryland raised a brow. "Why wouldn't we?"

"Your Grace." The valet tilted his head to the side.

Ryland's brows drew together. "What?"

"Only reminding you that you are a duke. I don't know a whole lot about the aristocracy, but I know they don't wear boots that look like this."

Normally Colin would have settled into the corner, content to gather as much information as possible from a personal conversation taking place in his presence. But this time he could not afford to misunderstand what was happening. It was simply too unbelievable.

He stood and grabbed Ryland's shoulder, unable to keep the shock from his face. "You've intentions to court Lady Georgina Hawthorne?"

Colin couldn't picture it. Ryland was a gentleman to the core, but he'd lived too long in the shadows for all of his edges to stay refined. He'd rip a delicate society flower to shreds.

"What? No." Ryland shifted in his seat, looking as uncomfortable as Colin had ever seen.

Colin turned an inquiring look to Jeffreys. Something was disturbing the normally unflappable duke, and being the good friend that he was, Colin couldn't wait to hold it over the other man's head.

Jeffreys frowned at the old boots. "The older sister, sir."

"Ah." Colin relaxed considerably and grinned. He hadn't heard as much about Lady Miranda, but he'd heard enough to know she'd be a much better fit for a man who'd spent the past nine years hiding in the shadows. Any woman willing to turn down multiple offers of marriage had to possess a considerable amount of courage. Something that could be necessary if danger decided to follow Ryland home.

Ryland glared at Jeffreys as the valet strode about the room gathering items. "Why are you telling Mr. McCrae my secrets, Jeffreys? Isn't your loyalty supposed to be to me?"

"Of course, Your Grace. That's why I didn't tell Mr. McCrae that you've been brooding over the young lady since you left your position at her house several months ago." Jeffreys threw the dilapidated boots into the trunk. "Only the least discreet of valets would reveal that you've actually paced the floor as you've contemplated what you'd do when she returned to London."

Colin laughed so hard he fell back into his chair, holding his right hand to his side. Ryland had left Riverton's house before Christmas, after sending the band of treasonists fleeing to hide in the large city. Spring was now nudging at London's edges. The idea that he'd been pining for a woman that long was entertaining indeed.

Ryland turned his glare from the valet to send a calculating look at Colin. "I don't suppose you received an invitation to this dance?"

Colin swallowed his laughter and nodded. He should have known he wouldn't escape being pulled into whatever scheme Ryland and his valet had concocted. In all honesty, if it included watching Ryland dangle on a hook, Colin didn't want to miss it. "I have. I hadn't intended to go, but if you're going to be there, I'll have to change my plans. The *ton* won't know what to do with such an interesting piece of gossip."

Ryland tapped the card into his palm. "I think a masquerade will do nicely. I can ease her into the idea of my being in Town without her recognizing me."

A groan trapped itself in Colin's throat. Lady Miranda had already met Ryland, only not in the form of a duke. She knew Ryland as her brother's valet, the role he'd played while he investigated the French spies in Hertfordshire. Obviously the woman had made a considerable impression on Ryland, and it was possible he'd made an impression on her as well, despite his posing as a servant. No amount of esteem was going to make a woman happy that she'd been deceived for months, though.

And there was no easing someone into a revelation of that magnitude.

Not to mention the fact that Ryland was still, as far as Colin knew, actively seeking the Napoleonic spy who had gotten away. "What about the case?"

The other man shrugged. "Every lead but one is stone-cold. Another agent of the War Office can follow Lambert as easily as I can."

Colin looked at Jeffreys, who shook his head, silently agreeing with Colin that there was nothing to be done to change Ryland's mind. Clearly, the duke wasn't thinking straight.

Ryland's life was about to get very complicated. And Colin planned to be right in the middle of it.

After all, watching Ryland muddle his way through such a revelation was going to be too much fun to miss.

Chapter 2

"I think I pulled the mask too tight." Harriette frowned as she slid a finger along Georgina's forehead, tracing the edge of the white jeweled mask.

"Leave it." Georgina put up a hand to stop Harriette from loosening the white silk ribbon. In truth, the edges were biting into her skin, but she didn't want to lose the benefit of the hours spent making the mask frame her eyes and hair to perfection.

"Very well." Harriette adjusted a curl on Georgina's coiffure as she frowned.

Georgina turned her head, making sure that the artful blond curls fell behind the mask in such a way that it hid the fact her ears weren't exactly even. Nothing could be left open to criticism tonight. She had only one chance to create the right first impression.

She rose to prance across the room, ensuring that her dress wouldn't bind or scratch during the dancing. The silken skirts swished pleasantly against her legs, but the bodice was going to take some getting used to. The structured front panel and dropped waist were very striking but also very restrictive to a woman who'd grown up with her skirts flowing freely about her middle.

The white-on-white embroidery that decorated the bodice felt stiff under her fingers as she ran a hand over the structured panels.

Thank goodness she didn't have to strap herself into a dress like this every day.

Georgina shook her head before turning to the mirror to check the fit of the mask once more. She tried smiling, laughing, and even pantomimed the act of drinking. Yes, the mask had been designed very well.

"This night is going to be perfect, Harriette. Everything is going to go according to plan."

Harriette said nothing as she helped Georgina arrange the white velvet cloak around her shoulders.

Curving her lips into the coy-yet-innocent smile she'd been practicing for the past year, Georgina curtsied before the maid. "How do I look?"

"Like an angel." Harriette's smile was as genuine as Georgina's was fake, but they were the only ones who knew that. Anyone who saw the maid wrap Georgina in a light hug, carefully avoiding the elaborately curled hair, would think both women were happy about the night's potential. "Good luck, my lady."

Georgina returned the hug. "I have a plan, dear Harriette. I don't need luck." She'd used up all her luck the day she met Harriette. Life hadn't seen fit to grant her any more since then, and it wasn't likely to start now.

The corridor was empty as she stepped out of her room and took a final, fortifying breath before moving to the stairs. Anxiety jumped around her middle, threatening to make her ill.

As her hand wrapped around the newel post and her foot landed on the top stair, her frazzled nerves were joined by heady anticipation. Three years of practice and planning were coming to fruition. The past year had thrown an obstacle or two in her path, but now everything was in place. All she had to do was execute the plan and all of London would fall at her feet.

Then her only task would be to keep them there.

Griffith, Duke of Riverton, Georgina's elder brother, was the first to greet her at the bottom of the stairs. "An angel in white. What a departure from your normal appearance."

Georgina tipped her head to the side, trying to appear bored by his sardonic statement. She'd worn nothing but white for the past two years. It was flattering on her, left a dramatic impression, and was easily altered so that she never appeared to wear the same dress twice. Exhausting, yes, but it only added to the impression of legendary elegance. At least she hoped it did.

He offered her his arm, and Georgina was grateful that she'd practiced this as well. Her brother was tall, broad, and imposing. An asset when dealing with ducal business, but incredibly awkward when a woman was trying to find a flattering way to take his arm, even if she was a bit taller than average.

Her mother looked her over with a small smile, so similar to Georgina's own. "Do not listen to him. You look delightful."

Lord Blackstone, the earl Mother married two years ago, murmured his agreement. Miranda gave the smile of an older sister. Even the blue mask tied across her face couldn't hide the fact that Miranda was less than thrilled to be sharing this evening with her younger sister. Georgina lifted her chin a bit higher and strode across the hall.

Each step toward the coach made everything a bit more real. The roses on the hall table smelled stronger the closer she drew to the door. The night air felt sharper as it rushed through the open portal to meet them. Even the rattle of passing traffic had an edge to it this evening. Everything was louder, brighter, as if the magnitude of the evening lent the world more intensity.

Georgina climbed the carriage steps behind Miranda, trying to shake herself of any fanciful thoughts. It was an evening like any other. She had a plan, and as long as she didn't allow emotion to cloud her thoughts as it had last year, she would execute her plan perfectly and all would be well.

Mother and Lord Blackstone settled onto the seat across from the sisters as Griffith shut the door and moved to his own carriage. Georgina would ride home with him, but Mother wanted to arrive with her youngest daughter. It was Georgina's first ball, after all.

A prickling numbness crept through Georgina's fingers and

up her arms as she smoothed her skirts onto the seat beside her elder sister. The sharp contrast of Georgina's stark white dress next to Miranda's bright blue one gave Georgina pause. Was she doing the right thing? Did her penchant for white make her appear unapproachable instead of valuable?

"How do I look?" she blurted before she could stop herself.

Assurance that her dress was flattering and her hair immaculate came from her mother and Lord Blackstone, but Miranda simply turned to look out the window. Georgina's eyes narrowed at her sister. It wasn't Georgina's fault Miranda was going into her fourth Season without a viable marriage prospect in sight. The woman was entirely too particular, turning away more than one perfectly acceptable proposal.

What if people assumed Georgina was of the same mind as Miranda? Would the gentlemen avoid her? Nerves tightened Georgina's stomach until there was a very real chance she was going to need the carriage to pull over.

There had to be something she could think about that would keep her from worrying herself into a simpering miss who held up the wall in the back corner of the ballroom.

"What are you again?" Georgina ran a hand over the gauzy overlay on Miranda's blue skirt. The color did wonders for Miranda's complexion. Their complexions were similar but just enough different that Miranda had never really been able to wear white well. Another reason Georgina had gravitated to it. People would never think she wasn't as good as her sister.

"The sky," Miranda mumbled.

Mother frowned. "I thought you said you were a bird."

Lord Blackstone laughed. "Told me she was the ocean."

Miranda grinned. "I guess I shall be a woman of mystery, then."

Her sister was a fool. How could Miranda leave so much up to chance? If she didn't take control and guide people's impressions of her, they might come up with anything. Confidence was an admirable trait, but not if it caused a woman to miss the many opportunities Miranda had.

Her foolish sister should have spent her time in Town last spring securing her future. Instead she'd poured her efforts into Griffith's new ward, turning her into an acceptable match for the Marquis of Raebourne. If Miranda had done as she should have, Georgina would have been making her bow alone this evening, the marquis would still be available, and all of her carefully laid marital plans would still have been intact. But Miranda hadn't done as she ought, and the whole situation had turned into a giant mess that threatened to topple Georgina's success before she'd stepped into her first ballroom.

The tingling in Georgina's fingers spread through her arms and down to her toes. What if she couldn't guide people to the appropriate impression? She curled her hands into fists and tuned out the rest of the conversation. Distraction was not what she needed after all. She needed to remember who she was before she stepped out of this carriage.

She was Lady Georgina Hawthorne, sister of the Duke of Riverton.

Lady Georgina Hawthorne was not lacking in confidence.

Lady Georgina Hawthorne knew every conversational trick there was.

Lady Georgina Hawthorne could tell you the pertinent information about everyone who was anyone and could easily identify those who were, for her intentions, no one.

A rush of fresh air swept through the carriage, drawing her attention to the open door, a yawning hole of noise, color, and movement. Darkness crept into the corner of Georgina's vision as she looked at the people cutting through the candlelight to enter the house.

She took a deep breath and admitted the truth, if only to herself.

Lady Georgina Hawthorne was scared.

⁓

"That is a brilliant shade of orange you're wearing." Colin tried and failed to keep the slight grin from gracing his face as he mocked Ryland's costume. The Duke of Marshington, recently retired spy and knife expert, was dressed in the shockingly eye-catching costume of an eighteenth-century French courtier.

The result was even better than Colin had imagined when he'd given Jeffreys the idea.

The corners of Ryland's mouth tightened below his mask as he adjusted the swaths of lace dripping from the sleeve of his garish orange brocade coat.

"The shoes are a nice touch." Colin bumped Ryland's clunky-heeled buckle shoe with his own more refined and considerably more comfortable-looking evening shoe.

"I'm glad you are enjoying yourself." The low grumble in Ryland's voice inflated Colin's grin even more.

He was enjoying himself, even though he'd done nothing but stand in this corner since they arrived ten minutes prior. For the first time in recent memory, Colin was attending a social function with the simple intent of having fun. Such society events were almost always enjoyable, but his enjoyment typically came from bettering his business skills, which involved pursuing advantageous connections and insightful gossip the way a fresh-faced debutante pursued an eligible earl.

But tonight he wasn't here on business. Tonight he was going to sit back and watch Ryland try to win the heart of the lady who had captured his attention.

Though nothing was going to happen if they lurked in the curtained alcove behind the refreshments all evening. Colin narrowed his eyes at his friend. Was it possible Ryland was nervous? Maybe he needed something other than the woman who had stolen his heart to focus on for a moment.

"You know what they say about you, don't you?" Colin leaned one shoulder against the wall and crossed his ankles.

Ryland glanced at him. "Who?"

"Them." Colin gave a sweeping nod, indicating the swirling crowd of London's elite. "It's one of their favorite games—trying to figure out where you've been."

Ryland grunted.

"Some say you're wasting away from some dread disease. Others assume you've a hideous disfigurement you're trying to hide." Colin pretended to brush some lint from Ryland's shoulder. "My favorite, though, is the one about you running off to be a privateer. It's grown rather elaborate. Did you know you've got an entire band of ruffians hiding out on a secluded island in the Orkneys? Some claim it's the Caribbean, but I like the Orkneys story better. It's more original."

Ryland grunted again.

Colin glanced around, hoping for inspiration. Eventually someone was going to see them and make things even more awkward. The distraction he needed stepped up to the punch bowl only a few steps away from their hidden alcove. Who better to spur Ryland into action than the brother of the lady he was here to see? Not the eldest brother, granted, but Colin had met Lord Trent a time or two and knew the man would welcome the conversation.

Ryland narrowed his gaze as Colin stepped to the punch bowl, but he followed without question.

"Do you remember Lord Trent?" Colin gestured toward the tall blond man while procuring his own glass of watered-down punch.

"Of course," Ryland said.

Lord Trent's eyebrows rose enough to cause wrinkles to appear above his black domino mask. His green gaze swept up and down Ryland's garish outfit. "That's an exceedingly bold choice of outfit. I applaud anyone daring enough to wear such an ensemble, but I can't quite place you. Have we met?"

Colin took a sip of his drink, reminding himself not to wince at the weak, sour flavor. "The Duke of Marshington."

Ryland sighed.

Colin grinned.

Lord Trent's jaw went a bit slack. "In truth? Were it anyone but Mr. McCrae, I'd refuse to believe it, but I've never known him to jest about such a thing."

Shaking back the lace, Ryland displayed the signet ring on his right hand. Everyone in England knew Ryland kept a tight hold on that ring. His cousin, Gregory Montgomery, had been trying to claim the title since Ryland disappeared, but it was hard to declare a man dead when he kept sending letters sealed with his crest. It was dangerous for the man to carry such a personal article on missions, but he hadn't been a day without it since he inherited the title as a child.

Lord Trent grinned as he clapped a hand on Ryland's shoulder. "It's been an age. I haven't seen you since Eton."

Colin sipped as the two men caught up on old times and school memories. At twenty-six, Colin was a year younger than Ryland and two or three years older than Lord Trent. The two men couldn't have spent much time together in school, though Ryland's close friendship with Lord Trent's elder brother probably allowed them to interact more than other students of that age difference.

Despite his personal vow for a business-free evening, Colin found himself looking over the ballroom with an assessing eye. Nearly all the ladies were in costume, as were most of the men. A few, including Colin himself, had simply added a domino mask to their normal evening attire. Lord Trent had put a bit more effort into the evening, donning a black medieval-styled tunic over tight breeches.

There were three men in the corner, no doubt talking horse races. Mr. Townsend rarely talked of anything else.

Lady Elizabeth, distinctly short and round even in her Grecian costume, was dancing with Mr. Burnside. That would make his father, Lord Trotham, very happy. And when Lord Trotham was happy, he tended to ignore some of his holdings.

Colin made a mental note to contact Trotham's estate manager to ensure Trotham's sawmill in Essex was being properly managed. The rest of the viscount's holdings were none of Colin's business, but he'd taken an interest in the sawmill last year. It had been a sound investment so far, but Trotham had been concerned about his son settling down for the past two years.

Mention of Gentleman Jack's boxing facility pulled Colin's attention back to the men in front of him. Lord Trent had always been an exceptional athlete, but Colin didn't know he'd been training with the legendary boxer. If Ryland's confession to Lord Trent's sister didn't go well, those skills could cause a problem for Ryland. The cup of punch wasn't wide enough to hide the grin that split Colin's face, but the sour smell and the weak taste were enough to help him control it.

The conversation lulled, and Colin opened his mouth to ask Lord Trent about his plans for the Season, but a blinding swirl of white entered their circle, robbing the words from his tongue.

"Good evening." A feminine voice rolled into his ears like the soft waves on the beach of a sheltered cove. He couldn't stop the accompanying shiver as he turned his eyes to the source.

The white blur settled into the most beautiful creature Colin had ever seen. Golden curls spilled over her head, woven through with a string of pearls. The mask covered a good portion of her face, but delightful green eyes were easily visible, the slight tilt to the corners making him curious to discover her secrets.

His gaze swept down, taking in the Elizabethan-styled white gown, trimmed with feathers in such a way that she appeared to be floating. God was certainly having a good day when He made this angel.

Lord Trent nodded to the lady and then smiled at someone over her shoulder. "Griffith, you won't believe who I've found."

Colin dragged his eyes from the vision in white to the enormous man standing next to her. The Duke of Riverton was dressed much as Colin was, though not for the same reason. As the man who handled a good bit of Riverton's investments, Colin knew the duke needn't be concerned about the cost of an outfit intended for a single evening. For that matter, neither did Colin, but the fear of destitution was hard to move past, even all these years later.

"What a splendid coat." Riverton looked over Ryland's outfit and didn't even try to hide his amused grin. "I was wondering if you would make an appearance tonight."

Ryland reached a hand to smooth the ruffles marching down his chest. The signet ring caught the light from a nearby candle, causing it to glint amongst the lacy frills.

A quick gasp parted the lips of the beauty at Lord Trent's side. Her eyes widened, and she briefly snagged her bottom lip between her teeth as she stared at Ryland's hand. Obviously she recognized the ring.

Ryland seemed oblivious as he answered Riverton. "I told you that I would see you in London."

Colin lifted the cup of punch to his lips to hide his smile as the lady's face and body melted into a position that flattered every curve and curl she possessed. He didn't dare drink any of the unpleasant liquid for fear the laughter he was holding back would escape.

As the three aristocratic gentlemen continued to talk about the effects of Ryland's return, Colin took in the increasingly agitated woman in their midst. Her smile never faltered, but her glare was becoming quite pointed as no one saw fit to introduce her to Ryland.

Brilliant green eyes. Golden blond hair. Her hand on the arm of the unmarried Duke of Riverton, but paying him little or no attention. This had to be Lady Georgina, the duke's youngest sister. A woman completely out of Colin's reach, not that such a quality gave her much distinction in this room. Colin rarely encountered a woman who would consider his station and position an acceptable match.

He'd rarely encountered a woman of this much beauty either. Even with the mask and the abundance of feathers, she was as magnificent as the rumors claimed.

And the rumors had claimed quite a lot. The woman was nearly legend. He'd never seen society anticipate a lady's first bow as much as they had Lady Georgina's. Given that the young lady had a sister out in the ballrooms already, he'd never understood the fascination.

Until now.

Chapter 3

Colin struggled to contain his amusement as the lady gave a dainty cough and glared at her brothers. No doubt their continued inane conversation about Ryland's unexpected attendance was intended to annoy Lady Georgina. It appeared to be working.

Colin took a few steps to his left to reach for a fresh glass of punch. He slid around behind Lord Trent and offered the cup to Lady Georgina. "Might I offer you some refreshment?"

Her eyes widened as they went from the cup to his face. Was she trying to place him? Wondering if they'd met? In all the times he'd visited Hawthorne House to see Riverton, Colin had never met the sisters, had only seen Lady Miranda twice. And since he took great care to keep himself out of the local gossip papers, she was unlikely to have even heard of him. Let her wonder. Maybe that would give Ryland time to escape and find Lady Miranda.

A glance at the trio of men now working to hide their own grins showed that Ryland had no intention of slipping off. Colin nodded toward the punch cup once more. "Terribly forward of me, I know, seeing as we've not been introduced, but I can't bear to see a lady ignored."

"Yes, of course." She took the punch as if she'd never seen a drink in her life. "Thank you."

Riverton patted Lady Georgina on the hand. "My apologies. Are we supposed to perform introductions? This is a masquerade, after all."

Lady Georgina tilted her head, managing to look at Riverton but smile at Ryland in the same motion. Most impressive. "I can hardly dance with a gentleman I don't know."

Riverton tilted his head. "That is true. Gentlemen, may I present my sister, Lady Georgina. Georgina, this is His Grace, the Duke of Marshington, and Mr. Col—"

Lady Georgina's gasp cut off the introduction of Colin. "Duke, is it truly you? I've heard about you for years, of course. What brings you back to London?"

Cheeky girl, but charming. Colin was, fortunately, well accustomed to being on the ignored fringes of society. He wasn't aristocratic, wasn't even gentry. What he was, was very, very good with money. He had an eye for investments, a good head for business, and a golden touch with new ventures. For a group of people who required a lot of money to maintain their preferred lifestyle, that made him a sought-after commodity.

That didn't make him popular.

Ryland set his punch down and reached for Lady Georgina's hand. "Might I have the next dance?"

Experience in restraint kept Colin's eyebrows from flying up. Ryland was here for the elder Hawthorne sister. What was he doing asking the younger one to dance?

Colin's gaze cut from his friend to the woman in white. There was more smiling and head tilting. Did she practice in a mirror? This had to be only Lady Georgina's first or second time out in society. That kind of confidence and skill usually came with experience.

"I would be delighted, Your Grace."

Within moments they were lost among the blur of other couples in the intricate steps of a quadrille. It was a fairly new one. When had Ryland had time to learn it?

Colin shrugged and finished his punch. Ryland never did anything without a plan, so there was a reason he'd asked Lady Georgina to dance. Even if Colin was fairly certain it meant the plan was a bad one, there was nothing he could do about it.

"I must apologize once more," Riverton said.

Colin waved a hand in dismissal. "It's not a bother. Women usually ignore me at these events, unless they have the misfortune of being sat next to me at dinner."

Lord Trent grinned. "I've sat near you at dinner. You managed to use all the correct utensils and didn't slurp the soup."

Colin smiled but didn't respond as there was no need to answer. All three men were well aware of the social ladder and where Colin sat upon it. That the Hawthorne brothers chose to ignore the vast chasm between his status and their own was a boon, but not one he expected from most others of their echelon.

"Have you been here long?" Riverton asked Lord Trent.

"But a quarter hour at the most. Hadn't time to do more than glance over the crush before I looked up and found Ryland looking ridiculous."

Colin grinned. "It looks even better than I'd hoped."

Riverton looked impressed. "You are responsible for that frippery?"

"Only the idea." Colin shook his head. "I'm afraid the brilliance of execution must be laid at Jeffreys' feet."

Where was Lady Miranda? Colin looked over the crowd, though there was little chance he'd recognize her in a mask. She was there somewhere, though, and Ryland probably knew what she was wearing, which made Colin wonder once more what Ryland was doing dancing with Lady Georgina. Given her obvious intentions a few moments ago, future family gatherings were going to be a bit uncomfortable if Ryland had his way in courting Lady Miranda.

"Will you be in Town for the Season, Colin?" Riverton asked, turning from the dance floor.

"I don't know yet. I may take a trip in a month or so to see some investments to the west." Colin hadn't planned on taking the trip until after summer, but a persistent itch had spread through him as

38

the Season approached. Restlessness was not something he really knew what to do with. Despite the fact that London didn't hold much in common with Glasgow, the Scottish port city he'd grown up in, when he'd all but run away from his family five years ago there hadn't been much question of where he would go. He'd felt at home in the big city the first time he'd set foot in it.

But five years was a long time. Part of him wondered if this craving to leave London had something to do with a hidden desire to venture north. If so, he was doomed to disappointment. There was little chance his father would welcome him home, even if he wanted to try.

"They've greatly improved the road west in the past few years," Riverton said.

Lord Trent nodded. "Especially if you're in a carriage with those new elliptical springs. I rode in one a few months ago. You can barely tell you're moving."

Colin knew about the springs. He'd missed the opportunity to invest in them but was watching to see what other innovations might be inspired by the new springs. Before he could add to the conversation, movement in the crowd caught his eye.

Several mothers were maneuvering their daughters closer to the refreshment table. The broad shoulders of the eligible Duke of Riverton had been spotted, and soon they were ensconced in polite conversation in which Colin was even more politely ignored.

It was possible this constant invisibility was the true source of his insatiable disquiet. Lady Georgina might be the most striking woman he'd seen of late, but she wasn't the only one he'd noticed. The urge to settle down, marry, pass on his faith to a new generation was growing.

And he didn't know what to do about it.

It was interesting to circulate among the cream of society, but very disconcerting to know that none of the young ladies he saw on a regular basis would consider him an eligible match. The exotic green eyes of Lady Georgina flashed through his head again.

Her brothers gave every indication of not caring about the social differences. Was there a chance she might feel the same way?

Riverton and Lord Trent selected women from the surrounding crowd to take on the dance floor. The rest of the mingling ladies dispersed, none of them interested in attracting Colin's hand.

Unable to stop the habit, Colin took the circuitous route to the side of the dance floor. Men, deep in their cups, confident they were safe among peers, talked openly about issues and successes. A little bit here, a snatch of conversation there, and Colin could piece together a vision of what would succeed and what would fail. It sounded as if Mr. Martin's plantation was finally starting to produce. Colin would pay the man a visit in a few days and see who was lined up to ship the goods.

"Thank you for the dance, Lady Georgina."

Ryland's voice drew Colin's attention away from the conversation behind him. His eyes narrowed as Ryland walked Lady Georgina to the pillar where Colin was standing. He was not gathering information for his friend. Not here. Not about this.

"It was my pleasure, Duke." Lady Georgina looked a touch confused as she looked around. No wonder. Her brothers and her mother—typical people for a gentleman to leave his dancing partner with—were nowhere to be found. Despite her confusion, she turned an adoring look on the duke. "I do love to dance with such a graceful partner."

"Have you met my friend, Mr. McCrae?"

Colin was going to kill Ryland. Well, not kill. They'd saved each other's necks too often for Colin to even jokingly consider harming him. But there was definitely retribution in Ryland's future.

"I don't believe I've had the pleasure." A small frown line appeared at the top of the lady's mask. Surely she remembered him from a few moments ago. Her gaze narrowed slightly, weakening Colin's slight hope that she would be as welcoming as her brothers.

"My lady." Colin bowed and accepted her hand from Ryland.

Ryland grinned. "I see someone with whom I must speak."

Colin glared. The black domino mask probably dampened the

impact of it, not that he had much chance of intimidating a man of Ryland's experience even if he deserved the icy glare. The scoundrel was leaving him standing in the corner of the ballroom holding the hand of the woman everyone expected to be the Season's Diamond.

There was only one acceptable thing to do.

There was a science to being popular. One had to have the right connections and be seen with the right people, of course, but there was a great deal more to it than that. Too much time spent with the less worthy would diminish your status, but too little gave a person an air of snobbishness instead of discretion. It was all about the proper balance.

Which presented Georgina with quite a conundrum, because she and Harriette had studied *Debrett's Peerage* in detail, and not a single McCrae had been listed that she could recall. Three years of poring over every society column in reach hadn't revealed his name either.

She resisted the urge to pull her hand from the man's grasp. He was certainly handsome—from what could be seen around the mask, at least. Chestnut brown hair with just a hint of red in it swept back from his forehead, a nearby candle flame revealed the clear blue eyes behind his mask. And though his smile looked a bit tight, it gave the impression that the man was friendly—a rarity in a London ballroom.

Not that any of that mattered. Good looks and personality were only advantageous if the man also possessed popularity. Dwelling in a corner with someone so far beneath her that he was practically off the ladder made the balance very precarious.

"May I have the honor of this dance?" He inclined his head toward the crowd of dancers.

"The honor is mine." She smiled her kind-but-disinterested smile and let him lead her to the floor. What else could she do? The Duke of Marshington obviously thought well of this man, as did her brothers. She couldn't risk offending him.

Unfortunately, they joined one of the simpler dances, which allowed adequate time for conversation between the couples. Why couldn't she and the duke have danced this one instead of such a physically exhausting one? Their dance had been much too rushed to do anything more than smile at each other.

"Have you known the duke long?" Georgina asked. She might as well utilize this time as best she could.

"Which one?" Mr. McCrae's grip was firm but gentle as they joined hands to circle another couple.

"Either. Both." His closeness to her brothers was nearly as important as his closeness to Marshington.

"I've known your brother for about three years."

They split and allowed another couple to pass between them. Georgina waited until they came back together to speak again. "And Marshington?"

"Longer."

Longer? That told her nothing. Marshington had been absent from society for the past nine years. How did this man factor in to that absence? "How interesting. You are not from London, then?"

She winced as one corner of Mr. McCrae's mouth tilted up. While she couldn't quite place the light accent that coated his words, it was very obvious he'd spent his formative years away from London.

"No. I spend a great deal of time here though. It is a convenient place to do business from, after all."

Georgina gritted her teeth as the tinge of accent thickened into a recognizable Scottish brogue. An unpopular Scottish businessman. Thank goodness this was a masquerade and still early in the evening. Anyone who did happen to recognize who she was dancing with would probably forget it by the end of the night. There was nothing to do but get through the dance. At least the orchestra was one of the good ones. She allowed the music to flow through her, finding enjoyment in the dance if not the company.

"He's made his choice already."

Georgina blinked. He couldn't mean . . . "Who?"

42

"Ry . . . er, Marshington. His interest was already drawn before he returned to London. 'Tis the reason he returned."

Thankfully the dance parted them again for a few moments. Georgina bit her cheek to keep from grinning. She had joked with her sister that she wanted to be amazing enough to lure Marshington from hiding, but she never thought she would truly be able to do it.

Mr. McCrae was talking about her, wasn't he? He had to be. The duke was here, at this masquerade, where very few girls were making their first bows in society. Lady Elizabeth Ferrington was here, but she was practically betrothed already. Besides, Georgina was the first person the duke had danced with. Her plan was going to work. She was going to be saved from the ruin she'd been hiding from since childhood.

It was enough to make her want to praise God like her brother so often did.

The comfort of success made her feel a bit more charitable toward her dancing partner. "The costumes this evening are most interesting."

He didn't pause as he circled behind her. "Yes, though I've had difficulty determining what some of them are."

Georgina tried to stifle her admiration of the man's dancing, but it really was superb. Even with the simpler steps, his grace and ease was evident. He might be on the fringes of society, but he seemed to be comfortable moving in it.

She envied anyone with that sort of confidence. Who was he that the normal pressures of society didn't affect him? He hadn't even altered his clothing to fit in with the evening. "What are you supposed to be?"

"An interloper." He leaned in and whispered the words with a sly grin.

She stumbled. The dratted man had made her stumble. She never stumbled. His hand shot out to hold her elbow and steady her.

"You . . . you were not invited?"

He laughed. A pleasant, rich laugh. So many men had irritating laughs that grated the eardrums or prickled along the skin. Mr. McCrae's was engaging, captivating, making her want to join in on a joke she wasn't sure she understood.

Was this how he'd gotten himself included in the gatherings of London's elite? Whatever charity she had managed to muster faded into a bitter sludge in the pit of her stomach. How unfair that such self-assurance and poise was wasted on a man with enough humor, looks, and likely intellect to circulate in high society. Mr. McCrae's smile showed an ease she'd never been able to attain no matter how often she practiced in the mirror.

"Have no fear, little angel, I am an official guest. Though I believe I am supposed to be dancing with the wallflowers, not the Diamonds."

How forward this conversation was getting. Georgina cast a glance at her fellow dancers to see if any of them had heard Mr. McCrae's statement. No one looked at them. She glanced back at Mr. McCrae, whose head was tilted to the side as he stepped around the formation, eyes wide as he waited for her response.

Not that she could make one. There was nothing she could respond. If she agreed with his assessment of her status, she showed an abominable amount of conceit. If she denied his claim, she would seem insecure or as if she expected him to fawn over her with compliments.

"I particularly like the Queen Elizabeth costume over there." She didn't; actually, the dress was entirely wrong, but it was the first costume that caught her eye. While her own dress only nodded at the fashions of the era, she wasn't claiming to be the monarch herself. If one were going to be a historic figure, she should get it right.

"I don't think it is very accurate."

Georgina cut her eyes to him. He could tell the distinctions? Had he too studied the portraits and paintings of the time period?

He continued before she could question him further. "What do you think the young lady in blue is supposed to be? There, on the edge of the dance area."

Georgina turned her head as they walked down the line of dancers. Miranda stood at the edge of the dancers, looking almost desperate as she searched the crowd for someone. "That is my sister."

"Lady Miranda?" Mr. McCrae grinned. "I didn't recognize her. Quite lovely. What is her costume?"

Annoying. Georgina was truly starting to dislike how flattering the brilliant blue dress was on Miranda. Normally, her sister looked pale and colorless wearing the light colors of the fresh-faced debutantes. If Mother allowed her to add more color to her wardrobe, Miranda would provide Georgina some considerable competition.

Mr. McCrae's eyebrow hitched up above his mask as they turned at the end of the line.

What had he asked? Oh yes, Miranda's costume. What had she said in the carriage? "A woman of mystery."

More of that intriguing laughter floated across the expanse as they once more allowed a couple to pass between them. "I would have thought that a costume that called for black, not blue."

Georgina sighed inwardly. If Miranda didn't have the decency to have married by now, couldn't she have at least continued to maintain her unassuming, near-spinster status? "I believe that adds to the mystique, Mr. McCrae."

The music drew to a close and he bowed. She curtsied. Had a longer dancing set ever existed?

"Where should I escort you? I fear our previous location would do you little good."

"My mother is over there." Georgina gestured toward a group of people containing several gentlemen she had danced with at her first assembly in the country. She truly had no idea where her mother was, but if she got close enough to those other gentlemen, she could entice one of them to ask for the next dance. Then she would be free of Mr. McCrae, his laugh, and his admiration of Miranda.

As they left the floor, she saw a familiar orange brocade out of the corner of her eye. It would be scandalous to dance with the duke again so soon after dancing with him before, but she was willing to risk it if . . .

He couldn't be.

He was leading Miranda onto the dance floor.

And Mr. McCrae was smiling.

Chapter 4

Georgina took a deep breath as she slipped into the alcove behind the punch bowl, allowing herself to relax for the first time all evening. The drink she held was probably supposed to be lemonade but tasted more like sour apples. Not that it mattered. It could be actual sour apples and she'd still drink it. Popularity was all well and good, but it did a lady little advantage if she were too parched to speak. She had partnered at least seven popular men on the dance floor, eight if one counted her brother, Lord Trent. Three of those men were considered extremely eligible bachelors. That had to be enough for anyone to forget she'd taken a turn around the floor with Mr. McCrae.

"Have you danced with anyone interesting this evening?"

Georgina bobbled the glass of lemonade. That enthusiasm was easy to recognize, and Georgina turned a genuine smile to the young woman beside her. "Several. My step into society is looking bright indeed. I didn't think your mother was going to let you come."

The slightly shorter woman clasped her green-gloved hands in front of her and leaned forward as if imparting a secret. Her tight, black curls dangled over the edge of her thin, black mask that did little to conceal her identity as Lady Jane, the eldest daughter of the Earl of Prendwick. She flicked her fan open and cast her pale blue-grey eyes to the ceiling. "I simply told Mother you were coming and that settled it. And I'm so very glad that it did, because I've met him."

Georgina was thankful for the mask as she couldn't prevent the surprise that flashed across her face. Had Jane danced with the duke as well? Georgina had been positive he'd danced only with her and her sister before leaving the party entirely. At the very least, that horrible orange coat had disappeared. "Who?"

"Him. The man whose home I shall keep, whose social engagements I shall manage, and whose title I shall sign on my letters." Jane swung her arms wide and twirled about on her heel, nearly knocking Georgina, a servant, and a potted lemon tree to the floor.

Georgina slid her arm through Jane's to stop the spinning and bring control to the situation. While she was certainly excited that her closest friend—other than Harriette—was already planning marital bliss, her past experience with Jane told her she should hold her rejoicing until she learned more particulars about the situation. "Who is he?"

Jane blinked and then craned her neck to look around the crowded ballroom. "Who is who?"

Georgina sighed. "The man whose home you're going to keep and all that."

"Oh!" She smiled and laid her head in the nest of feathers decorating Georgina's sleeve. "I don't know. He had a mask on."

"You don't . . ." Georgina snapped her teeth shut and bopped Jane on the forehead, careful to avoid the artfully arranged coiffure. "You can't marry him if you don't know who he is."

"I know. That's why I invited him to my house." Jane looked so proud of herself that Georgina hated to bring her down.

"Jane, after tonight, several men will be calling at your house." Hopefully not the same ones that would be calling on Georgina, but some men were bound to prefer Lady Jane. And she would flourish nicely wherever she landed on the aristocratic scale. Even if she had to settle for a second son bound for the army, she would do well.

The prospect of not being able to identify her mystery suitor didn't dim Jane's smile. If anything, it broadened with personal pride. "I know. That's why I invited him to our Friday salon next week."

Jane had never been overly bright. Sadly, it was one of the things Georgina liked about her. Even if Georgina were to mess up in front of the other girl, it was likely Jane wouldn't even notice that Georgina had revealed a life-changing secret. But this plan was too cork-brained for even Jane to think up. "You can't invite a man to our Friday afternoon salon. It's nothing but young ladies playing cards and pretending to gamble."

The Friday salons had begun last year as a group of girls not quite out but wishing they were decided to practice their social skills on each other. They'd gambled for real once, but their mothers had a collective tizzy and threatened to refuse to let them gather anymore. The plan was for the gatherings to continue even though all the young ladies were now out in society. Jane couldn't bring a man into their midst.

"Oh, but that's the brilliance of it. I've decided we don't need to play cards anymore since we'll be invited to *real* card parties now." Jane stood up tall and smoothed her green and blue skirt. "We're going to be a book club."

A book club. Georgina nearly dropped her glass of lemonade again. That was even worse. She could talk Jane out of it. She had to be able to talk Jane out of it. "You can't do a book club."

"Whyever not? They're very popular. I heard even Lady Brattleby's doing one."

"But one man and a bunch of ladies discussing romantic novels?" Even Jane could see how that wouldn't work. Couldn't she?

Jane frowned.

Relief sagged Georgina's shoulders, and she tipped the remainder of her lemonade into her mouth.

Jane shrugged. "I'll think of something else and send word around."

Georgina grunted a response. It was Jane's worst habit, sending letters to people she was going to see in a matter of hours. Who had time to do that?

Jane's attention snapped from Georgina to the ballroom beyond the alcove. "Oh, who's that? Do you think it's your brother Trent?"

Georgina glanced at the man who'd caught Jane's eye. As the man had brown hair it was most certainly not Trent, but it was very likely to be Lord Eversly, a man Jane would do well to dance with. Especially since Georgina had some misgivings about Jane's fascination with an unknown man. Anything that would redirect her attention would be a good thing. "It might be. Stand near the pillar there and he's sure to see you. Then you can find out if it's him while you dance."

Jane scurried out of the alcove to stand next to the pillar, her bright peacock-inspired dress making her difficult to miss. Sure enough, Lord Eversly asked her to dance.

Georgina stayed in the alcove until she spotted her own gentleman to target. Mr. Moreland, a younger son, popular with the *ton*. He was suitable to dance with and easily recognizable.

She stepped forward to stand near the pillar and catch his eye. As they stepped onto the dance floor, she saw more than one person look their way. Satisfaction made her smile as they stepped into the quadrille. This would be the dance people talked about when they discussed her mix of partners. No one would remember Mr. McCrae.

Especially not Georgina.

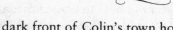

The dark front of Colin's town house greeted him as he paid the hackney driver and stepped to the pavement. As the hired conveyance drove away, it passed another carriage, one that had been decorated with pomp and station in mind. The contrast of the two vehicles was difficult to miss, and normally Colin chose to ignore it. He didn't see the point in owning his own carriage and horses. Though he could well afford it, the expense wasn't worth it for a single man who spent most of his time in London. This time, though, he found himself wishing no one had witnessed him arriving home from the ball in a hired hack.

The private carriage, gilded to the point of near gaudiness, rolled past Colin, the occupants' loud laughter scraping over him, making him shudder. He rolled his shoulders and shifted his weight, hoping the movement would ease the restlessness creeping under his skin.

It didn't.

He was accustomed to balls leaving him exhausted and tense, but tonight there was uneasiness in the fatigue. Instead of affording him a sense of accomplishment and a mental list of things to do the next day, his mind swirled with questions he hadn't allowed himself to consider in a very long time, if ever. It was going to take more than his usual cup of evening tea to distract him from his internal musings so he could rest tonight.

The door opened behind him, drawing him out of his reverie.

"Good evening, sir." Taggert, who acted as both Colin's butler and valet, held out his hands for Colin's hat and greatcoat. "Cook is preparing your tea tray. I shall bring it up directly."

Colin ran a hand through his hair. It was late and the financial world didn't keep *ton* hours. He would have to be awake and alert early tomorrow. He should go directly to bed.

But he simply couldn't.

"Bring the tea to the study. If there are any biscuits left, add those."

Taggert nodded. "Of course, sir."

Colin jogged up the stairs toward his study. The town home was narrow and modest, but still a ridiculous amount of space for a single man of his station. His first year in London, he'd taken rooms at the Albany, like many other gentlemen in his situation, but confining his life to two small rooms when he'd grown up with the sea as his backyard had slowly driven him to the brink of Bedlam. The terrace house gave him room to spread out, to walk, to not spend every moment at home staring at the same four walls. The fact that he never used two entire floors of the place meant little. He liked knowing they were there and he could use them if he wished.

If he were to marry, the extra space would be useful indeed.

He stumbled on the last stair. Marriage had entered his mind more this evening than the previous five years put together. Was that notion causing him such distress? It shouldn't. Plenty of men weren't going to get married this year, and there was no reason Colin should be ashamed to be one of them.

Two quick jerks loosened his cravat. The dishevelment was usually enough to indicate to his subconscious that his day was complete and it was time to relax. There would be no more guests this evening, no business associates claiming a sudden need for his attention. He could stop weighing his every word and deed to make sure they presented him in the way he wanted to be seen.

His body normally recognized this release and sleep would tug at him soon after. But tonight the freedom made him even more restless.

What was different this evening? Why was he in his study, eyeing the stack of correspondence he'd yet to go through instead of resting his head on his pillow?

Ryland had returned to society, and that had certainly changed Colin's evening. Perhaps his friend's intent to make a change in his life had affected Colin more than he thought. Even though the duke had left after dancing with Lady Miranda, Colin hadn't reverted to his normal evening routine. Instead he'd made every attempt to simply enjoy the evening, another significant difference.

He even danced a few more times, though with ladies considerably closer to his social class than the conniving Lady Georgina. His invitations had been better received than he had hoped. The idea of taking a wife, settling down, had niggled at the corners of his brain.

Taking a wife meant starting a family, though, and he wasn't sure he was ready to do that. He knew business, but families? He wasn't any good at those. His dealings with his own family certainly hadn't shown any marked skills in that area.

He wrote to them faithfully every three months, or at least he wrote to his mother and sister. They always wrote back, alternating between telling him the latest news and begging him to come home. More than once he'd considered it, but things had been tense between him and his father for years, even before he'd left Glasgow. That final argument had nearly destroyed the family's reputation around town. He couldn't risk the damage his return might do to his mother and sister. Bronwyn had come out this year and was hoping to find a husband soon. The last thing she needed was the gossip Colin's return would bring.

That was, of course, assuming his father would even let him into the house. Not once in the past five years had the man taken time to write him. Even when Colin sent inquiries about the family shipping business, Celestial Shipping, his father's office manager handled the reply.

If Colin were being honest, he'd have to admit that he hadn't written to Jaime McCrae during those five years either. At least not anything that had actually made it to the post.

The wild scent of Colin's favorite tea preceded Taggert into the room. He left the tea tray on the edge of the desk before gathering Colin's discarded jacket and cravat and leaving the room. Silent, efficient, and exactly what Colin normally wanted.

Tonight he wished he'd hired one of those chatty fellows as a butler. One of the nosy ones who pretended to be all stoic but was actually invested in his employer's life. Those butlers tended to gossip a lot though, which was the last thing a businessman such as Colin needed.

Since he certainly wasn't replacing his butler in the middle of the night, Colin would have to find a distraction elsewhere.

The pile of papers on his desk was the most likely location to find one.

He fixed his tea and dropped into the chair before selecting the *London Gazette* from the top of the pile. Perfect. His unusual mood was no doubt due to the increase in personal involvement this evening. He needed to get his mind back on business, and then everything would go back to normal.

With a steaming cup of tea at the ready and a large bite of cinnamon biscuit filling his mouth, he flipped to the paper's agricultural report. The Corn Returns, as the grain report was called, had brought him good news for the past two years. Last year he'd been able to live off the profits from his grain investments alone. Of course, if the war ever ended and France and Britain began trading again, grain would cease to be such a lucrative investment. He was more than willing to give up the influx of money if it meant an end to the fighting.

He finished perusing the papers while he ate the biscuits and drank a second cup of tea. He could probably force himself to retire now, but the stack of letters remaining was small. Fifteen minutes now would give him the luxury of starting with a clean desk tomorrow morning.

At the top of the stack of letters was one that made him grin. William Colgate was the perfect blend of business and pleasure. Colin had been a mere boy of eleven when William's family had left England on one of Celestial Shipping's ships. At the time, Colin had been sailing with his father more often than not—it was never too early to learn the business, after all—and a solid friendship had formed on that crossing and continued through regular letters. William's fledgling soap business in New York had been one of Colin's first investments. It was paying off nicely, though he had to keep his involvement quiet. Even Ryland didn't know Colin had such close ties to an American company. France wasn't the only country England was at war with, after all.

William wouldn't be expecting a reply for a few months. It wasn't easy to get mail to America. Still, responding to the letter gave Colin something to do, so he pulled a clean sheet of paper from his desk drawer and selected a new steel-tipped writing pen from another. He dipped the tip in the inkwell, marveling as he always did at how much nicer the pen felt in his hand than a quill did. There was a future in such pens, and he was on the lookout for the man who was going to take initiative and spread them to the masses. The elite would probably frown at them, but shopkeepers everywhere would rejoice.

Fancy new pen notwithstanding, Colin struggled to respond to William's letter. As the pen flowed over the page he found himself waxing poetic about the events of the evening and where he saw his life going. And it wasn't even the good kind of poetic. It was more the dreary, depressing, confusing sort of poetic that had grown men scrambling for the door at poetry readings and salons. Like an ode to the mold on the underside of a boat.

He threw his response in the fireplace and set William's letter aside. Answering it could wait for a day or two. Perhaps even a week.

The next letter in the stack was upside down, and the familiar three-star seal on the back didn't induce a smile.

Obviously he should have left the correspondence for tomorrow.

He supposed he still could. He could leave the stack and retire, but curiosity was a difficult thing to turn off. What if something was wrong with Celestial Shipping? Colin had gotten an update from the manager just last week. Why would he be writing again? Colin flipped the letter over and nearly knocked his teacup to the floor.

It wasn't the manager's handwriting on the front.

It was his father's.

Colin's emotions bounced around like a skiff in a storm as he ran his finger over the script he hadn't seen in so long he thought he'd forgotten it. He knew he was imagining things, but he swore he could smell the mix of salt water and cheroot smoke that always clung to his father at the end of the day.

The letter opener nearly sliced through his finger as he broke the seal with a bit too much aggression. Meticulous, even writing marched across the page in lines straight enough to make a Cambridge professor proud.

Colin's confusion grew as he read the letter. There was nothing profound or earth shattering on the page. No news of immense proportions, no impending doom. Not even a significant setback with the shipping company. There were a few sentences about the business, a couple of lines on his sister's ball, and then a paragraph on the new ship he was designing. That was it.

The news of the new ship design was exciting. Several of the men he managed investments for used Celestial Shipping to transport goods. There was no reason for Colin's father to know who had arranged the clients, but it let Colin have a hand in the company that had given him a love for business. A newer, faster ship would certainly increase their market share.

Part of his brain raced ahead, drafting a series of questions about the boat design, suggestions for materials, and ideas for the layout of the cargo hold. Before he could set nib to paper though, suspicion raised its head.

Carefully, Colin refolded the letter and set it to the side of his desk. Why had his father written now? Was he dying and didn't want to tell Colin? Despite the hard feelings between them, the idea that his father was ill made Colin's chest ache.

His mind seethed as he groped for the Bible on the edge of his desk. Opening it eased the ache in his chest a bit, but his thoughts couldn't settle enough to see where he'd opened it to. He stared blindly at the page in front of him, asking God what the letter meant, until his candle guttered out.

Then he sat in the dark.

His eyelids grew heavy, and it seemed easier to just lean his head against the back of the chair than stumble off to his room. He was sure to regret it in the morning, but he was suddenly too tired to care. In that hazy moment right before he fell asleep, he dreamed he was back at the ball, dancing through the night with an elegant creature in white. At least the dream version of Lady Georgina smiled at him.

Chapter 5

Georgina's eyes drifted shut, blocking out the morning sun as she inhaled the sweet steam rising from the large mug of tea. After a fortifying gulp, she squared her shoulders and nodded to Harriette. "I'm ready."

The rattle of paper filled the room as Harriette spread the morning's news sheets across the writing desk. "Everything appears to be following your plan." The maid looked up with a wide grin. "I still can't believe he was there."

"I know." Georgina returned the smile as she set the mug on her dressing table and began loosening the long braid she'd slept in. She loved mornings. Everyone else in the house thought her fast asleep, lazing the day away until noon, which meant in these early hours with Harriette she was completely free.

With hair swinging wildly about her shoulders, Georgina hauled Harriette to her feet and twirled the laughing maid around the room. "He was there, Harriette! All of my efforts to get proper mentions in the society columns last year have been worth it."

Harriette stumbled out of Georgina's impromptu waltz. She caught herself on the bedpost, barely stopping before she fell head-first into the lacy coverlet.

Georgina twirled on her own once more before dropping into a pink-and-white-striped chair, sending a flutter through the ruffles cascading from the seat to the floor. "Speaking of the papers. Is there anything else of importance in them today?"

Harriette flipped through the stack of news sheets. "Several lists of who has returned to Town and accounts of last night's ball. All mentions of you are quite favorable." She frowned and glanced up from the paper. "Who is Lord Canwell?"

Georgina paused, a comb halfway through her hair. "I don't know. We should look him up."

Their well-used copy of *Debrett's Peerage* was already in Harriette's hand. She flipped the pages while Georgina began pinning her hair to the top of her head. "Ah, he's a baron."

"Not very useful, then. We should add him to the book anyway if he's being mentioned in the columns. I want to know whether or not to avoid him." Georgina turned her head back and forth, examining her efforts in the mirror. This would be her first day receiving visitors at home. She needed to be perfect.

She frowned. That curl was certainly not perfect.

Harriette dipped a quill in the nearby inkwell and jotted a line in the leather-bound book that always rested on the edge of the writing desk. Keeping a log of the social actions of England's finest was probably not what her mother had intended for Georgina to do, but that book was Georgina's secret weapon and the key to making sure she never did anything to mar her carefully crafted reputation.

After setting the book aside, Harriette picked up a letter from amidst the many newspapers. "Lady Jane sent you a message about your Friday gatherings."

Georgina's eyes widened as she slid a final pin into place. "So soon? I only talked to her last evening about her ludicrous idea to turn our Friday salons into a book club. She promised to think of something else."

"She did." Harriette avoided Georgina's eyes. "It was apparently an epiphany on her way home last night."

The paper in the maid's hand shook slightly, and Georgina

frowned at it as if it were a vile snake instead of mere parchment. "What did she choose?"

"I'm afraid it's not much better." Harriette started to extend the paper as if she didn't want to say the words out loud. Her hand trembled for a moment before she dropped the note on the table.

Georgina couldn't stop herself from crossing the room and picking up the folded paper herself. She didn't open it though, knowing only one thing could make Harriette so nervous. "Does she want to form a group for a musicale performance? I admit pianoforte is not my best talent, but I can perform well enough if I practice."

"She doesn't want to do a musicale either."

Georgina was afraid of that.

Harriette took a deep breath before tossing her words out in a rush. "She still wants to do a book club."

The groan escaped before Georgina could stop it. It was bad enough when the conversation turned to popular books during an evening gathering. But to meet for the express purpose of discussing books? What she'd been looking forward to as a potential bright spot of each week was now a deep black gouge across her social calendar. "But we can't have men at a book club. She expressly wanted men to attend."

Harriette took the paper from Georgina's numb fingers as she nodded. "A book club with occasional salons where you will exhibit for the guests with a selection of readings and plays."

This new plan of Jane's was going to require careful handling. Until Georgina was safely married to a wealthy and titled gentleman, socially secure enough to appear as eccentric as she wanted, she had to be careful which invitations she turned down. If she didn't attend Jane's gathering, people would wonder why she'd turned on one of her oldest friends.

"You know she values your opinion," Harriette said quietly as she crossed the room to help Georgina into her dress.

Georgina frowned at the note before slipping the gown over her head and turning her back for Harriette to tighten the laces. Yes, Jane valued Georgina's opinion, but Georgina had already tried to talk her out of the book club idea. Should she continue to discourage her if it was what Jane truly wanted to do?

The Season, which had seemed so interminably long when she couldn't participate in it, now felt incredibly short. It was a feeling that had gnawed at her on the way home last night, the clicking of the wheels over the cobblestones sounding like a clock, eating away at the time she had left. Every event and invitation mattered because things were going to become more difficult with every passing day.

A throb in her left temple threatened to bloom into a debilitating headache, and the day hadn't even begun. She spun slowly on her heel. "How do I look?"

Harriette looked up and down with a critical eye before giving an approving nod. "Perfect, my lady."

Georgina leaned over to inspect herself in the mirror once more. It was indeed as close to perfection as humanity could get. Not that she could take credit for the evenly spaced eyes, the delicate nose, or even the straight teeth. The clear skin, exposed to a precise amount of sun to appear healthy but not tan, was something she could claim. As was the flattering cut of the gown and the artfully arranged curls that hid her slightly uneven ears. Now she had only to maintain that pretense for a few hours while they entertained callers.

The clock on the mantel chimed eleven. Mother was probably coming in the door at that very moment, exhibiting the punctuality she insisted a lady required. It was strange for Georgina, living without her mother, but the happy smile affixed to her face since she married Lord Blackstone made it all worth it. That Mother believed in traveling between the houses each day meant the two were still enjoying their married life. Or it meant that Mother knew Georgina would hate to give up receiving callers in a duke's house. Either way, Mother needed to chaperone her daughters' callers, and she'd said she would arrive at eleven o'clock this morning.

Georgina glided to the drawing room, restraining herself from a giddy skip as she took in the white-and-gold room. She'd decorated the room herself, a project her mother had given her to alleviate the utter boredom of remaining in London for a while after Miranda's first Season. It was the fireplace that had started it all. After Georgina had emptied the room, the white marble shot through with gold veins had inspired her. So vibrant yet untouchable and beautifully impractical. She'd done the room in white and then started in on changing her wardrobe.

Fortunately, the room's outrageous decor was well known around London. No one would know she'd coordinated her wardrobe and drawing room to create a formidable and lasting impression on anyone who came to call.

And Mother would never know that Georgina and Harriette had spent a great deal of time last year in the formal drawing room, adjusting the placement of the white-and-gold-striped settees and gilt armchairs to perfectly frame Georgina's all-white wardrobe, golden blond hair, and creamy complexion. It was the height of vanity, but who would dare accuse her of creating the entire thing on purpose?

Georgina settled herself onto one of the sofas and waited for the first visitor to arrive. While Mother looked over every detail of Georgina's appearance, Miranda walked past with nary a glance to settle on the other sofa and pull out her needlework.

Why hadn't Georgina thought to bring down something to occupy herself between guests? No, she couldn't think that way. There would be no time between guests. She would be in that much demand.

She had to be.

"The Duke of Marshington will be coming by today." Georgina wasn't sure why she'd blurted out that particular bit of information, but she had to bite her lip to keep from smirking when Miranda jabbed herself with a needle. Whether Georgina was attempting to bolster her own courage or impress Miranda with her social prowess, she'd clearly failed. She didn't feel any less anxious, and Miranda looked more annoyed than impressed.

"Darling, it was a masquerade." Mother gave a nod of approval after smoothing Georgina's skirt. "There are always one or two gentlemen claiming to be the esoteric duke at these things."

Georgina adjusted the skirts her mother had just smoothed. It probably looked spiteful, but it was simply that infernal urge to move. "He had the ring, Mother."

"The ring? I suppose that does make a difference." Mother sat in the adjacent gold brocade armchair and pulled out her own needlework.

Honestly, of all the unnecessary things her mother had taught her in the last eighteen years, she couldn't have found two minutes to say, *"A lady always brings something to occupy herself while she waits"*?

"Did you bring anything to occupy yourself between callers this morning?" Mother frowned at Georgina's empty hands.

Confidence. Confidence was the most important accessory a woman could put on. It made everyone think she knew what she was doing. "I don't think there will be any need. Several people mentioned calling on me today. We shall find ourselves quite busy. Especially when word goes around that the Duke of Marshington has come out of his self-imposed exile for me."

Miranda snorted.

Mother glared at her oldest daughter.

"You think it otherwise, dear sister?" Georgina didn't bother hiding her smirk this time. The truth was Georgina didn't really believe it either, but there was no reason Miranda had to know that.

Miranda set aside her needlepoint. "Has it not occurred to you, *dear sister*, that maybe he wants to call on me today? You are not the only eligible lady in this house."

And how well Georgina knew it. Miranda had had three years— *three years*—to get out of Georgina's way, but no. Here Georgina was, having to share a drawing room with a sister approaching spinsterhood.

"Oh, I am sorry to hurt your feelings. That was never my intention," Georgina simpered. Perhaps it had been, but she would never admit it. "But don't you think if you were the enticement he would have come back sometime in the last three years?"

If that didn't help Miranda remember the situation they were in, nothing would.

Her mother's voice cut through Georgina's triumph. "Georgina, that is uncalled for. A lady does not mention another's unwed status, particularly if they have been socializing for a while."

Georgina schooled her features into proper chastisement as she met her mother's glare. At least the admonishment should help remind Miranda that she was not the freshest flower in this particular bouquet.

She settled in to wait, biting her tongue to keep from saying anything else her mother might disapprove of.

It seemed an interminable length of time, but Gibson finally announced the first caller.

Georgina's heart plummeted in disappointment as Mr. Sherbourne appeared in the doorway. Dark, wiry, and nothing more than a mere gentleman. Not even the oldest son. He would never do for Georgina's plan.

But he was a nice enough man. Perhaps Miranda wanted an unremarkable man. Georgina looked at the carnations clutched in his hand, knowing her sister was about to be very upset with her and be entirely unable to do a thing about it. "The flowers are beautiful, Mr. Sherbourne. Were you aware that my sister, Lady Miranda, adores carnations?"

Actually, she didn't. Miranda's favorite flowers were tulips, but that was something she could set straight later if the two developed a *tendre* for each other.

Mr. Sherbourne's eyes clouded with confusion as his brows drew together, but he recovered quickly, turning to extend the bouquet to Miranda. "A lady should always have a bouquet of her favorite flowers. Please accept these, Lady Miranda."

Miranda looked much like she had the time Georgina decided to learn how to cook and she'd accidentally put too much salt in the biscuits. Her smile looked a bit sickly. "Of course. I am honored that you thought of me."

Georgina sat up a little straighter. Was it possible Miranda was actually intrigued by this man? If she was, it was Georgina's sisterly duty to try to make it happen for her. That Georgina herself would benefit from Miranda forming an attachment was secondary. Almost.

If she was wrong, her sister would be irked, and there was a certain amount of pleasure in that as well. Frankly, there was no way to lose. She tried to look attentive for politeness' sake but avoided any smiles that would encourage Mr. Sherbourne in her direction.

The man perched on the edge of a chair, looking unsure of which lady to direct his gaze to. He finally settled on Georgina. "The ball was splendid last evening. Lady Georgina, your angelic gown was divinely inspired."

Thank goodness Mr. Sherbourne wasn't an acceptable choice. She would listen to such insipidness for the rest of her life if she had to, but it wasn't her first choice. "Lady Miranda was the one with true inspiration. Her costume changed on a whim."

Confusion once more weighed his face into a blank mask before he turned that awkward small smile back to Miranda. "How did you manage that?"

Miranda glared at Georgina before answering. Georgina hid her shrug in a shift of her seating position, trying to look as if Miranda's answer was the most interesting thing in the world. Mr. Sherbourne apparently thought it was.

His next two comments were directed straight to Miranda, and when he took his leave, his good-bye was directed to her.

Georgina was quite proud of herself, though Miranda didn't seem to appreciate the gesture. Perhaps Mr. Sherbourne wasn't the man for her, but the encounter had given Georgina new purpose for the afternoon. Surely one of the men who came by today would be to her sister's liking, as long as he wasn't a man of great consequence.

She'd have to save those for herself.

Any man who didn't suit her purposes, though, would find himself with an expanded esteem for Miranda, thanks to Georgina's considerable practice and effort. If nothing else, Miranda's rise in popularity would keep her from dragging Georgina's reputation down.

If Miranda seemed to find the outcome less than helpful, Georgina was honest enough to admit her irritation made the whole thing more enjoyable.

As the third man departed, Miranda's ears glowed red behind her yellow curls. Yes, she was well and truly mad. And she couldn't do a thing about it.

Gibson strolled into the room once more. "The Earl of Ashcombe, my lady."

Georgina sat up a little straighter. He wasn't the duke, by any means, but the earl was young and titled, known to be plump in the pocket, and, most importantly, well-liked by men and women. He was considered a very good catch indeed.

Miranda sat up a bit straighter as well. Then she stood. What was going on? When she walked to the door at the back of the room, Georgina's concern grew. Everyone knew the two had considered courting during Miranda's first Season, but that had been years ago. Surely all feelings of animosity had faded by now.

The earl entered and winked at Georgina. Dreadfully cheeky of the man, but a light flirtation was a sign that the man was interested. The interest of a wealthy, titled, popular man was always helpful.

He was startlingly handsome, almost irritatingly so. His dark hair was perfectly combed, his bold blue jacket and tan trousers precisely tailored. Together they would make the most striking couple.

Georgina shoved Miranda's discomfort from her mind and flashed Lord Ashcombe the coy smile she'd practiced in the mirror for hours. "How nice of you to come."

God save him from idiotic lovesick fools. Colin reached down between his feet and plucked a few blades of grass. Ryland sat on the bench next to him in the middle of Grosvenor Square, growling at each gentleman who entered the house across the street instead of enjoying the beauty of the park.

Of all the things Colin could be doing with his afternoon, watching callers come and go from Hawthorne House ranked right below scouring the docks for a missing piece of cargo and right above telling Mr. Mathers again that he refused to seek investors for the man's preposterous scheme to build a floating pleasure castle in the English Channel. For pity's sake, there was a war going on. Who would want to sail into the middle of it for a party?

A group of *ton* women exited a carriage, packages stacked three high on top. Very well, this bored lot might get a thrill from partying in the middle of a war zone, but Colin refused to have anything to do with such idiocy.

Instead he'd embroiled himself in the slightly more palatable idiocy taking place in the middle of Mayfair.

Colin glanced sideways as Ryland growled once again, the tension in his shoulders threatening to rip his well-tailored jacket at the seams. While they weren't likely to die from this escapade, they certainly weren't going to accomplish anything. Was Ryland planning on sitting here all afternoon?

What was supposed to have been a brief visit on Colin's way to the club had turned into an entire day of moral support. Ryland had indeed talked to Miranda last night, but he'd kept his mask on. She still didn't know he was the valet she'd met last fall. That was going to change today.

If they ever managed to make it to the house.

The Earl of Ashcombe strolled down the street, a clutch of bright pink roses in his hand. He bounded up the stairs to Hawthorne House's door with a smug smile.

Beside him, Ryland ground his heel into the dirt.

Colin twined his blades of grass into a ring and tried to toss it onto a nearby tree branch. It bounced off. "Think any of them are here to visit her?"

"Only the smart ones," Ryland said.

"So none, then."

The pithy comment drew a laugh from Ryland, as it was intended to. There was a certain truth to the statement though. When it came to personal dealings, some of the trappings of London's high society seemed utterly ridiculous. Why had no one questioned them?

He supposed growing up and socializing in Scotland and at sea had given him a different perspective on the formal rituals. The Scots enjoyed their pomp and ceremony when the occasion warranted it, but they also appreciated simple things. When one was at sea, it was sometimes a celebration just to be alive when sailing into port.

After seven agonizing minutes—he knew because he'd counted the seconds—Colin pushed to his feet. "This isn't a campaign, chap. We either go in or we don't."

Another thirty seconds went by before the earl departed. That hadn't taken long.

Without a word, Ryland rose to his feet and crossed Grosvenor Square. Colin followed on his heels. Why had he agreed to this again?

The butler opened the door, and Colin handed him his card with a feeling of resignation swirling through his gut. The servant didn't look very impressed, but Colin hadn't expected him to. This was the butler of a duke. And while Colin had been to the house more than once for business, this butler was now manning the portal of a popular young woman. He saw the best of the best. A mere mister with a Scotch-Irish history wasn't going to impress him.

Ryland fumbled in his pockets.

This was why Colin had agreed to suffer through an afternoon social call. Ryland's social skills were more than rusty after nine years in the shadows, and there was a lot riding on this visit for him. He would likely either leave engaged or unconscious, depending on how things went with Lady Miranda and her brothers.

Women weren't usually forgiving when they learned they'd been fooled, and men were rarely restrained when a sister felt her honor had been slighted. Yes, it was very possible Ryland would end up on the wrong side of a fist before the afternoon was over, especially if Lord Trent was in residence. Riverton was a large man but not known for fighting. However, Lord Trent had been training with Gentleman Jack, and the man didn't take on anything less than the best pugilists.

Finally Ryland pulled a card out of his pocket. The butler was decidedly more impressed with this card, which was to be expected as even the servants would know about the great mystery surrounding the Duke of Marshington.

"If you will wait here"—the tall, thin man gestured them into the front hall—"I will announce your presence."

Ryland reached out a hand. "Hold, man," he said softly. "Who all is in the drawing room?"

Poor bloke. He was really nervous. Colin gave a mental shrug and waved at the rest of his afternoon as it sailed away. Ryland needed moral support if nothing else, so Colin would stay. He'd suffered much greater trials in the name of friendship over the years.

"Lady Blackstone and Lady Georgina, Your Grace," the butler said.

Colin nearly groaned at the reminder that visiting the love of Ryland's life meant spending time with that calculating busybody as well.

Ryland's heavy hand landed on Colin's shoulder. "Enjoy their company, my good man. I've business with Griffith to take care of first."

Colin's eyes narrowed at Ryland. He wouldn't. He couldn't.

Ryland strode off toward the back of the house.

He had. Colin gritted his teeth. They didn't normally keep score of who had helped whom last, but this time Ryland was going to owe him. Spending time in a drawing room with Lady Georgina was going to be far more excruciating than providing a night's shelter to a French informant or investigating estates and businesses to tell Ryland which smuggling suspects had more money than they should.

At the very least this was going to be enough of a favor for Colin to stop hearing about that knife wound Ryland had suffered on his behalf. Not that Colin would have been in danger if he hadn't been coming to meet Ryland, so in a way the knife wound wasn't Colin's fault at all.

Which meant Ryland was going to be deeply indebted to Colin for this visit.

"This way, sir." The butler stood at the entrance to a drawing room, ready to announce Colin's arrival.

Colin went, the resignation in his stomach boiling into dread. To leave now would be the height of rudeness. Besides, there was still the question of whether or not Ryland would be able to leave under his own power or if one of Miranda's brothers would knock him on his backside.

Colin stopped by the butler. "Is Lord Trent here?"

The butler simply raised a brow.

Right. Colin wasn't important enough to merit such information. He'd have to assume the younger man was here and would cause potential problems for Ryland. It might be messy, but the scene in the study was going to be much more interesting than making small talk with a woman who looked down on him.

The butler announced him, and with the silent hope that Lady Blackstone was more like her elder daughter than her younger, Colin stepped into the whitest room he'd ever seen.

White furniture, white walls, white everything, with only the occasional splash of gold to break the monotony. And in the center, perched like a queen on a white-and-gold-striped throne, was Lady Georgina. Dressed in white. *Good gracious.*

"Good afternoon, my lady." Colin bowed to the woman he assumed to be Lady Blackstone. She was very obviously Lady Georgina's mother. He then turned and bowed to Lady Georgina. "My lady."

Lady Georgina's nose wrinkled as if she could smell his lower social station. Maybe she could. Ambitious girls acquired peculiar talents. "Mother, may I present Mr. McCrae? Mr. McCrae, my mother, Lady Blackstone."

Lady Blackstone gestured for him to sit across from her. "I'm afraid we haven't met."

"I am a . . ." *Business partner? Friend?* "I am an acquaintance of your sons."

"Of course. A pleasure to meet you." She nodded her head, her eyes still curious.

Colin turned to Lady Georgina. "And you, Lady Georgina, how good to see you again." He fought back a devious grin as her eyes widened. Perhaps he could make this an enjoyable afternoon after all. "I enjoyed our dance last evening."

Chapter 6

Georgina dug her fingernails into her palm. What did the infernal man hope to accomplish by bringing up their dance? Mother was intrigued enough by his presence as it was. If she knew Georgina had deigned to dance with a man of his station, she would be positively overcome with curiosity. "As did I, of course."

Mr. McCrae settled into the seat Georgina's mother indicated. "The weather is pleasant this afternoon. I've been enjoying the fresh air in Grosvenor Square."

Georgina smiled, avoiding her mother's eyes. She did not want to talk to this man. What possessed him to come calling? He could hardly think their brief encounter the night before constituted interest on her side.

"It must have been lovely." Mother rushed in to rescue Georgina from a social disgrace. Though why it should matter, Georgina had no idea. Mr. McCrae's only significance came from his pocket-book. She knew because she'd made a few discreet inquiries at the ball last night.

"Yes, quite." Mr. McCrae cast a glance at the door.

Was he . . . irritated? It was the best description Georgina could think of for his expression.

Mr. McCrae addressed Mother again. "I'm afraid I missed seeing you last evening. Were you in costume?"

"Not really." Mother set aside her needlework. "I had my dressmaker re-create a favorite gown of mine from when I was Georgina's age."

"Nostalgia brings beauty, when the memory is a pleasant one. I'm sorry to have missed you. You must have looked lovely."

Was Mother blushing?

"Thank you, Mr. McCrae. I admit it was delightful to relive my youth, though my dancing partners have changed over the years."

Georgina's gaze flipped back and forth between Mother and Mr. McCrae. What was going on here? Was she being ignored?

Mr. McCrae leaned forward. "I don't know when we'll next be at the same function, Lady Blackstone, but I would be ever so honored if you would save me a dance when the event occurs."

Mother preened. Did Georgina look like that when men complimented her? She'd have to practice in the mirror more.

"If you wish, Mr. McCrae. Though I wouldn't want to take you away from the younger ladies. I've had my time—twice, if you will—and I'd not take the pleasure from one of them."

"He dances superbly." Georgina clapped a hand over her mouth, then tried to disguise the reaction with an ill-bred scratching of her nose. She never scratched her nose in public. One more sin to lay at Mr. McCrae's feet.

The man was laughing. To the innocent observer, which her mother apparently was, it was a humble laugh. The kind men give when they've been unexpectedly complimented and can't hide their pleasure.

Georgina knew better.

He was laughing at her. Odious man.

He smiled at her, his blue eyes crinkling at the corners. "I thank you for the gracious compliment, Lady Georgina. Our dance was so early in the evening I was sure you had forgotten about it."

She'd wanted to forget about it. Should have forgotten about it. He did not fit into her plan.

And she couldn't afford to step away from the plan.

"I never forget a pleasant interlude, Mr. McCrae." She tried to bite her tongue. Mother would be cross if Georgina finished the sentence as she wanted to. The words seemed to tumble out of their own accord. "Nor an unpleasant one."

Mother sucked in her breath.

Georgina glanced at her from the corner of her eye.

Cross didn't begin to describe her mother. Georgina was going to hear about this for the rest of the week.

Odious man.

"A good memory is an asset to a young lady, I'm sure. You wouldn't want to risk repeating the unpleasant memories," Mr. McCrae said.

"No." What was the man up to now?

"As I told your dear mother, I don't know when our paths will cross socially again, but feel free to claim a prior obligation to dance with me should you need an excuse to avoid one of those unpleasant encounters."

He was giving her a way out. How dare he do something nice when she was determined to dislike him?

"That is most generous of you, sir." It actually was. He was offering to come to her rescue whenever she wished. Her mother looked slightly appeased. Perhaps Georgina could avoid a lecture after all. "I hope to never need to take you up on your offer. Our encounters should only happen under the best of circumstances."

He sat back in his chair, one side of his mouth twitching. Was he fighting the urge to smirk? The cad. He was enjoying this veiled battle of wits.

A muffled crash echoed from the back of the house.

"What on earth?" Mother twisted in her seat to look at the door leading from the main hall. "Gibson?"

The butler appeared at the door instantly. "Yes, my lady?"

"Go find out what that awful racket was. And don't admit anyone else until we sort it out." She looked worried as she turned back to Mr. McCrae. "Mr. McCrae, I do apologize—"

He waved a hand in the air. "Think nothing of it, my lady. I arrived with a friend who had business with His Grace. I'm sure that was a reaction of . . . er, surprise that we heard."

Georgina's eyes narrowed. He was laughing. No sound emerged, but his shoulders were clearly shaking. He'd angled himself on the settee in an attempt to disguise it, but he obviously knew what the sound had been and found it humorous.

"Whom did you arrive with?" Georgina latched on to the most important information he'd revealed.

"Hmmm?" Mr. McCrae turned his head from the door with a smile still tugging at his lips. "Oh, Ry—the Duke of Marshington."

"The real duke?" Mother asked.

He'd started to call the duke by another name. What was the duke's first name again? Georgina couldn't recall but was willing to bet that's what Mr. McCrae had started to call him.

If he was that intimate a friend of the duke's, she might need to rethink her strategy. He could be useful.

"Yes, my lady," Mr. McCrae said. "He decided to return to London this year. I believe he's even planning on taking up his seat in the House of Lords."

"How wonderful! Griffith will be pleased. He's missed Marshington since school."

Mr. McCrae cleared his throat and shifted in his seat, the first sign of awkwardness he'd shown since he arrived. "Yes. I believe Marshington is also looking forward to renewing the acquaintance."

Georgina's eyes narrowed. What was the odious man hiding?

Another loud noise drifted through the house. Was that shouting? It almost sounded like Miranda. Georgina frowned. All the signs pointed toward Georgina having a brilliant chance to land the Duke of Marshington. If Miranda ruined those chances, Georgina would never forgive her.

A door slammed and quick, light footsteps crossed the hall to fade up the main stairs.

Mother rose from her seat, trying and failing not to appear worried.

Mr. McCrae rose as well, a decidedly lighter expression on his face. He looked amused.

"I believe I will . . . be back in a moment." Mother scurried out the door.

Mother never scurried.

Mr. McCrae released a full grin as Georgina's mother departed.

"You know something," Georgina said.

"Indeed I do." He turned the grin on her.

It was a shame that those handsome features were wasted on such an odious man. What were other words for *odious*? She'd have to ask Harriette, because if Georgina was going to continue to have interactions with Mr. McCrae, she was going to need every vile descriptor she could think of. "Marshington had business with my brother, you say?"

His grin widened. "Yes. Of a personal nature. Putting things in order to take up his rightful place and all."

Georgina's heart danced in her chest. It was happening! Everything was going according to plan. She'd be safe by Season's end for sure. If this Mr. McCrae was such a close friend of the duke's, it would be best to leave a good impression in his mind despite her dislike of him.

"Is he going to be long? I could arrange for tea."

Mr. McCrae shook his head. "I doubt it will be much longer now."

"What do you think he's doing in there?" Georgina plucked at the edge of the settee cushion.

"Why do you care?"

"Griffith is my brother. I care deeply about all his affairs. We're a very close family, you know."

His eyebrows rose. "Oh? Well, if it concerns you I'm sure he'll tell you."

Georgina's palms began to itch. Mr. McCrae knew why Marshington was here, she could tell. He was too amused. As if he knew what all the mysterious sounds indicated.

"Is he planning to marry this year? I can't think why else he'd end his seclusion."

"Can't you?" He looked at her, something unreadable passing his face. She didn't like not being able to guess what he was thinking. "No, I don't suppose you can. Fortunately for the world, Lady Georgina, the rest of us can think of important things aside from advantageous marriage settlements."

Georgina gasped.

Mr. McCrae grinned. Infuriating, odious man.

Suddenly the grin left his face and he rushed across the room to the door. "My lady? Are you well?"

Georgina rose to her feet. Her mother was in the doorway looking pinched and pale. "Mother?"

Mother pulled in a deep breath and straightened her back. "The Duke of Marshington is on the floor in Griffith's study. Unconscious."

Colin laughed. He couldn't stop it. Hearing that Ryland had been laid out on the floor was the funniest thing he'd heard in a long time.

He quickly got himself under control and assured the frantic Lady Blackstone that he could get Ryland home with no one the wiser. Understandably, she didn't want it known that the heretofore missing peer of the realm had to be hauled from her son's home like a dead body. Nor did she think it wise for the duke to remain in residence, given Lord Trent's current mindset.

It took some maneuvering, but they managed to bring Ryland's carriage down the alley behind the house. Colin, Riverton, and Lord Trent tried to nonchalantly carry the blanket-covered body of the Duke of Marshington through the back garden to the carriage.

Colin couldn't stop laughing at the ridiculous scene they were creating.

Riverton glanced over as another chuckle escaped Colin's lips. "It is funny."

"Aye," Colin said, grinning. He shifted his hold on Ryland's shoulder. A decade of spy work had left the man a tower of heavy, solid muscle.

They slid Ryland onto the carriage seat. He only suffered two additional bumps to the head during their efforts. Colin shrugged. Ryland was going to have a devil of a headache anyway. Getting knocked against a marble mantelpiece could do that to a man.

Colin climbed into the carriage but lingered in the open doorway. He shouldn't say anything. It wasn't his place. But Riverton had been a friend as well as a business partner, and Colin hated to see him caught off guard. "Ryland's made a career of keeping secrets, Riverton, but he's still a gentleman. No doubt you'll have an upset sister when this is all through, but it won't be Lady Miranda."

Riverton's look was hard. Colin could see the strength that made him a formidable duke. Colin knew from rumor and experience that Riverton was a good and fair man, but even the most noble of men had been known to bend their scruples when it came to protecting family.

"What do you know, Mr. McCrae?"

A helpful nudge was one thing, but Colin drew the line at spilling his secrets in a fountain of gossip. Knowledge was power, after all. "More than I should but not enough to say any more than I have, Your Grace."

He tipped his hat and sat back in his seat, praying Riverton wouldn't press him, pleased when Riverton slammed the door shut and the carriage pulled away.

Why did Colin keep opening his mouth to try to help these people? Normally he kept far away from people's personal affairs, but since Ryland had returned to London, Colin couldn't seem to stop meddling. He'd always felt God wanted him to change the world, be an example of integrity in business, but never had he felt God wanting him to reach into people's lives.

Part of him felt bad for Lady Georgina's forthcoming heart-break, though why it bothered him he couldn't say. By all accounts she was a girl who needed to be put in her place, but something stopped him from writing her off completely.

Ryland's head rolled.

Colin slouched and stretched his legs out to prop his feet on the facing seat. He didn't want the poor man falling to the floor. He'd suffered enough for King and country, not to mention saving Colin's life five years prior. The least Colin could do was see him comfortably home.

"Lady Georgina," Colin mumbled. She was a puzzle. He did have to admit the slightest bit of admiration for the way she seemed to be playing society to her advantage. Based on this morning's paper and the talk he'd heard at the club, everyone thought she was a spectacular young lady.

Her manipulations had an edge to them though. Mercenary? Desperate? He wasn't sure. Maybe that was what intrigued him. She had a hidden depth—very hidden but there nonetheless.

He shrugged. It was unlikely he—a mere mister, and a Scottish one involved in business, at that—would be the one to unravel her mystery. He would never be a suitable match for one such as her.

Not that he wanted to be.

Though Lady Georgina had a breathtaking face and form, and was enjoyable to sit across from at dinner or dance with for an evening, there was little more beyond that. It would take a beautiful woman, both inside and out, to entice him to marry. He refused to allow his marriage to be nothing more than another business transaction. No, if he ever married it would be to a woman who made his life fuller and desired the same things he did.

A groan vibrated against his feet, pulling Colin from his musings.

"I was hoping you'd stay out until I got you home," Colin said. He couldn't help grinning at the discoloration that was already forming around Ryland's eye. One had to assume that the grand reveal had not gone as hoped.

The carriage pulled up to Ryland's house, and Colin bounded out to get Jeffreys and perhaps Price, the butler, as well. Between them they should be able to get the now-conscious duke up to his room without much fuss.

He shook his head as he jogged down to the servant area behind the kitchen. Helping Ryland start a normal life was going to keep Colin busy. With any luck, he'd be too busy to have anything to do with pretty girls with intelligent green eyes and mercenary hearts.

Chapter 7

The smell of chocolate drifted through the layers of down and lace that Georgina had buried herself under during the night. As always it triggered a moment of excitement followed by heart-pounding trepidation. Morning chocolate was a special treat. One Harriette only brought if she knew Georgina was going to have a particularly difficult day.

Georgina nudged the covers down enough that she could see Harriette pull back the curtains, allowing a burst of morning sunshine in to blind Georgina.

The rustling of papers reached her ears before her eyes could adjust to the brightness. Georgina groaned and flipped the covers back over her head.

Harriette's voice was muffled, due to the thick covers around Georgina's head, but still understandable. "Stay abed if you wish. I can go through this morning's material with you even if you still wear your bedclothes."

Not bothering to hide her disgruntled frown, Georgina grabbed the top of the cover and flung it to her waist. Denial wasn't going to stop the morning or Harriette's news, so there was no sense in letting the chocolate get cold.

Wiggling to a sitting position, Georgina looked to the writing desk, expecting to see Harriette's normal stack of newspapers. The newspapers were there, but so was a basket filled with smaller papers. Letters of the more personal variety. "What is that?"

Harriette helped Georgina arrange the pillows into a more comfortable position and then slid a tray onto her lap with two steaming mugs of chocolate and a plate of toast and eggs.

Two mugs of chocolate? The little basket must be worse than Georgina feared.

"Your mother wants you to help with the invitations."

"Help with what?" Georgina took a large gulp of hot liquid, hoping it would thaw the icy fear lurking just below the surface.

Harriette avoided Georgina's gaze. "Answering them."

More hot liquid, more inhaled steam. "Those are all invitations?"

Harriette pulled a thick stack from the basket. "These are invitations. The rest are notes from your friends asking what your plans are. We knew this would happen if you were as popular as we hoped. The other girls want to be near you or to avoid you. Either way they want to know your every move, every thought, every man you've set your cap for."

When the maid finally looked toward Georgina, the sympathy in her eyes made Georgina want to crumble under the covers once more. It was definitely a two-mugs-of-chocolate kind of morning. "I suppose we'd best save the papers for last this morning, then."

Georgina munched on toast and eggs while Harriette went through the invitations in the stack. Balls were easy. Only those hosted by the most prestigious and well-connected merited Georgina's presence. Smaller gatherings such as dinner parties and soirees were a bit more difficult. How important was the hostess? What was the likelihood the men she wanted to charm would be in attendance? Was the entertainment set for the evening, or would impromptu exhibitions and games be expected?

Georgina did not do impromptu anything.

It took them an hour to sort through the pile of invitations. After that Georgina couldn't stand to stay in bed any longer and threw back the covers. She rolled off the mattress and shrugged into her ratty white dressing gown covered with a multitude of bright stains before stumbling over to the padded bench underneath her window. Her new sketchbook and pencil were tucked beneath one of the pillows. She settled in and began marking the lines of the park across the street.

"Shall we move on to the letters, then?" Harriette ignored Georgina's grimace as she always did.

Why did people waste so much paper on her? Letters from London to Hertfordshire she could understand, and she always had Harriette answer them in the briefest way politeness would allow. But when it was only a matter of streets, Georgina didn't see the point. She simply gave her friends a reply the next time she saw them at a function.

Harriette's lips flattened into near nonexistence as her eyes flew over the paper. "Lady Jane has decided that since she's yet to decide on a book for the club to read, the next Friday gathering will be an exhibition of sorts. She wants to expand the guest list and do a poetry reading."

"What?" Georgina dropped the sketchbook into her lap, shock draining all strength from her arms. Jane was moving ahead with her plans at an alarmingly fast rate. She must be truly hoping this mystery man would attend.

Harriette's eyes held something achingly close to pity. "You don't have to go, my lady."

But she did have to go, and they both knew it.

Georgina dropped her forehead to the cool glass. "We'll start practicing a poem by whoever is popular now. This is one area I don't want to stand out. Keep it simple and bland and make sure the book is small enough to fit into my reticule."

"I don't think there's much poetry in the library, my lady. Your brothers were never much into reading it, and Lady Miranda thinks it a dreadful waste of imagination."

"She would."

Harriette folded and unfolded the note. "We could stop by the bookshop this afternoon."

The hesitant tone in Harriette's voice matched that of a seamstress telling a client there was enough material to let the seams out an inch or two. Georgina would rather go anywhere than the bookshop. She'd rather have herself publicly weighed on George Berry's old coffee scale. A stroll through the fish market during the hottest part of the day would be more welcome. "Very well, we'll go to the bookshop. But we get the first acceptable volume we see."

"Agreed."

Georgina returned her attention to her sketchbook and added people to her picture, embellishing them with flower-bedecked hats and voluminous greatcoats. She liked looking down on them from her window where she couldn't see their faces and they couldn't see hers. Only when she was unseen could she truly relax. In this room she could pretend that she might still aspire to be as gracious a lady as her mother.

Harriette groaned. "Lady Sarah wants to do one as well."

"Wants to do what? A poetry gathering? If that is going to be the popular thing this Season, we'll need to start a new fashion immediately." Why couldn't the girls be happy with playing the pianoforte or sharing a game of cards? What was this sudden need to exhibit dramatic reading prowess?

"Perhaps a small gathering of your own? 'Tis the best way to . . ."

Harriette's voice dropped off, drawing Georgina's attention from her sketchbook. Small wrinkles formed at the corners of the maid's mouth as her eyes flew over another paper.

Georgina dropped her sketchbook and crossed the room to look over Harriette's shoulder. "What is it? What's wrong?"

Frustration curled her toes as she willed the words on the page to become something other than a dancing, winding trail of jumbled letters. She thought she saw the word *banquet*, but after a blink it turned into *piquet*. A moment later it was nothing as half the letters simply disappeared.

Harriette folded the note and dropped it back in the basket. "A note from Miss Clemens. It came yesterday, but we didn't have a chance to read it."

Georgina frowned. Lavinia Clemens was a friend from Hertfordshire. It wasn't odd for her to write while Georgina was in London, so what could be so distressing? Her hand trembled as she reached for the letter. She could, with considerable time and effort, make out the words in a book, but handwriting had always been beyond her understanding. There would be no way she could read the letter for herself, but she had to know what had made Harriette frown so darkly.

The maid wrapped her fingers around Georgina's wrist, stopping her from picking up the letter. "Mr. Dixon has proposed again."

"Hasn't she turned him down twice now?" Georgina propped her hands on her waist. Lavinia was a year older than Georgina, and her family a mere step above impoverished gentry, but they'd played together as children and enjoyed each other's company in the years since.

"She didn't precisely turn him down this time." Harriette pointed to one of the society pages lying on the desk. "They've made a comic about you. Seems the number of gentlemen calling at Hawthorne House yesterday drew a bit of notice."

Normally Georgina loved the comics. This was the first one she'd appeared in and they'd drawn her in a very flattering manner, which boded well for her plans and her carefully constructed reputation. But her delight was tempered by the idea that her childhood friend was planning to marry a man she'd never particularly cared for. True, she and Lavinia Clemens had grown apart in recent years, but Georgina still wished her well. A friendship as old as theirs didn't simply fade away because of a difference of interests. "Why is Lavinia accepting Mr. Dixon?"

Harriette picked up the letter with a sigh and smoothed it out on the table. "She hasn't exactly accepted him either. Her answer was more along the lines of 'possibly.' She intends to come to London and visit her aunt. If nothing comes of it, she'll go home and marry Mr. Dixon."

Georgina bit her lip, feelings swirling in her gut like the letters

84

she'd tried to read moments before. Lavinia didn't have the luxury of choosing spinsterhood. While a comfortable living with Mr. Dixon was better than none at all, Lavinia had confided that she hoped for another option.

But London? Was Lavinia hoping Georgina would help her? Lavinia was a gentleman's daughter. While their acquaintance in the country was perfectly acceptable, particularly since no one outside her family and a few villagers knew they still conversed, they would hardly move in the same circles in London.

Harriette smoothed Georgina's hair away from her face. "Don't worry, my lady. All will be well. I've looked over the papers, and everything is working to your advantage."

Georgina glanced at the letter from Lavinia once more before forcing her lips into a smile. "I'm sure you're right, Harriette. I'm worrying over nothing. Lavinia and I will meet a time or two for tea, and then she'll marry and everything will be fine."

It was a lie, and they both knew it. Lavinia would never be accepted in London. She was almost as broken as Georgina, and she had no way of hiding it.

While Georgina dressed for the day, they finished reading the notes. Harriette jotted one-line answers to those who couldn't be avoided, a short paragraph to those who lived outside London. Finally they were able to turn their attention to the society columns in the paper.

All the papers mentioned Georgina, and all of them said she was destined to make the match of the Season. One of the less reputable papers claimed the Duke of Marshington had already been round to see her. It was false, of course, since the duke had never made it past Griffith's study. But the fact that other people thought they'd make a grand couple boosted Georgina's confidence.

It was enough to send her worries to the dark corners of her mind. Georgina skipped from the dressing table to Harriette's side. "Today's the day, Harriette. I can feel it."

Chapter 8

Often, significant moments in life are only identifiable in hindsight, but every now and then something happens that announces its significance with trumpeted preamble and terrifying implications.

Such was the letter lying open on Colin's desk. He had half a mind to stop reading his correspondence altogether. What could possibly be going on in Scotland? Because he didn't for one moment think that this letter and his father's arriving so close together was coincidental.

It was obvious now why Jaime McCrae had written to his son. He must have known that Alastair Finley, Jaime's closest friend and staunchest rival, was going to extend this offer to Colin. What Colin didn't understand was why his father hadn't warned him, or asked him not to do it, or anything else that had anything to do with the shocking words now in front of him.

Alastair owned the Glasgow Atlantic shipping company. Glasgow Atlantic and Celestial were locked in a constant battle to be the biggest shipping company in Scotland. The rivalry had caused more than one rift across the city as the two friends dropped into feuding periods that would have made the Highlanders of old proud. And if the letter in front of him could be believed, Alastair had found a way to win the dispute once and for all.

That part of the letter was easy to understand. It was the rest that left Colin sitting in stunned silence. He'd become adept at reading the hidden messages, uncovering the real meaning behind a man's business proposal. Normally he trusted his instincts, but in this particular instance he rather hoped he was wrong.

Alastair wanted Colin to find him an heir. If the references to his youngest daughter, Erika, still being at home were anything to go by, the man wanted Colin to be that heir. Why else would he spend so much time reminding Colin how close the two of them had been before he left town?

Colin snorted at that. They had the same closeness as a barnacle and a ship hull. Erika had followed him everywhere that last year. He didn't mind it so much when they'd been younger, but as Erika turned fifteen, people had begun to whisper. So much so that Colin had thought about it. Even made the mistake of asking her what she thought about it. The last time he'd seen her she'd come down to the docks to see him off, knowing that both of their fathers were livid with him. It had been obvious then that she was more confident of their future than he was. Apparently five years' distance wasn't enough to make Alastair forget the idea.

Did Erika know her father was essentially offering her up as an incentive for Colin to return to Scotland?

Colin scrubbed his hands over his face and rose to pace the study. Was he reading too much into this? Letting his personal unease skew his thinking on the matter?

The letter actually stated that Alastair wanted a manager to help him in his old age. Someone young but experienced, from a respectable family, and familiar with shipping, Scotland, society, and business. He trusted Colin's judgment and gave him full leave to hire a suitable man. There weren't many people who could fill his requirements who hadn't been born into a shipping family themselves.

Which meant Colin was fairly certain Alastair had hopes of Colin filling the position himself.

Colin picked up the letter and slammed it into a pile of documents concerning other doomed ventures. He hadn't been home in five years, and the decision to leave hadn't been made on a whim. Alastair and Jaime had practically run him out of town, both men angry that Colin had interfered. Colin's father had certainly been the more vocal of the two, telling Colin that his attempts to salvage the family honor had done the exact opposite. That no one saw Jaime as the man of the family anymore. Alastair had added how ashamed he was that they'd agreed to let Colin join the ranks of men when he was clearly still a boy.

That Alastair even thought Colin would want to return and work underneath him after that meant the old man's memory was faulty.

That Colin had considered it as well, even if only for a moment, meant his own memory was weakening.

He needed some air.

His long strides had carried him five houses down the street before he realized he'd bolted from the house without a greatcoat, hat, or cane. Anyone seeing him would wonder at his sudden lack of proper accoutrements. Probably best to avoid the 'Change, then. He didn't need anyone he traded stocks with thinking he'd lost his wits. It was unlikely he'd be able to focus on the business transactions anyway.

A light breeze ruffled through his hair, sending one wayward lock curling onto his forehead. He could turn back. It wasn't as if he'd gone miles or taken a hack anywhere. His house was still visible, even.

But he couldn't. If he returned, he'd simply stare at the letter, wondering over the ramifications of his different options. One stroke of the quill could change his life forever. It could set the foundation for a business that would rival the East India Company, assuming Jaime still intended to leave Celestial Shipping to Colin. Jaime McCrae could follow Alastair's example and marry Colin's younger sister, Bronwyn, off to a man who would work alongside Jaime without questioning his business practices or challenging the way he handled the finances.

A man who wouldn't humiliate the family in order to prove Jaime wrong.

Colin couldn't see Bronwyn liking that prospect.

He couldn't deny there was something appealing about the idea of returning home, but the thought of going back under these conditions turned his stomach.

He should stop thinking about it.

Colin walked away from the house with purpose. The wind made him wish for his hat, but it wasn't worth turning back for it. He needed a distraction. Twenty minutes later he was standing in his club, listening to the raucous jibes of a high-stakes card game. A game not unlike the one that had driven the final wedge between him and his father.

Obviously the club was the wrong diversion.

Where could he go? Ryland was still nursing a carved-marble-induced headache. Colin's business associates wouldn't care about his personal life, nor did they want to hear about anything that could mean he wouldn't be making them more money in the future. He knew many other spies from the War Office, but aside from the fact that most of them were in France at the moment, they wouldn't be any good unless Colin wanted to secretly sabotage Alastair's new plans.

Colin was alone. And since being alone by himself was giving him a headache, he needed to be alone with other people. People who weren't about to lose the family fortune on the turn of a card.

He made for the nearest coffeehouse, shivering a bit as the clouds moved over the sun. It was a sign he'd lived too long in London if the crispness of the air made him cold. His Scottish friends would laugh him right into the nearest loch to show him what cold truly was. Then they'd haul him out and drag him to the local tavern.

If they were even speaking to him anymore.

He scoffed at himself. When had he become so utterly maudlin?

The aroma of coffee and chocolate hugged him as he walked through the door. Only the addition of salted sea air could have made the aroma more blessed.

"Ho, there! Good afternoon, Mr. McCrae."

Colin turned to see Lord Trent at a table in the corner and returned the younger man's greeting. With a brief glance upward, Colin sent a silent prayer of thanks floating up to heaven. What was his mother always saying? *"Trust God to give you what you need when you need it. If you get it too early, you might misplace it."* While Colin had never had much opportunity to interact with Lord Trent before, he couldn't help but notice how often he'd done so this Season. God's perfect timing indeed.

"Won't you join us?" Lord Trent gestured to the chair across from him.

Colin sat, grateful for the invitation. Whoever was joining them to make up the "us" would hopefully be as welcoming as Lord Trent.

Lord Trent leaned back in his chair. "What brings you out?"

"Air. My eyes were beginning to cross." Not an untruth. Colin's vision had been decidedly unfocused before he'd left the study and had yet to clear completely.

Lord Trent nodded. "Numbers were never my best thing. History and athletics got me through school, and I'm man enough to admit it."

A server delivered two cups of coffee to the table and took Colin's order for a third. "I recall His Grace boasting about your marks enough that last year of school."

With a laugh, Lord Trent leaned forward to wrap his hand around the coffee cup handle. "Griffith is still working out that fine line between father and brother."

An image of his own sister flashed through Colin's mind. Was he being a good brother to her? Was staying away helping her as much as he thought it was?

A feminine voice broke into his musings as the all-too-familiar glare of white filled the corner of his vision. "You'll never believe it, but Jane insists that—Oh. How do you do, Mr. McCrae?"

Colin looked up into the eyes of Lady Georgina. Lord Trent was standing, assisting his sister into the vacant chair in front of the other cup of coffee. Colin attempted to rectify his ungentlemanly behavior and stand as well, but his foot was hooked around the leg of his chair and the lady was seated by the time Colin could rise halfway out of his seat.

With a sigh he plopped back down. "I'm well, my lady. Are you enjoying the Season?"

Her eyes narrowed. "Yes, quite. Though I've only been in London a few days."

What could he say to that? Fortunately the server appeared with his coffee, giving him something to do besides stare at Lady Georgina and wish she were sweeter, nicer, and about a dozen steps lower on the social ladder.

Which meant the only thing he liked about Lady Georgina was her unfathomable beauty.

Which made him an unbelievable cad.

He took a large gulp of coffee, wincing as it singed his tongue.

"You were saying about Lady Jane?" Lord Trent sipped his coffee, his mouth curved slightly at the corners. It was hard to tell if his general good humor was creating the smile or he'd noticed Colin's overenthusiastic drinking.

Lady Georgina smiled at her brother. "Yes. She mentioned that Lord Howard was seen calling on Lady Sarah not a half hour ago, and if I'm not mistaken, she was jealous about it."

Lord Trent looked confused, no doubt wondering why he should care about a man calling on any young lady other than his sister.

Colin's mind, however, whirred to life like the experimental steam engine he'd seen in Leeds last year. If Lord Howard was paying a visit to a respectable young lady, it meant he was looking for a wife. Which meant he was preparing to settle down. Which was a good indication he was ready to pay closer attentions to some of his holdings. Which could mean making improvements and updating the lumber mill in Norfolk. Given its proximity to . . .

With a shake of his head, Colin forced his mind away from speculations and onto the people sitting at the table in front of him. He needed more in his life than business dealings, and that started with being able to set the business aside.

Lady Georgina frowned at her brother. "Honestly, Trent, Lord Howard is a viscount. Hardly the type of man I would allow to call on me."

Colin nearly choked on his coffee. Had Lord Trent suggested his sister wanted Lord Howard's attentions for herself? Colin grinned. Even he knew the lady's taste ran higher than that.

He couldn't resist the urge to rile her, though. "I called on you."

Two pairs of green eyes swung in his direction. One set laughing at his apparent gall, the other threatening to spear him through with a spoon.

The sip of coffee he took was more for show than anything else. He was too busy trying not to laugh to take a drink of any significant size. "I haven't a title to my name at all."

"Yes." Lady Georgina's eyes narrowed to slits. "We must tell Gibson to be more discerning."

Lord Trent's eyes crinkled at the corners, giving Colin a sense of safety in pursuing the teasing conversation. Their placement in the corner and the general noise of the coffeehouse kept their discussion private, and a moment of levity was certainly welcome after the morning he'd had. His eyes widened into what he hoped was an affronted expression. "You would deny me entrance after I've already been allowed to call on you? A call that lasted nearly an hour, I might add."

Lord Trent pressed his lips together but a laugh sputtered out nonetheless. He was well aware that the majority of Colin's time in the house had been spent seeing to Ryland's welfare. How much Lady Georgina knew of the afternoon was anyone's guess. After learning that the Duke of Marshington was, indeed, in her house, she'd drifted off in a daze, telling her mother to call her back downstairs if the duke awoke.

Lady Georgina placed her hands in her lap and sat a bit straighter. Her face almost appeared contrite. "I fear, sir, that any time dedicated to our drawing room would be a waste on your part. In all kindness, I must encourage you to spend your energies elsewhere."

Colin bit his cheek to hold in a smile. "Very prettily put, though I think you do yourself a disservice."

"I assure you I know my own value."

"Precisely. The mere fact that you allowed me into your drawing room raises my esteem in the eyes of many."

Lord Trent wasn't even bothering to hide his fascination. His gaze flew from Colin to Lady Georgina and back again.

All pretense of politeness dropped from her face. "Pray tell me whose esteem you wish to procure. I shall put in a good word if it will hurry you from my side."

"I seek no particular esteem, only general consideration. Though being seen with you in a coffeehouse is probably doing more for that than a mere afternoon call." Colin made a conscious effort to relax, or at least give the appearance of it.

Lady Georgina leaned in. "We did not purpose to meet you here."

Colin leaned in as well, wondering if they appeared to be having an intimate conversation with her brother as chaperone. Perhaps he would muse aloud on that next. "They don't know that."

She snapped back into an upright position in her seat. "Trent, we're leaving."

Lord Trent grinned. "Now? But it was getting so interesting."

"Now." She pushed to her feet and both gentlemen rose as well.

"Very well." Lord Trent turned to Colin. "Mr. McCrae, you and I are members of the same club, are we not?"

Colin nodded with a bit of trepidation. Had he pushed the exchange with Lady Georgina too far? It had been perilously close to several boundaries of propriety.

"Let's meet for billiards soon. I think you and I might get along famously." Lord Trent extended his hand with a grin.

Lady Georgina groaned. "Brothers. You are absolutely worthless."

Colin grinned back as he shook the younger man's hand. "Afternoon after tomorrow?"

93

"Splendid." Lord Trent offered his arm to his sister. "Come along, Georgina. You've a two o'clock appointment to have your claws sharpened."

The smile on Colin's face as he watched the siblings leave was no doubt wider than it should have been. He couldn't help it, though. That had been the most fun he'd had in a very long time.

Perhaps his frequent encounters with Lady Georgina weren't such a bad thing after all.

Chapter 9

"People are starting to stare, my lady." The quiet, subservient tone of Harriette's voice did more to remind Georgina they were amongst other people than the words did. Only in public did Harriette become the picture of an ideal lady's maid.

The street was crowded, and a brief glance around revealed that people were indeed beginning to notice that she was standing in front of a bookstore and not going in. Would they possibly be able to guess why? To the left of the window filled with colorful leather bindings and large antique books was a jewelry store, sparkling and familiar.

Surely Georgina needed a trinket of some kind. A birthday present? A new brooch? A hatpin at the very least. "What do you think of a new pin? I believe I could use a bit more sparkle with two of those evening gowns we purchased."

Harriette's brows drew together as she took a half step closer, pressing into Georgina's shoulder. "You didn't storm from the house determined to buy baubles. We're here for a book."

Yes, they were. She'd been putting off this errand, knowing the endeavor would put her in a foul mood. Since her encounter with Mr. McCrae at the coffeehouse had left her in a dismal temper, she'd hauled her maid out shopping as soon as Trent had seen her home. Time was running out for her to select a suitable reading passage, and there was no reason to ruin two days this week.

"You can do this, my lady. Just as we planned. We go in, go to the poetry section, and select the slimmest volume we can find. Then we pretend to look through a few more in case someone is looking before making our purchase and leaving." Harriette gave Georgina's hand a squeeze. "No more than twenty minutes."

"Good afternoon."

Georgina startled at the quiet greeting, noting the unspoken question in the phrase. Why did it have to be such a beautiful day? If it had only seen fit to rain this afternoon or at least threaten to do so, there wouldn't be nearly as many people out shopping. She smiled at Lady Sarah and her mother. "Good afternoon. Isn't the sun glorious today? I can't bear to leave it and go inside the shops. I should have taken a turn in the park instead of venturing to Bond Street."

Lady Sarah's eyebrows rose before she looked at the sky herself, a small smile erasing her curiosity. "It is a glorious day." She turned back to Georgina. "We've only one more stop to make. We could go for ices when we're done. It is certainly the type of weather to warrant such an outing."

"That sounds delightful." It sounded anything but delightful. However, if eating an ice would help Lady Sarah swallow Georgina's nonsense about enjoying the weather on the side of the road, she'd gladly partake of the cold treat. "Shall we meet you at Gunter's in an hour?"

Lady Sarah's agreement brought an end to the conversation, leaving Georgina once again standing outside the bookstore for no reason.

Harriette's smirk was barely visible in the corner of Georgina's vision.

"Not a word," Georgina mumbled as she pushed her way into the bookstore before someone else caught her and she found herself agreeing to a horse race.

The abrupt change of lighting had her blinking as they wandered farther into the store. Where was the poetry section?

"Left." Harriette's low whisper directed Georgina's attention, and she moved in that direction.

A slim book, already bound in blue leather with gold lettering on it, sat on display on a shelf at eye level. Georgina snatched it. "This one. Will this one do?"

The maid turned her head to read the cover. "It is poetry, my lady, but I've no idea if it's any good."

Georgina opened the book and flipped through the pages. Words were printed on each page. "Someone thought this person good enough to print an entire book of poetry by him. There's bound to be one decent poem in the bunch."

Harriette shrugged.

Georgina clutched the book to her chest. "That's settled. Let's go."

"But what about the plan?" Harriette's eyes were wide as she looked around the store.

"No one is paying us the least bit of attention." Georgina hoped, anyway. She was afraid to look around in case she accidentally caught someone's eye and found herself embroiled in a discussion about the latest gothic novel or some other such nonsense. "We've found a book. We're leaving."

"As you wish."

Georgina paid for the book and waited for the clerk to wrap it in paper. The smell of books surrounded her—leather and paper and ink, all foreign enough on their own, but combined left her feeling out of sorts and a bit woozy.

She left Harriette to wait for the book and fled back to the street. Something was certainly going to have to be done about Jane's new interest in poetry. Georgina refused to go through this every week.

Colin's agitation had settled greatly after his interlude with Lady Georgina and Lord Trent, but the inane conversation in the corner of Lady Buckton's drawing room was enough to try his patience all over again. This was a card party, and he'd somehow gotten trapped in a conversation with two men who were both terrified of and desirous to please the London elite bustling about the various rooms.

"Have you been asked to participate in Leatham's Cornwall project, McCrae?" Sir Robert Verney asked, trying and failing to look at ease.

Colin shook his head, both in answer to the question and in disbelief at the other man's attitude. People like Sir Robert could easily move in a lower social circle and be the most important person in attendance. Being overly notable never suited Colin's purposes, though, which made him perfectly comfortable to be the most inconsequential man in the room.

Most of the time.

Mr. Craven, the third man in their pitiful corner trio, laughed at Sir Robert's question. "McCrae wouldn't touch that if you paid him. We all know how McCrae feels about doing business with Leatham."

Colin looked around the room to avoid his companions' eyes. Leatham was still using slave labor in his northern mines. While Colin wasn't naïve enough to think he'd completely evaded the practice, Colin did his level best to avoid business ventures that utilized slave labor.

"I've made a tidy sum from Leatham's mines this year," Mr. Craven said.

Of course he had. It made Colin sick. Fortunately that was one of the few things Colin and his father had agreed upon. Whatever arguments they'd had over the running of the company, they'd at least agreed to not ship people.

"I've made a tidy sum off Celestial Shipping," Colin said, unwilling to let the conversation slide by. He liked Mr. Craven most of the time, at least when they weren't in social situations like these. Perhaps Colin could convince him to move his money away from Leatham.

Whatever else Colin might have planned to say got stuck in his throat as he once again found himself distracted by the eye-catching glitter of an all-white ensemble. Why was his gaze always drawn to her? She should have faded away, lost in the sea of colors and trimmings.

His internal musings died as the personification of narcissism advanced directly toward him, and there was nothing he could do about it. It was entertaining to contemplate, though. What would the great Lady Georgina do if her target simply walked away?

Which did beg the question of why he was her target. After the exchange at the coffeehouse, he would have expected her to give him a wide berth.

Sir Robert and Mr. Craven continued to discuss lucrative investment options, but the conversation wasn't enough to motivate Colin to look away from the lady's approach, even though he wanted to. She cut through the crowd like a beam of light. It had been mere days since she made her first bow at the masquerade ball and already people were calling her the Angel of the Season, confusing her penchant for dressing in the color of purity with the actual possession of a sweet demeanor.

Colin likened her to a lump of ice and would be perfectly happy to go the rest of the Season without risking frostbite again.

At least she was hauling Lady Miranda behind her. By all accounts the sisters had nothing in common but a set of parents. For Ryland's sake, Colin hoped that was true.

"I apologize for the intrusion," Lady Georgina simpered, as if she truly wanted to talk to Colin and the two gentlemen next to him. "But my sister insisted we come over here."

She smiled at Colin's acquaintances before turning the carefully constructed curve of her lips in his direction. "Mr. McCrae, she particularly wanted to meet you. Lady Miranda, this is Mr. Colin McCrae. I believe you know the other two gentlemen."

Lady Miranda's eyes widened.

Colin bit back a laugh. The gentlemen with him were probably known to her only by sight. While of higher rank than Colin, they were even less popular, invited to even out numbers or fill the ranks with less eligible gentlemen.

Their popularity, or lack thereof, could have something to do with their insistence on dwelling in corners.

"How do you do, Lady Miranda?" Colin bit his cheek to keep from grinning. "I was just telling Mr. Craven and Sir Robert about a shipping company I'm involved in. Very dry conversation, I'm afraid."

Lady Georgina scowled at him, no doubt angry that he'd circumvented her plan to embarrass her sister. Lady Miranda gave him a grateful smile for rescuing her.

He wished he were noble enough that saving Lady Miranda from potential embarrassment had been enough to motivate him, but the lady's honor had been a distant second thought in his mind. No, if he were honest, his goal had everything to do with getting under the skin of said lady's younger sister. Hammering at Lady Georgina's carefully constructed shell was too entertaining to pass up.

Admittedly, his actions toward the young lady were far from charitable, but did Georgina really deserve his charity? He'd rather reserve that for people in truly dire circumstances, not spoiled misses who didn't get the dancing partner they wanted.

He gave Lady Miranda a wink, further irking Lady Georgina.

Lady Miranda smiled and said, "I'm afraid I know nothing of shipping." The names he provided must have reminded her of past dealings, because Lady Miranda turned to the other gentlemen with a confident smile. "Mr. Craven, how is your sister? She married last year?"

The man with the thinning hair beamed. "Yes, she did. Doing splendidly. I hear from her occasionally." After an uncomfortable beat of silence, Mr. Craven turned to his companion. "Sir Robert, do you fancy a game of faro? I believe they are starting one in the library."

Colin held back a sigh as he watched the other men depart. They'd become accustomed to being ignored at these gatherings, and anyone of higher rank intimidated them, particularly the women.

Why did they come to these events in the first place if they weren't going to take full advantage of the opportunities presented?

Not that either of these ladies presented much of an opportunity. The majority of ladies in attendance weren't potential marriage partners, but that was one of the things that had to be endured for success.

And Colin needed success. Success brought money, and money brought the ability to help others and secure a future for his family. Most of the time that was enough.

He smiled at the sisters. "I suppose that leaves me to entertain two lovely ladies. Might I retrieve you a bit of refreshment? Or procure you a seat at a table?"

"No, thank you." Lady Georgina's graceful shell was back in place. She almost sounded civil. "I see someone I must speak with. Pardon me."

Colin held in a laugh as she turned and walked through the door. She must have the ability to see through walls if she saw someone in the other room to speak to.

His suppressed laughter made his smile a bit too big as he looked at Lady Miranda. "Do you need to speak with them as well?"

She smiled in return. "I believe I am good where I am, thank you."

Colin almost nodded in approval. "I am pleased to finally meet you."

"Finally, Mr. McCrae?"

Colin leaned into the corner, forcing her to turn her back to a good portion of the room and the numerous people who she would no doubt find more interesting than him. He might never get a chance to get to know her again, and if Ryland was making a mistake, Colin would rather know it now than after the wedding.

Not that he could change Ryland's mind. Colin's powers of persuasion weren't quite that good. "I've heard about you."

"All good things, I hope." Her smile wasn't as perfect as Lady

Georgina's, but it held an air of authenticity the Duchess of Ice had never possessed.

"But of course."

"Hmmm." Skepticism danced across her face, but she didn't challenge him. "Have you sat down to a game of whist yet this evening?"

"Sadly, no, I'm afraid I've been too deep in discussions since I arrived. Should we find a table and sit down to a game?" He started to offer her his arm, but a shadow falling across the wall beside him stopped his movement. He turned to see Ryland had appeared, crossing the room with his usual stealth. What was he doing here? And sporting a glorious discoloration around one eye, no less. Colin made a mental note to never spar with Lord Trent.

Lady Miranda and Ryland greeted each other—her with veiled hostility, and him with bored austerity designed to irk her further.

If these two ever found their way to the altar it would be a miracle.

Without warning, Lady Miranda pulled Colin back into the conversation. "Mr. McCrae, may I present His Grace, the Duke of Marshington? Your Grace, this is Mr. McCrae."

Ryland bowed his head. "A pleasure, sir."

Obviously no one had seen fit to tell Lady Miranda that Colin had been the one to see Ryland home the other day. Since Ryland wasn't correcting Lady Miranda's assumption, Colin wouldn't either. He didn't want to hinder any plan the man had. "The honor is mine, Your Grace."

As he executed the appropriate bow, a billow of white rejoined their circle. Lady Georgina. Of course she would find the most eligible bachelor in the place and be so wrapped in her own plans that she wouldn't notice the tension between that bachelor and her own sister.

Shameful.

"You looked in need of a rescue, dear sister. You couldn't possibly partner both of these fine gentlemen in a game of cards."

Colin groaned, but the other three people ignored him. He was going to have to play cards with a couple of spatting lovebirds and the white witch who wanted to split them up for her own grasping, nefarious purposes.

Resigned to his fate, he claimed Lady Miranda as a partner. He might have to sit with the conniving lass, but he refused to help her win anything.

The situation should have been perfect. The card table was situated to the side of the drawing room, away from most of the raucous laughter and disgruntled murmurs of the other card games. Georgina's back was to most of the attendees, which should have framed her well as a beacon of light in the midst of chaos. She was seated across from the Duke of Marshington at a card game that, if played carefully, could last for nearly an hour.

Yes, it should have been perfect.

If only Miranda wasn't ruining everything. Her sour frown indicated she was going to make this an unpleasant game.

As the duke settled himself in the chair across the table, Georgina relaxed her face into a pleasant half smile, lowering her lashes so she could examine her target without anyone noticing. Wherever he'd been hiding for the past nine years, he'd taken care of himself. Everyone was talking about him since his surprise return. Handsome, mysterious, powerful.

No one would dare cross his wife when he married.

He was perfect for her needs. Irritating sister or not, Georgina had to make the most of this opportunity.

Mr. McCrae dealt the cards with a sure hand, a slight tilt to one corner of his mouth. Odious man. Why did it always feel like he was laughing at her? As if he knew a secret joke and she were the subject.

The first two tricks were played in silence, broken only by the occasional overloud laughter from a nearby card table or the clink of glassware from the passing servants. Georgina considered and discarded many topics of conversation. The right topic could be the key to landing a successful match.

Miranda started the next round of cards.

"Fishing for something, are you?" the duke asked with a tap of his cards on the table.

"I beg your pardon!" Miranda sat up straighter in her chair, outraged.

Georgina cast a glance around to see if Miranda's outburst had drawn undue notice to their table. The duke's attention was certainly on the elder Hawthorne sister, which was not where Georgina wanted it. Georgina loved her sister. Sometimes she even liked her. But if Miranda's refusal to marry had proven anything, it was that she did not need the social protection of a powerful marriage.

"You aren't supposed to discuss the cards, Your Grace." Georgina gave him her best smile, the one she'd practiced for hours in front of a mirror. The one that had sent countless men scrambling for the refreshment table at the mere mention she might be thirsty.

The one that did absolutely no good now.

"My apologies," the duke said as Mr. McCrae slid the knave onto the pile. After a moment, the duke flicked the ace onto the table.

Since the duke had won the trick, Georgina gathered up the cards and added them to the stack the pair of them had already won. Neither he nor Miranda seemed to notice. They were talking about the card game as if it were a matter of great importance.

"You're going to rip that card," a low voice said in Georgina's ear.

Georgina released the cards immediately, her gaze flying to Mr. McCrae's clear blue eyes. "I will do no such thing."

She winced at the ridiculousness of her words. The wrinkles and dents of the cards bore witness to her rough treatment of them.

"Is the game not going well for you?" Mr. McCrae looked across the table to where Miranda and the duke were having some bizarre conversation about how to play cards. Miranda should know better. A lady never discussed strategy with a man, particularly in public.

Georgina turned back to Mr. McCrae. "I don't know what you're talking about. We've two tricks to your team's one."

His laugh was low and seemed to flow over her, raising the hair on her arm between her gloves and sleeve. "A bit of advice? You need to learn to evaluate the whole game, not just the cards in front of you."

Georgina had the uneasy feeling he was talking about more than whist. Did he know something? Did he know about her? He couldn't possibly know her secret, but he did seem to be everywhere, toting around that abominable confidence that he was welcome anywhere, despite his low station. Had he blackmailed his way into society? Perhaps he was trying to find something with which to manipulate her, or worse, Griffith.

The muscles in Georgina's neck and back tightened, pulling her shoulders into a painfully tense position. That would explain why he always seemed to be laughing at her. If he knew . . .

The duke slid his card onto the table. A foolish choice considering the cards played in the last trick.

Willing the tension, or at least any visible appearance of it, away from her shoulders, she smiled at her partner. No matter how hard Mr. McCrae looked, he'd never find anything. She and Harriette were too careful. "That was not well played, Your Grace, but you've been away from civilized gatherings for a while, so I won't complain."

Miranda spent a great deal of time contemplating her cards before playing the king on top of the duke's queen.

Frustration filled Georgina. Did her sister know nothing about men? They had two brothers and she hadn't learned yet that men were considerably more amiable when you let them win? It was all well and good for Miranda to put off every eligible suitor who tried to court her, but she wasn't the only Hawthorne seeking marriage this year.

Georgina needed to rectify things now. "How unkind, Miranda, for you to take advantage of His Grace's blunder."

Miranda raised her eyebrows, keeping her gaze on the duke in a most unnerving stare. Georgina was really going to have to talk to their mother. Miranda was losing all her poise as she attained spinsterhood.

Mr. McCrae coughed, though it sounded almost like a sputter as he collected the winning hand.

He contemplated her as he neatened the small pile of cards. "You look good in green."

Daft man. "Perhaps you should consider spectacles. I'm wearing white."

"Ah, yes, but the jealousy has livened your complexion."

The absolute gall of the man infuriated her. "Why would I be jealous?"

"Because you've lost."

Georgina looked at the table. Each couple had two stacks of cards in front of them. "We appear evenly matched at the moment."

"Then you aren't looking closely."

But she was. She was looking all too closely; she just didn't want to admit it. It was obvious to anyone with half a brain that the duke was, for whatever reason, giving his undivided attention to Miranda.

Georgina wasn't even under his consideration.

This was the second man her sister had ruined her chances with, even if she'd done so without intent. Georgina's voice was tight with unshed tears as she tried to move the game along. They were all stuck at this table until the game was finished "Sister dear, it is your play."

"What if I don't want it?" Miranda whispered.

"What do you mean you don't want it? You played the king, Miranda. Who did you think was going to have the next lead?"

The urge to slam her cards on the table and leave was strong, but that would create a scandal. Georgina needed the marriage of the Season, not the scandal of the year.

Very well, scandal of the week. Abandoning a card game wasn't worth more than a day or two of gossip. Assuming anyone even noticed.

Miranda plopped the queen of hearts on the table.

This was the strangest game Georgina had ever played. Was

her sister trying to flirt with a card? They were all acting as if the cards were some sort of life symbol. She threw down the two.

Very well, if philosophical was the way to the duke's heart, she would play along.

As soon as she thought of something to say.

The duke slowly laid the king on top of Miranda's queen.

Was the duke flirting back? Was this absurd game actually working for Miranda?

Miranda's cheeks flushed bright red and remained that way as they quietly played out the hand.

"I fear I must excuse myself." The duke gave no excuse, simply watched Miranda as he rose.

Georgina wanted to cry. Miranda had had three years—three years!—to make a good match. Did she have to suddenly become successful during Georgina's one and only chance? Because it was her only chance. One week into the Season, and Georgina was already exhausted from hiding her shortcoming. She'd never make it through a second Season.

The Earl of Ashcombe walked by the table as the duke walked away.

"My lord!" Georgina rose with measured grace. Another skill she'd spent hours perfecting, and it gained the earl's attention immediately. "We seem to be short a player. Would you care to join?"

"But of course. I would hate to leave the Ladies Hawthorne in distress." The earl took the duke's seat.

Miranda frowned at Georgina, but Georgina didn't care. It wasn't Georgina's fault that the man had dropped his courtship of Miranda during her first Season. He wasn't the greatest catch, but he was popular, wealthy, and powerful. If the duke didn't come up to scratch, Lord Ashcombe would do.

Mr. McCrae looked at everyone at the table, eyebrows inching higher.

Georgina ignored him as she dealt the cards. This was going to work.

It had to.

Chapter 10

He'd never been more grateful to lose a card game in his life. Shortly after Ashcombe joined the table, Lady Miranda had pleaded a headache. While Colin didn't doubt the truth of her statement, he had a distinct feeling the headache was more figurative than literal and most assuredly connected to the gentleman now sitting to Colin's left.

Lady Wrothington joined the game after Miranda departed. By then all Colin wanted was to be finished. He threw tricks and played as poorly as possible, but the others at his table seemed determined to stretch the game out as long as possible.

After the game, Lady Georgina drifted away. Colin watched her go and tried to convince himself he was glad to be free of her. It didn't work. The uncomfortable sensation remained that he was supposed to do something, which was a ludicrous idea.

It wasn't his business. He should leave it alone.

He wandered the edges of the rooms, exchanging banal social chatter with people on occasion, but mostly moving just to appear part of the party while avoiding brooding in a corner somewhere.

What were the chances Lady Georgina would listen to him even if he did say anything to her?

Nearly nonexistent.

Which meant the slightest possibility remained that he could get through to her. Colin drained the last of his drink and set the glass on a passing servant's tray, exchanging it for a fresh one. He needed something to occupy himself as he wandered around the rooms.

Did he really think Lady Georgina would listen to him? They'd yet to have an encounter that could be termed as anything less than a verbal skirmish.

God was going to have to create the optimal situation if He was going to keep prodding Colin to interfere in this family's relationships. Colin wasn't going to try to perform a miracle on his own. Simply playing cards at the same table as the lady had raised more than a few eyebrows. He could only imagine what seeking her out for a private conversation would do.

Content that he'd turned the matter over to more capable hands than his, Colin made an effort to make use of his evening. He listened to gossip, talked business, and observed people. It was amazing how many business deals fell through because the people involved didn't get along. Knowing who couldn't stand each other was a valuable part of his success.

Every woman wearing even a bit of white distracted him until he cast his eyes toward the ceiling in a prayer of submission. He couldn't take it anymore. Obviously God wasn't going to remove the notion that Colin was supposed to help Georgina until he gave in and did something about it. Downing the last of his lemonade as if it were a bracing shot of Scotch, he set off to find the lady in white.

That she was standing alone by a window was a miracle.

Colin frowned at the wording of his thoughts. He had asked for a miraculous sign. "How is your evening?"

Lady Georgina startled at his voice, her eyes darting around. Whether to see who might notice her talking to someone of Colin's ilk or looking for someone to save her he didn't know.

"Well. Thank you, Mr. McCrae."

"You remember my name. I'm flattered."

"I am endeavoring to forget it, but you keep appearing."

He nodded, searching, praying for the right words, wishing he'd been a little less obstinate in his prayers a few moments ago. He turned so they were standing shoulder to shoulder, looking out the window into the night.

"Your sister doesn't seem to care for Lord Ashcombe." Colin winced. That had been rather blunt.

"That is probably why they didn't marry."

Was that disapproval in her voice? "You think they should have?"

"He's a very eligible match."

Colin gave up pretending to look through the window and turned to lean his shoulder against the glass so he could see her face better. "But she doesn't care for him."

She flipped open her fan, a gorgeous creation covered in painted vines and roses, and stirred the air with small flicks of her wrist, managing to aim the breeze so that it didn't ruffle her coiffure. "What has that to do with anything?"

Colin opened his mouth and snapped it shut. While it was true that practical matches were still quite widespread, he'd seen more and more love matches over the years. It was a trend he heartily approved of, given the tense atmosphere his own parents' practical marriage had created.

"She's your sister."

"Yes. She is."

What had he expected? That she would open up and confide her deepest secrets to him? "May I give you a piece of advice?"

"Can I stop you?"

"You could walk away."

"And you might follow. I seem to keep encountering you, Mr. McCrae, and I think we both know you will not suit my purposes. If having this conversation will keep you away from me, I'd like to get it over with." The fan moved with a bit more vigor, sending the ringlets framing her face into a frothing dance of their own.

Colin crossed his arms over his chest and smiled. "I applaud your honesty."

"I despise your persistency."

"Fair enough." Colin collected his thoughts before plunging on. He was never this candid in public. He was well known for dealing honestly with people, but he never waded into personal waters. "Your family needs to come before your marital goals."

Lady Georgina's eyebrows rose. "Is that all? And where is your family? I would venture a guess that you are rather far from home. Not many people raised in England speak with such a brogue."

"Aye, I am far from home." And even farther from his family. "Which is why I know what happens when someone puts their own gain above their family."

"You know nothing about me or my family."

"I know you've been setting your cap for the duke since he returned to London."

She tilted her chin down and looked at him through her lashes. If he didn't know better, he'd think she was flirting with him. The fan slowed to a less agitated pace. "I've seen you as often as I've seen the duke this Season. More so. One might think you were jealous, Mr. McCrae."

"One might think you were desperate, Lady Georgina."

Her eyes widened and the fan stilled entirely. Had he hit the mark? Why would the daughter of a duke be desperate? She had years before people started whispering behind their fans.

She snapped her fan shut and shoved it into her reticule. "You hardly know my family. Why do you care?"

That wasn't entirely true. He'd done a good bit of business with her elder brother. She wouldn't have reason to know that though. "Consider me a concerned romantic."

"Romantic? You wish to see me marry for love?"

As Lady Georgina obviously cared more for social status than anything else, he couldn't care less if the schemer saddled herself with an ancient aristocrat with a penchant for gambling away the family coffers. But Ryland was a close friend and Colin was fast coming to like Lady Miranda. "Has love found you?"

She scoffed. "Hardly."

"Then I have no opinion one way or the other as far as you're concerned. But I'd hate to see you trample on your sister's heart, as she seems the kind to be searching for love."

Lady Georgina's eyes narrowed. "What makes you think Miranda is in love with Lord Ashcombe?"

Was the lady dense? "Nothing. She's in love with someone else entirely."

"What makes you the expert?"

Colin cast his eyes around the room, noting the couples that seemed more enamored with each other than their surroundings. "Observation."

"Of a single night?"

"Of a single moment. Women in love have a certain look about them when the object of their affection is around."

Lady Georgina turned to look over the room as well. Was she noting the same couples he did? "Simpering and weak?"

"No. Murderous. Love and hate are two sides of the same coin, you know." Colin grinned as he pulled a coin from his pocket and flipped it in the air. "It's always a gamble to see which way it will land."

He caught the coin and placed it on the back of his hand, but nearly fumbled as he realized the description would fit Lady Georgina and himself. But there was no softer side to his disdain for the lady. There couldn't be, for that way led to nothing but frustration and heartache. No doubt Lady Georgina was the emotional exception that proved the rule. One didn't particularly need a heart to be angry.

Shoving the coin back into his pocket, he returned to his goal of getting through to Lady Miranda's thickheaded sister. "I'm guessing it landed poorly for her with Lord Ashcombe. Don't be the reason it goes wrong for her this time."

Lady Georgina frowned. "I think we're done here."

"As you wish." Colin bowed, hoping he'd said enough to at least make her think.

It was the longest carriage ride of her life, but Georgina kept her ire contained until they got home. Well, most of her ire. She might have berated Miranda's social skills a time or two on the way home, but compared to how she really felt about the evening, it was a mild chastisement indeed. Once home she rushed through the house to the safety of her room, sighing as she saw Harriette setting a hot mug of tea on the dressing table.

After dropping onto the chair, Georgina wrapped her hands around the mug. The warmth from the first sip flowed through her body and brought her a sense of calm.

Georgina took deep breaths while Harriette pulled pins from the coiffure that had taken nearly an hour to create. "She's going to ruin everything, Harriette."

Harriette's eyes flitted to Georgina's reflected gaze. Her forehead scrunched in confusion beneath her smoothed-back hair. "Who?"

Georgina sighed and took another sip of tea. "My sister. She's determined to ruin me."

"Oh." Harriette's confusion was obvious as she began unlacing Georgina's dress. "I don't think your sister would ruin you, my lady."

"No?" Georgina rubbed her hands over her face. "I'll be lucky if the Duke of Marshington ever speaks to me again. How am I supposed to convince the man he wants to marry me if my sister continues to act like a simple-headed ninny in his presence?"

Harriette's hands paused. "Lady Miranda?"

"Unbelievable, I know." Georgina nibbled on her lip until she caught Harriette's disapproving glare in the mirror. Right. Nibbling would make her lips look flaky and craggy. "Maybe he didn't notice. He has been gone for nine years."

Harriette made soothing noises as she helped Georgina change clothes.

Georgina pulled her hair free of the night rail's neckline. "He wouldn't have come back to London if he weren't looking for a bride."

More encouraging noises came from the maid.

Was Harriette being condescending? Georgina narrowed her

eyes in the mirror as she sank back into the chair. "All I have to do is show him I'm the best candidate."

The maid began pulling Georgina's hair into a long braid. "You've put considerable effort into making yourself the best possible lady in the ballroom this Season. I don't think you'll have to worry about drawing the notice of an attractive match."

Georgina burst from the chair and began to pace. "I need the best match, not an attractive match. I have to be the envy of everyone if I am to protect myself."

She swung around to face the maid, who looked on with dark, sympathetic eyes. Georgina hated the note of panic that was creeping into her voice, but everything was turning out to be a bit harder than she had anticipated. "I have to be above reproach by the end of this Season, Harriette. If they find out . . . One day I'm going to get caught, Harriette, and if I'm not married when they find out I can't do the things a lady is expected to do, my life will be over. No one will want me."

Harriette said nothing as she urged Georgina back into the chair and set about redoing the braid her lady's outburst had interrupted.

Exhaustion and relief that in this room at least she didn't have to pretend brought a slump to Georgina's shoulders. "If only I were one year older, Harriette. I know I could have made it work with the marquis if I had been out in society last Season."

Harriette tugged Georgina's hair a bit tighter than necessary, drawing forth a squeak of surprise. "Lord Raebourne fell in love. There is nothing you could have done to convince him to marry you instead."

Georgina averted her face so Harriette couldn't see the disgruntled pout. With her braid completed, she stood and began the process of shaking out her dress from the evening, examining the trim for tears and holes. "We don't know that."

Gentle hands removed the dress from Georgina's fingers. "Yes, we do. Even you have to admit what a lovely woman Lady Raebourne is. She's been quite nice to you, despite your attempts to ruin the match."

While it might be true, Georgina didn't really have to admit it.

"Would you like to practice your poem for Lady Jane's gathering?" Harriette gestured toward the dressing table, where the slim book rested, mocking Georgina with its very presence.

The blue leather binding drew the eye, and more than once today Georgina had yearned to toss the thing through the window.

With arm extended as far as possible, she flipped the book open to the marked page. At this distance the words looked like an indistinguishable river of black bleeding across the page. Given enough time she could make out a printed page using some cumbersome techniques she and Harriette had devised, but it always brought on a headache.

She'd long ago given up praying for relief. Considering God was the one who'd given her the curse in the first place, she didn't hold out much hope of Him fixing it.

As she squinted her eyes, struggling to pick out individual words she'd already memorized, the prick of pain started directly behind her left eye. "Not tonight, Harriette. I'm too tired."

Tired, yes, but also restless. She yanked her dressing gown from the wardrobe, finding comfort in the colorful streaks and smudges that mottled the white silk. Once the sash was yanked tight, she plopped a sketchbook into the circle of candlelight on the dressing table.

Harriette picked up Georgina's slippers and dress but remained standing where she was, her lip caught between her teeth.

Georgina narrowed her eyes at her friend. Twelve years together, fooling the world, perpetuating the lie that Georgina could do what every other normal young lady of wealth and breeding could do, meant they'd gotten close. There was no one Georgina trusted more or knew better.

And a bit lip meant there was something worse than Lady Jane's poetry recitation.

"You'll make your lips craggy and flaky doing that, Harriette." Georgina pretended she wasn't preparing for forthcoming doom, hoping her apparent ease would help Harriette vocalize the problem.

"It's your mother, my lady."

Georgina's eyebrows shot up as she looked up from her box of pastels. Her mother? She'd been managing her mother for years. It was amazing how little people expected of you when you cultivated an air of arrogant disdain for everything around you.

Harriette shifted her weight. "She wants you to help with the invitations."

"I know. We've been taking care of them in the mornings." Georgina turned back to her pastels and danced her fingers along the soft, oily edges. She selected a medium brown and slid it across the paper, mollified a bit by the bold stroke of color.

"No, not those, my lady. The ones for your ball. She wants you to help address them."

Georgina paused in the act of trading the brown pastel stick for a red one. "When?"

Harriette shrugged. "Your ball isn't for seven more weeks. You have a few weeks to prepare, I would imagine."

"We'll have to do them beforehand. She'll be amazed at my initiative." The bitter words were soothed by the swirls of red mingling with the strokes of brown.

A nod was Harriette's only response. Likely she'd already formed a plan for getting her hands on the invitations. Georgina would have to take care of her own toilette for a few days to allow Harriette time to do the actual addressing, but it was nothing they hadn't done before.

Smudging the colors with her fingers, Georgina grimaced at more than the feeling of gooey pastel on her skin. "We'll have to make sure we have a complete list of invitees." She speared Harriette with her gaze. "I can't afford to have her ask me to add someone else at the last minute."

"You can get out of it."

"True." Georgina had mastered the art of getting out of things. Occasionally it was something she actually wanted to do, but if she didn't maintain an air of bored selfishness, she could get caught.

Harriette nodded and disappeared into the dressing room.

Georgina looked down at her drawing, expecting to see the face of the duke, the man she'd set her cap for as the best candidate for the role of social savior. He was an even better alliance than the marquis would have been.

Instead of the startling grey eyes and dark hair of His Grace, she saw the red-tinged curls and laughing blue eyes of Mr. McCrae.

With an angry growl she crumpled the picture and hurled it into the cold fireplace. That man was hindering her focus. It was insupportable.

She crossed to the wash basin and scrubbed the pastel residue from her hands. The colors bled into the basin, swirling and crashing against each other like the dancers at a ball, before blending into a murky mess. That was her life these days. A beautiful, well-thought-out plan with a thousand moving pieces, and it could all come crashing down in an instant.

Sleep. She needed sleep. Everything looked better with sleep.

Dropping the stained dressing robe on a nearby chair, she crawled into bed.

And proceeded to stare at the ceiling, reliving every humiliating moment since she'd met the infernal Scotsman.

It was painfully obvious she was going to have to add a new swirl to her life, because one thing was certain—she had to avoid another encounter with Mr. Colin McCrae.

Chapter 11

A strange feeling overtook Colin's limbs as he strolled down St. James's Street toward his club. His heart was beating just the slightest bit faster. A sensation that fell somewhere short of an actual itch ran across his skin. There was an almost overwhelming urge to hurry. He nearly broke into a jog as the doors of Boodle's came into view.

So he stopped where he was, on a public street awash with afternoon sunlight. He refused to walk into a situation with an unknown quantity. Especially if that unknown was his own self.

The feeling wasn't completely foreign, but it had certainly been a long time since he'd felt it.

Anticipation.

He was excited to go in those doors today. Despite the fact that his routine brought him by the club no fewer than three times a week and frequently as many as six, he was anticipating today's visit in a way he hadn't in a very long time. Today there was nothing more pressing to do than shoot billiards with Lord Trent.

And it was making him behave like a young lady waiting for a caller.

Had his life become so much about plans and agendas that he'd stopped doing things for simple enjoyment?

Yes. Yes it had.

He shook his head as he entered the building. Even though he'd been spending a great deal of time with Ryland since his return, the visits had been with purpose. They'd been visiting Hawthorne House, trying to ascertain Lady Miranda's social schedule, or trying to tie the last loose string on Ryland's final case.

Supposedly Ryland was off the case, but leaving things undone had never sat well with him. Technically, Colin had never even been on the case, since he didn't even work for the War Office.

The War Office was much more concerned with getting results than with being official.

Which was how Colin had gotten the required sponsors to join this club in the first place. The domain of the more business-minded gentlemen, a club such as Boodle's was still considerably out of reach for a man of Colin's social status. The men of the War Office liked the way Colin's mind worked, though, and they wanted to provide him with access to enough people to connect the dots they might be missing.

If Colin made a profit from the same information, so be it. He invested money for more than one agent of the Crown. They would find themselves well off when they hung up their cloaks and pistols.

But today wasn't about information or clandestine meetings. It was about something that had been missing in his life for far too long. Fun. He was going to an appointment without having anything on the line or even a secondary motive. A novel concept.

Lord Trent was already racking the billiard balls when Colin entered the back room.

"Have you seen? The betting book is already filling up for the Season." Lord Trent slid the cue between his fingers and sent the balls scurrying across the felt.

"It's more fun to bet early in the Season. Waiting until the matches are obvious doesn't present the same challenge." Colin gritted his teeth to keep from grinning at Lord Trent's skill. He wouldn't have to hold back for appearance's sake. This was turning into a brilliant day.

They took turns knocking balls into the pockets. The club was quiet that afternoon. They were in fact the only men occupying the billiard tables, leaving them free to enjoy the simple sounds of the balls clacking against each other before they thunked into the pockets.

They'd each won a game and were setting up the third before Lord Trent spoke again.

"Do you know what I just realized?"

Colin raised a brow as he positioned his cue.

Lord Trent propped a hip against the billiard table. "I have nothing to attend this evening. No obligatory escorting of sisters."

Once Colin had sent the balls rolling, Lord Trent spoke once more. "Have you any siblings, Mr. McCrae?"

It wasn't surprising that Lord Trent had chosen Colin's least favorite topic. The Hawthornes were a notoriously loyal family. They would never comprehend the idea that a man could consider gambling away his livelihood and his children's future and well-being along with it. "I've a sister."

"She married?"

"No." At least not that he knew of. "She's out this year, though." And he wasn't there to protect her. He placed his aim carefully but put too much force behind the cue, and the tip clanked against the ball, sending it careening into the bumpers. He should be there making sure she was courted by the right sort of man. But the scandal that had driven him from town in the first place still lurked in people's memories, waiting to be recalled the moment he showed his face again. If he returned, it could ruin any chance she had at a decent match.

"Why don't you bring her down to London? I'm sure Mother would love to take her around." Lord Trent's cue connected with a solid thump, and two balls dropped into the pocket.

The chaos that would cause brought a smile to Colin's face as he imagined it. "My father doesn't care for London."

That was putting it lightly. Oh, his father didn't mind the docks, though they were annoyingly overcrowded. It was the actual city itself. The hustle and bustle that Colin had thrived on for the past five years made the old Scotsman grumble and grouse and look mad enough to chew nails for at least a week after each visit.

Lord Trent leaned on his cue, considering Colin for a long moment. Was he guessing that was the very reason Colin had settled in the city? Whatever his thoughts, Lord Trent didn't voice them, just nodded and went back to the game.

Lord Howard stumbled through the room in worn and wrinkled evening clothes. Had the man not been home yet? It was early afternoon.

Lord Trent circled the table to stand beside Colin. "His name's in the books at least three times. Hard to believe there are women out there who actually want to marry that man, isn't it?"

Collin shrugged. "Most of the time he's well put together. Now, of course, he's a bit worse for wear." Though his family had money, Lord Howard didn't have a pence to his name. Some woman was going to wake up to a harsh reality when she discovered that.

"Praise God neither of my sisters have set their caps for him. Don't think I could stomach him coming round that often." Lord Trent sank the last ball, winning the game.

Colin stored his cue in disgust. He'd barely touched a ball that round.

The two men ordered drinks and dropped into two of the tufted burgundy leather chairs near one of the upper-floor windows. "What about you?"

Colin looked at Lord Trent with raised eyebrows. "What about me?"

"Any plans to marry soon?"

With a shrug, Colin took a large swallow of brandy to buy himself time. "I'm not opposed to the idea. But I've time yet." Colin prayed that was enough to satisfy the man and that Lord Trent wouldn't feel the need to bring up his sisters in relation to Colin's matrimonial prospects.

Lord Trent nodded, apparently in agreement with Colin's views of pending matrimony. "It will be nice, though, once my sisters have married. Having both of them out is exhausting."

Colin couldn't have agreed more.

In the name of getting his life back to normal, Colin left the club and strolled farther down St. James's Street in the direction of Ryland's Pall Mall mansion. Perhaps it was the mellow mood he found himself in after spending a few hours relaxing instead of thinking, but Colin had almost convinced himself that Ryland was ready to discuss a reasonable, straight-forward progression for his courtship of Lady Miranda.

As hard as Ryland was working for the lady, Colin was beginning to suspect that Ryland was having to overcome more than simply lying about his identity. Which meant it was likely that Colin was about to witness the unfurling of another campaign scheme.

Which was almost as entertaining as engaging the younger Hawthorne sister in a battle of wits.

Where had that thought come from?

Yet more evidence that he needed Ryland to get married so Colin could stop thinking about anyone's personal matters. He was becoming entirely too involved in them.

The butler opened Ryland's door, replacing the wooden blockade with his own sizable bulk. His craggy face and nonexistent neck probably scared away the majority of callers.

The majority of callers didn't know that the giant former smuggler was keeping an abandoned kitten in the kitchen and feeding drops of milk into its mouth every few hours.

Colin handed the butler his hat, praying Ryland's next scheme was harebrained enough to engage Colin's mind for the next several hours, if not a day or two. Anything to keep from thinking about Lady Georgina. Maybe he couldn't shake her because Colin had just left her brother. The whole family bore a marked resemblance to each other. "Good afternoon, Price. Is he in?"

"Of course, Mr. McCrae."

He took Colin's coat and led the way down the hall to Ryland's study. "Mr. McCrae is here to see you, sir."

Colin clapped Price on the shoulder as he sidled around the man to get into the study. "You'll have to start using *Your Grace* instead of *sir* if you want to be a proper butler, Price."

Price grinned as he backed out of the room. It made his face look eerily boyish. "I think that's the least of my problems, Mr. McCrae."

Colin looked the other man up and down, taking in the muscles stretching the tailored coat, the cravat attempting to delineate some sort of neck, and the pale scar that slashed its way above the stiff collar. "You may have a point there."

Price pulled the door closed as Colin threw himself into one of the Chippendale wing chairs that flanked the cold fireplace.

Ryland was rising from a desk sprawled with account books. Colin tried to gauge his mood, but despite the fading discoloration around the eye, his face was remarkably blank.

Colin stuck his booted feet out in front of himself and crossed them at the ankles. He was going to have to rattle the cage a bit. "Didn't expect to see you at the card party last night."

Ryland shrugged as he came around the desk to settle in the other chair. "I couldn't bear to hide out in my room any longer."

He looked calm. Too calm. The kind of calm that indicated he had a plan he felt certain of.

Colin's prayers had been answered. Normally a master strategist, this whole business with Lady Miranda had knocked Ryland off course. It was entertaining to say the least.

Making him stew about it was even more so. Colin redirected the conversation as much to prolong Ryland's agony as to tease him. "Is your aunt delighted you're home?"

"Hardly. I think she coddled the eggs with her glare this morning."

"And Mr. Montgomery?"

Ryland shrugged, apparently not interested in discussing his cousin.

Sweat formed beneath Colin's collar. He was no longer amused and now a bit anxious to hear the plan. If discussing the aunt and cousin who hated him wouldn't distract Ryland, then his plan required Colin's involvement. So much for being an entertained bystander.

"Have you found anything more about that mine investment inquiry?" Ryland asked.

Relief flooded Colin's gut. It wasn't anything to do with Lady Miranda, but about that fake investment Colin had given Ryland to use in a spy case.

Colin frowned. "I thought you were off the case. You said you turned everything you had over to another agent."

Ryland dropped his head onto the back of the chair. "I don't like leaving things unfinished."

Silence stretched.

"You're supposed to be moving on with your life," Colin finally said.

Colin understood the unbearable itch of leaving things undone, but the man was in the middle of courting a lady who lived the epitome of a normal life. If Ryland continued to dabble in his old affairs, would Lady Miranda be dragged into it? How long could Ryland keep the two completely separate?

Colin gave in and told Ryland everything he knew about the doomed investment he had built the fake one on. There wasn't much, but if it helped Ryland finish this case and leave the world of espionage behind, it was worth it.

Eventually Colin couldn't take it anymore. He had to know if things were as bad with Lady Miranda as they appeared to be. "How fares your latest project?"

"I assume you refer to my courtship of Lady Miranda."

When last Colin had seen them it more closely resembled the harassment of Lady Miranda, but *courtship* was probably still the most accurate word. "Aye. Unless you've decided the younger sister is more appealing after all."

Simply joking that someone of intelligence would find Lady Georgina preferable to Lady Miranda left a sour taste in Colin's mouth.

Ryland's lips curved into a half smile. "Not at all. Are you intrigued by the younger?"

"Are you daft, man?" The sour taste crawled down his throat. "It takes only a moment to tell her head is filled with fashion and frippery. I'd rather court your parlor maid."

"Jess is actually quite fetching. She likes to read Shakespeare."

"Maybe I'll take her for a drive." Colin laughed. There were days when the idea of packing it all up and taking a simple maid and running to the country was appealing.

Too bad the idle life would bore him within days.

Ryland leaned forward and braced his elbows on his knees. "I was wondering if you would take Miranda."

Collin's laughter stumbled to a halt in his throat, all but choking him. "I beg your pardon?"

"You didn't reveal last night that we know each other." Ryland lifted a single eyebrow, daring Colin to contradict the assumption that he enjoyed the intrigue.

"Old habits, you know. I never knew what you were up to on the rare occasion I saw you in public. Seemed safer to pretend I didn't know you." Colin leaned forward, mirroring Ryland's posture. He was not going to get dragged in to Ryland's scheme. Not under any circumstances.

Still, he really wanted to know what it was. "Please don't tell me you want me to spy on this woman."

"Yes."

What must it be like in Ryland's head? Colin's lips flattened. "I refuse to interrogate a lady as to whether or not she's forgiven you. Besides, as you said, she doesn't know we know each other."

Ryland examined his fingernails. "You could ask her about the card game."

Colin burst from the chair and paced across the room. "You want me to go to this woman's house, ask her to go for a ride, and then proceed to embarrass her thoroughly so that you can have more information with which to create your plan of attack?"

"Yes."

"No. This is a courtship, not an army invasion." Besides, if he went to Hawthorne House he'd have to see the social-climbing Ice Princess as well as Lady Miranda. *No, thank you.*

"One should always know the factors involved when creating a plan of action. Information is power, and I'm going to need all of the leverage I can get to bring her around. She's being stubbornly female about the whole thing."

Colin scoffed. "How dare she?" He glared at Ryland. "Find yourself another lackey. I won't do it." This time he really meant it. Colin would not get involved.

Not any more than he already had.

The two men stared at each other. Time stretched on, the clicking of the mantel clock the only sound.

"This is about more than your spying, isn't it?"

Ryland frowned. "It's possible I obtained some of her personal papers during my investigation."

Colin waited. His inner resolve had already crumbled, and he knew he was going to agree to Ryland's request, but he refused to admit it yet. His agreement was the only bargaining power he had at the moment, and as Ryland had said, information was power.

"I wrote to her," Ryland mumbled. "As the duke."

"While you there as the valet?"

Ryland nodded.

Colin gave a low whistle. That was a lot of deception for one woman to forgive. Ryland rather deserved to go through the gauntlet to get her back. "'Twas a fine piece of horseflesh you got at Tattersall's this week."

Ryland frowned. "You can't have the horse."

Colin simply grinned.

Chapter 12

Georgina plucked a stray thread from her skirt before fanning the fabric across the gold-and-white settee. She smiled as Lord Andrew made his bows and good-byes. Being heir to only a viscountcy, he wasn't marriage material, but he was handsome and well-liked. It was important to have a group of acceptable dance partners.

Otherwise she might end up dancing with Mr. McCrae again.

"My lady, Mr. McCrae has arrived."

Had she conjured the man up from thin air? Georgina's eyes widened as she searched the butler for signs that he was lying or taking part in an elaborate joke. That Gibson had never been anything but serious and competent about his job meant nothing. The man had to be lying now.

"Odious man," she hissed under her breath. "I don't wish to see him, Mother."

Gibson cleared his throat. "He asked to see Lady Miranda, milady."

"Oh." Georgina turned to Miranda, who looked equally as stunned.

After a moment Miranda's expression turned smug. Did she

think to make Georgina jealous because that man was calling? As if Georgina would ever desire his company.

Miranda looked gleeful as she answered the butler. "Thank you, Gibson. Please show him in."

Maybe Georgina's sister just wanted to torture her. It wouldn't be the first time.

Gibson bowed and returned to the hall. Mr. McCrae strode in moments later.

Part of Georgina admitted that he made a very striking picture entering the drawing room. His clothing was impeccable. Cut with an expert hand and worn with care. The lines of his cravat were sharp enough to cut someone.

Maybe even himself.

Then he'd be too busy nursing his wounds to hinder Georgina's plans.

He bowed to Georgina's mother. "Good afternoon, my lady."

"Same to you, Mr. McCrae. I didn't know we would see you again so soon."

Georgina's mouth tightened at the warm smile on her mother's face. Did she really want this man in the family? Miranda's spinsterhood was better than marrying this lout.

The lout bypassed her completely.

What was he up to? Hadn't he just been warning her off the duke, suggesting that Miranda had feelings for him?

"Lady Miranda, I know this is quite presumptuous of me, but would you care to go for a drive?"

"Yes." Miranda popped up from the settee. "Yes, I would love to."

Entirely unlike a woman in love. Tension Georgina hadn't even known she'd been carrying around released. The duke was available after all.

Miranda laid her hand on Mr. McCrae's arm, smiling as he covered her hand with his own.

Georgina's stomach tightened up once more.

Now that Lady Miranda was in the carriage, Colin wasn't sure what to do with her. He was fairly certain Ryland wanted Colin to pretend to want to court Lady Miranda himself, but chances were he'd be seeing this woman for many years to come and they didn't need that sort of history.

"I enjoyed meeting you last night. I haven't played such an interesting hand of whist in years." Not since the night his father had gambled away a quarter of the family shipping company.

Lady Miranda flushed and turned her face away. "I confess that I have not either."

He hated bringing up that absurd card game. To most people the conversation Ryland and Lady Miranda had held over a hand of cards would have been nothing but strange, but Colin knew enough of the situation to follow their coded statements.

Not that Lady Miranda would know that.

A few people looked his way with narrowed eyes as they drove down the street. What were they thinking? Colin never took a woman out for a drive. That he was doing so now might be seen as significant. If people started calling him grasping and thought him intent on truly courting Lady Miranda, they might become wary of his presence on the fringe of their circles.

He shouldn't have done it. No matter how good a friend Ryland was.

"Lady Miranda, may I be ruthlessly honest with you?"

"Of . . . of course."

Colin shifted in his seat. "We both know there was more afoot than a game of cards last night, and we also know that I could never compete with a duke as far as social status goes."

He was playing right into Ryland's plan, but there was no other way to have this conversation and not make things worse for the duke. While it was true he shouldn't have agreed to do this, he was here now and might as well make the best of it.

"Mr. McCrae, I can assure you that I find you a most interesting gentleman."

Colin had a feeling God was not happy with his behavior at the moment. Why was he doing this? It had been obvious last night that Lady Miranda felt strongly for the duke. Shouldn't that be enough for Ryland to move forward?

A nervous laugh threatened the back of his throat. He coughed in an effort to keep it away, but he couldn't stop his brogue from thickening as he restrained the threat. "It's glad I am to hear that. I was more wondering if you would say that the duke was an interesting gentleman as well. As I said, I don't have much to compete with him."

A scoffing noise of utter dismissal caught Colin off guard. She was more irked with Ryland than Colin had realized. No wonder the man was having a difficult time.

With the topic of the duke in the air, there was no stopping the awkward conversation that followed. There was no hiding the fact that Colin knew Ryland, though he tried to soften any indication of how strong the relationship was.

It was apparent that Lady Miranda's emotions were significant. Her feelings were cloaked in a great deal of anger, but she obviously cared for the man. It was a refreshing, if bumbling, conversation.

Why couldn't his encounters with Lady Georgina be more like this? Forthright, honest, bold.

He shifted in the seat of the curricle. Why did he care how Lady Georgina acted? It wasn't as if her prickly, socially obsessed personality was the only thing keeping him from courting her.

Suddenly the whole thing seemed like too much. London. Society. Even Ryland and Lady Miranda's bizarre courtship. He was going to do what he'd promised to do and then cut ties to this entire thing.

"The thing is, Lady Miranda, I'm considering looking into some investments out of town." The fledgling idea sounded brilliant. He normally saved his trips for when the majority of his investors had returned to the country, but perhaps he should do things differently this year. "I know this is terribly forward of me, but I need to know if I should postpone my trip."

He really would hate to miss Ryland's wedding.

"Mr. McCrae, I—"

"Do call me Colin. It's the least I can offer considering how personal I'm being at the moment."

Lady Miranda swallowed. "Colin, I don't know what to say to this. I have known you for a mere day."

He watched her, debating. Should he unfurl the sails and make a run for the shore? As much as he hated that Ryland had convinced him to do this, he also understood his friend's need to know that there would, eventually, be success at the end of this endeavor. And if Colin was already going to be begging God's forgiveness for the matter, some good might as well come of it. Flawed logic that, but part of him wanted to believe it.

"There's something between you and the duke, isn't there? You're a beautiful lady, but I have a sense I shouldn't waste my time courting you. Am I right?"

He couldn't shake the idea that part of him was saying these words to her sister. Nothing in him wanted to have a relationship with Lady Georgina. Did it?

"I'm sorry, Colin, but I think maybe you are."

Victory elated Colin on Ryland's behalf even as another part of him cracked in pain. It didn't make sense.

"I'm not entirely sure what will happen with the duke, but I owe it to myself to find out." A sad smile curved her lips.

Now that he'd decided to be done with the entire situation, Colin felt a little more charitable toward the uncomfortable girl next to him. "I understand. Shall we simply enjoy this sunshine, then, as I take the route back home?"

"That would be wonderful, yes."

He would grant himself a boon as well and push away any thoughts of goals or motivations and sit back to enjoy the ride. The silence was comfortable, broken by the occasional comment or observation. As he pulled up in front of her home, though, reality came crushing back.

In some ways, he'd jeopardized his reputation for Ryland this afternoon. At the very least he'd temporarily given up his invisibility.

Ryland would get his information and, with effort, the love of his life.

What would Colin get?

He jumped down and walked Lady Miranda to the door. The restlessness that was becoming all too familiar worked its way from his gut to his toes. He looked over the vehicle, wondering why he'd never bothered with curricles, coaches, and horses of his own. Wouldn't it be a sign that he was settling down? Setting up roots? Odd that enhanced mobility could indicate that. "It is a fine curricle, isn't it?"

Miranda nodded with a small smile. "It is. I hope your friend will allow you to borrow it again when you find another young lady to take for a drive."

That wasn't likely to happen anytime soon, even if he did purchase his own conveyance. The stares their ride had garnered proved he was going to have to be very sure before he openly courted any woman. That made him feel old and tired. He didn't want to feel old and tired. Ryland would get the information he wanted from this endeavor, but it had been gained through dishonesty.

Colin could at least correct that.

The grin that spread across his face felt familiar, fun. More like him than he'd felt in a long time. More like the young man who'd once laughed with his friends and thought his future secure.

"I think I'll keep it." Though he had no idea where he'd store it. Probably part of the reason he'd never looked into getting his own. "It's the least Ryland can do after putting me in a position to anger such a lovely woman as yourself."

The door opened behind Lady Miranda, even as her shocked mouth gaped farther open.

Colin continued to speak as he bowed and backed down the four steps to the street. "Do tell him for me at the ball tonight, won't you? That I'm keeping his horse and curricle? He'll understand."

He tipped his hat as Lady Miranda's teeth snapped together with a wince-inducing click. She whirled and entered the house.

Colin chuckled to himself as he turned back to the curricle. The reopening of the door drew his attention around once more. Lady Miranda must have thought of a response after all.

But it wasn't Lady Miranda coming down the steps.

Chapter 13

Colin nodded his head at Lord Ashcombe as the man made his way down the steps. "Good day, my lord."

Ashcombe looked over the conveyance, a half sneer on his lips that was probably intended to be something of a smile. "Mr. McCrae, I had no idea your taste in horses was so fine."

Colin stroked the horse's hindquarters. "Horses are an investment like any other. It is important to get a good return."

Ashcombe glanced at the house and then back to Colin. "One can surmise what payoff you hope to obtain."

"Not everyone has the same objectives in life." Five years of working with aristocrats in addition to twenty years living with a stubborn father had given Colin the ability to keep the stiffness and distaste he felt out of his voice. He even managed a natural-feeling smile.

"You've directed me well in the past, Mr. McCrae. Allow me to return the favor." Ashcombe pulled his gloves on, seeming completely at ease with the conversation.

Colin grew increasingly nervous. If the man insulted Lady Miranda . . . Well, he didn't know what he was going to do. Nothing if he was feeling charitable. Inform Ryland if he took a more vindictive line.

Ashcombe nodded his head back toward Hawthorne House. "She isn't worth the work. You're a man of business, as I am. If your wife is not an asset to your dealings, she will be the millstone that sinks your wealth. Lady Miranda is too uncertain. 'Tis best to look elsewhere."

Ashcombe tipped his hat and walked down the street.

Colin shook his head as he gave the horse one last pat on the neck. He'd keep quiet for now. With any luck, Ashcombe's presence at Hawthorne House meant Lady Georgina had changed her matrimonial target. She and Lord Ashcombe deserved each other.

Miranda's stomps echoed through the hall and up the stairs. As much as Georgina wanted Miranda to marry, she was quite glad the outing with Mr. McCrae had gone poorly. If Georgina were forced to welcome that man into the family, she'd marry Napoleon just to get away from him.

Well, perhaps not Napoleon, but someone who would take her far, far away from Mr. McCrae and the temptation to upend a punch bowl over his head.

Fortunately, Miranda's initial interest in Mr. McCrae seemed to have waned, and things with Lord Ashcombe were coming along very nicely. Georgina hated having to put so much effort into her alternative plan, but her first choices weren't turning out the way she'd hoped, and the earl was so easy to bring to heel. Feign a bit of interest in his plans for his sheep and the man would do almost anything.

Georgina crept to the window to peek around the curtain. Lord Ashcombe was just now walking away from the steps of Hawthorne House where Mr. McCrae was still standing. Whatever the men had been discussing had pulled a small smile from Mr. McCrae. It brought a warmness to his handsome face that made Georgina's stomach whirl into a waltz with her heart.

No. No. No. No one was going to give Georgina those ridiculous sensations her friends were always going on and on about.

Especially not a man who wasn't even on her list of possibilities. Georgina wasn't averse to love, she knew it existed, but she wasn't going to let such a mind-numbing emotion cloud her judgment. Colin McCrae provided nothing but a handsome face and sharp conversation. If things were different, she might consider those beneficial qualities.

But things weren't different, and that made him a mere nuisance. And a distraction. She should be thinking of Lord Ashcombe, not admiring the fit of Mr. McCrae's coat.

Why wasn't the man leaving?

She looked back to his face and froze. He was looking right at her, the amused grin spreading into a full-blown smile.

The lacy white curtain fluttered back into place as Georgina stepped away from the window.

Ashcombe. She was going to focus her efforts on Ashcombe and get him to propose as soon as may be.

She couldn't afford to wait any longer.

Georgina felt more than a little guilty at how happy she was to see Jane's bright red nose Thursday morning. Her efforts to secure Ashcombe's attention over the past three days had been less successful than she wished. Now that Jane was too ill to host her gathering, Georgina would be free to attend the opera with her mother and sister, an opera she'd heard Ashcombe discuss attending as well. The potential benefit added to her guilt, making it easier to keep her face and voice contrite. "How awful to catch a head cold so early in the Season. You'll have to cancel your poetry reading."

Jane sniffled and burrowed deeper into the pillows on the settee in her family parlor. "I know. Mama's sending out rescheduled invitations as we speak. We can't do it next Friday, though, because Father has some important dinner scheduled."

She punctuated her sentence with a ghastly blow into her handkerchief.

"We'll have to push it out two weeks, then." Georgina tried not to be disgusted by her friend's illness, but really, what was she doing here? Jane's missive had said it was urgent that she see Georgina as soon as possible. Knowing Jane, an urgent message could have meant anything from difficulty choosing new wallpaper for the drawing room to having the maid singe off her curls. Apparently it had been a horrible late-season cold and the wonderful news that Georgina wouldn't have to recite a poem tomorrow night.

A two-week postponement was even more delightful. Jane had been known to forget the name of her cat in a two-week span. With a little help from Georgina she could certainly be made to forget a poetry reading.

"No," Jane said, her voice thick and rough. "Mother is going to move it to next Wednesday. At first I thought that a silly idea, but it's actually quite genius. Since Parliament won't be meeting that day, more men will be available to attend."

Georgina hoped her feigned excitement was convincing. Moving it to a Wednesday was perfect. Now it was a special event and their Friday salons could return to normal. After Jane got better, of course.

Jane flopped one hand through the air. "That's not why I brought you here, though."

There was more urgent news than the postponement of Jane's pet project? Georgina couldn't think of a single thing Jane had talked about more over the past two weeks.

"He wrote me," Jane whispered excitedly, pulling a piece of paper from the tray on the table next to her. "Look."

Georgina allowed her distaste for the extended piece of paper show clearly on her face. She wouldn't want to take the paper on a normal day, but particularly not from an infirm Jane. "I'd rather not get that close if you don't mind."

Jane frowned and then sniffled. "Oh, I understand." Her fever-bright eyes brightened further with excitement. "It's from him."

"Who?" Georgina kept up with every piece of gossip, every

morsel of information, and she had no idea who would be causing this much excitement in Jane's life.

"*Him*. The man from the masquerade. I told you I was going to marry him."

The answer to the one question only served to raise many others. "You found out who he was?"

"Well, no." Jane's face grew a bit sheepish as she looked back down at her note. "But he mentioned our conversation at the ball and that he was looking forward to my poetry gathering. That means, despite your concerns, he's a properly eligible man because he received an invitation."

Georgina was fairly certain every single man with a connection to someone of higher rank than baron had been invited. "He wrote you but didn't sign it?"

It didn't sound as if this man had much going for him other than a potentially respectable rank. Shouldn't Jane require more than that?

A niggling voice at the edge of her mind tried to point out that she wasn't requiring anything more for herself, so why should Jane?

Georgina shifted uncomfortably in her seat. Fortunately Jane fell into a fit of coughs at the same time, making her oblivious to her friend's sudden discomfort.

After taking a long drink of tea, Jane waved the letter in the air once more. "He signed it *H*. Isn't that romantic? He's keeping the mystery alive for a while longer."

Romantic? Was she serious? Georgina sputtered, trying to find the right words. This wasn't romantic, it was disturbing. This man could be anyone.

"Do you think I should write him back?"

Georgina sighed. "You wouldn't know where to send it."

Jane sighed. "That's true."

"Has no other gentleman caught your eye?" Georgina could recommend several. As the daughter of an earl, Jane was a very respectable match and could afford to be selective in whom she married. Foolishness was, for better or worse, not much of a liability when it came to marriage. Jane would have no shortcomings to hide from a potential suitor.

Jane frowned. "Mr. Givendale has been by a time or two. He's second in line to a viscountcy, you know, and likely to inherit, given how sickly his brother is. But he only brings roses."

Georgina frowned as well. "What's wrong with roses?"

"They're predictable, Georgina!" Jane flopped over the arm of the settee. "Where's the romance in roses?"

This cold had obviously addled Jane's mind. "I think you should rest, Jane. We can revisit this discussion when you're feeling better."

Jane yawned and stretched out across the many pillows. "I want romance, Georgina, like in books."

Yet another reason not to read. "I know you do."

"It's like you've always said, Georgina," Jane mumbled. "Marriage cannot be left up to chance. I have to make it happen."

Struggling with an even stronger sense of guilt, Georgina stayed until Jane had fallen asleep. Jane was, in her own way, following Georgina's example when it came to finding a husband. The problem was, what made so much sense when she and Harriette discussed it sounded so wrong when Jane said it. At least Jane's romance scale wasn't as cold as Georgina's popularity and power requirements.

For the first time, Georgina wondered if she was truly doing the right thing.

Colin strolled into the kitchens of Ryland's house as casually as if he always entered that way. The cook lifted her brow and shook a knife in his direction. Her threatening motions were betrayed by the laughter in her eyes and small smile at the corner of her lips. "You know better than to sneak through my kitchens, Mr. McCrae."

"Where else could I get the best biscuits in London?" Colin winked and snagged a sugar-dusted biscuit from the plate on the worktable before jogging up the servant stairs to the main part of the house.

Price was waiting for him at the top of the stairs, arms crossed over his massive chest. "Didn't he send you a message?"

"Yes." In a move that was fast becoming tradition for the two of them, Colin pushed his way right past the enormous butler. "A very cryptic message that said only 'Stay away.' Obviously I took that to mean I should come straightaway."

Price sighed. "He's in the ballroom."

In the ballroom? What could Ryland be doing in the ballroom? Colin nodded and headed for the main stairs.

"Oh, Mr. McCrae . . ." Price called.

Colin turned.

"Your hat and coat?"

After relinquishing the items to the butler, Colin took the main stairs two at a time. What could possibly have put Ryland in such a mood that he felt the need to tell Colin to stay away? Had Lady Miranda decided she couldn't forgive him after all?

At the entrance to the ballroom Colin froze, his concern rising to disastrous levels.

Four dummies had been pulled into the ballroom. Ryland stood several feet away from them, throwing knives into various parts of the straw bodies. Once he'd emptied his hands, he collected the knives and started again.

"You might as well come in since you're here," he said after emptying his hands once more.

Colin strode into the ballroom as Ryland collected the knives. "I thought things were going better?"

He'd been deliberately staying away from all things related to the Hawthorne females for the past week, but his friendships with Ryland and Trent meant he'd still heard how things were going. The last he'd heard concerning Miranda was that she was on the verge of not only forgiving Ryland but admitting she loved him as well. What had gone wrong?

Ryland slung a knife through the air with particularly heavy force. It buried to the hilt in the chest of the tallest dummy. "I love her too much to let her get killed." He speared Colin with a glare. "You aren't supposed to be here either."

"I took a smuggler ship to France so you'd have food to bribe those villagers with. After that, sneaking in through your kitchens seems simple." Colin crossed his arms over his chest.

Ryland scoffed. "It was your own ship, and you made me take a rowboat to the edge of the cove."

Colin shrugged.

"The case has gone bad. He knows we're after him, and he's threatening us."

Colin waited. Ryland had been a spy for nine years. His life had been threatened more times than Colin wanted to count. There had to be more to the story.

"He threatened *her*."

Air whooshed from Colin's lungs. This was what he'd been afraid of when Ryland didn't truly walk away from the case. "Is she safe?"

"She should be. As long as I stay away from her. I haven't seen her for three days. If I continue to stay away, our man might think she isn't that important to me after all."

It was possible Lady Miranda would think the same thing. Now Colin understood the knife throwing.

"Do you know who?"

"I have my suspicions, but until he's caught, I can't do anything."

Colin shifted his weight from foot to foot as Ryland threw three more knives in quick succession. "What can I do?"

Ryland sighed and rubbed a hand over his forehead. "Nothing. I've got a man checking on a suspect's estate, like you taught me to do. Once he gets back I'll know more. Until then, stay away. We aren't publicly connected. The fewer targets this maniac has, the better."

Chapter 14

Georgina's misgivings continued the next day. The weather obliged her sour mood and opened the skies to pour a deluge of rain across London.

She couldn't afford second thoughts. Ashcombe wasn't exactly tripping over his feet to call upon her, but he was showing more interest than anyone else on her list. As much as she didn't believe the duke was pursuing Miranda, Georgina also didn't truly believe that he wanted her either. Other than the dance at the masquerade, the duke had all but ignored Georgina. She'd made the mistake of not encouraging any of the other men earlier this Season, choosing to focus on the duke instead. Now any marital intentions those men possessed were being directed at other young ladies.

Panic nibbled at Georgina's toes, sending a restless energy across her shoulders and down to her fingers. She set off for the solarium, where she'd set up her paints earlier that morning. A few well-placed slashes of color and all of this would start to make sense. Everything made more sense when she was painting. At least then things turned out the way she wanted them to.

The canvas waited, pristine and untouched, a perfect surface for her to create anything she wished. If only life were as easy to construct. But life had more than one painter, and the picture seemed to be changing faster than she could adjust.

She yanked open the drawer of her paint box and withdrew her palette and brushes. The colors blended as she fixed her paints with less care than normal. Muddy browns and greys marred the edges of the vibrant colors as they infringed on each other's space. She would have to select the paint she used with care.

Just like her husband.

Not that she was entirely certain she had a choice, but it was possible the earl wouldn't suit her needs. It was one reason why he originally had been so low on her list of potential suitors.

He was rich, handsome, and many ladies sought his attention. But once he was married, would his position remain supreme? If his popularity was tied to his bachelor status, it would dissipate upon marriage, and then where would she be?

In a better position than pitied spinster—that's where.

The fact that the earl wasn't always a very nice man could not even be allowed to enter the consideration.

Georgina swirled her paintbrush in a dollop of pink paint.

The waratah in the conservatory was the perfect muse for her current mood. She'd never seen such an ugly flower in her life. What had possessed the caretaker to plant such a thing?

Vibrant colors sliced across the canvas, their lines a bit harsher than the plant actually called for, but she wasn't feeling soft at the moment.

She was feeling desperate.

"Don't marry Ashcombe."

At first Georgina thought the strangled, whispered words had come from her own mind, so her paintbrush never stopped moving. Conversations with herself were a fairly common occurrence after all. When one kept as vital a secret as she did, her options for honest discussion were limited.

Then she realized the interruption had been Miranda, who appeared to have come to the conservatory for the express purpose of dispensing her sisterly advice.

Georgina kept the paintbrush moving. "Whyever not? He's extremely eligible. I would of course prefer a marquis or a duke or even one of those foreign princes, but they seem to be out of town. If I must settle for an earl, let him be a rich and popular one."

"But he's awful."

Hearing her sister voice the same concern she herself had brought up mere moments earlier strengthened the panic. The earl was a good idea. He had to be.

Georgina turned to glare at her older sister. "Because he didn't want you? There are a hundred reasons why he might not have offered for—"

Miranda stepped forward. "He did."

"No, he didn't." Georgina swallowed. He couldn't have. If Lord Ashcombe had offered for Miranda and been turned down, that made Georgina a paltry second choice. It was bad enough to accept a man who'd been turned down, but turned down by one's own sister . . . ?

Miranda sat on the vacant stool beside Georgina. "Yes, he did. He went to Griffith to work out the details."

Georgina turned back to her painting but didn't apply the brush to the canvas. Maybe things hadn't truly progressed as far as Miranda thought. After all, Georgina hadn't known about it and she'd hung on every possible piece of gossip for the past three years. "What happened? Obviously you didn't marry him."

"He wanted . . ." Miranda swallowed. Whatever tale she had to tell was clearly difficult.

Should she take Miranda's hand? Make one of those humming noises Harriette used so often? Georgina had never been cast in the role of comforter.

With a deep breath, Miranda was once more her strong collected self. "He wanted land. It was his condition. If the estate from Papa's mother wasn't included in the dowry, he would rescind his attentions."

So he hadn't ever truly made Miranda an offer. Georgina applied herself to mixing more pink paint. Honestly, if a small parcel of land bought Georgina permanent acceptance, she'd pay it gladly.

Miranda wasn't done making her point though. "He didn't care about me. All that mattered was what he could gain from Griffith through the match."

The words sliced into Georgina's heart, laying open a place she rarely allowed herself to look. It didn't matter if her future husband cared about her. It couldn't.

She gently dabbed against the canvas. The choking feeling in her throat made her words low. "He must have cared a bit. He was willing to marry you."

"He was willing to marry Griffith's connections." Miranda licked her lips. "He's still willing to marry for them."

And Miranda didn't want Georgina being a pawn like so many other young ladies.

As if Miranda could understand Georgina's problem.

That's because you haven't told her.

The new voice in her head made her jump. She covered the jitters by exchanging her brush for another, amazed she didn't fumble the entire box to the floor.

What was Mr. McCrae doing as the voice of reason in her head? His one moment of good advice did not give him the right to set up permanent residence in her mind.

She stabbed at the painting. "Get out."

Miranda winced and turned to leave the room.

Georgina hadn't been directing the command at Miranda, but she didn't call her sister back. The truth was her plan was beginning to lose a bit of its appeal now that she was actually in it. Marrying for love was a family tradition.

Her mother had even managed to do it twice, surprising herself most of all when she ended her widowed status a year and a half ago.

Miranda refused to settle for anyone who didn't want her for herself alone. An unreasonable requirement, but then again, she had no reason to relinquish her ideals.

Miranda wasn't fundamentally flawed.

Neither are you.

Georgina dropped the brush and it bounced against the canvas before falling to the floor. How had the man gotten inside her head? He'd never even said such words to her. What made her think he would be more supportive than anyone else? He didn't even know her secret.

She picked up the brush and frowned at the canvas. A deep green streak sliced through her partially completed flower. Another endeavor failed because of the interference of Mr. McCrae.

This was getting ridiculous.

Colin's neck was stiff from spending the night carefully positioned in a chair so as not to muss his clothing overmuch. He'd gone away as Ryland requested, but only the short walk to his club. His home was a twenty-minute hackney ride away, and if Ryland needed him, Colin wanted to be able to get there quickly.

Lord Trent's arrival had been a welcome distraction. Especially when the rain began to fall in torrential buckets.

Since the rain had never let up and neither man had pressing engagements, they'd both stayed. It was now approaching midnight. Before long Colin was going to be making himself comfortable in a club chair once more.

The number 6 billiard ball dropped into the pocket with a satisfying thud. Colin grinned at the scowl on Lord Trent's face. They'd been meeting regularly for billiards, and those pressure-free moments were fast becoming Colin's favorite times of the day, even when he wasn't trying to forget that his closest friend was tracking down a criminal in a monsoon.

Lord Trent was uncomplicated. Colin rather appreciated having a friend who didn't risk his life on a regular basis and had little to no interest in Colin's investment acumen.

"I believe you've been deliberately deceiving us, Mr. McCrae. Word around the club is that your billiards game is only slightly above mediocre." Lord Trent leaned on his cue stick and raised his eyebrows.

Colin choked on air, and his next shot went wide, bouncing erratically against the edges of the table. "The club discusses my billiard prowess?"

Lord Trent lined his shot up with a grin and a scoffing laugh. "No. Well, not often. It was a passing remark." His cue connected with the balls, sending a red orb swirling into a pocket. "Probably because Sir Humphry so rarely wins."

"Perhaps I was preoccupied that day."

"Perhaps you were trying to calculate the potential profitability of his new arc lamp."

Colin couldn't keep the grin off his face, though he knew it had to look smug. "I already knew the potential profitability of the arc lamp. Why else would I have invested in mining potash?"

Lord Trent's low whistle accompanied the sinking of another ball. "Maybe we should be talking business instead of billiards."

"Only if you want to get us kicked out of the club."

Lord Trent's next shot went wide of the intended pocket. "Not that I have much to invest. I leave the bulk of my funds in Griffith's hands."

"Then it's doing well." Colin rounded the table, looking for the best play.

"How would you know?"

"His Grace and I don't play billiards." Colin lined up his shot and sank two more balls.

Lord Trent laughed. "How long have you not been playing billiards together?"

"More than three years. Long enough to know your money is in good hands."

"True. But it's probably time to grow up and handle it myself." Lord Trent propped his hip against the table. "He gave me an estate, you know. Well, sold it to me, but we both know the price he charged was insanely low."

"And the lease on a house in London as well, no?" Colin had

wisely kept his mouth shut about both transactions, even though Riverton could have made considerably more in both cases.

"Yes." Lord Trent leaned over the table but didn't take his shot. "So tell me, Mr. McCrae, if I were to take control of my own financial assets, what would I do first?"

Colin leaned against the table and crossed his arms. Even though the place was quiet due to the rainstorm, Colin chose his words with care. Who knew when the wrong ears would be listening? Despite the War Office contacts that had gotten him the club membership, he would be evicted in a moment if he violated the rules.

The servant approaching with a single piece of paper on a silver tray kept Colin from speaking further. "Pardon me, my lord. This message arrived for you."

Lord Trent raised the crookedly folded and poorly sealed paper with lifted eyebrows. Whoever had sent it must have been in quite a hurry.

Which usually meant bad news.

Lord Trent's face paled and his cue clattered to the ground, drawing the attention of the handful of men scattered about the other end of the room.

Colin scooped up the cue and pressed it into Lord Trent's hand. "Finish the play."

Lord Trent's eyes were glazed as they looked up. "What?"

"Finish the play. Whatever's in that note, it's personal. And unless you want everyone in here nosing around in your business, you'll shove it in your pocket and finish the play." Colin made sure to keep his voice low and firm so to break through the haze that appeared to be engulfing Lord Trent's thoughts.

As he looked around the table, Lord Trent's eyes cleared and his posture stiffened. "Isn't it your turn?"

Colin gave the younger man a mental pat on the back. He'd recovered nicely. "Doesn't matter. Hit the ball."

"Right." Lord Trent leaned over the table to send the balls crashing into each other with no real direction. "I need to leave."

"Of course, but let's do it right."

Colin was struggling with his own composure but managed to sink two balls before deliberately missing to give Lord Trent the final shot. The fact that the hasty note had come for Lord Trent and not Colin meant it had probably come from Riverton.

Which meant Lady Miranda might have become involved despite Ryland's safety measures.

The last ball finally dropped into a pocket. The game had been played entirely out of order, but the table had been cleared.

"Ah, you win." Colin pitched his voice loud enough to be heard by those nearby but not loud enough to draw undue attention. "I owe you those figures then. Do you want them now?"

Lord Trent's grin was more wooden than normal, but genuine gratitude was in his eyes. "Of course. Can't have you backing out. I'll have a carriage brought around."

Colin felt a bit sorry for the footman who had to plunge into the rain to find them a hack. Hopefully this wasn't a pressing emergency and Lord Trent would have time to take Colin home first. Finding two hired carriages in the rain would be impossible.

The idea of walking in a downpour was unappealing to say the least. He hated being wet. Ironic for a boy who'd grown up around the ocean and playing on boats.

Maybe it was because getting wet on a boat was a bad sign.

They climbed into the carriage, shaking the water from their greatcoats.

"Hawthorne House," Lord Trent told the driver. As soon as the door closed, he turned to Colin. "Miranda is missing."

Colin's heart clenched. His fears had become a reality. What about the rest of the family? Obviously Lord Trent was safe, but what about Lady Georgina? "Missing?"

Lord Trent nodded and pulled the paper from his pocket. "Griffith said he received word from Ryland's butler that Miranda was in trouble and they were heading to Marshington Abbey."

That wasn't good. Wait, Marshington Abbey? The criminal had taken Lady Miranda to Ryland's childhood home? The man must be insane. And insane men were dangerous.

The hack pulled up to Hawthorne House and Lord Trent threw the door open and jumped to the ground before the carriage had settled onto the stopped wheels.

After a brief conversation with the butler, Lord Trent jumped back into the hack. "He's already left."

Colin considered suggesting Lord Trent wait for word, but if their places were reversed he'd punch the man who suggested such a thing.

And Lord Trent was a practiced pugilist.

"Raebourne," Colin suggested instead.

Lord Trent dragged his hand through his hair before punching his fist into the upholstered seat cushion. "What?"

"Lord Raebourne. He's a friend of the family, isn't he? He can be trusted, and he'll have a carriage and horses available."

"Perfect." Lord Trent stuck his head out the door and gave the driver the new direction.

He was shoved back into the carriage by a large bundle of white. Lord Trent fell back into his seat with a grunt.

"I'm coming too." Lady Georgina shook the hood of her cloak back and reached out to slam the hack door shut. She plopped herself on the seat beside Lord Trent as the vehicle moved forward.

Colin was torn between relief that she was safe and ire that she'd thrown herself into the middle of a potentially dangerous situation. Surely her brother would insist she return to the house.

Lord Trent glared at her but didn't stop the carriage.

In moments, they were in front of Raebourne's house, pounding on the door. Colin tossed a coin to the hackney driver. Time and discretion were both of the essence in a situation like this. They didn't need a hired man hanging around hearing more than he should.

The butler opened the door with bleary eyes and a smothered yawn.

Lord Trent pushed past him, bellowing for Anthony. Lady Georgina swept in behind him, her cloak billowing around her like a cloud, complete with raindrops dripping from the wet hem.

Colin followed them into the house with a wince. The butler was fully awake now and preparing to toss all of them out on their ear.

Lord Raebourne appeared, tying a dressing gown around him. His dark brown hair was mussed, and he kept blinking as if he weren't quite ready to be among the conscious. "What the blazes is going on?"

Lord Trent bounded up the stairs. "I need your carriage."

Lord Raebourne's wife appeared behind him, looking slightly more aware of her surroundings. "What's wrong?"

"Miranda. She's possibly in danger. I need to get to Kent."

It was the kind of statement that broke through sleep's last hold on the brain. Lord Raebourne transformed into a noble marquis before Colin's eyes. "Hughson, get the carriage ready. And wake Cook to throw together a basket." Lord Raebourne nodded at Colin and Lord Trent. "Wait in the drawing room. I'll be dressed momentarily."

Colin tried his best to rest his eyes while they waited. He could go home. Probably should go home. It was one thing to insist on coming to Ryland's aid, but this was a family matter. Colin had no part in it, except possibly the fact that Lord Trent needed a keeper. Ryland was likely halfway to Kent now, and the last thing he needed was Lady Miranda's brothers getting in the way. Colin couldn't stop Riverton, but maybe he could corral Lord Trent, and now, it appeared, Lord Raebourne.

This could turn into a veritable circus.

Lady Georgina sat in a chair on the other side of the room. She'd yet to acknowledge his presence. Was there any chance they could convince her to stay with Lady Raebourne? There was nothing to gain from her presence on this escapade. In fact, there was potential to great loss of reputation, depending on the outcome.

She appeared serene with the exception of her bottom lip, caught between clenched, even white teeth. Should he go over? Talk to her? There was little that could be done for Lord Trent right now, but if Lady Georgina was concerned, he could console her, tell her Ryland would protect Lady Miranda.

151

Did Lady Georgina even know the truth about Ryland? The other siblings knew, but Colin wouldn't put it past Lady Georgina to miss the news entirely.

"No."

"Yes."

Lord and Lady Raebourne burst into the drawing room, both dressed in warm traveling clothes, Lady Raebourne's redingote buttoned crookedly.

"No." Lord Raebourne put his hands on his hips.

"You can't stop me." Lady Raebourne crossed her arms over her chest, the insolent posture looking a bit hilarious on her tiny frame.

Colin knew better than to laugh.

Lord Raebourne leaned down to speak into his wife's face. "What makes you think I can't keep you here?"

"Because James won't take you anywhere if I tell him not to."

Lord Raebourne dragged his hands over his face. "I thought we agreed you wouldn't manipulate the servants."

"This is too important."

"This is too dangerous."

Lady Raebourne huffed. "I'm not leaving Miranda to the care of a bunch of panicked men."

Colin took exception to that. He wasn't panicked in the least. Concerned, yes. Aware of the importance of efficient usage of time, yes. But panicked? No.

Lord Raebourne echoed Colin's thoughts. "We're not panicked, we're concerned. And we have Georgina."

Lady Raebourne raised her eyebrows, clearly unwilling to point out that Lady Georgina might not be the most calming female presence for Lady Miranda. "I'm going."

Lord Trent stepped between them. "Can we leave?"

Moments later they were hurtling down the road to Kent. It was a bit impractical to squeeze five into the traveling coach, but no one volunteered to stay behind. It was also impossible to fit the three men to a single seat, leaving the other for the ladies to ride in comfort.

As the smallest of the three men, Colin found himself sitting on the ladies' side, pressed against Lady Georgina, and trying to keep his facial expressions clear of the internal struggle between his physical appreciation and his intellectual distaste. He stared out the window, praying for sleep but knowing he wouldn't find it unless he turned his turmoil over to the Lord.

He was still awake when the first rays of sun crested the horizon.

Chapter 15

Raebourne's coach was new, equipped with advanced new springs, and outfitted with a set of prime horses and a speed only the panicked can induce. One of Raebourne's grooms rode ahead, ensuring that fresh horses were ready in the inn yards. With the faster coach and faster horse changes, the group caught up to Riverton at an inn about two hours away from their destination.

Knowing the aristocrats wouldn't listen to reason, Colin grabbed the two coachmen and convinced them to approach Marshington Abbey with caution. If Ryland did have a plan in the works, he didn't need anyone blundering in and ruining it.

Expecting Lady Georgina to move to her brother's coach, Colin climbed back into Raebourne's, only to find himself sharing a seat with the lady he was trying to avoid. Apparently Lord Trent was the one who opted to gain more room by switching to Riverton's carriage. Colin couldn't even call on propriety to ask Lady Raebourne to share the seat with Lady Georgina. The married couple across the way was far too engrossed in their debate to notice they were sharing their carriage, much less that the other seat wasn't properly filled.

Lord Raebourne was trying to convince Lady Raebourne to stay in the carriage when they arrived at the Abbey. Given the mutinous expression on the lady's face, that wasn't going to happen. Trying to give them privacy, he turned to Lady Georgina. His mind went utterly blank of discussion topics. What could they possibly find to talk about?

"The sun is rising."

Admittedly not his best conversation starter.

Lady Georgina leaned against the window, eyes widening as color streaked the sky. "It's beautiful. The way the reds and oranges blend together. It's like the night sky is a curtain pulling back to let the sun through. I wish I had my paints. We don't get sunrises like that in London."

Colin opened his mouth and shut it again, taking a moment to absorb what she was saying. He latched on to the most tangible part of her revelation. "You paint?"

She nodded. "All of my fans and most of the fire screens in the house. The borders on Lady Jane's cerulean shawl."

He'd seen the fire screens when visiting Riverton. They were exquisite works of art, blooming with color and detail. "You like color."

It wasn't a question, but Lady Georgina answered him anyway. "What's not to like about it?"

"But your traveling cloak is white."

She looked at him for a long while, as if contemplating whether or not his inane comment merited an answer. "Everything I have is white."

Colin half turned in the seat and settled into the corner. "I've noticed. Why is that?"

Lady Georgina looked annoyed enough to ignore him but finally gave a shrug. "Because you've noticed."

Colin began to scoff at her nonanswer before realizing the truth of her statement. While white was a color found in every young lady's wardrobe, it was never the only color. The fact that Lady Georgina didn't even trim her dresses in any color but white was quite famous among the *ton*.

It was rather ingenious, actually.

"Why did you come?" Since she seemed to be in the mood to explain herself, even if vaguely, he decided not to waste the opportunity.

"My sister is in danger, Mr. McCrae. Whatever else you may think of me, I've never given you reason to doubt that I care about my sister." She turned her nose up and stared on the window.

Colin laughed. "You haven't? Not even when you tried to catch the eye of the man she loves?"

When Georgina's response finally came, it was very quiet. "Miranda's feelings have not yet been determined."

The carriage pulled into Marshington Abbey's long drive. Colin grinned. What was the poor dear going to do when she couldn't fool herself anymore? "I have a feeling we'll soon see otherwise."

The front yard of the Abbey was in complete chaos. Something had certainly happened. Colin's breathing thinned as he waited for the carriages to stop. He knew that things didn't always turn out well in spite of well-laid plans and determined protectors.

Jeffreys, Ryland's retired-spy valet, and Price, the former smuggler turned butler, were overseeing an army of villagers beating rugs and cleaning items from the house. The fact that they didn't look the least bit worried or distressed eased Colin's chest considerably. If something bad had happened, the men's scowls would be dark enough to put out the sun.

Price came over as Colin and Riverton climbed down from their respective carriages. "Good morning, Your Grace. I didn't expect to see you, Mr. McCrae."

"Right place, right time."

Price grinned. "Story of your life."

Colin could do no more than nod. God had certainly guided his steps over the years.

Lady Raebourne tumbled out of the carriage, ripping her cloak from her husband's hand. "I am Lady Raebourne, and you are . . . ?"

"Price, my lady." Price's eyes widened as he took in the little lady.

Colin sucked in his cheeks to keep his grin hidden. He didn't know much about Lady Raebourne, but the woman was showing herself to be considerably more formidable than she appeared. It was amusing to watch.

Lady Raebourne smiled sweetly up at the butler, appearing completely oblivious to his intimidating form. "Good morning, Price. Is Miranda safe?"

Price nodded, glancing from Colin to Riverton and back to Lady Raebourne and her husband standing behind her, looking cross. "Yes, everything is taken care of. We've hauled Mr. Montgomery to the magistrate already. Ry— His Grace and Lady Miranda are in the drawing room."

Colin frowned. Mr. Montgomery? Ryland's cousin had been the criminal mastermind? That didn't make any sense, although it did explain the location a bit better as Gregory Montgomery had grown up in the house as well.

Trent and Riverton were already halfway to the house when Colin broke free from his considerations. The Raebournes were right behind the brothers, still arguing about whether or not Lady Raebourne was going to wait in the carriage.

Where was Lady Georgina?

Colin turned to find her hovering in the doorway of the carriage, lip caught between her teeth. Despite her brave declarations in the carriage, he knew she didn't have the best relationship with Lady Miranda. Was she more worried about her sister or about having to finally admit that Ryland wasn't available?

Without a word, he helped her from the carriage. She set her shoulders and nearly ran after her brothers. Colin followed at a slower pace, appreciating the drama filling the yard as villagers set about airing rugs and linens and cleaning furniture. The Abbey hadn't been occupied in well over a decade, and it suddenly had a slew of potential overnight visitors.

Chances were Ryland and Lady Miranda were engaged already. If not, they would be by the end of the day.

After all the ups and downs, the couple would finally be happily settled, or at least on their way to being so.

It would also irk Lady Georgina.

The thought brought a smile to Colin's face as he ambled into the house.

The last thing he expected as he entered was to see Lady Georgina actually caring for her sister.

Lady Georgina sat on the settee next to Lady Miranda, her skirt bunched on one side and her traveling cloak draped over the back, trailing down to pool on the floor. Never had he seen her disregard her appearance that way.

There was no pretense in her bearing, no practiced smiles or postures. She smoothed Lady Miranda's hair with a gentle hand and complete focus. Colin had never seen her like that. She looked . . . genuine. Approachable in a way she hadn't been before. This was Georgina without any artifice, and Colin wasn't sure what to do with it.

It was only when she thought no one was looking that she would glance at Ryland and a bit of sadness would flitter across her face.

Had there been any real feeling there? Colin would have sworn she wanted Ryland strictly for his position and influence. Was he wrong?

The idea that Lady Georgina was actually in love with Ryland didn't sit well with him. The sensation almost felt like jealousy. But that was preposterous. Wasn't it?

Colin distracted himself by pulling Ryland aside. "What happened?"

The other man shook his head but didn't take his eyes off Lady Miranda. "We caught our spy yesterday, but this was something much more mundane. My cousin wanted the title—thought to lure me here and arrange a way to inherit it. Miranda was the bait."

Colin winced. It was a tale as old as time and one that many aristocratic families had to deal with daily, though fortunately the jealousy didn't often end in murder. "What does that mean for you?"

Ryland raised an eyebrow and cut Colin a brief, questioning glance. "It means I'm getting married."

Colin laughed quietly as the duke strode back across the room. It was good to see Ryland happy. A darkness that Colin had never fully realized had settled on his friend seemed to now be lifted. Leaning his shoulder against the wall, Colin did what he did best. Observed.

The men were talking, joking, enjoying the time together now that the danger was gone. The women were joining in. Lady Georgina fixed her skirt and her posture before reaching a hand up to smooth her mussed coiffure.

The laughter and love flowed as easily and plentifully as the tea, but Colin stayed on the fringe—watching, waiting, and wondering if he would ever again see his own family like that.

"If I ever claim to be falling in love, Harriette, I give you permission to knock me over the head with a chamber pot." Georgina flung herself across the foot of the bed, weary from spending the bulk of the past twenty-four hours in a carriage. They'd returned to London after spending less than three hours at the Abbey. There were reputations to consider, after all.

Harriette bustled around the room, draping towels over the fire screen and pulling clothes from the dressing room. "What's wrong with love? I've always thought it a delightful notion."

"Love has ruined not one but two perfect plans." Georgina pushed up into a sitting position. "I had exclusive access to the Marquis of Raebourne for nearly two years while he stayed in the country visiting no one but Griffith. When it came time to look for a wife, it would have been so easy to choose me. But no, he had to fall in love with someone who doesn't know the first thing about being a marchioness."

Harriette met Georgina's eyes, a look of practicality stamped on her face. Georgina tilted her chin up, daring the maid to bring up the fact that Georgina had not yet been out in society when Anthony had chosen his bride. With a shake of her head, Harriette turned back to the closet.

Georgina picked at the laces on her white leather traveling boots. "And if a duke were suddenly to come out of hiding, why wouldn't he select the most popular and successful woman of the Season as his wife? I'm telling you, Harriette, love makes people do things that don't make sense."

Harriette frowned at the dirt on Georgina's shoes. "Perhaps that is why your mother continues to let you buy such impractical footwear."

A knock at the door prevented Georgina from having to come up with an answer. Family love was all well and good. She loved her family. But that didn't keep her from making logical plans and following through on them. If only other people would cooperate with her plans, she might be able to get out of this Season with her dignity and reputation intact.

While Harriette directed the filling of the tub, Georgina considered her options. Now that the duke was well and truly out of reach, where did that leave her?

Lord Ashcombe. Although she had to admit the knowledge that he'd done more than simply call on her sister made things the slightest bit awkward.

There was also the question of what he would do when he discovered her secret.

Georgina wasn't foolish enough to think her shortcomings could be hidden from a husband as easily as they could from the rest of her family. Ashcombe's pride should keep him from telling the world, but he was known to be quite ruthless in business matters. How would he handle a wife who lacked a basic skill necessary to run his household?

"The water is ready, my lady."

Georgina sank gratefully into the bath. Traveling always exhausted her, and she'd never traveled so hard or fast in her life. They must have used every spare horse between London and Kent to make the round trip as fast as they did. "Do I have anywhere to go tonight, Harriette?"

"Lady Jane's rescheduled poetry recitation party is tonight. Would you like to use your recent travels as a reason to send your regrets?"

With a groan, Georgina sank deeper into the tub until only her head remained above the water. "No. We don't need everyone knowing about Miranda's little adventure. A scandal is the last thing I need right now."

Harriette nodded, laying out clothes for the evening.

Georgina groaned as the heat from the water soaked into her tired muscles. "Perhaps I can graciously allow the other ladies more chances to exhibit their skills instead of me." She tilted her chin down and opened her eyes wide. "Modesty is a virtue, after all."

A grin tugged at Harriette's lips as she pulled a chair closer to the bath and opened their thick notebook of secrets. It never ceased to amaze Georgina that writing things down wasn't an abhorred chore for other people.

"Let's see, Lady Jane will be in attendance, of course." Harriette flipped to a page at the front of the book. "Last week you said she danced with Lord Howard twice and spent an unfortunate amount of time talking to him in the corner."

Georgina grimaced. "Yes. He's apparently very romantic. Ugh. Her mystery man would be a better choice. Did she have any significant connection to any other gentlemen?"

"No." Harriette flipped a few pages. "Although she and several other ladies were trying to talk to you about Lord Trent." The maid looked up, confusion on her face. "Not His Grace?"

Georgina shook her head. "No. Despite the fact that every lady in the realm would like to catch Griffith's attention, he is quite famously unattainable. In order to be caught he would have to actually socialize."

"Perhaps he's waiting until he falls in love."

"Bite your tongue!" Georgina couldn't help but grin. She supposed, when it came down to it, she wanted her siblings to find love. It seemed to matter to them, particularly Miranda. Then again, they had the luxury of holding out for the mindless emotion. "Who else will be there?"

The sound of pages turning scraped through the room. What would the *ton* think if they knew about that book? No doubt some of them would go to great lengths to get a look at it. She and Harriette had been accumulating gossip and news for three years now.

There wasn't much she didn't know, socially speaking.

"What about Ashcombe? Has there been anyone serious since Miranda?" Georgina was almost certain there hadn't been—one of the things that had led her to think his intentions of settling down had never been very serious. If Miranda was right, it was his attachment to Griffith that was strong enough to last the years.

"No." Harriette's voice faded, looking surprised that they didn't know more about the man. "There's very little about Ashcombe in here that would be of any use. Bits and pieces of information, but nothing of much importance."

Is there anything about me in there?

The internalized voice of Mr. McCrae startled Georgina into a sitting position, sloshing water over the side of the tub.

"My lady?" Harriette set the notebook aside and started to rise.

Georgina waved her back down and reached for the cake of scented soap. How did that man keep getting in her head? True, she'd spent several hours in close proximity to him, but as he was nowhere nearby now, she should be able to ignore his existence.

She cast a glance at the reopened notebook in Harriette's lap. Did she know anything about Mr. McCrae? The only way to know was to ask. Never before had she wanted to hide something from Harriette this badly.

"Harriette, do we have anything about Mr. McCrae in that book?" She slid the soap over her skin, trying to sound nonchalant.

"Mr. McCrae?" Harriette's eyebrows drew together as she looked through the book. "I don't recall anything about him. Is he on the list?"

"No!" Water sloshed over the side of the tub again as Georgina twisted to face Harriette. "He is most definitely not on the list."

Harriette looked as if she was trying to decide how to ask her next question. Georgina didn't know exactly what the maid was going to ask, but she was very certain she didn't want to answer it. She began to rinse. "Why don't we go over the poem again? I'll have to leave soon."

Georgina busied herself with the linen drying cloth as Harriette retrieved the slim volume of poetry. It was all Georgina could do not to dunk the thing in the cooling bathwater.

⸺

"I've changed my mind. We should do a play." Lady Jane bounced on her toes, blessedly oblivious of the way her bouncing curls made Georgina feel ill.

She refused to admit it was Jane's suggestion causing the discomfort.

"A play?" Georgina handed her coat to the waiting maid but kept a tight hold on her reticule. The extra weight of the small poetry book made the bag a constant drag on her arm that she couldn't ignore.

"Yes, isn't it genius?" Jane hooked her arm through Georgina's. "I know I said poetry, but a play would be so much better, don't you think?"

"No," Georgina bit out. She tried to keep the panic from her voice. They couldn't do a play when she'd prepared for a poem.

Jane's smile fell away. "You don't think it's a good idea? Why not?"

"Because . . ." Why not? There had to be a good reason for not doing a play. Something that would appeal to a marriage-minded female, because Jane thought of very little else. "Because with a poem you will be the focus of the attention. If we do a play, someone might steal the attention away from you."

"Oh." Jane's face cleared into a smile. "You're right. I wouldn't want to risk that."

Georgina's shoulders relaxed. Crisis averted.

"Good evening, Lady Georgina."

Tension spiraled back up her spine. Was Mr. McCrae really in attendance or was she imagining his voice again? She turned to see him looking disgustingly fresh considering he'd taken the same wild carriage ride she had. She only hoped she looked as rested. "Good evening. Mr. McGrue, wasn't it?"

He smiled as if her childish attempt to put distance between them were more amusing than annoying. Oh, how she despised that beautiful smile. "Close enough. Will you be reciting this evening?"

"Of course she is." Jane squeezed Georgina's arm. "She's simply wonderful. I couldn't convince her to do more than one though, so make sure you don't miss it."

"I'm sure yours will be equally as captivating, Lady Jane. I shall refrain from leaving the room for the entire evening so that I don't miss a single performance."

Jane giggled as Mr. McCrae bowed and headed for the refreshments laid out along one wall of the drawing room.

"What is he doing here?" Georgina whispered.

"Mr. McCrae?" Jane's eyes widened. "Father insisted. Said it was the only way to get him to talk about some tin mine."

Georgina relaxed again. If the man had been invited under the guise of business, he wouldn't remain in the room long.

Chapter 16

Poetry recitations were normally dreadfully dull and the bane of any gentleman's social existence. This one was no different. Yet Colin wouldn't have missed it for anything. Nothing short of an explosion was going to pry him out of his seat in the back of the room. For one thing, if he left, Lord Prendwick would corner him to talk about that dreadful chemical investment he wanted to make. Colin wasn't going to have anything to do with it but didn't want to damage the connections he had with those who did. By his calculations, if he managed to avoid them for another week, they'd move on to something else.

Mostly, though, he wanted to see which poem Lady Georgina would choose to recite.

He winced as a young lady squinted at the book she was holding. She obviously needed spectacles but refused to be seen in public with them. Didn't she realize her scrunched-up eyes and stumbling words were far more distracting than the frames and lenses would be?

Finally, Lady Georgina rose, to a very enthusiastic reception. After the stuttering young lady, anything would be an improvement.

"'I wandered lonely as a cloud,'" she began, "'that floats on high o'er vales and hills . . .'"

Colin sat a little straighter. The other young ladies had chosen frippery and romantic nonsense about doomed loves and handsome suitors. Though it was entirely possible this poem would end in the same place, the opening line shot through him like a dagger.

The girl was truly amazing. Her words were clear, she didn't stuff her face in the book, and she even managed to inject some inflection and emotion into her words. Why would such a consummate reciter only perform once in an evening? Lady Jane, an accomplished but not astounding presenter, had already been up twice.

As she started the second verse, he realized it was a poem about flowers.

He also realized she wasn't reading it, despite having the book open in her hand. The woman had memorized her poem. No doubt it made for a flawless performance, but why would she take the time to do that?

"'For oft when on my couch I lie in vacant or in pensive mood . . .'"

Colin grinned at the idea of Lady Georgina flopped on a couch, contemplating the mysteries of life. It didn't fit with the composed, polished young lady he'd encountered so many times.

As she came to the last line, however, a suspicious wetness seemed to form in her eye, and he wasn't sure it was all an affectation. "'And then my heart with pleasure fills, and dances with the daffodils.'"

Applause filled the room as she closed the book and curtsied. It was a bit faster, a touch louder than the polite clapping for some of the other young ladies. No doubt Hawthorne House would be overrun with daffodils over the next few days, every gentleman believing he was being clever. William Wordsworth would probably sell a few more volumes of poetry as well.

When the exhibitions were finally complete, the mingling began. Though he knew he should slip out and leave the others to their courtship dance, he couldn't leave without speaking to her. It was becoming a compulsion, to see if he could rattle her glamorous cage the slightest bit. "Well done."

She started a bit at his voice in her ear before spinning to face him. "Thank you."

He waited for the witty comment to form on his tongue, but none came. She had done genuinely well tonight. The glow of accomplishment made her even more beautiful than usual. With nothing to criticize, Colin could do nothing but stand in admiration. "I was hoping you'd grace us with an encore."

"You're very gracious, Mr. McCrae."

He used a small cough to clear the sudden tightness in his throat. "Is that poem a favorite of yours? You seemed to know it well."

Her smile was slight, but it looked softer, more real than any smile he'd seen on her face before. "I like the idea of dancing in a field of flowers."

"By yourself?" Was he flirting with her?

A hint of color tinged the edges of her high cheekbones. "Sometimes."

Was she flirting back? She looked as stunned as he felt. Their customary barbs and cutting remarks seemed to have disappeared. After seeing her with Lady Miranda at Marshington Abbey, Colin couldn't quite keep her in the conniving, calculating box he'd originally placed her in. She was real. Human. Beautiful.

And leaving.

With a wide smile, she extended her arm to a man behind him, stepping around Colin to receive more accolades.

Colin sighed with relief as he heard her simpering behind him, giggling over the gushed compliments. The moment had been just that, a moment. The lady had no reason to use her wiles on him, and his admiration for her poetry recitation had been genuine. That was all there was to it.

He spent the rest of the evening doling out vague appreciation for the other young ladies and occasionally talking business with some of the fathers who had been dragged along to the event. If he purposely avoided a certain woman in white, no one knew it but him.

"That is a stunning amount of daffodils."

Georgina glanced up from her canvas to find Miranda standing in the doorway, her mouth gaping at the scene in the upstairs parlor. Bouquets of bright yellow flowers had been arriving all morning. It had taken a while, but Georgina had arranged them across the table, sofa, and floor until the flowers had a waterfall appearance. Now she was painting them, and the effect was rather beautiful.

Miranda strolled into the room and ran her finger along the edge of one flower. "What are they for?"

"I'm painting them." Georgina felt a bit ashamed as the wonder on Miranda's face faded into annoyance. "I read a poem about daffodils at Jane's last night."

Miranda's eyebrows rose. "You went out last night? I fell asleep and didn't waken until ten this morning."

Georgina shrugged. "I didn't spend the previous evening running from a madman and getting engaged." She waited for the sting at the reminder that the Duke of Marshington would not be her salvation. It didn't come. In fact, she felt something suspiciously similar to happiness for her sister.

One glance at the dreamy smile on Miranda's face proved that, yes, Georgina was pleased that Miranda had found the love she'd sought.

The association with another powerful duke couldn't hurt Georgina's standing either.

"When is the wedding?" Georgina turned back to her canvas. She had avoided having any meaningful conversation with Miranda for years in fear that her older sister would discover her shortcomings. Now that Miranda would be moving out, Georgina mourned the lost moments. Perhaps she could spend the next few weeks forging a stronger relationship.

"Saturday."

Georgina dropped her paintbrush. "Saturday? But . . . that's the day after tomorrow."

Miranda nodded. "Ryland got a special license nearly a week

ago. We're going to get married and move out to the Abbey, start setting it to rights."

"But . . . that's so soon." Georgina set aside her pallet before she dropped it as well. The paintbrush had managed to mar nothing but her easel on its trip to the floor. She wouldn't be so lucky a second time.

"I know. But it's for the best. You'll have the drawing room all to yourself now. My few callers won't bother you anymore."

"I-I think I'll miss you." It was hard to say who was more stunned by the statement, Miranda or Georgina, but as soon as the words left her mouth, Georgina knew they were true. No matter what had happened between them in the past few years, Georgina knew Miranda would always be there for her.

Perhaps even if she knew the truth.

Could Georgina possibly tell her? Could she find the words? She'd never told anyone. Only Harriette knew.

Miranda eased onto the sofa nearest Georgina's chair. She looked a little unsure. "Mother and I went to visit Lady Yensworth this afternoon."

Georgina nodded. "She would be the one to spread the news of your coming nuptials the fastest."

"That is what we figured." Miranda glanced around the room and then sat forward excitedly. "Oh! We stopped for coffee on our way home, and you'll never guess who we saw."

"Who?" Georgina leaned forward as well.

"Miss Lavinia Clemens. Do you remember her?"

Georgina blinked. She'd actually forgotten that Lavinia was coming to Town. With everything going on, she and Harriette had never gotten around to answering the letter. Not that Lavinia would be surprised. Georgina often made a point of not answering letters. "She wrote me a while back, said she was coming to London to visit her aunt."

Miranda's eyebrows rose. "I didn't know you actually read your correspondence. I always imagined you tossing it right in the fire."

Georgina deserved that, she supposed. It did fit the image she'd worked so hard to cultivate. Again the urge to tell Miranda the truth made her tongue swell. She sacrificed Lavinia on the altar of awkwardness instead. "Lavinia's gotten an offer from Mr. Dixon."

"Truly? I suppose she could do worse."

"She could also do better." Georgina sat back, assuming the powerful role of the person holding the gossip. "She's come to Town to see if she can make that happen. No one expects her to land a title, of course, but Lavinia's quite pretty."

Miranda's eyes widened. "Does she still . . . ?" Her hand fluttered in front of her mouth.

"Does she still what?" What could Miranda possibly be trying to signal with her hand? It looked as if she was trying to play some strange imaginary violin. Lavinia had many good qualities, but musicality was not one of them.

"Does she still stutter?" Miranda's voice lowered to a whisper. "When she speaks, does she still do that thing with the *d*'s and *t*'s?"

"I believe so." Georgina began gathering her painting things. Yes, Lavinia stuttered, but she'd done a marvelous job of working around it. It gave her the reputation of being exceptionally quiet, but surely her other assets would overshadow that. "Do you think it will matter? I mean, she manages to do everything. Clearly she's not stupid. I've seen her do sums in her head faster than the dressmaker can."

Miranda smiled. "She does have a strong head for maths. And did you see her at the hunt last year? Her horse cleared that fence and she never even bobbled. I didn't dare try it."

"I don't remember that." Georgina had been too busy trying not to appear too enthusiastic about the hunt to notice much else. Riding wasn't her favorite activity, but she didn't abhor it as much as she let everyone believe. It was exhausting to appear aloof sometimes. "I do remember Trent tripping into the hedges while playing blindman's bluff with the children."

They giggled over memories for the next ten minutes, but Georgina couldn't quite forget Miranda's face when she'd asked about Lavinia's speech.

"Miranda, do you truly think the way Lavinia speaks will hurt her chances of getting a husband?"

Miranda considered Georgina. "Don't you?"

"It shouldn't." Perhaps it was because they'd met as children, but Lavinia's speech issue had never been much of a problem for Georgina. Lavinia could bring a great deal to a marriage, wouldn't she? Shouldn't that be what was considered? To be honest, Georgina had never thought much about other people's marriage prospects unless they affected her own. What did that say about her? Yes, it was getting her closer to her goal, but the trait wasn't attractive in the slightest.

Miranda sighed. "I know it shouldn't, but the fact is most men in London are going to want a wife who can stand up with them in society."

Georgina looked at Miranda, waiting, hoping, to see something that told her that her sister didn't really believe that. That she didn't think Lavinia's inability to speak perfectly was going to make her less worthy.

It wasn't there.

Georgina saw distaste over the truth of the observation. She saw grief over the death of Lavinia's prospects. But she also saw acceptance of the fact of life that would limit Lavinia's potential.

If Miranda thought that about Lavinia, what would she possibly think if Georgina admitted she not only wouldn't bring as much substantial value to a marriage, but would actually cause her husband more trouble than he'd started with? Lavinia's stutter was an inconvenience to be sure, but she could do all the things a wife was supposed to do.

Georgina couldn't.

She scooped up the brush and began dabbing at her painting once more. "I think Lavinia's a lovely girl and any man would be lucky to have her."

"I had no idea the two of you were so close." Miranda stood, looking sad that the conversation had turned into an argument like so many of their talks before. It made Georgina sad too, but she didn't know what else to do.

Miranda walked to the door. "I'll leave you to your daffodils."

Georgina watched another bloom form on the canvas. Lavinia might have a lot to offer, but her stutter had kept her on the fringes of the community, where her social skills had developed to a mediocre level at best. And while Georgina wasn't prepared to throw her own reputation away to improve Lavinia's stakes, there had to be something she could do to raise the girl's lot.

Maybe then Miranda would revise her opinion.

Until then, Georgina was going to keep any urges of confession sealed tightly away.

Sunday morning dawned bright with sunshine and brilliant with bird song.

Georgina awakened, angry at the world and despairing of ever finding what she needed. Miranda wouldn't be at the breakfast table that morning or in the family pew at Grosvenor Chapel. She had gotten married yesterday, evading the pending gloom of spinsterhood with remarkable flair, dropping the *Lady* and gaining *Her Grace*.

A styling that Georgina would never be able to claim, for there wasn't another duke showing interest in marriage this Season. The reminder that Georgina's plans were crumbling left a sour taste in her mouth.

It didn't help that an unfamiliar face was delivering her breakfast tray. The scent of chocolate set Georgina's nerves on edge. Harriette wasn't there. And she'd sent chocolate.

"Who are you?" Georgina bit out the question, not caring that she should probably know who the maid was. The girl was employed at the house, after all, and was likely even an upstairs maid.

"Margery, milady." Wisps of brunette curls trailed out from beneath one side of Margery's cap. They trembled as the shaky maid attempted an awkward curtsy while still holding the tray.

Georgina's frown deepened. "Where's Harriette?"

The maid brought the tray over to the bed. Usually Georgina

placed it on the dressing table so she could partake of the breakfast while she dressed her hair. Not this morning, though. Tales
of the spoiled daughter of the house pinning her own hair up
would make the maid queen of the servants' quarters. Georgina
tucked the covers around her legs as she sat up in the bed. Until
she found out what was going on, she'd have to lower herself to
Margery's expectations.

Now unencumbered, Margery bobbed a considerably more
graceful though no less fearful curtsy. "I'm afraid Harriette is
unwell this morning."

Georgina's steaming chocolate turned into dread as it slid down
her throat. "She is unwell?"

"Yes, milady. I'm afraid she had a fall coming down the stairs
this morning. She had to be carried back up to her bed."

A second sip of chocolate did little to ease Georgina's trepidation, but she did her best to make the maid believe it had.
Based on the look of relief that crossed Margery's face, the
efforts were successful. She turned and walked to the dressing
room, loose curls bopping under her cap in a way that irritated
Georgina because Harriette would never allow herself to look
so disheveled.

Ripples appeared in the chocolate as Georgina's hand began to
tremble without the maid in the room. Georgina carefully set the
cup aside and folded her hands into the coverlet. She forced deep
breaths through her nose, imagining all the panic sinking into her
toes, leaving her in complete control of her emotions, at least on
the outside. "Has anyone sent for a physician?"

It was not the first time Harriette had been unwell in the past
ten years, but it was the first time she'd been injured badly enough
to be put to bed. How badly was she hurt? Harriette knew how
much Georgina needed her, so she always did whatever she could
to be available. If she was staying in bed, it must be bad indeed.

Margery looked confused as she emerged to lay out Georgina's
clothing for the day. "No, my lady. She insisted that she wasn't
hurt. It wasn't until she nearly fell down the stairs a second time

that Mrs. Brantley threatened to tie her to the bed if she didn't stay there."

A deep flush worked its way across Margery's cheeks as she shared the information. It was probably the longest conversation the maid had ever had with one of the family.

What should she do? Georgina wanted, needed, to see to the care and comfort of her friend, but she had a reputation to maintain, even among the household staff. She couldn't give anyone a reason to look at her relationship with Harriette too closely.

"Have the physician called for immediately. I don't trust you or anyone else to do my hair correctly. I want Harriette back on her feet as soon as possible." Georgina turned her head and devoted her attention to the toast so Margery wouldn't see Georgina wince over the callousness of her declaration. The near silent swish of the maid's skirts leaving the room was her only answer.

There was some truth to the statement. It would annoy Georgina to have to sit patiently while Margery did her hair, knowing Georgina could have done it herself in half the time. She'd been doing everything but the most elaborate of coiffures since she was fourteen. She would also have to start her day completely uninformed, without Harriette to read the papers and correspondence.

Fortunately it was Sunday. The family would be gathering for church, so there wouldn't be time to linger with her temporary maid. The actual attending church part of the morning she could do without, though. After yesterday's wedding she felt like praising God even less than normal.

As if the marriage itself weren't torturous enough, the wedding had been utter misery. Georgina had stood by her sister, across from Mr. McCrae. She'd known the two men were close but had no idea how they had gotten close enough that the duke would choose a mere gentleman to stand with him at his wedding.

Of course, until yesterday she'd also been the only member of the family unaware of the duke's clandestine activities while he'd been missing. Perhaps it was a good thing she hadn't married him. Keeping her secrets from an experienced spy would have been impossible.

She nibbled on her toast, trying to work up some enthusiasm for becoming Lady Ashcombe.

The maid returned to the room and laid out a pair of slippers.

Georgina raised her eyebrows at the woman. Had she honestly returned to the dressing room instead of seeing to Georgina's request? "Margery? The physician?"

Margery blushed again. "Now, my lady?"

"Yes. Now." Georgina frowned, sending the maid scurrying from the room, considerably less silent than a few moments before.

It wouldn't take long for her to dispatch a footman for the doctor, so Georgina scrambled to exchange the selected dress and shoes with ones she actually felt like wearing. It was going to be difficult to allow someone else to dress her when she normally did much of it on her own. Except for the tying. Even Georgina wasn't nimble enough to do up her own fastenings.

When Margery returned, Georgina was sitting in same position she'd been when the maid left. She sipped the chocolate to hide her giggles as the maid looked over the new outfit in confusion. She ran a finger over the lace, probably trying to convince herself that she wasn't crazy for thinking she'd laid out a dress trimmed in ribbon a few moments earlier.

Let her wonder. It would keep her from looking too closely at Georgina. Getting through a Sunday without Harriette wouldn't be unbearable, though the constant watchfulness was sure to exhaust her. She could only hope her lady's maid wasn't too badly injured and was feeling better by Monday.

She wasn't.

By the time Margery delivered a breakfast tray Monday morning, Georgina was ready to eat her art pastels. Her stomach had been grumbling at her for two hours and she'd even considered risking taking a drink from the water pitcher next to the wash basin. The rest of the house was convinced that Georgina regularly slept well past ten on any morning, not requiring her attendance elsewhere.

That she was normally up and halfway dressed by eight was her and Harriette's secret.

Margery had gained a bit of confidence overnight. Her hands didn't tremble as she prepared a dress. She didn't cast furtive glances toward Georgina every few seconds, as if seeking approval for the very act of breathing.

She even smiled as she assured Georgina the doctor had come by. "He assured us the leg wasn't broken, though the pain kept Harriette up all night and left her in a sweat this morning. He put her on laudanum until the swelling goes down. She should be up and about in a few days."

Georgina waited until Margery turned her back before stuffing her mouth as full of toast as possible. A few days. What was she going to do?

Chapter 17

Colin turned the page of the book and settled deeper into the leather club chair. He should have returned home a half hour ago to dress for the evening, but for once he didn't feel like playing along with the socially elite. He didn't feel like talking business, which was why he'd ensconced himself at the club, where he'd hear nothing but gossip and banter about horses, hounds, and the occasional family squabble.

That was part of the reason why Colin paid the enormous annual fee. It was a haven for a man like him. A place where he wasn't allowed to do business.

Maybe he'd stay here all night. It was a halfway decent book. He could always practice his billiard game if he got bored.

He grinned as he turned another page.

"Pardon me, Mr. McCrae, a message has arrived for you."

Colin looked up at the porter who was extending a silver tray with a square of folded parchment on it. There was no question about accepting the note, but he still hesitated before reaching out and plucking it from the tray. "Thank you."

He broke the seal with no small amount of trepidation. The number of times he'd been summoned from the club wouldn't even require a whole hand to count, and each and every one of those dire emergencies had been from someone in the War Office.

The note was from Trent, asking Colin to stop by Hawthorne House this evening. His stomach untwisted as he realized King and country had no immediate need of his services, but a fair amount of apprehension remained. The note was more vague than cryptic, but after five years of War Office associations, Colin braced himself for the worst. Was someone sick? Was Lady Georgina hurt? Ryland and Miranda should have reached Marshington Abbey yesterday, but what if something had gone awry?

Hawthorne House wasn't all that close to the club, but the distance was short enough that Colin would probably have walked there on a normal day. Given that he had no idea what he would be called upon to do when he got there, though, he hired a hack.

The butler opened the door as Colin jogged up the steps. He still didn't look too pleased to see Colin, though the slight frown that usually marred his face when Colin called on the women was gone. There must not be too much of an emergency then, or the butler would be welcoming his assistance.

"Good evening, sir. Lord Trent said you might be joining them. May I take your hat and coat?"

Colin handed over the items, worry turning to curiosity. *Them?* Who was he joining?

Trent entered the hall, a wide, easy smile on his face. "Good, you made it." He stopped and looked Colin up and down. "I should have been more specific. There was no emergency. Georgina decided to stay in this evening, so Griffith invited several men over for dinner and cards. No women around. Sounds delightful, doesn't it?"

It did, actually. As long as they didn't expect him to talk business all evening. The regret lacing Colin's voice was genuine. "I'm afraid I didn't dress for dinner."

Trent gestured toward the stairs. "I still have some clothing here, though it's a bit out of date. I'm afraid anything of Griffith's would be too large."

That was an understatement. Griffith was the size of a small boat. Trent's clothing might hang a bit on Colin, but it should be wearable. And if he tied the cravat in the latest style, no one would think twice about the cut of the coat. Colin's grin matched Trent's. "Where's your room?"

"Up the stairs and to the left. Fourth door on the right. Need me to show you?"

Colin laughed as Trent edged his way toward the masculine laughter spilling from the drawing room. The man must truly be tired of escorting his sisters around Town. "No, I can find it."

"Join us when you're ready. I don't think dinner is supposed to be served for another hour." Trent waved and entered the drawing room.

Colin climbed the steps and started down the corridor. A door suddenly wrenched open, releasing a distraught woman into the hall like a cannonball.

He flattened himself against the wall to keep from being knocked over by the little maid with brown hair escaping her cap and fat tears streaking down angry red cheeks.

"So sorry, sir." She wiped her cheeks with her sleeves. "Can I help you?"

A shake of his head was all the permission the maid needed to scurry down the hall. Colin looked at the open door a few steps away. Only one person in this house would ever treat a servant in such a way that they'd leave a room in tears.

Colin had nothing but respect for Riverton, and he was coming to admire Trent as well. How a woman like Lady Georgina managed to grow up around them astounded Colin. Didn't she see what she was becoming? Didn't her family see it?

Why had no one done anything? It was possible they thought her too set in her ways. A week ago he might have agreed, but he'd seen her determination to help rescue Miranda, seen the way she tried to offer comfort. Those were not the actions of someone too far gone to change. God could work wonders with a little willingness. Maybe a little encouragement would send her in the right direction.

At any rate, something had to be done before she terrorized the entire staff.

Three long strides brought him to the door the maid had left open. A glance inside revealed a bed swathed in pink and green ruffles and lace.

Her bedchamber.

Heat crept up Colin's neck as he forced his gaze away from the bed. He'd been hoping for the family parlor. No matter how lofty his goal, he couldn't enter her bedchamber. The sense of disappointment and failure surprised him. He didn't know why it bothered him so much, but the prickly pear in the midst of the gracious Hawthorne family seemed wrong somehow.

Even though he couldn't enter, he couldn't bring himself to leave either. At a glance everything was normal, but he couldn't shake the idea that something was very wrong with what he was seeing.

The room was a riot of color. Aside from the various shades of pink and green in the decor, vibrant paintings hung on every wall, with more leaning against the cabinet near the window. A large curling G graced the bottom corner of each painting. He had admired her fire screens, but these were breathtaking. Did no one know she was such an exceptional painter?

And in the middle of the color, like a bright beacon of white light, was Georgina.

She sat at a pale-wood writing desk. Her head was bent over a paper that she kept turning every few seconds. Twisting her head to look at it sideways, she ran her finger along the surface.

What was she doing?

She growled—actually growled like a dog in an alley—and shoved the paper across the desk.

A thought flitted through Colin's mind, too incredible to even fully form into conscious words. It couldn't be. It simply couldn't be. Not in a family as loving and well-off as this one. No matter how indulgent they might be, they'd have made Georgina get an education.

Wouldn't they?

She slid a piece of paper toward her and dipped the quill in the ink. After squaring her shoulders like a soldier marching to battle, she set quill to paper.

Her movements were slow. Painfully slow.

After what couldn't have been more than two words, she threw the quill on the desk and crumpled the paper into a ball. Her toss missed the fireplace, and the balled paper scraped against the wall before skidding along the floor toward Colin, allowing him a glimpse of the messiest, most unreadable writing he'd seen since he'd asked a group of illiterate sailors to sign a contract. No, this was even worse than that had been.

Colin dropped against the doorframe, thankful for its solidity. There was no ignoring the evidence before him.

Lady Georgina Hawthorne couldn't read. He glanced down at the paper. Or write.

Thoughts raced through Colin's head, each trying to capture his attention, like young boys playing a game of keep-away. Should he leave? Stay? Did this knowledge actually change anything? She was still obnoxious and mercenary.

He looked over his shoulder, as if he'd be able to see Trent and Riverton through the floors and walls. Did they know?

Too many questions existed for Colin to sweep into the room as the maid's avenger, challenging Lady Georgina's treatment of the rest of humanity. He backed into the passageway, choosing to leave her to her struggles and pray for the opportunity to broach the subject with Riverton. What else could he do?

His place as a friend of the family wasn't nearly established enough to handle a secret of this magnitude.

A muffled sob sent chills down his spine and froze him midturn. He couldn't do it. He couldn't leave her. Not like this.

The very idea of the haughty and socially superior Lady Georgina in tears threw him off-kilter. The reality of it was enough to send his brain spinning, leaving him to rely on instinct.

Instinct said he should offer aid to a crying woman. Apparently there was a reason important enough to drive him into her chambers.

With a deep breath and a plea for God-given compassion, he crossed the threshold.

Georgina stabbed at her eyes with a handkerchief. Stopping the tears would leave her face red and puffy, so she knew better than to try. When tears came it was best to give them rein, mop up the mess, and move on as if it never happened. Most of the time she even felt better afterward.

No, there was nothing wrong with crying, as long as one only allowed the perceived weakness in private. How many times had she cried into Harriette's shoulder, despairing that she would ever learn to cope with her imperfection?

While she had dampened Harriette's shoulder on countless occasions, she hadn't cried in front of anyone else since she was a little girl. Not since she'd found Harriette and the two of them had made their plan, determined to fool everyone into thinking that Georgina was as bright as any other aristocratic young lady.

At such a young age neither girl was able to comprehend what they were making Harriette give up. The sacrifice had been so great, and where had it gotten them? Harriette was working as a lady's maid, nursing a swollen ankle, mind muddled with laudanum, while Georgina sat in the midst of a possible emergency but without a way of discovering what the problem even was—much less come up with a solution.

She'd gone to Harriette, but there was no breaking through the laudanum-induced stupor. Even when Harriette managed to open her eyes, she seemed to think Georgina was twelve and they were plotting to fool the governess into thinking Georgina had written the essay on Greek history.

Georgina remembered that essay. Harriette had enjoyed writing it, gushing to Georgina about all she'd learned. When it came time to hand them in, Harriette hadn't even blinked as she placed the paper with Georgina's illegible writing attempts into the governess' hand with *Harriette* scrawled across the top. She hadn't flinched when the governess called her stupid or when the woman lamented having to teach a wretched village girl because of Georgina's strange insistence.

Harriette had even smiled as the governess scooped the beautifully written essay off Georgina's desk, praising the penmanship, the opening lines, and even the choice of subject matter.

And now, it could all be for naught. All the mislaid insults, all the hiding. What would become of it now? Because it was either maintain the façade that Harriette had given everything to build, or break it down on the chance that Jane was truly in trouble.

How horrible would it be if Jane's urgent message was merely another brilliant idea for her Friday salons? Despair brought a fresh wave of tears to Georgina's eyes.

She felt a little guilty sending Margery from the room in tears, but what choice did Georgina have? The tears had been burning her eyes, threatening to spill over at any moment, and she couldn't let the maid witness them. She didn't trust Margery like she trusted Harriette.

Georgina searched for a dry spot on her handkerchief to catch the new flow of tears. What could she possibly do without Harriette?

"May I be of assistance?"

Georgina gripped the handkerchief tighter. The lightly tamed brogue traveled from her ear across her entire body. Even her toes went on alert, curling tightly in her slippers. She was not in the proper frame of mind to deal with this man.

If he was even real. The blasted man had been the voice of her conscience more often than not lately.

"Lady Georgina?"

She turned on the stool, surprised to find an expression of concern on his face and a clean handkerchief dangling from an extended arm. He wasn't going to chide her? Make a subtle insult about her intelligence or lack of ambition? She narrowed her eyes, searching his face for a hint of his thoughts. Had he come in when he heard her crying? Or had he been there long enough to see her struggle with the letter?

Because the sodden mess in her hand was useless, she accepted the offered handkerchief. "Thank you."

He shuffled his feet and cast a glance around the room as she dabbed at her eyes, more delicately than she had when she thought herself alone. There was no need to impress Mr. McCrae, but some habits were too deeply ingrained to ignore.

"May I be of assistance?" he repeated.

"You have provided a clean handkerchief. That is a gentleman's duty when a lady is crying, is it not?" He had to be talking about the crying. She would never be able to face Harriette if this were the man to finally bring them down.

"Yes, of course." He looked at the writing desk and the letter she'd been trying to make out moments earlier. His eyes traveled from the letter to her quill and on to her face before returning back to the letter.

Her tears dried instantly.

Everything in her dried. Her heart was pumping shards of glass through her veins, cutting her to ribbons from the inside out.

He knew.

What was she going to do? What was *he* going to do? He'd made no secret he disapproved of her calculated hunt for a husband. If he wanted to, he could make all of her work for naught. No one would want a wife who couldn't read the household accounts, keep up with her own correspondence, or even accept an invitation on her own.

Spots danced before her vision, reminding her to breathe, even if the act was painful.

After another look around the room, Mr. McCrae rubbed a hand along the back of his neck and sighed. He hooked his foot around a leg of the nearby straight chair and pulled it over. The chair scraped along the floor, jarring Georgina's nerves once more.

He sat, his knees almost brushing her own.

She watched his face, looking for a clue, an indication of what he meant to do. Because sitting beside her at the writing desk wasn't what she expected.

Then he picked up the letter.

He cleared his throat and shifted his weight in the chair as if he couldn't get situated. Georgina knew it to be a most comfortable chair, which meant the situation had him out of sorts.

It was confusing her as well, though she managed to maintain proper posture. A hollow victory at best.

"'My dearest Georgina,'" he read.

Heat swelled from Georgina's ravaged middle to her cheeks. He was going to read her the letter.

"'How you will laugh when you learn what I have done. (I loved that line, didn't you?) You always said we'd have to be great schemers to land ourselves the best possible husbands.'" Mr. McCrae speared Georgina with a scathing glance.

His condescension was oddly comforting. It felt a great deal more normal than his assistance.

He cleared his throat and continued. "'Well, I've done it. I have truly done it, and we leave tonight for Gretna Green.'"

"What?" Georgina and Mr. McCrae uttered the question in outrage at the same time.

His eyes went straight to the bottom of the letter to discover the writer's identity.

Georgina knew the writer to be Lady Jane, but she desperately needed to know who made up the other half of the "we" headed to Gretna Green. She prayed it was not Lord Howard. If there was a God in heaven, surely He would protect Jane from that scoundrel.

Unable to wait for Mr. McCrae to keep reading, she snatched the letter from his hand and searched the words, desperately hoping a name would form amongst the swirling letters.

But no. The more she tried, the more they swam, changing on her even as she tried to read them, blurring and moving until she wasn't even sure where she was looking. Then the word would disappear completely and she'd be left blinking away spots.

She pushed the paper back to Mr. McCrae, who was still blinking in surprise. "Who?"

He pointed to the bottom of the note. "Lady Jane Mulberry."

"I know it is Lady Jane, who is the man?"

"Oh, uh . . ." He looked over the letter. Jealous bile rose in Georgina's throat at the obvious ease he felt searching the words for the desired information.

"Her mysterious H?" His handsome face scrunched into a frown of confusion.

Georgina groaned and popped up from the stool to pace the room. "Does she say when she was leaving?"

Another glance at the letter. "Eight o'clock. Her father thinks she is going to a party in Hampstead Heath, so they'll get many miles from town before he knows they've fled."

Georgina's eyes flew to the clock, grateful that letters were the only thing that spun around when she looked at them. It was nearly nine.

She swiped the handkerchief over her cheeks to rid herself of any lingering tears. "Come along."

It was possible Mr. McCrae was in too great a shock to follow her immediately, but he would catch her soon enough. Curiosity alone would spur him to follow her, so she flounced from the room without a backward glance.

Later she could worry about the ramifications of him knowing her secret. Just thinking about it made her breathing quicken, and right now she needed all of her faculties to be in working order. She would try to simply be thankful he'd happened along when he did and keep him too busy to do anything about what he'd learned.

Once Jane was safe at home, then Georgina could panic.

There had to be a way to get Jane safely home. Georgina had begun to suspect that Jane's mystery man was none other than Lord Howard. The man had been a simpering fool at the poetry reading and he'd sought Jane out at every ball for the past two weeks. Even if the man had ideas of settling down, he was first and foremost a cad. If he thought he could get something from Jane, he wouldn't hesitate.

Not that it would be difficult. Hieing off to Gretna Green probably seemed incredibly romantic to Jane.

The chime of the large clock in the downstairs hall echoed up the stairs marking the ninth hour. There was still time to save her friend, but just barely.

Chapter 18

Colin trotted after Georgina, the preposterous letter gripped in his fist. Did women really write this sort of thing to each other? Telling each other in advance of their plans to ruin themselves? And Lady Jane expected Lady Georgina to be happy about it.

Thank goodness she wasn't. The squared shoulders marching down the corridor did not belong to someone reveling in her friend's good fortune. Lady Georgina appeared so determined that he could almost forget how dejected and broken she'd appeared earlier. Almost.

"You." She snagged the attention of a footman carrying a pitcher of water down the passage toward the bedchambers. "See that the traveling coach is brought round fitted with our sturdiest, fastest horses. The one without the crest."

She continued walking before the servant could stammer out, "Yes, my lady."

Colin lengthened his stride to keep up with her. How was she moving so fast? She was practically running, but you wouldn't know it to look at the perfect posture gliding down the stairs. The hem of her dress was barely fluttering.

A maid carrying candles across the front hall scurried to the side as Georgina flew down the last few steps. "Pack me a bag."

"Me, my lady?"

"Yes, you. Or Margery, if she thinks she can do it right. Just a small bag. Simple things. Country clothes. Ones I can manage myself."

Colin took pity on the panicking maid and relieved her of the candles.

"Bless you," she whispered before hustling to the back of the house. If she were running to get Margery, Colin could only wish her the best of luck. He assumed Margery was the crying maid he'd encountered earlier. If she'd curled into the darkest corner to lick her wounds Colin wouldn't be surprised.

He dumped the candles on a nearby table and jogged across the large front hall to catch Georgina's retreating form, skidding to a halt as she came to the same doors Trent had disappeared through earlier. She wasn't going to tell all of those people, was she? Lady Jane would be ruined before she lost sight of London.

Lady Georgina poked her head in the drawing room. "Griffith?"

Colin blinked. The tone was honeyed and simpering. Gone was the steadfast general, ordering the servants to prepare for battle. In its place was the softer posture of a woman who knew her welcome and believed it her due. No one in that drawing room would know anything untoward was going on.

"Brother, may I have a word with you?"

"Georgina, we have guests." Riverton's voice was equal parts exasperation and condescension.

Realization crashed through Colin. Georgina wanted her brother to see her as a child, to treat as if she were incompetent. How many things had she avoided because the family simply assumed she wouldn't or couldn't do them?

Respect, something he never thought to have for the young lady, bloomed in his chest. None of the spies he knew, not even Ryland, could switch character as fast as Georgina. He found himself in the surprising position of being awed by more than her appearance. It was disconcerting.

Riverton stepped into the hall, pulling the drawing room door closed behind him. The indulgent look on his face was now equal parts love and exasperation.

Georgina grasped his hands. "You have to leave right now. You have to save her."

Concern replaced the underlying irritation on Riverton's face. "What's wrong?"

"Jane has run off. You have to stop her, Griffith, catch her and bring her home before she ruins herself."

Riverton's eyes glazed over. Colin had sat across from that look on more than one occasion as the duke considered a new business opportunity. No doubt he was thinking through all the complications and possibilities. "When? Who with? Where was she heading? Did she go on horseback or by coach?"

Colin winced. He'd never got to finish reading the letter to Georgina. She wouldn't know the answers to those questions. While he couldn't begin to understand why or even how she'd kept this secret from her family, this was not the best time to be forced to reveal it. Time was of the essence.

Should he step in? Offer what he knew?

Before he could make a decision, Lady Georgina started to cry. She ripped the letter from Colin's hand and shoved it at her brother's chest. "Here." She sobbed. "Everything I know"— hiccup—"is in here."

Colin gave her a mental round of applause. If she ever decided to throw propriety to the wind, she could find a career on the stage.

Trent stepped into the hall. "What's going on?"

"Lady Jane is making a colossal mistake." Riverton waved the letter in the air. "I'd send round to her father, but they've already been gone an hour."

"Not to mention her father is rubbish on horseback and doesn't own his own coach." Trent grimaced as his eyes flew over the letter.

"Who is her 'mysterious H'?" Griffith looked disgusted by the secretive pet name.

Lady Georgina hiccupped. "Lord Howard. They've been inseparable for weeks."

Colin glanced back at Georgina, sniffling delicately into a handkerchief. He knew his mind should be consumed with the problem at hand, but it was stuck on the fascinating revelation about Lady Georgina. How had she reached adulthood without learning to read? Why?

Riverton folded the letter, using his thumb and finger to sharpen the creases. "I have to go after her."

"And let the biggest gossips in London wonder what took you away?" Trent took the letter back. "No, I'll go. No one will miss me."

Georgina's hand tightened on her handkerchief until the knuckles paled. "We have to hurry. She could be halfway to Scotland by now."

Riverton shook his head. "No more than a few miles down the road, assuming she actually left when she said she would."

The glare from Lady Georgina's narrowed eyes would have gored a bloody hole through Riverton's chest if he gave credence to the intangible. Colin leaned against the wall, watching the family byplay with increasing interest.

Lady Georgina sniffled. "Regardless, we should depart immediately."

Trent's eyes widened. "We? I'll travel much faster without you."

"And once you've found her? How will you get her home?" She jabbed her fists onto her hips.

With a frown, Trent conceded the point.

The footman Georgina had sent for the coach entered the hall, trying desperately not to appear curious, and failing. "My lady—"

"Charles, have the traveling coach brought round. The unmarked one," Riverton said.

Alarm and confusion filled the footman's face as he looked back and forth between the brother and sister. Colin pressed a fist to his mouth, hoping the sharp pinch of teeth against lips would keep the threatening laughter contained.

Georgina lifted a single brow.

"Right away, my lord." The footman scurried away.

Colin shook his head. When he'd walked in the house an hour ago, he'd have said Lady Georgina was riding the tide of her brother's influence. It was very obvious now that she was controlling her own destiny in this family, despite what many would term a shortcoming.

Did that mean he was wrong about other things when it came to this woman?

Trent ran a hand over his cravat. "I'll change coats and cravats. Everything else will pass well enough, but we don't want to make it obvious that we're leaving town in a hurry."

"I'll pack a bag." Lady Georgina followed Trent across the hall to the stairs.

Riverton looked to the drawing room door, no doubt dreading the curious people he'd face when he returned.

"What will you tell them?" Colin asked.

Riverton's eyes widened in his serious face. He gave a one-shouldered shrug. "Nothing."

What would it be like to walk in a room and not strategize his way through the evening? "Must be nice to be the duke."

"It has its moments." Riverton straightened his jacket and reached for the drawing room door as Lady Georgina scampered back down the stairs.

Riverton looked at the bag with raised eyebrows but said nothing before he returned to the gathering.

Colin debated joining him, just to witness the men trying to get the duke to gossip like a society matron. Colin's sudden presence would no doubt add to the speculation. Fun though it would be, he didn't need his name in the gossip mill. When people were talking about you, they were less likely to talk to you.

"Are you ready?" Lady Georgina asked.

Colin looked about the entry hall. Apparently she was talking to him. "For what?"

She rolled her eyes. "To go?"

Trent joined them, a tan coat in place of his dark evening one. "You mean for Colin to come with us?"

Colin's surprise exceeded Trent's. Why on earth would he go? He wasn't family, had barely even spoken to Lady Jane on two less-than-memorable occasions.

Georgina glided to the door, a clenched fist on the handle of her valise the only outward sign of her distress. "If you get beat to a pulp rescuing Jane from Lord Howard's clutches, we'll need Mr. McCrae to escort us home. It's not ideal, granted, so do try not to become incapacitated."

Colin liked to think he had a decent grasp of how the softer side of the population thought, but he was beginning to think he didn't understand them at all. If all their minds worked liked Lady Georgina's, it was a wonder that any man could maintain a sensible conversation with a woman.

Trent crossed to the door with a shrug. "Care to join us on this little adventure? At least you'll provide me with some pleasant company."

Trent glared at Georgina as they settled into the coach seats. He was probably mad at her for that crack about his getting beaten. Her brother did like to pride himself on his pugilistic skills, and Lord Howard wasn't known for being very athletic. The fact was Georgina needed Mr. McCrae on this trip. Like it or not, he knew her secret and had thus far shown no intention of revealing it.

Her heart pounded against her chest once more as the fact that her secret was exposed now insisted on being addressed. She gritted her teeth and shoved her fears away. With Trent in the carriage she couldn't risk a conversation with Mr. McCrae. Unless he began to share with Trent, she could wait for a more secluded opportunity.

She hated having to bring him with her, but she needed to keep an eye on him and learn what he planned to do with his new-found information. Besides, with Harriette unfit to travel, Georgina needed him in case she came across another note from Jane or some other missive in need of attention. Relying on the insufferable man for anything made her unsettled, but it was better than bringing someone else into her confidence.

Instead of pulling straight out of London, the coach crossed the square and headed deeper into Mayfair.

"Where are we going? This isn't the North Road." Georgina jerked away from the window as the coach rolled down St. James's Street. She couldn't be seen in this area of town. Her reputation would be ruined.

"I have to pick something up." Mr. McCrae watched out the window, perched on the edge of his seat.

The coach turned onto Pall Mall, and Mr. McCrae jumped out before the vehicle had rolled to a complete stop. Georgina tried to see where they were but couldn't risk showing her face in the window. The coach was unmarked. They didn't need anyone wondering why the duke's family was traveling in an unmarked carriage.

Before she could slide across the seat to get a better look out the window, Mr. McCrae was climbing back in. The carriage began moving again as he pulled the door closed. His arm was wrapped around a small leather bag. A long strap dangled nearly to the floor.

"What is that?" Trent and Georgina asked at the same time, the siblings craning their necks to see the bag as Mr. McCrae settled into his seat.

"Let's hope I don't have to tell you." He slid the bag between his hip and the wall, covering it with his coat as if hoping his companions would forget it was there.

Little chance of that, but nothing more was said about it as they rolled out of town.

Trent turned the discussion to sport, which suited Georgina fine. Whatever kept the men occupied suited her. She hadn't the faintest idea of how to rescue Jane. Though she hated to admit it, she was simply along for the ride, next to useless until they actually located the fool girl.

"We're an hour out of London." Trent pushed the curtain aside to watch the trees fly by. "Let's start checking inns. At the very least they'll have to stop somewhere and change horses or take a meal. They may not even push very far, thinking anyone coming after them would race right past."

The road to Gretna Green was littered with inns, and the men spent a great deal of debate over which ones to check. Visiting them all would take too long.

There was also the question of who should go in and inquire after Lord Howard. They couldn't mention Jane or her reputation would be ruined, whether they found her tonight or not.

In the end Georgina stayed in the coach with the footman standing guard at the door while both men went in. If it looked like they planned to meet Lord Howard there, their inquiries would garner considerably less suspicion. The ruse took all too much time as far as Georgina was concerned. It was somewhat frightening to sit in the carriage alone.

After the fourth inn, the men looked grim as they climbed back in the carriage.

"What if he didn't come this way?" Trent leaned forward to rest his elbows on his knees. "Jane seemed to think they were going to Gretna Green, but what if they weren't?"

Mr. McCrae shrugged. "There are other roads to Scotland. Any town across the border will get the ceremony done."

Assuming Lord Howard even intended to take her to Scotland. The men exchanged glances, leaving that last bit unsaid, but Georgina knew what they were thinking. Her shoulders slumped. That was it then. "They could be anywhere, couldn't they?"

Trent nodded, suddenly looking tired and defeated. "That's even assuming they headed north. Howard's low enough to take her west long enough to ruin her so he can force more money out her father to make the scandal go away."

A low thumping noise broke the silence of the coach as Mr. McCrae drummed his fingers against his knee. Such an uncouth habit, but Georgina was thankful that he appeared more in thought than distress.

His fingers stopped moving, and he pressed closer to the window to look up and down the street. "How close are we to Elstree?"

Trent looked out the window as well. "About five miles or so. But that's back toward London. We checked the Flying Pig there, remember?"

Colin shook his head. "Howard's maternal grandfather owns a house in Elstree. I can't believe I forgot about it. I don't know how often Howard goes there, but it's enough that the staff wouldn't question his right to use it."

Georgina sighed. Wasn't that just like a man? "Mr. Fleckmire died years ago. Any house he had has surely changed hands."

Mr. McCrae shook his head, a smile tugging at his lips. "No, he's not dead, just very irritated with all of his daughters' choice of husbands and his wife's efforts to spend him into debtor's prison, so they left the country."

Trent was laughing as he stuck his head out the window and instructed the driver to turn back toward Elstree. "Where did they go?" he asked as the coach started rolling again.

Mr. McCrae gave his smile free rein, and as it spread across his face, Georgina was tempted to smile as well. "Canada. His wife keeps threatening to move to India and claim she's been widowed. He lets her redecorate the house while he goes off to hunt bear, and that seems to settle things for a while."

"How do you know all this?" Georgina hated herself for asking, but she couldn't contain the curiosity.

"I trade stocks on the 'Change for him. He's doing rather well."

Was there anyone's financial situation this man didn't know about? No wonder all of society kept him close. He could ruin them all. "Where is Canada?"

He tilted his head in thought. "Think north of America, only colder and more French."

"Sounds barbaric." Georgina shuddered and adjusted her skirts to wrap them tighter around her legs. All the in and out the men had been doing for the past hour left the coach a bit chilly, and just thinking about cold weather made her shiver.

Trent frowned. "But if he's in Canada, won't his house be closed up?"

Colin shook his head. "Mr. Fleckmire keeps it open for his grandchildren to use. Says they deserve a place to get away from their fathers."

"Sounds like the perfect place for Howard to go."

Georgina turned to the window to hide her agitation from the men. If the couple had gone to a private home, it might already be too late for Jane. The lovely but dimwitted Jane had been Georgina's closest friend in London for years, ever since the other girl had been standing three feet away from two gentlemen coming to blows in Regents Park and missed the entire thing.

Nothing made Georgina feel safer than an unobservant soul.

Georgina glanced at Mr. McCrae and found him watching her. He'd been watching her since they'd read the letter. What was he seeing? They were going to have to talk soon, and she hoped she got through it without making a fool of herself. Panic curled her toes, threatening to take over her body. What was he going to do now that he knew her secret?

He couldn't do anything if he was busy defending himself. "Tell us, Mr. McCrae, where are you from?"

His eyebrows lifted as his lips twisted in amusement. He knew what she was doing. "Glasgow. And I think, lass, if we're going to make a habit of hurtling through the countryside together in the middle of the night, you can call me Colin."

She didn't want to call him Colin. He already knew too much about her. To acknowledge their relationship as being more than circumstantial would put her in a very precarious position. She might actually start to like him. "That would hardly be proper, Mr. McCrae."

"Oh, give over, Georgina." Trent nudged her foot with his boot. "The man's hied off after your friend without a single protest. The least you can do is offer the use of your name."

The odious man's smirk was almost a grin.

"Very well. In private company only, you may call me Georgina, and I will call you . . ." She swallowed. Her gaze slid across the carriage to connect with his eyes. They weren't laughing anymore. "Colin."

Their eyes stayed locked together as he nodded. "Georgina."

A shiver started somewhere in her middle and worked its way to her fingers and toes, one that had nothing to do with panic and everything to do with . . . Well, she wasn't sure, but it was rather pleasant. Was he doing it on purpose? Adding the additional brogue to her name? It wasn't as if he'd never said it before. All he was doing was dropping the *Lady* from the front. It shouldn't have sounded so intimate.

"Good, good." Trent's loud joviality broke the spell. "Now that we're all friends and have a definite destination in mind, what shall we do while we race along hoping highwaymen don't waylay us?"

Chapter 19

Colin had only been to the house once, not long after he came to London. He was fairly certain they'd found the right one, though—unless there were many houses in the area with medieval gargoyles flanking the entrance. It was hard to forget those ugly carved beasts.

The front drive was closely lined with trees, closing it off from the rest of the house's grounds. They maneuvered the carriage to the other side of the gate and into a grove of trees. He didn't know if they were fruit or nut trees, but Colin really didn't care. They kept the carriage hidden from anyone passing by on the road or the main path to the house. It left them with a significant distance to cover on foot, but they could hardly roll up and announce their presence. They had no idea what kind of situation awaited them.

Colin jumped to the ground and slung the strap of the small leather satchel over his head so it lay across his chest. He hoped he didn't need it, but it was better to be prepared.

Trent was right behind him, holding one of the carriage lanterns aloft. Colin felt no surprise when a third thump indicated Georgina had disembarked as well.

"What are you doing?" Trent growled.

Georgina's eyes narrowed. "I'm coming with you."

"You're staying in the coach."

"Do you know how awful it was waiting in that coach while you went into the inns? And that was only five minutes!" Georgina's voice was growing considerably louder than a whisper.

"I've a better idea," Colin grumbled. "Let's stay here and argue until we draw their attention."

Trent frowned. "Come along, then."

Colin choked on the urge to send both of the siblings back to the carriage. Didn't they know they were supposed to be sneaking up to the house, not barreling through the underbrush like pigs hunting truffles? He redirected them to the lane, figuring the silence a clear path afforded outweighed the risk of exposure.

Fortunately, the Hawthorne siblings seemed to find the art of walking lightly by the time they reached the house.

Georgina held her breath as they approached the building. There wasn't much sign of life, but at least one room was ablaze with light on the north end of the house. Someone was in residence. They didn't dare try the front door, and the kitchens were bound to be busy. Only one door was accessible on the darkened south side, but it was locked.

With a sigh, Colin opened the leather bag at his hip. "Hold that lantern over here, would you?"

Trent shifted their dim lantern so a little beam of light fell into the bag. Georgina tried to peek, but all she could see was various leather and metal bits. Was that a knife?

Colin pulled out an iron hoop with several strange-looking keys on it. He then took the lantern and inspected the door.

Georgina looked over at Trent, who just shrugged.

The jangle of keys, a few grunts, and then the telltale scrape of the lock.

Georgina lifted her brows in Colin's direction. He who always seemed to think himself a little better than everyone else knew how to pick a lock? "You have hidden depths, Mr. McCrae."

"I'm beginning to think I'm not the only one."

He mimicked her condescending expression as he pushed the door open.

They were in.

Colin slid the ring of keys back into the bag and stepped inside. Trent and Georgina followed. It was difficult to tell what kind of room they were in, since all the furniture was covered in sheets. Colin extinguished the lamp and set it outside the door before easing it shut once more. "Let's see what we can find."

They didn't have to look long. The dining room was across the main hall and there sat Lord Howard and a giggling Jane.

Georgina wanted to strangle her.

"Is the pudding to your liking, my dear?" Lord Howard leaned toward Jane and ran a finger down her cheek.

"It's delicious." Jane giggled some more.

Georgina was never telling that girl a joke again.

"Why don't you go on and retire? I'll see to the house, and we'll set off again at first light." Lord Howard helped Jane to her feet and pulled her into a loose embrace. "I cannot wait until I'm married to you, my sweet."

Jane wrapped her arms around Lord Howard's neck and kissed him.

A burning sensation crawled up Georgina's throat. She was going to be ill. With eyes squeezed shut, she willed the mental image to fade away. What did Jane possibly see in that man? Perhaps Georgina should have stayed in the carriage.

"They've readied a room for you. Upstairs, to the right."

Georgina snapped her eyes back open as Howard's voice indicated an end to the press of lips.

Jane nodded and giggled some more before easing herself away, trailing a hand along Lord Howard's chest. Could she truly be attracted to the man? His appearance was dapper enough, but his mannerisms left a great deal to be desired. Apparently Jane didn't require as many qualities as Georgina did.

Such as a lofty title and enough money to silence the masses?

Georgina nearly groaned. Even when the real man was right next to her she heard him in her head. It was unfair.

Colin pulled Trent and Georgina deeper into the shadows as the couple stepped from the dining room. Georgina could not be the only one in their party who wanted to simply snatch the silly girl and run, but caution was necessary if they wanted to avoid Lord Howard. They were, after all, trespassing on his family's property. And, though foolish, Jane was obviously here of her own free will.

Lord Howard watched with narrowed eyes as Jane crossed the hall to the stairs. He actually licked his lips before going back into the dining room and closing the door.

The burning sensation crept to the back of Georgina's mouth.

Once the hideous man was out of sight, Colin pulled Georgina after him toward the stairs, Trent bringing up the rear of their little party.

It didn't take long to make their way to the room Jane had been sent to. It was the only room with light seeping underneath the door.

"You go first." Colin nudged Georgina toward the door.

Georgina frowned at him. "Why me?"

Trent groaned. "In case she's . . . undressing."

They had a point. Georgina eased her head into the door and saw Jane turning circles in the middle of the room, fully clothed. Georgina pushed her way in and dragged the men in after her.

Colin wasn't sure how he felt about breaking into someone's home, but the perplexed look on Lady Jane's face made him glad he'd come. A man's dressing gown, presumably Lord Howard's, was thrown over the end of the bed. A scattering of personal effects covered the writing desk. It was obviously not a guest room, and Lady Jane looked completely bewildered.

"Georgina?" Lady Jane actually smiled as she took Georgina's hand. "Did you come to see me married?"

"No," Georgina said through gritted teeth. "I've come to take you home. What is this nonsense?"

Lady Jane's eyes softened as she stared hazily off into nothingness. "Lord Howard said true love didn't wait for things like banns to be read. That is for people with less passion than we have."

Colin groaned. He didn't think Lady Jane and Lord Howard were communicating about the same kind of passion.

"Jane, you'll be ruined if you do this." Georgina tried to pull Jane toward the door. "Let's go home and talk about this."

"Oh, no, I see what you're worried about." Jane smiled again. Did she even realize Colin and Trent were in the room? Could she be that obtuse? "John has promised to keep me pure until we say our vows."

Colin couldn't take it anymore. "Is that why he sent you to his room for the night?"

"Well, I . . ." Lady Jane looked around again. Her face changed from confused to hurt to scared as she accepted where she was. "I'm sure it's a mistake."

Trent shook his head. "Mistake or not, you don't want to do this."

More glazed staring. Did Lady Jane live in the real world at all? "But it's love."

Colin cleared his throat. "It will be nice, won't it? You and, er, John joining with your family for Christmas, visiting each other's homes during the Season. Your father showing his grandchildren how to . . . to . . . whistle?"

Had Colin McCrae lost his mind? They were supposed to be convincing Jane to leave, not encouraging her to marry the hideous man downstairs. And whistle? Who dreamed of having their children whistle?

"Oh, yes!" Jane clasped her hands together. "My family dances by the light of the yule log every year. That's the only time Mother lets Father whistle so that everyone can dance and no one has to play the pianoforte."

Colin nodded his head enthusiastically. "Yes, yes, and do you think your father will be as welcoming if he doesn't have a chance to give you away at the wedding? He'll be hurt."

Hurt? The earl was going to be furious, not hurt. Georgina covered her eyes in defeat. Why had she insisted on bringing him?

Jane's soft wail had Georgina snapping her head up again to find Jane's trembling hands covering her heart. "Georgina, what have I done?"

Colin McCrae was apparently a genius.

"Nothing. Which is how we're going to keep it." Georgina started across the room. "Let's go."

Heavy footsteps sounded in the hallway. Colin's sappy speech had taken too long and Lord Howard was about to enter. Colin looked at Trent and nodded at Lady Jane. Both men grabbed a lady by the arm and hauled them to doors on opposite sides of the room.

Colin shoved Georgina through and slid the door closed with a barely audible *click*. He turned from the door to find himself surrounded by shelves and hooks filled with clothing. They had managed to escape into the dressing room. Was this all Lord Howard's? The man must be doing more than occasionally visiting. Was he living here? It could explain the long hours at the club. Lord Howard was notoriously low on funds, but Colin hadn't realized it was bad enough for him to try to live off his grandfather.

Not that Colin cared overmuch about Howard's living arrangement at the moment. What mattered was that he and Georgina were trapped in a room with one door, one window, and no weapon. With any luck Trent and Lady Jane had passed through to another bedchamber and were even now making their way down a set of stairs.

Any moment now, Lord Howard was going to realize his quarry had escaped and go after her. Hopefully he wouldn't need to change clothes in order to do that.

Georgina stood a foot away, hands clasped in front of her, not moving. He wasn't even sure she was breathing. For a woman who plotted everything down to the perfect mix of dance partners, this situation must be intolerable.

The moonlight through the window was enough to make out the hulking shape of a large skirted chaise lounge on the far side of the dressing room. He pulled Georgina across the room and pushed her down behind the furniture. "Get back here in case he comes in."

"What about Jane? What are we going to do?" Her whisper was barely audible, forcing Colin to lean in until his nose brushed her curls. She smelled like lemons.

"Trent has Jane." He aimed his whisper at her ear. "Don't worry. I'll get you out of here."

Georgina sank to the floor and crossed her arms over her chest. "Thank you."

Kneeling behind a chaise lounge in the dressing room of a man who may or may not be dangerous didn't exactly make him feel as if he had earned her thanks. She needed to be prepared that he might not be as sure as he wanted to be. "You can thank me when I've managed to actually get you home with your reputation intact."

She sighed. "While I dearly hope we accomplish that, I want to thank you for trying. Even if we fail."

Colin lifted an eyebrow, though he doubted she could see it in the dark closet. "Your faith in my ability astounds me."

He felt her arms shift in a shrug. "It will be quite ironic if Jane manages to get home unscathed and I suffer the consequences."

"I'm going to get you out of here and back to Trent."

"Good."

Did she believe him? Did it matter? Colin searched the dark. Her breathing reached his ears, quick and shallow. Too quick. "Everything will work out. All we have to do is get outside and we'll have smooth sailing."

"Given our location a good ten feet above the ground in a room with no outside door, forgive me if I don't find that comforting."

A heartbeat passed before she spoke again. "You can't tell anyone."

Colin frowned at the rushed words that had come spilling from her mouth. "Of course not. The whole point of this is to hush the entire night up."

He actually heard her swallow. "No . . . you can't tell anyone about me. About . . . about the reading."

A shout from the other room had them hunkering down behind the chaise before Colin could answer. Lord Howard was mad. Colin leaned over Georgina. If anyone or anything came busting through that door, she wasn't going to be the one it caught.

Her hair tickled his chin, and her hands pressed lightly against his chest. Even through the coat, vest, and shirt he could feel the pressure.

His heart jumped.

Then it stopped beating. It was simply the situation. He was not attracted to Georgina. She was conniving, calculating, grasping, and a host of other things he didn't admire. The fact that she was also smart, caring, and brave didn't negate those things. They only made the picture more complex.

"So why the desperate husband hunt?" he whispered into her ear.

"What? You want to talk about this now?"

"We have to wait—we don't have to be bored. Keep your voice down and he won't hear us."

"It's what women do." She'd turned her head to whisper straight into his ear. Suddenly this talking plan didn't seem like such a good idea.

"What?" He cleared his throat and shifted his weight so that he wasn't pressing along her body in quite as many places.

"Get married. What else would a woman of my station be doing?"

She had a point, but her actions seemed to go well beyond that of the average marriage-minded female. "Yes, but why so determined? First Raebourne, then Ryland, now Ashcombe. It's obvious you're hunting titles."

Lord Howard bellowed from the other room, calling for someone named Jasper. His stomps echoed through the dressing-room door, going back and forth across the bedchamber.

They weren't going anywhere any time soon.

With a sigh, Georgina shifted, pressing closer to Colin's chest before sinking lower to the floor. She wiggled up until her back was to the wall and her shoulder against the raised back of the chaise lounge. She slid her legs under the skirted furniture. She was completely hidden from the door.

Colin relaxed back onto his heels, allowing the moonlight to come between them, giving him a clear view of her face. Could she see his as well? Or did his angle to the window keep him in shadow?

Her lips curved softly as she snared him in her direct gaze. She lowered her voice to a whisper, not that Lord Howard could hear anything over the racket his pacing march was making. "Tell me something about you first."

Part of Colin prayed for very heavy cloud cover to roll in. All of him prayed for a miracle to get them out of there.

"What do you want to know?" he asked, even as he told himself to change the conversation.

She thought for a moment. "Why you're in London."

Colin's eyebrows rose. "If I tell you why I live in London, you'll tell me why you want a husband so badly?"

Her head tilted to the side as she considered him. "I'll trade a question for a question."

That seemed fair enough, but was it a good idea? There wasn't much she could ask that he wouldn't willingly answer. His father, of course, but she didn't know enough to ask about him. Even his connection to the War Office could be talked about in the vaguest of ways, since she was already aware of it.

Lord Howard started screaming, and loud crashes indicated his temper had a physical element to it. The summoned Jasper had apparently arrived, though the servant didn't seem very concerned about the missing woman. He actually had the gall to ask if Lord Howard had checked under the bed.

Apparently he hadn't. And would he then check the dressing room? Colin hung his head. Why couldn't the man just run after her so he could get Georgina out of this overgrown closet?

Surprisingly, his fellow trespasser didn't seem perturbed by the ruckus on the other side of the door.

There was nothing else to do while they waited but talk, or whisper, in their case. He sat next to her, back against the wall. "All right. I'm in London because that's the center of business. The stock exchange is there, the people with the investment money are there. Lots of shipping, lots of news. It's the hub of life for a man like me."

"I want protection."

The whispered confession slipped into Colin's heart, making him want to pull Georgina close even though he didn't understand her statement. Their talk didn't seem so harmless now. "Protection from what? You're the daughter of a duke."

"Who can't read or write. What do you think would happen to me if Society knew that I can't address my own invitations? That I can't read a cook's menu? That the household accounts and correspondence of any man I married would have to be handled by someone other than the lady of the house?"

"*Shh-shhh.*" Colin wrapped his arm around her, trying to calm her as her voice crept louder than a toneless whisper. He pulled her close and rubbed a hand along her back. He'd never thought about what it meant for a woman to be able to do things like that, but most of the things that an aristocratic husband would expect of her would require her to read.

"And I need you not to tell them." The whisper broke as if she were holding back a sob.

"I won't. I won't." He'd planned to talk to Riverton as soon as they got back, but now it didn't seem quite so important. She managed so well, did it really matter if her brother knew?

She leaned into him a moment before pulling away slightly. "I have to marry before everyone finds out, and it has to be to a man powerful enough to protect me when they do."

Which certainly wasn't him.

His arms dropped to his side at the sudden thought. Why would he think such a thing? Marriage might be something he'd thought about with more frequency of late, but marriage to her had never entered his mind. At least not seriously.

"Why can't you read?"

"No, no, Mr. McCrae. A question for a question."

Colin didn't want to play anymore. The men in the other room had stilled, their voices lowering to normal level, which meant Colin couldn't hear them. "I'm going to check on Lord Howard."

Easing away from Georgina was harder than anticipated. He felt chilled where she'd been pressed up against his side.

He pressed his ear to the door, hoping he hadn't missed a vital part of their plan.

". . . going to find her." Lord Howard's flat voice sent a chill down Colin's back. "You search all of the rooms up here. She can't have gone far."

"Of course, sir." The servant sounded bored. Colin didn't think he'd be putting much effort into the search. Not that Colin could blame the man. It was doubtful that the servants had much respect for Lord Howard, especially since they weren't even really in his employ.

More stomping and then a door opened and closed. Only one man had left. Even if the servant wasn't willing to exert himself in the search, he wouldn't ignore two unknown people emerging from the dressing room.

Enough noise passed through the door for Colin to know the other man didn't immediately leave the room, but not enough to know what he was doing. Colin pressed his ear closer to the crack between the door and the wall, hoping to hear something definitive. His ear grew warm and the wood bit into it, but he learned nothing. All was quiet on the other side of the door. Had the servant left? They were trained to be quiet. Perhaps Colin had missed his exit.

Wincing at the slight *click* of the latch, Colin eased the door open enough to line up one eye with the opening and peek into the other room.

Jasper was certainly doing a thorough job of searching the upstairs rooms. If Lady Jane had decided to hide in the pages of the book, the servant would have her in hand within the hour. Chances were he wouldn't care about Colin and Georgina sneaking or even walking boldly across the room, but it was possible Howard had sent more servants searching as he left the house. Time for a new plan.

He eased the door shut and looked around. They had a chaise lounge. And clothes.

"Gather up his trousers. As many as you can." Colin crossed to the window. He was about to ruin some clothes, but Georgina's reputation was considerably more important than Lord Howard's trousers, assuming they were in fact his and not one of the other grandchildren's.

The window hadn't been opened in a long time, if ever, and it took quite a bit of effort to raise the sash. There was at least fifteen feet between the window sash and the ground. Even though the wall beneath them was edged with bushes, it was too far to jump.

"Here." Georgina dropped a pile of trousers at his feet.

He tied one pair around the chaise lounge and then tied them leg to leg until he had a decent line of them hanging out the window, scraping the top of the hedge. He pulled them back up and offered the end of the makeshift rope to Georgina. "Hold on tight, and I'll lower you down."

She looked over the line of trousers. "Will it hold?"

"If it starts to rip I'll get you as low as I can before you fall."

"Comforting." Despite the flat tone of her whisper, she stepped up to the window.

Colin stood on the trousers to keep them from falling and wrapped his hands around her waist. Her quickly indrawn breath told him she was as affected by their situation as he was.

He rather wished he hadn't learned that.

He lifted her to his chest and she slid her feet through the open window. Her skirts fell away, baring her stockinged leg.

He almost dropped her.

"Colin!"

"Sorry." Colin tried not to laugh as he watched her, clutching a trouser leg in her hands, glaring over her shoulder while her legs dangled out the window. She was never going to forgive him for this indignity as it was. If he laughed, she'd hate him for sure.

And he didn't think he wanted her to hate him anymore.

He lowered her out the window. She whimpered as he released her weight, and only her grip on the trousers kept her from crashing into the hedge below.

Colin lowered her as fast he could, listening for any sign that Jasper was growing curious. At least Lord Howard would credit Lady Jane for the ladder of trousers left dangling from the dressing room.

Georgina tried to push off from the wall as she neared the greenery below. She almost cleared the hedge, but her shoulders ended up buried in the side of the bush. Still she seemed happy with her escape, looking up at him with a brilliant smile of relief, even as she struggled to roll out of the bush.

Colin slung his leg over the windowsill and tried to work his way down the trouser legs. Easing his way over the knotted fabric was difficult. A ripping sound filled his ears as his knees cleared the top of the ground-floor window.

The pants gave way, and he tumbled down, his momentum sending him crashing through the bush and rolling to the lawn below until he landed in a heap at Georgina's feet. If anyone were actively looking for them, they'd have heard that. He could only hope that all the servants were as apathetic to Lord Howard's plight as Jasper was.

He looked up to see her smile, wide and unpretentious. Possibly the first genuine expression he'd ever seen on her face.

She nudged his shoulder with her foot. "And you thought you'd never be one of the men at my feet."

Chapter 20

An answering grin spread across Colin's face. Amazing how easy it was to think of him as Colin now.

The smile fell off her face. It was too easy. She cleared her throat. "I find myself in need of rescue once more, Mr. McCrae."

He picked himself up off the ground. "I thought I was Colin."

"Oh, very well. Would you care to remove the bush from my hair, Colin?"

Instead of immediately moving forward to extract her from the hedge, he stayed where he was, staring, his grin growing the slightest bit wider. "You look good in green."

Georgina rolled her eyes. It was the only part of her she could move, since the hedge's hold on her hair was forcing her to stand at an angle that made moving her hands impossible unless she wanted to burrow farther into the foliage.

He laughed softly but moved forward to inspect her situation. After a few tugs he gave a low whistle. Georgina tried to twist around, as if she'd be able to see what he was looking at.

"Stay still, won't you? You've got limbs stabbing straight through your, er, arrangement."

She tried to breathe calmly while he contemplated how to release her. But then he pulled the knife she'd seen earlier out of his little leather bag. Her heart pounded, and she tugged against the bush. "Oh, no, please don't cut my hair. I'll have to hide away for the rest of the Season."

Heavy hands held her shoulders still. Where had he put the knife?

"Calm down. I'm going to cut the bush. I assume you have no objection to traveling home with a twig or two in your coiffure?"

"Of course not." Now she felt ridiculous.

He retrieved the knife from the ground and leaned into the limbs behind her. They were going to leave quite a dent in the hedge, along with the ruined clothing. It would certainly give the servants something to talk about in the morning. A few quick tugs and she felt the pressure on her head release. She moved several steps away, shaking out her skirt and smoothing her hair as best she could, which wasn't well given her new accessories. "Which way do you think?"

He looked both ways and then pointed. "Let's try that way. I'm pretty sure we're on the opposite side of where we went in."

They walked, Colin adjusting his steps to match her own. He was very considerate like that. She was very thankful he'd come along. Despite her attempts to wrangle him, he could easily have declined, as evidenced by the way he detoured the coach in London.

He dropped the knife back into the bag. That was as good a topic of conversation as anything else. She cleared her throat. "Where did you get the bag?"

He lifted an eyebrow. "Playing again, are we? Very well. I stopped by Ryland's and borrowed it from his parlor maid."

She hadn't been thinking of starting the game again, but if he wanted to . . . Wait, what had he said? "His . . . Marshington's parlor maid picks locks? Does he know this?"

"I'm fairly certain he taught her."

Interesting. But still not as intriguing as the fact that Colin possessed such a skill. "Who taught you?"

"That's another question."

The grass felt soft under her feet, like the plushest of rugs. With the warm night air and just enough moonlight to keep it from being oppressively dark, she found she was comfortable. Right now there was no risk that anyone would discover her secret, even if she were to talk about it. She'd never felt so free. Even alone in her room with Harriette there was the chance that another maid would enter, or even her mother. She'd never truly been alone before. She was safe. "Ask me anything."

He seemed to consider his words for several steps. His speech was slow when it finally came. "How is it your family doesn't know about . . . you know?"

"My deformity?"

He put a hand on her arm to pull her to a stop, bringing her attention to his scowling face. "Don't call it that."

"My shortcoming? My failing?"

His lips thinned. They started walking once more. "Your inconvenience."

An interesting choice of words. She considered the fact that she was in slippers instead of boots inconvenient. As was the fact that, should they encounter Lord Howard on the grounds, her white dress would give them away instantly. Her inability to read, however, always seemed much more of a hindrance than a mere inconvenience. "Harriette."

Wrinkles deepened across his forehead. "Harriette?"

"My lady's maid." Georgina trailed a finger along the edge of a blooming rose as they passed. "I was six before I realized that everyone didn't struggle the way I did. I thought getting the letters to stay in one place was part of learning to read. My governess thought I was lazy and spoiled. So I used that and insisted on having my own lady's maid. Mother thought it was adorable, especially when I chose Harriette."

"Harriette is quite young herself."

Georgina nodded, wondering once more what would have become of Harriette if she hadn't joined Georgina. "Two years older than me. She lived in the village. I took a book out to the lake one day to see if I could read it without anyone around. She found me and waited for me to try. When it didn't work, she read the book to me."

"And you asked for her as your maid."

"She was brilliant. Took my lessons with me and everything. We would trade slates when the governess wasn't looking. She called Harriette horrible things. Harriette tried to tell me Miss Winston didn't really think those things, it was just because Harriette was a nobody from the village, but I knew. I knew every word she said was really meant for me."

Where were these words coming from? She'd never even admitted such a thing to Harriette before, wasn't even sure she'd admitted as much to herself. But it was true. Georgina had felt the weight of every disparaging remark that had been directed at the maid. Even her mother hadn't understood why Georgina kept insisting that Harriette was the perfect companion, had gently suggested that perhaps Harriette wasn't suited to the aristocratic life, even as a lady's maid.

"And now?" Colin's gentle voice broke through Georgina's memories.

She glanced at Colin. Here, finally, was someone who could know exactly how smart and loyal Harriette was. "She does all of my writing. Reads me the society pages every morning and goes through all of my correspondence. I don't know what I would do without her."

"Where was she when Jane's letter came?"

"On laudanum for an injured ankle." Now that Jane was found, Georgina could smile at the memory of Harriette's antics. The woman did not handle her medicine well.

They walked in silence. If the sun had been shining and they weren't in imminent danger of being caught in a compromising situation of questionable legality, it would almost have seemed they were taking a stroll through her garden in London. What would it be like to take such a stroll with Colin? The conversation was certainly coming more easily than—

"Well, that's a problem."

Georgina looked up from her toes to find they'd come upon a wall. A wall with no gate in sight. "A walled garden, perhaps?"

Colin nodded. "With any luck we're already in it and jumping this wall will get us out."

Georgina swallowed hard. The wall was brick that had been mortared into a completely smooth surface. Not even a vine of ivy dared to mar the surface. "Jump it?"

He bent his legs and cupped his hands together. His jacket pulled taut across his shoulders. "Give me your foot and I'll boost you up. Then I'll climb up and lower you down the other side."

Georgina looked from Colin to the wall and back again. "Have you lost your mind?"

"Unless you would like to try going through the house again. I, for one, would like to make it back to the carriage before sunrise." He nodded toward his cupped hands. "Your foot?"

She couldn't do this. She couldn't place her foot in his hands and, well, jump over his head. Everything she'd done for the past twelve years had been to create the image of a dignified, sophisticated, perfect young lady. This would be scandalous.

It's only a scandal if anyone knows about it.

Why did she have to spend the evening dealing with two Colin McCraes? That was insupportable. She needed to get back to London.

Before she could talk herself out of it, Georgina lifted her skirt, wincing at the mud and grass stains crawling along the hemline. Her slippers were ruined as well. She slid her foot into his joined hands. Until that moment she hadn't known she was cold, had in fact thought the night rather warm, but the heat that cocooned her foot left the rest of her shivering. She looked down on his head as she placed her hands on his shoulders, curling her fingers into his coat to keep from running them through the mess of reddish brown curls.

He looked up, probably to make sure she was ready, and their eyes met. She was close enough to see the individual lashes, feel the mingling of their breath. If she brushed her lips against Colin's, what would it feel like? Would that incredible warmth that surrounded her foot and seeped through her hands find its way to her lips as well?

"Up we go," she said brightly before she could give in to the temptation.

Colin lifted her, and she immediately felt the sensation of falling. She bit her lip to keep from squealing but couldn't prevent herself from wrapping her arms around his head in a fit of self-preservation.

Once Colin was upright, he waited silently while she searched for the nerve to unwind herself and reach for the top of the wall. It was only a foot or two over Colin's head, easily reachable from her position if she could convince herself to let go of his jacket.

"All you have to do is sit on the wall. I'll do the rest." Colin slid one hand up to her knee and hoisted her higher, forcing her to sit on the wall or topple headfirst over his shoulder.

Once her backside was settled, she actually felt quite secure. Secure enough to smile down at Colin, who was rubbing his hands over his face and mumbling. Wait, was he praying? As if God was going to help them out of this mess. If He'd wanted to intervene, He could have let them flee through a door that led to a corridor instead of the dressing room.

Finally Colin looked at her, then down at her ankles peeping out from her skirt. There was nothing she could do about it in her current position. Considering he'd had his hand halfway up her skirt—something she was truly trying not to think about—she didn't see why a bit of ankle would send him into a panic now. "Are we going to stay here all night?"

Colin groaned before jumping and throwing his arms along the top of the wall. He grunted, working his feet up the wall until he could throw a leg over. He sat up, breathing hard.

"Very impressive." Georgina grinned.

"Hmmm." Colin grabbed her under the arms. Really, was there anywhere this man's hands weren't going to go this evening?

There was no gentle coaxing this time. He tugged her to him

and flipped her legs to the other side of the wall as if she were a rag doll. With one leg on either side of the wall, he leaned over and dangled her along the back side of the wall. Then he let go.

Georgina sucked in her breath to scream, but then her feet were on the ground. It couldn't have been more than a few inches.

Colin swung his other leg over and dropped down beside her. "Onward."

He stomped off and Georgina scrambled after him. "Were you a spy too?"

"What?" He looked confused, but at least his pace settled back down to something she could keep up with.

"It's my turn to ask a question. You and Ryland are close enough that you stood up with him at the wedding. Were you a spy?"

"No."

She waited for him to expound. While he had, strictly speaking, answered her question, they'd embellished on all the other ones.

After several moments of silence, Georgina pressed for more. "How do you know Ryland, then?"

He glanced at her but quickly turned his face away. "That's another question."

"Ask me one, then." She would give his question a curt response as well, and they'd be right back to him within seconds.

"What were you thinking back there, before I threw you up on the wall?"

Georgina stumbled. Had he noticed her intention to kiss him? Was it something she'd done? Did a person change when they thought about kissing? She'd never had to worry about it before. Not that there hadn't been a man or two who wanted to take her aside for a stolen kiss, but she had merely sidestepped the situations. She had no way of knowing if she would be a good kisser, and she would not risk her reputation in order to find out. Now she was wishing she'd tried to study the subject a bit more. She always figured that by the time it mattered she would already be married or at least engaged.

She glanced at Colin. At some point they had both stopped and were standing in the quiet, waiting on her to answer. She opened her mouth to tell him the truth. It was what she'd been doing all evening, and part of her wanted to hold on to the novelty, to let him be the one person she never lied to. But her tongue couldn't form the words. "Er, that I had no idea I was afraid of heights."

"I met him in Spain." He started walking again.

He knew she was lying. She didn't know how she knew he knew, but she did. Otherwise he'd have given a more complete answer.

Georgina took in a deep breath, oddly compelled to know how he'd met the duke and knowing that now was her only opportunity. She bartered with her tongue for a partial truth instead of a complete lie. "I wondered how your hair would feel."

It was his turn to stumble. "My hair?"

She nodded but kept walking, using the motion as an excuse to keep her face averted. "Is it soft? It curls in the most interesting way. Griffith's and Trent's hair just sort of lays there. Yours seems to have . . . life."

He tipped his head sideways as they rounded the corner of the house. "Why don't you see for yourself?"

"No, I think I'd rather not."

He smiled at her as he straightened, the tension seemed to leave his shoulders, and he strolled beside her once more instead of stomping. "My father owns a shipping company. I hitched a ride to Spain and ended up stumbling into the middle of a group of people trading slaves for guns. I didn't know what to do, but I couldn't leave those people. I tried to free them, but the traders caught me instead, throwing me in with the lot."

Georgina sucked her breath in. This was not the fun story she was expecting. "And Ryland was there?"

Colin nodded. "He was . . . one of the traders. But not really. He was trying to get information. Some of the slaves had come from one of Napoleon's palaces. They already had a plan in place to try to get the slaves free, but it wasn't foolproof, and I'd managed to make the gun men angry."

"Ryland saved your life?"

"At the possible expense of his own, yes. It was close. Ryland and another spy were shot, but the slaves scattered across the port. I hope they managed to find work or make their way home. Spain was no longer safe for Ryland and his cohorts. So I smuggled them onto my ship in packing crates. I spent the trip back to England slipping them food and medical supplies. I've never been so scared. The captain barely tolerated having me on board. I didn't know what he'd do if he found stowaways."

This incident, the way he talked about it, was about much more than meeting Ryland. It had changed something in him. It couldn't be a coincidence that he'd been living in London since it occurred. Georgina's voice dropped to a whisper. "Have you been home since?"

His gaze snapped to meet hers, and his response was immediate. "Have you considered telling your family?"

"There you are!" Trent burst through the trees and wrapped Georgina in his arms. "I've been so worried. I started to go back in the house three times, but I don't have Colin's bag of tricks and there were no open doors or windows. The place is locked up tight."

Colin clapped Trent on the shoulder. "We had to go the long way around. Lord Howard is out searching for Lady Jane. I was a bit worried he would have found you."

Trent shook his head. "He tore down the main drive on a horse a while ago and took the road toward the village. He must think Lady Jane headed there to find assistance."

Georgina glanced around but saw no one besides the three of them. "Where is Jane?"

Trent gestured toward the trees behind him. "Sleeping in the carriage."

Colin filled Trent in on the basics of their adventure, leaving out a few details such as their encounter with the wall. Georgina didn't correct him.

They reached the carriage, and she climbed in to arrange herself on the seat next to her friend while Trent and Colin saw to waking the coachman and helping him reharness the horses.

In minutes they were barreling back down the road toward London. With every mile, she made the conscious effort to pull her mind away from the man sitting across the carriage. Their walk through the garden had been the most relaxing, enjoyable time she'd had in years. It was a luxury she couldn't afford, though, because it had also been the most frightening. Colin couldn't keep her safe. Colin couldn't make people overlook her eccentricities. Colin wasn't the man she needed.

Georgina avoided his gaze as the conversation faltered. Trent's snores were soon mingling with Jane's heavy breathing, leaving Georgina alone with Colin, but not as alone as they'd been mere hours earlier. The urge she felt to continue their game scared her. The questions had been venturing into things so personal she didn't even talk about them with Harriette, and yet . . .

These urges were dangerous. Too dangerous to toy with anymore. It was time for Colin to stop being Colin.

They pulled up to a modest town home a few streets over from St. James's Square. What were they doing here? The door swung open and Colin rose from his seat. He lived here? Not in rented rooms or a hotel, but in a terraced house? Would she ever cease being surprised by what she learned about him?

He caught her eye before he stepped down from the carriage. The first rays of the rising sun hit his face through the open door. "Good morning, Georgina."

She swallowed and felt her heart hit her toes. "Good-bye, Mr. McCrae."

Chapter 21

It was a shame, really, that one couldn't go to the store and buy a play to watch at home like one could purchase a book. Maybe then there wouldn't be so many conversations about popular books at *ton* gatherings. Georgina could certainly do with a few less of them.

"She was a complete simpleton for holding out on Mr. Collins." Lady Theodora Clayton stuck her nose in the air, disdain dripping from her voice as if she were talking about a real person.

"Nonsense. What were his lofty connections going to gain her?" Georgina snapped her fan open as she vocalized her opinion. She'd spent most of the day sleeping off her midnight adventures but had woken in time to prepare for tonight's gathering. Sleeping through the day had kept her from missing Harriette too much, though Margery had told her that Harriette insisted she'd be back in the morning.

Georgina hadn't really felt up to the effort of a gathering such as this one, but when they'd deposited Jane at her house, she'd begged Georgina to come tonight. Jane had to attend to quell any rumors that might have started from her journey. She insisted she couldn't face the evening without Georgina.

So here Georgina was, being pulled into a conversation about a popular book. Sweat was beginning to dampen her lower back.

Lady Theodora frowned as she rethought her opinion. "Lady Catherine de Bourgh didn't seem to move about much, did she?"

"No. Where I believed Lizzie was cork-brained for turning down Mr. Darcy the first time." Georgina fluttered the fan a little harder as Trent and Colin entered the room well within conversing distance. Did the man always have to look so fresh and rested after driving across the country all night?

She would ignore them. Maybe they wouldn't come greet her. She and Colin—Mr. McCrae—had to become nothing more than nodding acquaintances again. She devoted herself back to the conversation. "He was of considerable better society than she. Refusing his offer was unthinkable."

Jane sighed, a dreamy look on her face as she stared off at nothing. "But what about love?"

Georgina scoffed to hide her inner cringe. Only people without flaws and secrets could afford to hold out for love. And for Jane to be simpering over the feeling less than a day after it nearly ruined her was enough to make Georgina declare the entire emotion absurd. "What of it? Consider how much time you'll spend with your husband versus the amount of time you'll spend doing other things related to your station in life."

Jane's fan fell limp as her eyes widened. "I never thought about that."

Given her ridiculous notion to run off with Lord Howard, Jane's lack of thought was more than obvious. Georgina bit her tongue to keep the retort inside. Lady Jane was personable and beautiful enough to provide competition if she ever set her mind to it. Her general empty-headedness wouldn't deter anyone.

Many might think it an asset. She'd be able to have children, run the house, and attend social gatherings without putting too many demands on her husband.

She could even handle her own correspondence.

The unfairness of it all made beads of perspiration break out on Georgina's chest and neck. She flicked her fan a bit faster. Why was it so infernally hot in this room?

Lady Theodora looked around the room at the conversing groups of London's elite. "Perhaps I should rethink some things."

Her eyes lit on the two men talking quietly to the right of the trio of ladies. She pitched her voice a little louder. "Good evening, Lord Trent and um . . . Good evening."

Trent and Mr. McCrae turned to the ladies, smiles at the ready. Trent bowed and greeted the group.

Georgina wanted to smack the coquettish smiles off of her companions' faces. She supposed Trent was a worthy suitor, even as a second son. But he was also her brother and had taken to spending entirely too much time with the man who could ruin her life. She refused to think kindly of him at the moment.

Trent gave Georgina a hard look, reminding her of her manners. One more sin to lay at Mr. McCrae's door. Georgina hadn't forgotten a social nicety since she was seven years old. "May I present Mr. McCrae? Mr. McCrae, this is Lady Jane and Lady Theodora."

Bows and pleasantries were exchanged, while Jane's blush grew brighter and brighter. She was trying to pretend she hadn't met Mr. McCrae on the road back to London, but she wasn't doing a cracking good job of it.

Mr. McCrae, however, performed admirably. As much as Georgina would like to think him self-centered enough to have forgotten Lady Jane, she had to admit he was just being nice.

"We were discussing the romantic tale of Elizabeth Bennet and Mr. Darcy." Lady Theodora tilted her head to look up at Trent through her lashes. "Have you by chance read the book, my lord?"

"I'm afraid I haven't had the pleasure, but I've noticed both my sisters carrying it around." Trent looked around the little group. "Is it one you'd recommend?"

Jane and Lady Theodora set themselves on either side of Trent, forcing Mr. McCrae to step back or be trampled. He moved around the circle to Georgina's side.

Watching her friends simper over her brother was unbearable, particularly when they simpered about a book. It wasn't because she thought Trent didn't deserve it but because it left her with no way to maneuver the situation. She was left powerless on the fringe.

It felt eerily foretelling.

Her fan churned the air around her, making her ringlets flutter. She forced herself to slow the flicking to a respectable, sedate speed. She couldn't let everyone know she was flustered.

"There are quite a few people on the terrace this evening," Mr. McCrae said, leaning in so the words went to her ears only. "Would you like for me to escort you?"

"No." She bit her lip at the lie.

Lady Jane edged closer to Trent, as if he didn't know she'd tried to run off with Lord Howard. It was almost nauseating.

Georgina snapped her fan closed. "Yes."

Colin bowed and offered his arm.

In deference to the warm night, their hostess had lit the terrace almost as well as the drawing rooms. Several couples mingled on the other side of the thrown-open double doors. It was the perfect place for a semiprivate conversation.

Georgina glanced at Col . . . Mr. McCrae. If only her conversing partner were more advantageous.

"You carry a book around?" Mr. McCrae leaned on the stone balustrade in a circle of light.

The shifting shadows from the lantern flame licked at the red tinges in his brown hair. She shouldn't notice. She told herself not to notice. Finding this man's hair more compelling than Ashcombe's brown-on-brown locks wouldn't help her achieve her goal. "Every young lady keeps a book lying around. You never know when you will need to entertain yourself for a moment of two."

Mr. McCrae's eyebrows shot up and a smile tweaked the corner of his lips. "That is true. Most young ladies can find momentary solace within the pages of a novel." He leaned in a bit, lowering his voice to a conspiratorial whisper. "But not you."

Georgina twisted her head to look over the terrace, ensuring that no one was close enough to hear his words. "Have a care with your words, if you don't mind."

"I don't mind."

They stood in silence for a moment. Why didn't she walk away from him? It wasn't as if she wanted to be spending time with him. She should claim a need for refreshment or even a necessary visit to the retiring room. Anything to get away from his side and in the vicinity of someone more suitable. Preferably Ashcombe.

"Why haven't you told them?" His whisper rolled over her ear, soft as the roses that lent their heavy perfume to the terrace air.

Were they still talking about that? She made herself busy adjusting her glove so she wouldn't have to look him in the face. If she saw pity, it would kill her. "We already addressed this. I would be the laughingstock of London. I'd be lucky for an offer to run away with Wickham."

He laughed low and it skittered across her skin and beneath the glove she'd just smoothed. "Hang London. I'm talking about your family. Trent truly believes you've read the book."

"I have read the book." She finally looked at him to ensure he believed her.

His lifted eyebrow indicated he didn't.

"Very well, Harriette has read it to me, but that's as good as reading it myself."

"Why haven't you told them?"

The man was like a spinster trying to hold the attention of a third-tier bachelor. Why couldn't he let her be? "Tell me, Mr. McCrae, what purpose would that serve?"

He blinked, appearing caught off guard for the first time since she'd met him. "They would be able to help you."

She leaned in, hoping if anyone glanced their way the conversation would appear light and friendly, not serious or personal in any way. "Help me do what?"

If he said they could help her learn to read, she'd risk the scandal and poke him in the eye with her fan right there on the terrace. She'd tried everything over the years from smuggling in instruction primers to having Harriette write words in gigantic letters. Nothing had made reading any easier. Eventually she'd managed deciphering a line or two in a printed book, but it had taken her hours.

Only slightly better would be the idea that they could assist her in making an advantageous marriage. Didn't he know any overt efforts on their part would make her look desperate and cause everyone to wonder what was wrong with her?

He shifted his weight, doing his part to appear a man compelled to escort her outside. Maybe it wasn't an act. What if he had only brought her outside because he felt it his gentlemanly duty?

"They could help you be yourself."

It was Georgina's turn to blink, to reveal the shock she couldn't contain. Of all the things he wished her to do, be herself was the last thing she expected. No one expected you to be yourself in London. They wanted perfection, the epitome of a lady. "Colin, I—"

"Ah, Lady Georgina, I was wondering if you intended to grace us with your presence this evening."

Colin held her gaze for but a moment more before acknowledging the man behind her. "Lord Ashcombe, good evening."

"Mr. McCrae." The unspoken question was written all over his face. He wanted to know what she was doing on the terrace with someone of so little consequence.

"Mr. McCrae was kind enough to escort me out here when Trent became an overwhelming center of attention." She cast the earl her most flirtatious smile. If the loosening of his own smile was an indication, he swallowed the bait like a trout in her brother's fishing stream. "Having an eligible brother can be quite tiresome."

"Perhaps we could find some more pleasant company? There has been talk of starting up dancing in the drawing room." He offered his arm.

Georgina laid her hand on it. "That sounds delightful, Lord Ashcombe." Part of her wanted to stay on the terrace with Colin, and she wondered at that. Wasn't Ashcombe her goal? Her options were running out. She couldn't afford to lose this one.

She cast a glance over her shoulder as she re-entered the house. Why did it feel like Colin was the actual loss?

He told himself to look out at the garden, at the other couples on the terrace, his shoes, anything really besides the white swish of Georgina's skirt as she entered the house. It didn't work. His gaze stuck to her until she disappeared. Only then did he turn to look over the garden, his lips pressed into a grim line. Had he truly thought things would be different now? He'd come to this party particularly to see her, had maneuvered Trent into bringing him since Colin hadn't actually been invited. And for what? Another cold brush-off from the Ice Queen?

After everything that had happened in the past twenty-four hours, Colin had thought it would be different. Thought she would be different. He liked the girl who had dropped everything to save her friend, manipulating her brothers and even himself into preventing a young woman's ruin. He'd been impressed by the Georgina who had hidden behind a chaise lounge, climbed down a rope made of trousers, and been daring enough to bare her own secrets to learn a few of his.

If he didn't know better, he would be convinced that there were actually two women of like name and appearance, switching places at will for the express purpose of driving him mad.

Colin traced Georgina's path into the drawing room. He should leave. One of the cardinal rules of a man on the fringe of high society was that he knew how to keep his place. Draw too much attention to yourself and they were likely to cut you off. Attending parties you weren't invited to was a very good way to collect attention.

She was dancing with Ashcombe. She was smiling her perfect smile, the one Colin hated, the one she used to keep anyone from getting close enough to discover her secret. The dancers went in a circle, and Ashcombe's appreciation of the smile was evident. He was enjoying being the focus of the prettiest girl in the room, the one everyone said would make the match of the year. At least they had before Miranda's marriage to Ryland had hit the papers.

"Save me."

Colin turned to find Trent, wild-eyed and panicked. "From what?"

Trent's gaze darted around the room. "Whom."

Colin rolled his eyes. "From whom, then."

"Lady Jane."

"The woman we resc—" Colin snapped his teeth shut and swallowed. They didn't need to go through the trouble of saving the girl only to start rumors about the event. "The young lady Lord Howard was calling on recently?"

"The very one. She has, shall we say, decided to direct her attentions elsewhere after recent events."

Colin laughed. The disgruntled look on Trent's face was too funny not to. He couldn't quite find it in his heart to feel sorry for the beleaguered man.

Trent nudged Colin in the shoulder. "I'm serious."

"What would you have me do? Your rescuing her could be seen as rather romantic."

"You were there too." Trent frowned.

"I'm afraid I am not aristocratic, secluded, or destitute, and we all know a romantic hero must possess one of those qualities."

Trent's eyes widened in new desperation. "Come up with something to distract her from me. Anything will do, really."

Colin looked around the room, wondering what could possibly divert a woman's attention from a man she now viewed as her reputation's savior. His eyes lit on the slightly rounded figure of Lord Howard on the other side of the drawing room. "I believe your distraction has arrived."

"So help me, if she runs off with that lout again, I'll let her be ruined."

Colin was inclined to agree. But he was more worried that Lord Howard would confront Lady Jane and she would give up the names of those who had helped her escape. What would Lord Howard do with that information? Colin didn't have any direct association with the man, but the cad had a title and could certainly make life rough if he chose to. All it would take was a well-placed comment or two.

"You should ask her to dance."

Trent glared at Colin. "Didn't you hear me? I'm trying to avoid her, not encourage her."

"She'll move on to someone else by the end of the week. What's important now is that Lord Howard thinks her out of his reach and in the company of people who make it worth his while to leave it alone."

A laugh to Colin's left grated across his skin even as he appreciated the perfect cadence and melody of the sound. Did she practice that too? Ashcombe wasn't a funny man, so he couldn't have said anything worth truly laughing about.

"I suppose you're right." Trent rubbed a hand over his face, and Colin had to think back to what they'd been talking about a few moments ago.

He had to get out of here before he did something stupid. Colin clapped Trent on the shoulder. "Get to it, my man. I'm heading home."

Trent's eyebrows rose. "But we've only been here twenty minutes."

"I remembered some urgent business I left undone when we left town last night." That wasn't completely untrue. He'd left things unfinished on his desk, but all of it had been taken care of this afternoon.

Without waiting for Trent to acknowledge his statement, Colin headed out the door, bypassing saying good-bye to the hosts, who hadn't actually wanted him there in the first place.

When he got home, he went to his study even though he had nothing else to do there this evening. The letter from Alastair Finley still sat on the corner of the desk, right next to the one from his father. He'd left them there, too sentimental to toss them in the fire, yet unable to bring himself to actually answer either one.

His fingers danced over the request from Alastair. With his instincts screaming at him to put the paper down and not get pulled into the feud once more, Colin opened the paper and read the offer again. It was still there, the request for an office manager, Alastair's concerns over not having a suitable heir, his not-so-subtle hints about Erika's availability. The old seaman was offering a way home, a new life, even a little bit of revenge on Colin's father. For the first time, Colin saw a bit of appeal in all three things.

Chapter 22

"This is different." Harriette edged a bit closer to Georgina. The maid was still pale with pain, but her limp was barely noticeable. Georgina had tried to convince her to stay home another day and rest, but Harriette wouldn't hear of it. She felt bad enough for not being able to help during the entire Jane debacle.

"We're still in Mayfair." Barely. Georgina hoped she had infused that sentence with a bit more confidence than she felt. The coffee-house, busy but not overly crowded, was in a respectable part of town, but not one Georgina frequented.

Georgina led Harriette to a table in the back. She'd selected this shop because it was nowhere near St. James's or Bond Street, where her friends and acquaintances were likely to gather. A quick glance around the shop revealed a few curious stares but no familiar faces. Even her simplest dress was drawing notice among the clientele filling the establishment.

"Why couldn't we have gone to our usual shop?" Harriette sat next to Georgina, looking around as if she expected to find the customers had turned from gentry, barristers, and the occasional shop owner into hardened sailors, ruffians, and dangerous scar-faced thugs.

"Because we're meeting Lavinia." Georgina had ignored Lavinia's presence in Town as long as she dared. It felt wrong to

231

not acknowledge their friendship, but at the same time Georgina couldn't risk marring her own reputation with Lavinia's.

Colin's voice had chided her for hours after she'd sent Lavinia an invite to meet her here at this out-of-the-way coffeehouse, but Georgina couldn't do anything else. Lavinia was a fine companion in the country, where everyone in the area knew her and had grown accustomed to her stilted speaking. She wasn't the most popular girl in the village. No one scorned her, as evidenced by the marriage offer from Mr. Dixon, but at the same time, even there, she wasn't always welcomed with warmth.

Lavinia looked as if she belonged with the crowd as she entered the shop, her light brown ringlets framing an easy smile. She rushed across the room, her brown eyes crinkling at the corners when she reached Georgina's table.

"Good t-to see you!" Lavinia reached across the table and clasped Georgina's hand.

Georgina glanced around. Lavinia was alone. "Where is your maid?"

"Mother is shopping. She'll walk home with me."

They ordered coffee, and the conversation was stilted for the first few moments, but it didn't take long before the two fell into their normal pattern, sharing stories and telling jokes. Eventually Georgina didn't even hear Lavinia's stutters anymore.

A curl of jealousy hit Georgina in the heart. She'd never been jealous of Lavinia before. Pitied her, yes, since the other girl was unable or unwilling to hide her affliction, but never jealousy. Yet here Lavinia was, talking about her plans and opportunities in London seemingly without concern of what would happen when people heard her speak.

"Aren't you worried? Even just a little bit?" Georgina asked after Lavinia had laid out her hopes that someone more suitable than Mr. Dixon would come into her life during her six weeks in London. As much as she tried, Georgina couldn't shake the thought that Miranda might have been right about Lavinia's poor prospects.

Lavinia gazed out the window over the other patrons' heads. "D-did you know that Moses didn't speak well?"

Moses? Was Georgina supposed to know someone named Moses? "Oh?"

With a nod, Lavinia sat forward in her chair, leaning over the table as if she were about to gift Georgina with the most amazing piece of gossip.

Georgina couldn't help leaning in herself. Even Harriette, who had set her chair back from the table and busied herself with a bit of knitting, tilted her head to hear better.

"Moses couldn't speak well, and God used him anyway. I understand he's responsible for the first five books of the B-Bible."

Georgina hated the man already. He'd started that book her family seemed to obsess over. "What has that to do with anything?"

"Well, the way I see it, if a man of G-god has the same affliction I d-do, then I d-don't think G-god wants me to worry about it."

Georgina wasn't sure that was how it worked, but if it gave Lavinia the confidence to move about London, she wasn't going to argue. It wasn't fair that God gifted some people with whatever they needed to feel good about themselves. Of course He frequently seemed to give out gifts through that book of His, which meant He didn't have anything for Georgina or He'd have made it so she could read it.

No matter what they said in church on Sunday, it was obvious to Georgina that she wasn't one of His special children. She'd done something so wrong as a child that God had blocked her out of the family when she was still learning to walk.

"I wish you the best of luck." Georgina squeezed Lavinia's hand, knowing it was the truth. "I don't know when we'll be able to meet again. Mother has my schedule sewn up for the next several weeks." And that was a lie.

"I'm happy we were able to meet t-today. My aunt secured a few exciting invitations, so p-perhaps we will meet again while I am here." Lavinia's eyes relayed the understatement she was making. If her wide-eyed anticipation was anything to go by, her aunt had been invited to an event or two well above their normal circle of acquaintances.

That made Georgina a bit nervous. They were bound to be large parties, though, or even balls, so it shouldn't be too difficult for Georgina to convincingly avoid Lavinia at those events. "I'll keep an eye open for you."

Guilt turned the coffee she'd drunk into a toxic sludge in her midsection. She would keep watch for Lavinia, though not for the reason the other girl probably thought. Georgina would look for Lavinia because Miranda was right. Even the server walking by their table had looked askance at Lavinia as she stumbled over her words. Imagine what the *ton* was going to do to her.

When Lavinia's mother joined them, Georgina kept the conversation as brief as possible before making her good-byes.

In deference to Harriette's ankle, Georgina hired a hack to take them back to their normal section of Mayfair. The silence was thick as they watched the town homes grow taller and nicer.

"I've nothing to feel guilty about."

Harriette's tilted her head in confusion. "My lady?"

Georgina shifted in her seat. This hack could certainly do with some fresh cushions on the seat. "There's country life and Town life. A girl shouldn't have to live both of them in the same set of streets."

Harriette said nothing, and Georgina avoided looking in her direction. Colin's voice was already berating her. She didn't need Harriette's sad eyes joining the party.

"Did I see you speaking with Miss Clemens in a coffeehouse yesterday?"

Georgina startled at Ashcombe's statement. It was the first words he'd said since picking her up for a drive nearly ten minutes ago. She'd been sitting next to him, letting her mind wander as it did so often for the past two days. Two days in which she hadn't seen Colin McCrae at all, though he'd seen fit to pop into her mind at the most inopportune moments.

"Lady Georgina?" Ashcombe prodded.

What had he asked about? Oh yes, coffee with Lavinia. How had he known about that? "I did have coffee with Miss Clemens. She and I know each other from the country."

Ashcombe's mouth pressed into a thin line as he nodded. "You'll not be seen with her again."

Georgina's eyes widened. Not even Griffith had been so demanding as to refuse to allow her to spend company with a person. It didn't matter that Georgina had come to a similar conclusion herself. For Ashcombe to dictate such a thing when they hadn't even spoken of marriage was absurdly high-handed. "I beg your pardon."

The smile that twisted his lips didn't curl in any natural way—it gave off a sinister feeling instead. He should practice it in a mirror. "We both know I don't take many ladies out for a drive. If I'm to associate myself with you, I require you to maintain a certain image. Image is key to a man's success, you know, and his wife's behavior reflects on him even more than it reflects on her."

She was torn between giddiness that he'd referred to her as his potential wife and anger over the presumption that his reputation mattered more than hers.

Isn't that why you're seeking a man of high regard? So that his reputation can save yours from future damage?

Georgina formed the mental image of a tiny Colin McCrae tumbling over the side of a cliff. How did Lord Ashcombe even know who Lavinia was? Georgina was depending on no one recognizing her even if they happened to see Georgina with her. "What is wrong with Lavinia Clemens? Her father owns a successful set of lumber mills."

Ashcombe nodded. "Yes, I know. Clemens is a good man. Such a shame he had a stupid daughter. I do wonder at his judgment in sending her to London."

Her jaw dropped open for a moment before she recalled how inelegant surprise looked. Had he called Lavinia stupid? "Lavinia is brilliant."

"I can see where you would think so. She dresses quite smartly and paints a pretty picture from across the room, but she reveals her true intelligence whenever she speaks a sentence over four words. You must have noticed. While it is kind of you to overlook it, I must ask that you confine your works of charity to more obvious and helpful causes."

Her works of charity? Georgina sat back against the curricle seat. Did she consider Lavinia charity work? It was possible. In the country she considered the other girl a friend, but she had walked halfway across town to meet her somewhere she thought none of her other friends would be about. Apparently Lord Ashcombe had been.

That sounded considerably more selfish than any charity work would be.

"Has your brother spoken of any plans he has for going to Gloucester any time soon?"

The change of subject caught Georgina off guard. "My brother?"

"Riverton. Has he plans to travel to Gloucester?"

When had they stopped talking about Lavinia? Ashcombe made a declaration and that was the end of the discussion? Why would he discount her opinion? Why just assume she would abide by his wishes when they had no formal or even informal agreement between them? What would he say about her own failing if he felt so strongly about her distancing herself from Lavinia's? Georgina's head spun from the abundance of questions. "N-no. I haven't heard of any plans."

"Hmmm. Do keep me informed if you hear otherwise. I have holdings of my own in Gloucester I should like to discuss with him if he makes the trip." Ashcombe turned the horses around.

Georgina was surprised to feel relief that they were on the back end of their journey together. He'd made yet another declaration. How much worse would it get if they got married?

And when had she started thinking in terms of *if*?

"Good evening, Colin."

Colin nearly dropped his drink. When Trent had issued the

236

invitation to an informal dinner, Colin never dreamed Georgina would be in attendance. Trent was living in bachelor lodgings after all, not exactly the place one expected to find unmarried young ladies, even if they were related.

He'd been doing his best to avoid this particular young lady and having great success at it, though it meant he was having to work considerably harder at his club to keep up with the latest gossip and happenings.

Wishing he'd seen her before she'd noticed him, he gave her his attention and immediately felt like he'd been without drink for days. Her dinner dress was the simplest gown he'd ever seen her wear, the clean white silk decorated only with a garden of embroidered white flowers across the bodice and hem. The short puffed sleeves were nearly transparent and only a single perfect curl draped down from the hair piled atop her head. It was obvious her beauty didn't come from embellishments.

He took a quick swallow of drink before responding. "Good evening, Lady Georgina."

She arched her eyebrow. "I thought we'd dispensed of this lady nonsense."

Colin's eyes narrowed as he took another slow sip of his drink. What was she after? "I don't think Lord Ashcombe would take kindly to the familiarity."

Georgina pointedly looked about the room. "Ashcombe isn't here, is he?"

What was the young lady up to? Despite the number of times they'd been thrown together, she had never sought him out. Even though the party was decidedly small, there were enough people about that they could have busied themselves with other conversations for most of the evening. Georgina obviously wanted something, and Colin was in no mood to be toyed with. She bewildered him enough as it was. "What do you want, Georgina?"

She looked down at the drink in her hand, giving the liquid a swirl before glancing up at him through her eyelashes. "I was hoping you would know of a businessman looking for a wife."

Colin had fallen off a boat once. The current had pulled him under and dragged him against the wooden hull until he didn't know which way was up. Georgina's statement left him swimming in a similar state of discombobulation. Feelings warred with questions and bumped against logical skepticism. The clenching of his gut left him wondering if she'd begun to look at him a bit differently. The practical businessman in him poked at the sentence, looking for her scheme, trying to figure out what she hoped to gain by such a request. Most of him, however, was left in a state of confusion, asking the same question over and over. "What?"

"I asked if you knew of a businessman looking for a wife."

That was what he'd thought she said. It didn't make any more sense the second time around.

Colin set his drink on a nearby table before he spilled it. "Why?"

"Because I thought it would make an interesting conversation." She rolled her eyes and turned to look across the room. "Why do you think I'm asking? Because I know a woman who would make a wonderful wife to a business-minded man."

Colin blinked. Would this woman ever do what he expected her to? She wanted to play matchmaker? "What kind of a businessman?"

"How should I know? I didn't even know there were different types of businessmen."

He turned to look across the room as well, standing so that their shoulders almost brushed. The other occupants of the room mingled freely, smiling and laughing with each other. Colin had definitely stumbled into a family affair. A pang of longing hit him in the chest as he thought how much his mother and sister would enjoy such a gathering. His father would have set sail in order to miss it. "Maybe I'd like to meet her myself."

She frowned. "You?"

The idea grew in his mind, nourished by the consideration he'd been giving Alastair's proposition. Even if he didn't choose to return to Scotland and court Erika, there was no reason why he shouldn't find someone else to marry. He could easily support a family. "Why not me?"

"She wouldn't suit you at all," Georgina spit out in a rush.

Colin's brows drew together. "Why not?"

"Oh look, my mother has arrived."

Colin was fairly certain Lord and Lady Blackstone had been in the room for at least ten minutes, but he didn't stop Georgina from rushing to her mother's side. To be honest, he didn't really want Georgina to answer that question. There wasn't an answer that wouldn't make his life infinitely more difficult. Either she saw a problem with him and knew he would make a horrible husband or she shared just enough of his attraction that she didn't want to see him with anyone else, even though she didn't actually want his attention herself.

Not that he'd offered it.

But he was coming to discover that Georgina was a jewel with hidden depths, facets that made themselves known at the oddest moments. She intrigued him. That was a good word for it. Intrigue was safe. He simply wanted to figure her out, how her inability to read fit with her social savvy and the occasional burst of goodwill toward other people. She was a puzzle he wanted to solve, not a woman he wanted to spend time with.

Ryland and the newly titled Duchess of Marshington arrived. They were in Town for only a handful of days while Ryland finished a few things he'd been unable to complete before the wedding. Colin assumed their presence in Town had prompted this family gathering, though he had no idea why he'd been invited.

The happy couple was swarmed by the family. Colin remained in his corner, knowing that eventually Ryland would break free of the smothering affections.

Before he could, the tall, balding butler appeared in the doorway to announce that dinner was ready.

Everyone milled into the small dining room, but no one sat. Trent hadn't seen fit to mark the seats, and Lady Blackstone was splitting her sentences between berating Trent for planning a party without her assistance and figuring out where everyone was supposed to sit. With two dukes, a marquis, and an earl in the room, Colin was confident in his appropriate placement. He made his way to the foot of the table and stood behind his chair to watch the rest of the show. Because it was family and informal, they eventually decided to sit wherever they wished despite Lady Blackstone declaring it highly improper. Miranda's smile was a bit smug as she plopped down into a chair halfway down the table.

Lady Raebourne, who had been a ward of the Duke of Riverton before her marriage, sat next to her, leaving her husband to sit directly across from Colin.

Somehow Georgina ended up on Colin's left.

Colin tried to remember if he'd prayed for the Lord to teach him patience recently because he could think of no other reason why God would constantly be throwing Lady Georgina into his path.

Trent stood at the head of the table, waiting until everyone was seated before playing host. "Thank you all for coming tonight. I wanted us to get together and celebrate Ryland and Miranda's new marriage without all the danger and rush. I thought it only fitting that we celebrate with those who were there to rescue Miranda, even if she was safe before we ever got there."

Everyone smiled at the happy couple.

Trent raised his glass. "To Ryland and Miranda!"

The toast was echoed around the table, and the clink of glassware followed.

Colin fell into his normal habits, sitting quietly and paying attention to his surroundings. It didn't take him long to see that Georgina had well and truly fooled everyone at the table.

"Have you subdued the masses yet, Georgina? Gotten all of this year's bachelors standing in a line?" Lord Blackstone smiled at his stepdaughter.

Georgina smiled and swept a pointed look at Ryland. "Not all, obviously. But I've not been lacking for flowers to decorate the house with."

Lady Raebourne leaned forward. "Have you had a chance to

spend time with Viscount Cottingsworth? He has an extensive collection of books on classical paintings."

Miranda snorted. "Georgina's more interested in the loftiness of a man's title than in what they have in common."

"Contrary to the uncommonly happy people in this room, most married people are quite fulfilled leading separate lives." Georgina glared at her older sister.

"How sad for them." Miranda covered Ryland's hand with her own.

Lady Blackstone sipped her wine. "There's no need to rush, my dear. It took Miranda four years, but she found the perfect gentleman for her."

Riverton seemed to pale a bit at the thought of Georgina remaining at home for another four years. Colin didn't blame him. According to Trent, Hawthorne House had been more overrun in four weeks of Georgina's Season than in all of Miranda's Seasons combined.

Trent grinned from the head of the table. "You should consider Mr. Glover. He spends most of his time in his library, so you would be assured of never seeing each other."

Colin leaned back in his chair, looking from person to person and trying to place everyone in their respective family roles. It was obvious they were all embedded in each other's lives and affections. Even the teasing was loving and well-intentioned. How could Georgina have kept such a secret from them even with Harriette's help?

His gaze returned to Georgina, and he noticed a tension in her smile that wasn't there before. His position allowed him to see her fingers curling and uncurling repeatedly under the table. Was the conversation upsetting her? They weren't saying anything he hadn't heard her say before. They believed exactly what she wished them to.

She curled her hand into a fist so tight the knuckles paled. Slowly she unfurled her fingers and lifted her hand to pick up her fork. "Are you implying, brother, that my best marriage prospect is the heir to a mere baron? I assure you that I need not set my sights so low. Once I decide the man I want, there will be no question of my getting him."

Uncomfortable silence filled the room. It was understandable given that at one point or another she had declared her intentions to marry two of the men now seated at the table. Was she now saying that in spite of the trouble she'd caused, she hadn't devoted her full measure of skill into winning them?

The conversation stumbled on until dinner finally came to a conclusion. Once the women had departed for the drawing room, the men collected their port. Ryland came to sit in Georgina's vacated seat.

Colin took a sip. "How are things at the Abbey?"

Ryland had avoided the country estate for years because of the unpleasant childhood memories attached to it. Now he and Miranda were working to set it to rights once more.

The duke smiled, a rarity in the time Colin had known him but an event that was occurring with more frequency since meeting Miranda. "Miranda is magical with the tenants. I wouldn't be able to do it without her."

"I'll have to come out and see the place soon."

"You're welcome anytime."

Once the thought had taken root, Colin couldn't shake it. A visit to Marshington Abbey would get him out of town, away from Georgina and all of the problems knowing her seemed to bring. It was also in the opposite direction as Glasgow, which could possibly curb this nagging notion that it was time to go home. Yes, five years was a long time, but there might never be enough time for his father to forgive him or for him to forgive his father. When a man attempted to gamble away his family's livelihood, it wasn't something his son was going to laugh off.

Ryland set his glass on the table and spun it so the crystal caught the candlelight. "I've heard Georgina is considering Ashcombe as a suitor."

Colin laughed. "You've been back in Town a matter of hours. How did you hear about this?"

"It's true, then?" Ryland's mouth flattened into a grim line.

Colin shrugged. "Though that's not the kind of thing I usually concern myself with, it appears so."

Ryland shook his head. "Not something I normally concern myself with either, but Miranda was stomping about the house mumbling about it all afternoon. She was so preoccupied she forgot to fire Jess today."

Port nearly sputtered through Colin's lips. Jess was the parlor maid Colin had borrowed the lock-picking tools from. She and Miranda had never gotten along very well, and Miranda usually fired the woman at least once a day when they were in the same house. Since she was an old spy friend of Ryland's, everyone, Miranda included, knew she wasn't going anywhere until she was ready.

Under the pretext of worrying about Colin's health, Ryland pounded him on the back while a smug smirk twisted his lips. "Ashcombe wouldn't be my choice of future relatives. Miranda thinks even less of him. The idea upsets her to the point I considered getting rid of him."

Colin choked. Again. He was going to have to stop drinking around Ryland.

Ryland lifted a corner of his mouth in a smirk before taking a smooth sip of his own. "Not like that. I'm sure it would only take his removal from London to drive Georgina's attention elsewhere. The effects of proximity, you know."

"He has certainly spent a great deal of time with G—" Colin cleared his throat. "Lady Georgina."

Ryland frowned once more. "I'm not sure Georgina would care even if she knew how much Miranda disliked that man."

Colin frowned as well, because to be honest, he wasn't sure either. For the first time he saw just how much Georgina was willing to sacrifice to protect her secret.

She was willing to give up her family.

Chapter 23

It was a sad thing when someone was desperately obvious in their desire to appear popular.

Georgina eased her way around the ballroom, resisting the urge to roll her eyes at the guest list. Everyone of any respectability had been invited, making it dreadfully crowded and explaining how Lavinia's aunt had landed what she perceived to be a prize invitation.

Regardless, the crush meant that Lavinia was in attendance. It might be Georgina's only chance to help her. She wasn't sure why she wanted so badly for Lavinia to find a good marriage. Harriette suggested it was Georgina looking for hope that her own situation might turn out well. Georgina had scoffed at that notion and told the maid she must still be feeling ill.

Are you trying to impress me with this?

The little Colin in her head was even more annoyingly wrong than her maid. She was starting to get used to him now though, even occasionally talking back. Sometimes he had good advice. Which Georgina took, since the advice had to have originated in her own head despite the strange second personality she seemed to have picked up.

"Oh, Georgina, there you are." Jane stepped into Georgina's

path, blocking her migration to the south side of the ballroom, where the lesser-quality gentlemen were mingling with the new faces in the crowd. Putting a few of those men on her dance card would give her the chance to send them Lavinia's way.

But first she had to get away from Jane. "Good evening, Jane. Have you danced yet?"

Jane's giggle made Georgina groan. "Lord Howard is here."

"Jane!"

"What?" Jane pouted. "I told him I simply couldn't marry in a way that would disappoint my family, and he called on me the very next day. Even talked to father for a quarter of an hour."

"But . . ." Georgina couldn't think of a thing to say to change Jane's mind. As nothing too untoward was likely to happen in the ballroom, she'd have time to think of something later. Right now she needed to arrange a suitable match for Lavinia. "Have you seen Trent yet? He's here tonight as well."

Jane's eyes lit up, and Georgina silently begged her brother's forgiveness. Jane's attentions could be a bit daunting.

"Is he over near the punch? I usually find him near the punch."

That was because having his hands full gave him an excuse not to dance. Of course, it also gave young ladies an excuse to be near him as they drank their own glasses of punch. "I believe so."

Jane disappeared in a swirl of light green skirts.

Why were her friends intent on settling for marriages so far beneath their worth? Jane had a gracious heart and Lavinia had a sharp mind. Shouldn't they want men who treasured those things?

Shouldn't you?

She stomped across the edge of the ballroom, taking care to make it a graceful, elegant stomp. With each step she imagined herself tromping all over her mental Colin's toes.

"What are you doing?"

Georgina ignored the voice until she realized it came from beside her instead of inside her head. She was going to have to make the real Colin wear a bell or something. "Oh, good evening, Colin. You're exactly who I need."

Colin's eyes grew wide and he looked at a complete loss for words. Georgina would have loved to stop and savor the situation, but she needed to accomplish her goal and return to the more appropriate side of the ballroom. "Which of these gentlemen would appreciate a smart wife?"

"Are we talking about your friend again? The one I'm all wrong for?"

"Yes." Georgina squirmed. Colin was probably perfect for Lavinia but Georgina refused to introduce the two of them or waste any time examining why she felt that way. No matter what Harriette or the little man residing in her head said, Georgina knew that her hesitation was simply because Colin was aware of her secret and she didn't want him to share it with someone she knew.

Colin sighed and looked around, standing on his toes to see over the crush. "There's a man over there in a green coat. Mr. Coles. In town for only a few weeks, but he's my best suggestion."

Georgina frowned. "I don't know Mr. Coles."

His eyebrows lowered. "Why would you?"

This was a problem Georgina hadn't foreseen. The men Lavinia would need wouldn't be the men Georgina knew. "Introduce us."

"I beg your pardon?" Colin looked like he'd swallowed his own tongue.

"Introduce us." It was a simple concept. People did it at balls every day.

"You want me to introduce you to Mr. Coles. I, a man that you rarely like admitting you know, am going to introduce you, a woman that all of society is watching through opera glasses, to him, a man who'd rather be herding sheep than standing in a ballroom."

Georgina pasted on the smile she wore when she pretended she had no clue what was going on. She was going to brave through this and see if Colin would follow. "Good. You'll do it, then. He sounds perfect for Miss Clemens."

They worked their way through the crowd to a spot about a foot behind their target. Colin was ready to reach past another man to

246

tap Mr. Coles on the shoulder. Georgina grabbed his finger before he could. "Are you crazy? We have to make it look like we're just happening by or he'll wonder what's wrong with me."

Colin looked her up and down. "What is wrong with you?"

If only she knew. "We need to stroll by."

"The only way to 'stroll by,' as you put it, is to join the dance. If you haven't noticed, it's a bit crowded over here."

Georgina smiled at him again. She was using her entire repertoire on him and it seemed to do nothing but annoy him. "How kind of you to ask."

They stared at each other again. Her wondering if he was going to capitulate, and him . . . Well, she didn't know what he was thinking. Any other man of her acquaintance would have been much easier to manipulate. A horrible thought occurred to her. What if all businessmen were less susceptible to her ploys? How would she convince one of them to dance with Lavinia?

Colin offered her his arm and they stepped out to join the forming dance set. After three goes through the pattern, in which time Colin said not a word, they found themselves next to Mr. Coles. "Ah, Mr. Coles, how do you do?"

Georgina's mouth dropped open. He was actually going to do it. She hadn't truly thought he would. Who introduced someone in the middle of a dance?

The two men talked in hushed tones for a moment before Colin stepped aside. "My apologies, Lady Georgina, but I see someone with whom I simply must speak. This is Mr. Coles. He has agreed to finish the dance with you."

Georgina nodded graciously at the men. Inside she was marveling at Colin's genius. What at first seemed absurd now revealed itself to be inspired. Was it possible Georgina could use the same trick to get men to dance with Lavinia? It was worth a try. Two more patterns and they had traveled very near to where Lavinia stood smiling and swaying along with the music.

So Georgina tripped.

Mr. Coles caught her by the arm and righted her, but Georgina gave a squeal of pain and grimaced. Lavinia rushed over to ask after her welfare. Georgina couldn't have planned it better.

She sighed and cast a weary look at her foot. "Mr. Coles, I don't think I'll be able to finish the dance."

He looked almost relieved. "May I escort you somewhere?"

"I would hate to deprive you of the remainder of the set." Georgina hooked her arm through Lavinia's. "This is my friend Miss Clemens. She would be delighted to finish it with you."

Without waiting for a response, Georgina limped away, hoping Lavinia would make the best of the opportunity and that Mr. Coles was indeed a good choice for her.

As Georgina was swallowed up by the crowd lining the dance area she returned to her natural, graceful gait.

The whole ordeal had been more exhausting and taken more time than she'd anticipated. As much as she wanted to help Lavinia, she couldn't afford to venture to this side of the room again tonight.

A servant approached her. "I beg your pardon, Lady Georgina, but the gentleman asked me to deliver this message to you."

Georgina took the folded paper and frowned. Who sent a message in the middle of a ballroom? What could possibly be worth taking the time to find quill and paper instead of just crossing the room?

It must be detailed or urgent or both. What if Trent were hurt? She unfolded the note with trembling fingers, but all the noise and movement distracted her. She couldn't focus on a single word. Everything changed the moment she looked at it. Despite muddling her way through a book paragraph or two over the years, handwriting remained a hopeless endeavor.

She folded the note and stuffed it into her glove.

It looked like she was going to need to finagle another dance with Mr. McCrae.

"I need your help."

Colin turned to find himself once more looking into the bright green eyes of Lady Georgina Hawthorne. "That seems to be happening with increasing frequency."

Georgina sighed. "Would you mind dancing with me again?"

"But we've already danced once." Colin wasn't averse to taking a turn on the dance floor, but he'd always been careful to dance only once with any particular lady. Anything more would draw gossip he didn't need or want. That no one had mentioned his earlier desertion of Lady Georgina on the dance floor was something of a miracle.

"Our talking in the corner will draw even more attention."

"Then go away." Colin was done being her servant. There wasn't a puzzle in existence that was worth this much trouble.

Georgina smiled at a passing matron. The older woman looked from her to Colin with a gleam in her eye. For Georgina to be off the dance floor at all during an event such as this was an anomaly, but to be seen in extensive conversation with Colin could ruin all her hard work. It didn't matter if Colin thought her goal a ridiculous one, he had to admire her dedication to it.

Which meant whatever she needed him for meant more than her goal. And he hadn't seen anything that she cared about that much.

"Please."

What had it cost her to say that word? The look on her face, the first genuine one he'd seen on her all evening, punched him in the middle with the desperation in her eyes. That unnerving sense of skepticism, hope, and self-loathing hit him in the stomach again. Despite his better judgment, he offered her his arm. "Shall we?"

He escorted her to the floor, where the strains of a waltz were beginning to play. He scooped her into his arms and onto the floor. It would be a waltz. He made it a point to avoid waltzes. Did he have any personal rules that hadn't been broken for this woman?

"There's a note in my glove."

Surprise had him jerking his arms, knocking her off balance until he had to tighten his hold to keep her from falling. "What?"

She righted herself with an exasperated sigh. "A note in my glove. It was delivered to me a few minutes ago."

The light and airy music turned tinny, like the pings of his sister's music box. Georgina was using him again. He'd known she was, but somehow the blatant evidence of it bothered him. He didn't know why, though, because most people of his acquaintance only sought him out when they needed something. He'd made a living out of being available when people needed him. Was it because her requests were more personal than anyone else's?

Colin pressed his lips together to keep from groaning. "You want me to read your note."

Her eyes narrowed as if she were questioning his intelligence. Had she just sniffed his breath? Did she think he was drunk? "Yes. I believe that's what I said."

"You said only that there was a note in your glove, which would be terribly awkward for me to retrieve if you think about it." He spun her through the curve of dancing couples. "What would you do if I weren't here? If I were not privy to your most precious secret?"

She frowned. "I don't know. It's never happened before."

"Consider your options and then choose one." He gave serious consideration to leaving her in the middle of the dance again. It was unlikely to go unnoticed this time. "I will no longer be party to your deception, though I'd be happy to escort you to Trent, should you wish to ask for his assistance."

Her head tilted to the side and her eyes widened. Colin braced himself for unshed tears to appear. He wouldn't put it past her to manufacture that gut-wrenching sheen on command.

"What if the note is from Trent? He could be hurt, or called away, or in possession of some dreadful news about the family."

"Then finding him will be considerably more expedient."

Georgina stomped on his foot. "Why must you be so awful? Isn't a gentleman supposed to help a lady in need?"

There was no dignified way out of that question. Colin sighed. "If you can retrieve the note, I'll read it."

It took a few steps but she managed to slide the note out without much difficulty. Someone was sure to have noticed, though. At least one third of the ballroom's occupants were probably watching them right now. They were the most potentially scandalous couple on the floor.

Colin unfolded the note and hid it in their joined hands. It was short, but long enough to anger him all over again. This was the kind of man she wished to marry? Her precious pride was more important than avoiding this sort of high-handedness?

"It's from Ashcombe," he ground out through clenched teeth.

She bit her lip. "What does he say?"

"That you should find someone—anyone—else to marry."

She blinked. "Truly?"

Colin sighed. "No. That's me offering a personal interpretation. The man is telling you to take more care of the company you keep. He says you have an agreement."

"I never actually agreed." Georgina looked at the toe of her slipper appearing and disappearing from beneath her hem as they danced. The song was drawing to a close. Colin fought the desire to dance her right out the door and away from the ball.

Colin did not like the instincts boiling in his middle. "Was this before or after you asked for my help with Miss Clemens?"

She swallowed hard enough for her throat to ripple visibly. "Before."

The burn rose to his chest. "Did he tell you to stay away from Miss Clemens?"

Her head swooped up, defiance in her eyes. "And what if he did? He is looking out for my reputation, which is what I need in a husband. He's worried Lavinia's . . . malady will reflect poorly on anyone spending time with her."

"Because she stutters? And you want to marry this man?" The song ended. Colin leaned forward to hiss in her ear. "You cannot possibly hide your secret from your husband for the rest of your life."

"I'm counting on his own pride to motivate him to help me hide it." She straightened and raised her voice to a normal level. "Thank you for the dance, Mr. McCrae. I'll see myself to the refreshment table."

With a growing sense of hopelessness, Colin watched her walk away. Her white skirts swished through the crowd, taking her straight to Ashcombe's side. He didn't look happy, but whatever Georgina was saying seemed to appease him. She was right. Ashcombe's pride would probably keep him from revealing her secret in public, but what would he do to her in the privacy of their own home? Could she survive the derision and neglect he was sure to serve her when he realized he'd been fooled? Would she become a pretty shell to be twirled around at parties and then shoved back into a corner?

And why was he bothering himself with these questions, anyway? There wasn't a thing he could do about it. The decisions were hers to make. He just didn't want to see her make them.

He thought of his own sister. She'd be in the midst of her first Season now. Was she thinking clearly? Making good decisions? Was their father looking out for her interests or his own?

Perhaps he should return to Scotland after all.

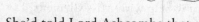

She'd told Lord Ashcombe that she wouldn't be available to ride the next day. By the time she'd arrived home from the ball, panic had set in. She was missing a chance to convince the earl to marry her. Because of, what, his arrogant assumptions? She'd do well to get used to those.

Thank goodness Harriette had taken it upon herself to save Georgina from contemplating her fallacy all afternoon. She invited Lavinia over to paint. Rather, she'd sent a note under Georgina's name inviting Lavinia to come paint.

Georgina looked up from her fire screen to see how Lavinia's was faring. They'd set up in the conservatory for inspiration but the blob of pink and red on Lavinia's screen didn't resemble any plant that Georgina could see. "How is your, er, rose?"

Lavinia tilted her head to the side and contemplated her screen. "Very f-far from an accurate f-flower, I'm afraid."

Georgina giggled. If Lavinia's attempt were supposed to be a rose, it looked like it had fallen in the road and been trampled under a few dozen horse hooves. "It's not your best work, I'll grant you."

"Yours is gorgeous." Lavinia stood from her stool and moved to stand behind Georgina.

"Thank you. When I finish it, it shall be yours."

Lavinia gasped. "Oh, I c-couldn't."

"Yes. You shall. Honestly, I paint more of these than we could possibly use. Even the servants' fireplaces have screens."

Georgina flicked her brush along the screen, adding a green leaf to her vine of climbing roses. Harriette's idea had been a perfect distraction. Especially since Ashcombe had already sent word that he was canceling their riding engagement for tomorrow as well.

Do you really want that in a husband? A man who will punish you for caring for other people?

No, he wasn't punishing her for caring. He was reminding her that her actions had consequences. He hadn't said she couldn't see Lavinia, only that she couldn't be seen with her. A problem Harriette had solved nicely.

You think that's a significant difference?

Perhaps not a significant one, but it was a difference nevertheless.

Georgina swirled the paint into the center of one last rose. She'd given in to the fact that, for now at least, she was stuck with this strange inner voice that had taken the form of a miniature Colin McCrae. It didn't surprise her anymore when he appeared, and she no longer berated herself for answering.

You deserve more than that.

Of course, sometimes she still ignored him.

"There!" Georgina stepped aside so Lavinia could view the full painting. "It will look lovely in your home."

Lavinia nodded and smiled. "Better than my own efforts."

"You can claim it as your own."

"Then I would have to explain to Mr. D-Dixon why I couldn't replicate the effort on anything else." Lavinia laughed softly as she ran a hand along the edge of the screen, admiring the twists of roses and winding vines.

Georgina's brows drew together and she busied herself with packing away the paints. "Mr. Dixon? Why should he matter?"

"I'm going home to marry him."

"But . . . didn't you come to London to find someone else? Because you didn't want to marry Mr. Dixon?" Georgina dropped onto Lavinia's vacated stool.

"I've been here t-two weeks, Georgina. No one will d-dance with me twice, and the only visitors we have are my aunt's friends. They're very nice ladies, but d-don't tend t-to bring eligible gentlemen with them." Lavinia shrugged. "Mr. D-Dixon knows me. It will work well. I shall simply enjoy London for the next four weeks and then return home and cease being a burden on my father."

Anger flashed through Georgina. Over the years she had pushed most of her childhood friends away, but Lavinia had remained, clinging to the hem of Georgina's life like a thorny burr. They'd never been close enough for Georgina to share her shortcomings with Lavinia, of course, but she'd felt comfortable having Lavinia over for tea or visiting the village shops together.

Perhaps because you assumed her struggles would make her more likely to accept your own if she were to find them out.

Georgina rolled her eyes. Her inner Colin was as annoying as the real one. The point was, Lavinia was her friend, and no friend of Georgina's was going to settle for a husband who wouldn't raise her lot in life. Georgina had saved Jane, at least for the time being, and she would save Lavinia.

"You mean he knows of your speech." As soon as she'd blurted the words, Georgina wished them back. They'd never spoken about Lavinia's problem before.

Wide brown eyes looked at Georgina. "Y-yes. I sup-p-pose that is a significant thing."

"But you can't marry someone simply because of that."

How is that any different than what you're doing?

Georgina imagined shoving the little man into her paint box

as she slammed the lid shut and flicked the latch to keep it closed. She and Lavinia were in very different situations.

Lavinia reached out and hugged Georgina, driving thoughts of imaginary men from her head. When was the last time someone other than Harriette had really hugged her? "You're very sweet, Georgina, but so is Mr. D-Dixon."

"But listen to you! You won't even be able to say your own name properly," Georgina whispered, stunned that tears were threatening to cloud her vision.

Lavinia gave a watery laugh and wiped away a tear of her own. "No. But he says I c-can help with the estate. He knows I'm not st-stupid. It won't be a love match, but it will be a good match."

Georgina blinked. Why did she care who Lavinia married? She was right. Mr. Dixon wasn't a bad man for someone of Lavinia's situation. Lavinia wasn't doing anything that hundreds of women in England didn't do every year.

Maybe because you're hoping for more than just a respectable match yourself.

He was supposed to be drowning in watercolors. How had he gotten out of her paint box? She shoved him back into her mental closet and added an iron gate for good measure. He was right. Of course he was. Georgina was feeling desperate about her own situation. But the fact was, Lavinia was stronger than Georgina. Lavinia had no choice but to tell the world about her problem. She'd had to be strong in the face of society's derision.

Georgina had not. Georgina had manipulated and fashioned her life so she could pretend that she wasn't fundamentally damaged.

What did that say about her?

Before Colin could add his own thoughts, she built a mental wall about the iron gate, keeping him out of sight. Whatever he had to say about this revelation, she didn't want to hear it.

The first commission Colin had ever made came from Mr. Dunbar, the owner of a general store in Glasgow. Colin had tipped the man off that his sons, famous for their witty shouting matches and sporadic fistfights, were one of the store's biggest draws. People shopped just to watch the boys battle.

Mr. Dunbar had then told his sons that one of them was going to have to muck the barn all summer and they had to decide which one. The fight had gone on for two weeks, and Mr. Dunbar made more money than in the previous two months combined. He'd given Colin a nice bonus.

From that time on, Colin's fate was sealed. He'd lost himself in numbers, in patterns, in fluctuations, and how events impacted sales and shipments. He'd found what God created him for, and ever since he'd been able to throw himself into the predictions and calculations with abandon.

Until now. His trusted escape was failing him.

When he should have been studying weather patterns and grain returns, he was remembering waltzes and green eyes. Instead of considering the impact of various shipping records, he was contemplating how people's secrets drove them to desperate measures. Wasn't that how he'd ended up in London after all?

He set the pen aside with a sigh. Lady Georgina Hawthorne had managed to do what no one and nothing else had ever done—distract Colin.

For the tenth time that morning Colin read the first line on the report in front of him. An hour had passed while he stared at the numbers. No matter how he looked at them, no matter how much he reprimanded himself for his lack of concentration, they remained just that. Numbers. They didn't take on a life of their own, as they always had. They just sat on the page as cold, calculated information.

The knock on his study door drew a sigh of relief. Anything was better than this struggle to accomplish something that had always come so easily.

Was that what reading was like for Georgina? An impossible struggle to achieve something that should be simple?

He bid the butler to enter with a spark of hope in his voice. Perhaps the man was going to bring him something more captivating than numbers to banish the thoughts of Georgina from his mind.

"There's a Mr. McCrae here to see you, sir."

Colin blinked. "A Mr. . . . But I'm Mr. McCrae. Are you feeling all right, Taggert?"

"Top-notch, sir. The man says he's your father."

Colin stared at the butler until the clock on the mantel ticked over the minute, snapping him out of his reverie. The butler's news was certainly mind-consuming. Blinking to relieve his dry eyes, Colin rose from behind his desk. "Er, drawing room. I'll see him in the drawing room."

"Very good, sir." The servant bowed and left the room.

His father was in his home. It wasn't so surprising that his father was in London. Colin knew of at least three times in the past five years the man had been in Town. But he'd never been to see Colin.

Irritation rose, a burning sensation in the center of Colin's chest. Five years of silence. Five years of pretending nothing had happened, that he'd never had a son born to witness his shortcomings. But now that there was the possibility Colin might come back and work under Alastair? Now he found the time to visit.

Colin straightened his sleeves and retrieved his coat from a nearby chair. Thankfully he made a habit of making himself presentable even when he had no intention of seeing anyone. He grazed his hand over the Bible on the desk as if it were a touchstone and closed his eyes, unsure what he was hoping God would do but needing the reassurance that He had some sort of plan.

As Colin stepped from the study, his heartbeat had calmed, but his mind still spun with scenarios of what would happen when he got to the drawing room. The endless number of options made it impossible for his thoughts to land on any one idea for long. It was enough to make him dizzy, but at least he could be grateful for one thing. For the next hour he wouldn't be thinking of Lady Georgina.

Chapter 24

Within a quarter of an hour of his father's arrival, two things occurred to Colin. One, his skill for planning multiple steps ahead had not come from his father, who seemed to have shown up on Colin's doorstep on impulse, and two, not only was he going to agree to find Alastair a manager—he was going to take the job himself.

Somewhere between Jaime McCrae's stiff greeting and their shared consumption of half a pot of tea, Colin had settled on the fact that it was time to go home. Time to see his family. Time to do something about starting one of his own. Time to see if he could make a go of something more solid than a handful of investments and stock trades that could be gotten out of when the going got tough.

Colin watched the older man across from him stare down into his tea. Did his father have a purpose to his visit? Was he ready to mend things? In hopes of getting a meaningful conversation started, he asked, "Is the *Raven* still scheduled to come through London in a few weeks?"

Jaime's shaggy eyebrows lowered into a frown. "What do you know of the *Raven*?"

Colin took a long, slow sip of tea while he considered his father's reaction. The *Raven* wasn't carrying anything sensitive or even all that unusual. She was loaded to the deck with tea and spices. Colin had received the report on her just last week. "I read the reports I'm sent."

"Those are owner's reports." The gruff mumble caught Colin off guard. Was his father refusing to acknowledge the fact that Colin owned one quarter of the company?

"I'm aware of what they are." He regretted the ice that lined his words, but Jaime—for Colin wasn't sure he was willing to call him Father at the moment—deserved a bit of coldness for the way he was acting in Colin's home. Jaime wasn't even going to acknowledge Colin owned part of the company due to Jaime's folly. Did he feel any remorse for it, even knowing the ramifications of five years? The essential loss of his son?

The lingering hope Colin had of returning to the family company floated away. He hadn't even realized he'd been harboring such a hope, but he let it go with more sadness than he would have expected.

"This is good tea." Jaime poured himself another cup. It was the third time one of them had commented on the tea. They'd also covered the changeability of weather and the annoyance of traffic. Inane topics covered in drawing rooms all over the city. Usually between mere acquaintances, though, not family.

"How is Mother?" Colin finally asked. He might as well get some benefit from this awkward visit. News of his family would do. The discussion might even ease open the door to talk about whatever had truly brought his father here.

"Do you mean to take me out of business?"

Well, that door opened considerably faster than Colin had anticipated. "I beg your pardon?"

"If you team up with Alastair, he won't let you keep working with Celestial. Are you going to run me out of business by taking your portion of my company over to him?" Father plunked the cup on the saucer and shoved the set across the side table.

Colin swallowed. There were so many things wrong with Jaime's statement that Colin didn't know where to start. "Why would you think I would do that?"

"It's what ye've been wanting, isn't it?" His father's thick brogue was tinged with anger, and perhaps a bit of desperation. "For the past five years ye've been looking for a way to pay me back."

"I've done nothing of the sort." Although the thought had crossed his mind once or twice, the knowledge that ruining his father would ruin his mother and sister as well had always stayed his hand.

Jaime pushed from the seat and began to pace the room. "What do you call that move you made three years ago, sending word to my manager that he was to set two ships on the trade route to Jamaica?"

"I call it shrewd business sense. We've both profited from that decision." Colin sipped his tea, even though nothing but dregs remained in the cup.

"But the order didn't come from me."

"No one knows that." Colin made sure all of his ideas went through the main office of the shipping company. If the manager agreed with the idea, he made it happen. If he didn't, he claimed that Jaime's greater share of ownership had overruled Colin. Only the manager knew what instructions originated from Colin and what came from Jaime.

"But I know." Jaime dropped into his seat. "Tell me what you mean to do."

Colin lifted a brow. Had his father always been this paranoid? This unstable? Mother's letters always made it sound as if life was going well for them, but was she covering up the truth? "I mean to go on as I have been for the past five years."

The curl of his father's lip showed what he thought of Colin's activities. "Dabbling in your little investments?"

"Setting aside enough money to care for Mother and Bronwyn should you wager the business away on a hand of cards again." Colin set aside his cup and rose, taking a moment to smooth his jacket and waistcoat.

The angry man stood as well, bracing his legs as if Colin's drawing room were the deck of a ship. "You'd like that, wouldn't you?"

Colin lifted a single brow, hoping he looked like Ryland. This was the kind of situation the man excelled in, cutting through emotional fronts to lay the man behind them low. It didn't seem to have any effect on Jaime.

"You'd like me to be proven the irresponsible wastrel you believe me to be. It was one time. I've only wagered as such one time." The man looked down with a wistful half smile. "I'd never had a hand so pretty."

"Alastair's was prettier."

His father looked up. "But not as pretty as yours."

"For which I thank the Lord daily." Colin looked his father in the eye, trying to dig in his own soul to find the forgiveness he knew God wanted him to extend. He couldn't find it. "Why did you do it?"

Eyelids wrinkled and lined from years on the sea slid closed over sad blue eyes. Jaime aged before Colin's eyes, the anger seeping out along with what seemed to remain of the old man's strength. "It doesn't matter." He sank back into his chair. The look on his face was resigned as the eyes opened once more. "You've done well for yourself. Living all fancy in London, like a proper gentleman."

Colin considered throwing the teacup. Didn't Jaime owe him some answers after all these years? Colin wanted to lash out, demand that the old seaman explain what he'd been thinking, why he'd been willing to take such a risk, even if on a pretty hand of cards.

Before Colin could figure out a way to say what he so desperately wanted to, his father stood. The movements were slow and looked painful. "For what it's worth, son, I'm glad you were there that day."

Colin said the only thing he could, the only thing that kept running through his mind. "Why did you do it?" It came out as a whisper this time, and in truth, he didn't expect any more of an answer than he had received moments earlier.

Jaime was silent for a moment before a ghost of a smile curled around the wrinkles at the corners of his lips. "Did you know Alastair sent his future son-in-law down to university in Cambridge? Not that he's getting a benefit from that. The couple moved inland after they married. He's a barrister over in Edinburgh now."

With a look around the drawing room, Jaime laughed. "Not doing nearly as well as you. I doubt it means much, but I'm proud of you."

Colin didn't want it to mean anything. He wanted to explore the niggling idea that Jaime had bet the business in hopes of increasing his cash holdings in order to look better than Alastair. But as much as he wanted to think of the man as Jaime, he was still his father. The tinges of red and brown in his greying curls were the same color Colin saw in the mirror. The blue eyes, faded by years of squinting on the sea, were so very similar to Colin's own. This man was still his father, and what he thought was still important.

One mistake. The man had made one mistake, and it had cost him a quarter of his company and a third of his family. Could Colin really fault the man for a single mistake? When he'd made so many himself?

Jaime headed for the door, his steps spry, even though he looked old and weary. The weight of unspoken remorse, perhaps, rather than age?

Was there a chance this could be mended after all? Colin swallowed against the emotion in his throat, so thick he couldn't quite name it—wasn't sure he wanted to, because he was fairly certain part of it was guilt for his own part in the separation.

"Da," he said quietly.

Jaime stopped but didn't turn around. "Your mother has them set your place at the table every night."

Colin would not cry. The empty place setting had been a tradition growing up. Whenever Jaime was away at sea, his place at the table would still be set. Colin's mother always said it was because even though he wasn't there, he was still family.

It was as close as Jaime was going to come to asking Colin to return home. But Colin couldn't ignore what had happened.

Perhaps if he came to understand what had motivated his father he could find the first steps toward forgiveness.

"If I come to Scotland, do you think . . . I'd like for us to talk about that day. I deserve that much. We all do." Had Jaime ever told his wife what had happened? What had she thought when Colin's letter had been the only part of him to return from that last trip?

Father turned enough to look Colin in the eye, a glimmer of hope making the wrinkled face a little less sad. "I suppose you do."

Both stood there, still as statues, each lost in his own thoughts. Was his father thinking about the implications of Colin's return to Scotland? Was he considering how reuniting his family could come at the cost of his position as head of the largest shipping company in Scotland? Because while Colin might be ready to come home, might even be ready to forgive his father, he wasn't going to let things return to the way they once had been.

It was painfully obvious as Jaime left the house that a return to the old way was what he wanted, because of all the things his father hadn't said, the fact that he hadn't offered Colin a position at Celestial Shipping left the largest hole.

"Isn't he handsome? He had a new piano shipped in from Italy."

Georgina bit the inside of her lip to keep her mouth from dropping open at Jane's simpering declaration. While Georgina was thankful her friend's fascination with Lord Howard seemed to have waned, it appeared the fool woman had learned nothing from her escapade. She'd become enamored with the equally as worthless Mr. Givendale. "He's up to his ears in gambling debt," Georgina mumbled.

Jane's eyes widened. "How do you know?"

"Because he's dancing. Last week I was returning from the ladies' retiring room and I heard them banning him from the card room until he'd made good on his IOUs. Since he's dancing tonight, I assume he has yet to return to those gentlemen's good graces."

Georgina flicked her fan, enjoying the brief respite from dancing. When had the balls turned into such tedium? Was it the worry that accompanied them? Each event was one day closer to the end of the Season and one less opportunity to secure her future.

"So you think I shouldn't—"

"Exactly." Georgina cut Jane off. She refused to run after the girl again. "Or at least require him to marry you in a church this time."

Jane had the decency to blush.

"Pardon, Lady Georgina, but the gentleman asked me to give you this."

Georgina turned to the footman at her side, extending a silver platter with a folded piece of paper on it. Had Ashcombe sent her another note? Was the man incapable of crossing a room? She'd done nothing this evening that could possibly draw his censure. She took the paper and stuffed it in her glove. "Thank you."

Jane looked from Georgina's glove to her face, which Georgina hoped was exuding serenity and not panic. "Aren't you going to read it?"

Georgina cut her eyes to look at her friend. "Honestly, Jane, anyone who hasn't the time to cross the room and talk to me in person does not deserve my immediate attention."

"But aren't you curious?"

Thankful that Jane was still as predictable as ever, Georgina made a production of sighing and considering her friend. "No." She slid the note from her glove. "But if it bothers you so much, feel free to read it."

Wide blue eyes met Georgina's as delicate fingers wrapped around the folded paper.

Georgina waited while Jane opened the paper. She immediately squealed and clapped one hand over her mouth to stop the sound. She looked up at Georgina. "It's from Lord Ashcombe."

She'd figured as much. If the man insisted on relaying every communication through written correspondence, she might have to reconsider his suit. Frustration that she would be right back where she was at the beginning of the Season—only without a list of prospects—made her want to rip the paper from Jane's fingers, but she maintained an appearance of nonchalance until Jane finished reading the infernal note.

Jane gasped again before gritting her teeth to hold back another squeal. "He wants to you to meet him." She nudged Georgina in the arm. "Things must be going well with the earl."

Georgina rolled her eyes and retrieved the paper. Things were going well with the earl but not well enough for her to risk her reputation on a clandestine meeting on the terrace or, worse, in the garden. He would simply have to do his courting in front of everyone else like a normal gentleman.

She tucked the paper back in her glove and smiled at Jane. "If he wants to speak to me, he shall have to find me. I am not a servant to be summoned. Now, if you'll excuse me, I've promised this next dance to Lord Eversly."

Jane almost swooned at the mention of the handsome viscount. Georgina left to await her partner, trying her best to push the note from her mind.

Lord Ashcombe whirled Georgina across the floor in her first waltz of the evening. Georgina gave herself over to the music and movement, enjoying the fact that the earl did not speak for the first circle of the dance floor. As they rounded the corner, he broke the silence. "Did you receive my note?"

Georgina's eyes widened. That was how he chose to open the conversation? No words of how nice it was to see her or how beautiful she looked tonight? She was even wearing her most flattering ball gown. She'd been saving it for when she felt it time to encourage her chosen man to take the next steps. Ashcombe was moving considerably slower than she'd expected him to.

"Yes," she said carefully. "Your note was delivered."

He frowned. "And you ignored it?"

Georgina smiled, knowing the things that would be said if anyone noticed both of them frowning at each other. "I am not a servant to be summoned, my lord." The line had impressed Jane. Maybe it would have a similar effect on Lord Ashcombe.

"And I am not a man to be ignored."

Not impressed, then.

The flowing music washed over Georgina as she waited for Lord Ashcombe to continue. It was probably best to wait for him to direct the conversation. He didn't seem to be in any rush to do so, choosing instead to look out over her head as they continued twirling their way down the floor.

"I have limited time to spend here this evening. My request was reasonable."

What could she say to that? All she knew was he'd requested she meet him. Had there been anything else in the note of import? She had assumed it was for a private meeting, but what if it wasn't? A response was required, if the growing irritation in his angry face was any indication. She erred on the side of vagueness. "I have my reputation to consider, my lord."

His eyebrows rose as he spun Georgina with extra vigor. "Your reputation?"

Georgina swallowed and made an effort to look bored with the entire thing. His reaction meant the meeting location had probably been appropriate, even if his summoning her was not entirely so. Haughty disdain had helped her brazen through more than one difficult situation, though never with as particular a subject matter as this one. One misstep on her part and he would know she hadn't read his note.

Such inconsideration on her part could have him dropping his courtship of her entirely. The edges of her slight frown trembled. Her eyes burned on the edge of panicked tears. She cleared her throat. Now was not the time to fall apart. She'd stared down governesses in the schoolroom, peers at poetry readings, and more than one hostess who had requested she sing at the pianoforte. Surely she could face down one partially besotted earl. "My lord, this is better than a secluded meeting, is it not? Much better to be seen in the midst of the crush so that everyone knows the man I have a preference for."

A little bit of a lift to a man's ego never hurt either.

His eyes narrowed. "I agree. Much better than a clandestine meeting on the terrace."

So he had requested her to meet him on the terrace.

"As I said, my lord, I have a reputation to consider."

They danced on in silence for a time, but the enjoyment was gone. To everyone else they looked as graceful as always, but Georgina was well aware of the stiffness in his arms. As the dance drew to a close, Lord Ashcombe bowed over her hand. "Have you the note still?"

"But of course." They were still talking about that blasted note? Lord Ashcombe was quickly becoming more than she wanted to deal with. Was there someone else—anyone else—who could save her from herself?

"Perhaps you should have taken the time to read it, then." His gritted teeth made the words tight, but she understood them clearly.

"My lord?" Sweat trickled down Georgina's back. Noise from the ball swirled around her, filling her ears and making her dizzy. Or was that due to her racing heart?

"May I see the note?"

She pulled it from her glove as they reached the edge of the ballroom. He opened it and extended it back to her.

His eyebrows were arched high, his gaze was hard.

Georgina swallowed and looked at the paper. It could have been the fact that the paper shook slightly in his extended hand, or that panic surged through her chest, or the lighting that was dim enough to cause deep shadows across the earl's body. It could have been any number of things, but the fact was Georgina couldn't make out the first thing on the paper. Even the scribblings that she knew made up her name refused to come into any kind of focus.

What was she going to do? She swallowed hard. "I see."

Only she didn't see. She didn't see a thing, and if this conversation continued, Lord Ashcombe would know that something was very, very wrong. She plucked the paper from his fingers, folded it, and slid it back into her glove.

His eyes narrowed further. "You did not care for my request to meet you in the garden?"

Garden? Hadn't he said *terrace* a moment ago? Was he actually testing her? Georgina swallowed, darting her eyes sideways to find an escape. She had to reassert her power in this relationship. "The fact remains, my lord, that I do not care to be summoned. Next time I request you take the time to cross the room if you wish to speak with me."

Mr. Sherbourne crossed the corner of her vision. A pang of guilt struck her even as she opened her mouth. "And there is Mr. Sherbourne."

The man spun toward her with shock evident on his face.

"So it is." Lord Ashbourne's eyes narrowed even further, becoming little more than menacing slits.

"I've promised the next dance to him."

"You have?" both men asked at the same time.

Georgina gave Mr. Sherbourne her best smile. "Of course."

"Of course. Yes." Mr. Sherbourne tripped over his feet as he offered Georgina his arm.

Georgina sighed as she escaped to the dance floor. As she curtsied to her partner, she glanced over to the side of the dance floor where Lord Ashcombe still stood, watching her with a thoughtful look on his face.

The dance seemed to go on for hours. As soon as Mr. Sherbourne escorted her to the side, she pled a headache and had Trent take her home. It wasn't a complete lie. The heavy beating of her heart was sending shooting pains through her head and neck that would soon render her incapacitated with pain.

Georgina couldn't meet Harriette's worried eyes as she pulled the gloves free of her hands. Lord Ashcombe's note fluttered to the carpet.

Harriette picked it up and unfolded it. "What's this?"

Groaning, Georgina fell back onto the bed, eager to relieve the pressure in her head. "A note from Lord Ashcombe asking me to meet him on the terrace."

"The terrace?" Harriette's voice was shaky enough to convince Georgina to pry her eyelids open and look at the maid.

"It's not?"

Two slow shakes of Harriette's head sent dread crawling across Georgina's skin, skittering along her spine until it pooled in her throat, making it difficult to breathe.

Harriette held up the note. "He wanted you to come to the refreshment table."

Chapter 25

How was it that an idea could seem completely wrong a mere two hours after it looked completely right?

Colin ran a hand over his face as he stared into the cup of untouched coffee in front of him. Alastair had asked him to find a manager for his shipping company. This morning Colin had sent him a letter confirming that he would have someone en route to Alastair's office by the end of next week.

As there were no known prospects for the position other than himself, he'd all but committed himself to returning to Scotland. He hadn't been able to put that down on paper though. Writing it down felt too much like a contract, an agreement he couldn't get out of.

But his mind was made up, wasn't it? He didn't want to get out of it. Did he?

Colin stifled a groan. Though he was sitting at the back corner table of the coffeehouse, that didn't mean he couldn't draw attention to himself with such a guttural sound as he wanted to make. Every emotion a man could feel was coursing through his veins right then. Excitement, relief, worry, fear. All at the mere thought of going home.

How would his father react? His family? The town? Would they accept his return or see him as the ultimate traitor for betraying his family? Not many people knew about the card game. To them, he'd simply left.

"Could I interest you in a business proposition, Mr. McCrae?"

Perfect. Yes, business was always a good distraction. He looked up and once more fought the urge to sigh. He could do without this interruption. Still, business was business. And even though he was returning to Glasgow, he had no intention of giving up his investments. "I'm always interested, Lord Ashcombe."

Ashcombe settled into the seat across from Colin. "I believe it will prove very lucrative, but it will require careful management."

Colin lifted a brow to convey interest without excitement. Whatever his personal issues with the Earl of Ashcombe, the man had made some astute business decisions in the six years he'd been managing his family's estate. Colin had worked with him more than once in the past, mostly because he never had to work directly with Ashcombe.

The earl had an amazingly capable and personable estate manager who had as much to do with Ashcombe's success as anything else. Colin even considered the man something of a friend. Despite the fact that they'd only met twice in person, their business correspondence often contained personal elements among the numbers and updates.

"I'll be looking to expand my operation in Cheshire soon. I have reason to believe the sheep pastures of Crestwood are being underutilized."

"No doubt they are." Hairs rose along Colin's arms, rubbing uncomfortably along his shirt sleeve. Crestwood was one of Riverton's estates. Their underutilization was at Colin's instigation. The land's potential went far beyond what most people thought. Not that Colin was about to share that information with the earl. Instead he tipped his head in a motion to continue.

"I'm afraid I don't have the funds at the moment to develop appropriately." The earl cast Colin a cold sideways glance. "An investor or two would be welcome. Discreet ones, of course."

Colin bit his cheek to refrain from making a derogatory comment about the earl maintaining the social façade of old family money, despite the fact that he'd inherited little but a debt-ridden title and a crumbling estate in Cheshire. He'd done well in the past few years but had spent almost as much as he'd made. Everyone had bought into the illusion of grand success. Even Georgina. "Discretion is the mark of every good business decision."

The earl's smile was smug, no doubt thinking he was maneuvering Colin neatly into his plan.

A careful sip of the lukewarm coffee combated the burn of bile in his throat. Was this really what God wanted Colin to do? All the intrigue, whispers, and flimsy images were becoming harder and harder to stay away from. He'd worked his way into the aristocracy in the hopes of being a solid Christian example of a good businessman, but it didn't seem that anyone was noticing his efforts. Maybe this was God's confirmation that it was time to leave London.

But he still needed to know if Ashcombe was planning something. Colin was too close to the Hawthorne family to ignore any potential threat.

Ashcombe leaned back in his chair. "I've considered setting up a factory. There are good roads running through that land."

Colin pursed his lips, adopting a confused look. "Don't those lands belong to Riverton?"

The smile on the earl's face slid from smug to slimy. "For now."

Thankfully, surprise was an appropriate response because Colin couldn't refrain from expressing his shock on his face. "He's indicated repeatedly that he has no inclination to part with it."

And with good reason. If these new steam engines ever became something more than a lark or flimsy amusement ride, the land would be a prime spot to utilize their shipping capabilities. The inquisitive men who were obsessed with the smoke-churning energy were one day going to make something that could actually transport goods more than a foot or two, and Griffith's land in Cheshire would make a perfect connection point when that happened. It was worth holding on to.

Ashcombe set his empty glass on the table. "Never underestimate the power of reputation in changing a man's mind."

Colin scoffed. The earl intended to blackmail the duke? He had quite a bit more nerve than Colin had realized. "You have nothing on Riverton."

"I know. The dangers of being a family man, hmmm?" Lord Ashcombe stood and straightened his coat sleeves. "And I'll even gain a pretty wife in the bargain. Useless, but pretty."

Colin forced himself to breath evenly, though it felt as if very little air was actually making it into his lungs. The earl was going after Griffith's family? And as for the wife . . . Georgina? It certainly appeared that the earl was Georgina's first choice, but that preference wouldn't be enough to sway Griffith to part with the land.

Unless . . . Colin choked. *"Useless but pretty."* Ashcombe knew. There was no other explanation.

"Lady Georgina has shown a preference for you as her waltz partner, as I hear." Colin forced himself to continue his calm sipping of coffee.

"Yes. Society considers her quite a catch. It's amazing what fools we can be." Ashcombe rose. "Be thinking of my offer, Mr. McCrae. I know you've worked in that area before, and I would prefer to work with a man who is familiar with the land."

"Of course." Colin nodded his head even as his thoughts went in three different directions.

Ashcombe tipped his hat and left.

Colin gulped the last of his coffee and then went for a walk. He didn't know where he was going or what he hoped to find. All he knew was that staying in one place wasn't an option. The churning emotions, his equally unbalancing thoughts. Dear God, what was he supposed to do with it all?

Eventually he found himself in the gardens beside Grosvenor Chapel. A peaceful oasis, mere steps away from Hawthorne House, the center of the anguish he'd drowned in over the past month. He didn't know what to think anymore.

He sank down on to a bench, looking at the side of the chapel, admiring the windows framed with lush plants. It looked different from the outside. Still beautiful and God-honoring, but different. Perhaps that was what he needed in this situation. A new perspective, particularly one from God.

Yes, some time alone with God was exactly what this situation needed.

Georgina slammed her bedchamber door hard enough to make the latch bounce and the door swing open once more.

So she kicked it.

Harriette stood in the middle of the room, eyes wide. "My lady?"

"He's gone." Georgina threw her reticule onto the dressing table. "We're halfway through the Season, Harriette. What am I going to do?"

The maid reached a hand out to try to catch Georgina's shoulder as she paced by. It did little more than graze a sleeve. "Who is gone, my lady?"

"Last night Lord Ashcombe told me to make sure Griffith was available this morning. He's been by twice to see him this week, but my brother has apparently been too busy." Georgina stopped and waved a hand toward the door. "What could he possibly be doing that is more important than settling my future?"

Harriette folded her hands together in front of her. "Perhaps he didn't know that's what the request was for."

"Of course he knew." Georgina resumed pacing. "Why else would Lord Ashcombe be requesting an audience with him?"

Silence met Georgina's question as the maid waited patiently by the dressing table. Of course there were other reasons for a man to request an audience with Griffith. Men were in and out of her brother's study all day long, but for some reason he'd always been too busy for Lord Ashcombe. Georgina had had to beg him to set aside time this morning for the earl. She'd never had to beg Griffith for anything before.

And then the man hadn't shown up.

She'd been prepared to lecture him on it at that evening's dinner party, but he hadn't shown up there either.

What was it with men disappearing? She hadn't seen Colin in well over a week. Even the little Colin in her head had made fewer and fewer appearances in the past few days. Tonight she'd given in to curiosity and discreetly mentioned him to Trent. Her brother hadn't even seen the man in a week either, and they'd been meeting at the club every other day before that.

"He's gone, Harriette." Georgina plopped onto the stool in front of the dressing table. She didn't have the energy to keep the despondency from her voice.

"Who?" Harriette approached Georgina slowly, as if she were an unpredictable horse.

"Lord Ashcombe." Yes, surely it was *his* absence that had her so melancholy. Colin's absence was nothing more than a curiosity.

Georgina sighed. "And according to Lord Eversly, it could be a very long time before he comes back."

Georgina refused to admit out loud that it was something of a relief. He hadn't sent any more notes across the room this week, but he'd kept looking at her strangely, watching her even more closely than before. She'd been more careful than ever, and it had left her exhausted.

Harriette began plucking pins from Georgina's hair. "Where did he go?"

"Home to Cheshire. Apparently the man overseeing his estate and interests up there got a better job offer and left for it immediately. Jane said the man sent notice that he was packing and moving his family with the intention of being gone by the time the letter reached London." Georgina began to brush her freed locks.

"That must be quite a job." Harriette undid Georgina's laces and encouraged her to stand and remove the dress.

Georgina grunted. "Lord Eversly said the man left to manage a shipping yard in Glasgow. I know Cheshire isn't the most

275

civilized of counties, but to leave it for Scotland? Who wants to go to Glasgow?"

I'm from Glasgow.

Georgina frowned at the little man in her head. Now he chose to make a reappearance? She shooed him away with a large mental broom. She wasn't interested in his version of her conscience.

"You spent a lot of time with Lord Eversly this evening, then? He's very popular. They mention him in the paper nearly every day." Harriette slid Georgina's dress over her head and moved to place it in the wardrobe.

"He's a viscount, Harriette. He won't do at all."

"Neither will the earl."

The maid's quiet words snatched Georgina from her sullen reverie. "What?"

Harriette rushed forward and caught Georgina's hand in her own. "You don't truly want to marry the earl, do you? It doesn't seem as though you like him very much."

Without a word Georgina moved toward the bed, avoiding Harriette's gaze until she was lying down, blankets pulled up to her chin, and tears threatening to spill over her lashes. "What am I going to do, Harriette?"

Harriette smoothed a hair back from Georgina's face. "What we always do. Find a way."

It was what Harriette had said since they were children, sitting on the side of a lake, reading children's stories. They'd become a team that day, Georgina and Harriette against the world. Tonight, however, the confident assurance didn't make Georgina feel any better. She was standing on a cliff, watching her last bridge start to smoke. What if the only way left was down?

Colin grumbled at the knocking sound that interrupted his sleep. He was blissfully enjoying a morning in his own bed for the first time in well over a week, and he did not care to be interrupted. "Go away!"

The butler opened the door instead. "I do beg your pardon, sir."

"Is the house on fire?" Colin grumbled into the pillow.

"No, sir."

"Has someone fallen down the stairs?"

"Er . . . no, sir."

Colin was fast running out of options to merit the butler's interruption. "Did the prince regent come knocking?"

"Very nearly, sir."

Colin lifted his face out of the pillow and turned his head to look at the butler. "I beg your pardon?"

"You've a summons from the Duke of Riverton."

A groan ripped from Colin's chest as he dropped his head back into his pillow. He had traded on Riverton's trust and friendship when he'd sent the message asking the duke to avoid the Earl of Ashcombe for a few days. What he hadn't been able to do was come up with a good reason for the request. He'd had several days to think about it, knowing the duke would demand answers eventually, and he'd yet to think of anything besides the truth.

A truth he couldn't share, because then he would have to reveal Georgina's secret.

"The footman is belowstairs waiting for your reply, sir."

With another groan Colin rolled out of bed and grabbed the note from the butler as he crossed to the desk on the other side of the room. The paper had a single line on it.

Please see me at your earliest convenience. —R

The underlying command jumped out from the overly polite words.

He scribbled his answer on the bottom of the paper and returned it to the butler. "Send breakfast up so I can eat while I dress. And coffee. Lots and lots of coffee."

"Very good, sir. Perhaps I should arrange for a bath as well?"

The breeches and shirt Colin had fallen asleep in were covered in road dust and wrinkled beyond hope. And he was beginning to itch. "Yes, I believe a bath is in order."

The butler nodded and left the room, leaving Colin alone with thoughts he didn't want to dwell on.

He rubbed rough hands over his face. What was he going to tell Riverton? It needed to be something good, because he was also going to have to come up with a story for Ryland as well, though he probably had a few days before that happened.

Not that the past eight days had been all that helpful.

After spending well over an hour praying in the chapel garden, Colin had come to the realization that he had to save Georgina. He had the means and the overwhelming feeling that God wanted him to use them.

Even if it changed the very course of Colin's life.

Part of Colin wanted to leave her to her fate. A fate she'd sought with her every breath. The fact that it wasn't going to happen quite the way she'd envisioned wasn't his business.

Why was he forever landing in the middle of other people's disasters, or at the very least, Georgina's disasters? Did God think Colin had all the answers, or did He simply get pleasure from making Colin uncomfortable?

Faced with deciding between protecting his family and maintaining his honor would have been very hard on Riverton. It wouldn't have been the first time someone had tried to force Riverton into doing something. Never before though, to Colin's knowledge, had someone threatened the duke's family.

It wasn't right.

And Colin liked things to be right.

So he'd sent the message about Ashcombe round to Riverton, and then he'd borrowed the best horse Ryland had in London. Ryland's man hadn't questioned Colin's use of the animal, but he had no doubt sent word to Ryland about it immediately. Even now there was probably a letter from Ryland on Colin's desk.

He'd ridden the horse as hard as he dared all the way to Cheshire.

During his hour of prayer, bits and pieces of Colin's communications with Ashcombe's estate manager had come to mind.

The man had grown up playing in the sea, on the coast of

Northumberland, very near the Scottish border. He'd started in shipping before moving into estate management to better support his family.

He'd mentioned hoping to eventually do something more than oversee Ashcombe's meager holdings, but he had been unable to grow them as he'd intended because Ashcombe kept spending the profits.

Alastair may have wanted Colin for family purposes, but when it came to managing the Glasgow Atlantic, Hugh Carson was as good a choice as Colin was.

Hugh had jumped at the chance to utilize his skills at the shipping company. The bonus Colin had paid him to resign and move immediately hadn't hurt.

The plan had been risky, but it had paid off. Colin passed Ashcombe on his way back to London, though he'd taken pains to make sure the earl hadn't seen him. The earl was going to have a hard time replacing a man of Carson's caliber. In the meantime, Ashcombe would have to see to managing his own holdings.

With any luck it would be enough time for Georgina to safely marry someone else. It couldn't guarantee that Ashcombe wouldn't still use the information to try to force Riverton into selling the property, but his power would be decidedly diminished if Georgina were already settled.

At the very least the girl would be free from a man willing to use her as a pawn in a business deal.

Because he'd run the horse ragged on his way to Cheshire, Colin had taken three times as long to return home, and his door had been a welcome site indeed.

Even that leisurely journey home hadn't provided enough time to figure out what to say to Riverton. He couldn't even think of a viable lie. He didn't feel right about lying to explain this situation, but he couldn't tell the truth either.

As he soaked in the tub, he wondered what he was going to do now that he'd given up the job in Scotland. What did that do to his convictions that it was time to go home? Should he simply go home and manage his investments from there? It would be difficult to stay abreast of the things that didn't find their way onto reports.

The answers to his questions weren't in the near-scalding bathwater.

Nor were they in the clouds as he meandered across the square toward Hawthorne House.

As the mansion's columned façade came into view, Colin took a moment to drop his head forward in prayer, begging God to put the right words in his mouth. His mind was still blank as he climbed the stairs and knocked.

Chapter 26

Harriette held the door open with her hip as she carried in the tray with Georgina's morning chocolate and the collection of society papers sitting atop a large book.

Georgina was already up and dressed, with her hair rolled into a simple chignon. "Will you tie me, please?"

After setting the tray down, Harriette fastened Georgina's dress before crossing her arms over her chest. "What are you doing up this early?"

"I couldn't sleep." Georgina spun around on her stool. "Is there anyone remaining on our list? Anyone who hasn't married, fled the city, or turned into an absolute and total wretch?"

Harriette gave Georgina an assessing look. "We've marked off marrying wretches, then, have we? I don't remember that being a requirement before."

Georgina became very interested in her mug of hot chocolate and the ripples caused by her short, shallow breaths. "It isn't too much to ask that I have some modicum of happiness in my marriage, is it?"

"Of course not. I've always said as much. I just don't know that you ever have." Harriette took the book and the papers over to the desk.

Distracted by curiosity, Georgina set her mug on the dressing table and crossed to the desk to open the book. It was a ledger. "What's this?"

"Oh." Harriette looked up from sorting the papers. "The household accounts."

Georgina lifted her brows in silent inquiry.

"You're going to be getting married soon, and those lessons your mother gave you on running the household were one of the few things I didn't always get to sit in on." She shrugged. "I've been helping Mrs. Brantley with them so that I could learn before you marry and we're taking care of a house on our own."

Tears threatened to spill across Georgina's cheeks. She reached for the maid and wrapped her in a tight hug. "You could do so much more than this, Harriette."

"Something more than fool the entirety of the civilized world?" Harriette scoffed. "Anything less would be an utter bore."

Georgina smiled as she returned to her chocolate and savored a long, deep drink. Then she frowned. Why had Harriette brought chocolate? "Harriette? Has something happened this morning?"

Harriette flicked the edge of one of the society papers but didn't pick it up. Her gaze caught Georgina's in the mirror, and the maid refused to look away. "Mr. McCrae is downstairs."

Georgina's eyes widened. "He is?" She set down her mug and turned halfway around on the stool before remembering that she shouldn't care if Colin was downstairs. She picked up her mug again and sipped. "Why would I care about that?"

She didn't care about that or wonder where he'd been for the last week—and if she repeated it enough someone was going to believe her. The fact that she'd been able to go about her business without running into the man had been bliss.

Harriette rearranged her papers. "He is in His Grace's study."

Of course he was. What would Colin say if he knew Lord Ashcombe was no longer an option?

Ashcombe should never have been an option in the first place.

Had she actually entertained the thought that she'd missed her

282

infernal imaginary friend? "I believe I need a change of scenery, Harriette."

"Change of scenery, my lady?" A poorly hidden smirk decorated Harriette's face as she set the papers on the desk in the corner. "Perhaps you'd care to take breakfast downstairs this morning?"

"Yes. Breakfast downstairs would be ideal." But not because Colin was here. "I'm sure a change of routine is all I need to come up with a solution to my latest problem."

Harriette gave up pretending to hide her laughter. "I'm sure it is, my lady."

Georgina frowned and flounced out of the room. Who knew agreeable servants could be so frustrating?

The footmen threw questioning glances at each other as soon as she entered the breakfast room. When she chose a seat at the table, they started whispering.

Let them whisper. From this seat she could see the doorway to Griffith's study. She took small bites of her breakfast, unsure of how long she'd need to linger before Mr. McCrae made an appearance. She told herself it was mere curiosity that made her want to see him.

The man in her head laughed.

She pretended to stab him with her fork.

Her mouth was full of toast when the door across the hall clicked open and Colin and Griffith emerged laughing. Her heart picked up speed, and the toast seemed to swell until it filled her entire mouth. Why hadn't she considered what to do when she actually saw him? What if he didn't see her? She could hardly call out an invitation for him to join her. Crumbs coated her mouth as she tried to chew, swallow, and take a quick drink all at the same time.

Hacking coughs ensued as the soggy mess lodged itself part way down her throat. It was not the way she'd intended to draw the men's attention, but she suddenly had it, as they had both been drawn to the breakfast room door.

"Georgina, are you all right?" Griffith circled the table and pounded her on the back. As if bruising her spine was going to help her breathe.

She nodded, waving a hand in front of her face in some sort of request for the air in the room to make its way into her lungs.

Colin appeared on her other side, setting a glass of water next to her mug of chocolate. "Perhaps this will help."

After a few gulps of water, Georgina had control of herself once more. Deciding her best option was to pretend the entire incident hadn't happened, she turned a bright smile to her brother. "Won't you join me?"

Dark blond eyebrows arched over suspicious green eyes. She couldn't blame him. She hadn't come down for breakfast since they'd arrived back in Town.

"I would enjoy that." Griffith straightened. "Won't you join us, Colin?"

Colin looked from brother to sister as if he'd like nothing better than to decline, but it wasn't easy to say no to a duke, even one you were friendly with.

"Do join us, Colin," Georgina added. The widening of Griffith's eyes made her instantly aware of her mistake. Griffith had no idea Colin had given her permission to use his name. Or that she considered them close enough acquaintances to accept the offer.

Colin bowed his head. "I would be honored."

There was an awkward moment as the men decided where to sit. Georgina's placement in the middle of the table made conventional seating impossible. "Oh, bother," she mumbled as she rose and took her plate to the seat to the right of the head of the table.

Griffith looked worried as he sat in the head seat. Colin looked like he wanted to laugh as he settled into the chair across from hers.

It's funny. Admit it.

Georgina nearly choked on a laugh of her own.

"So, Mr. McCrae, what brings you here so early?" Hopefully Griffith would forget her earlier use of Colin's name.

Both men sent looks her way that told her there was nothing

at all wrong with their memory. Breakfast downstairs had been a colossally bad idea.

Colin exchanged a glance with Riverton. "I had business with His Grace."

Georgina nodded her head as if the answer had imparted some great information instead of simply restating the obvious. He could hardly tell her that he had been summoned to explain why he'd told her brother to avoid her suitor while Colin arranged an emergency to draw said suitor away from London for an extended period of time.

He hadn't even been able to tell Riverton the whole truth. The entire business made him uneasy, but for some reason he felt a sense of loyalty to Georgina, a requirement that he keep her secret as long as possible even though he felt she should share it with those closest to her. If she'd had a few more people in her confidence, Ashcombe might never have suspected it.

Which would have put Colin in Scotland right now, having an awkward breakfast with his family instead of hers.

Riverton turned to his sister. "What brings you down at such an hour? You rarely poke your head above the covers this early, much less grace us with your presence."

One delicate shoulder shrugged. Colin had a suspicion that Georgina was in actuality a very early riser. If she and her maid did half the things she claimed they did—such as read novels, memorize poetry, and collaborate on correspondence—they would need time. What better time than morning when no one would disturb them, thinking her still abed?

The woman was diabolically clever.

"Whatever the reason, I am happy to see you up and about. You've been rather dejected since Ashcombe left town. He's no great loss, you know."

Georgina's eyes widened. "You think I've been pining for Lord Ashcombe?"

Riverton looked to Colin for help. Colin stuffed an inelegantly large bite of ham into his mouth. The duke sighed. "You haven't been?"

"Hardly."

He leaned back in his chair. "What's with the long face and the yelling at the servants, then?"

One brow lifted in a look of disdaining superiority that only a sister could get away with giving a duke. "I've always yelled at the servants."

Colin choked on his ham. This family was going to be the death of him.

Gibson, the butler, entered the room and crossed to Riverton's side for a quiet exchange. Riverton stood. "Pardon me. I shall be but a moment."

Georgina watched Riverton leave the room.

Colin watched Georgina. She did seem more subdued than normal this morning, though that could be attributed to the early hour.

Despite her claims to the contrary, was she upset over the loss of Ashcombe, or was it her plan's lack of success that was giving her a melancholy air?

"Ashcombe has left town."

Georgina's words startled Colin. "So I've heard."

She didn't suspect he'd had anything to do with it, did she? He was hoping very much that his absence several days before and after the earl's departure would keep anyone from connecting him to the issue.

She leaned forward. "Have you heard why?"

He matched her posture, leaning in as if the two were conspiring over coddled eggs. "Have you?"

Her eyes narrowed. He shouldn't have prodded her. Now she was suspicious. "I've heard it had something to do with an urgent business issue."

"I have heard the same." Colin made himself take his time as he cut another bite off the ham.

"He was my last hope, you know." She stabbed at her eggs, sending a river of liquid yolk across her plate.

Colin bent over his own eggs. The longer he knew Georgina, the more convinced he was that she didn't require a man to make herself the most elite personage of the *ton*. She could perform the feat married to a baronet. "I know nothing of the sort."

She frowned at him. "You think I'm being nonsensical."

"What time do you get up every morning?" Colin placed his fork down on his plate. It was time they had this out once and for all. Did she truly not understand what she'd been able to accomplish? How much more she was capable of?

"I beg your pardon."

"What. Time. Do. You. Arise?" Colin said slowly. "On average, of course."

She swirled her fork across her plate. "Harriette brings me tea and toast at half seven every morning. Sometimes she brings chocolate instead."

"Yet your family is under the impression that you spend an additional four to five hours in bed each day. So, yes, my lady, I do think you are being nonsensical."

"You think I should tell them."

"Yes, I do." In the past few weeks he'd seen her genuinely mad, tired, worried, and a host of other emotions her carefully practiced veneers were not prepared for. Those moments of authenticity were the only thing that kept him from washing his hands of her completely. Sometimes he felt that the Georgina he'd seen in those moments, the real Georgina, was begging him to help free her. To help her escape from the cage she had created for herself.

The woman had turned him fanciful.

"You are mad. That is all there is to it." The moment of vulnerability disappeared, shuttered behind her cool exterior once more.

He sighed at the loss of it, even as he knew he should welcome it. When she was cloaked he found it easier to keep his distance.

"What was that for?"

Suddenly finding himself without appetite, Colin pushed his plate away. "May I speak frankly?"

She scoffed. "As if I could stop you."

He had to nod an agreement on that one. Their time together had never rested on ceremony as far as he was concerned. "I think you do yourself a disservice. I think you're afraid to let people see who you are, the girl who loves art, who adores color. The fiercely loyal friend with all the vulnerabilities of the average person. Sometimes I think you're even afraid to face her yourself."

"You're quite philosophical in the morning, Mr. McCrae." She took a sip of chocolate. "Are we friends, then, Colin?"

"I suppose one might call us that." In truth he didn't know what they were. He had a growing suspicion of what he'd like them to be, but the chances of that happening were less likely than a blizzard in July. And it wasn't just because he was nowhere near her idea of an acceptable suitor. No, he was interested in the girl beneath the veneer, the one he caught glimpses of every time he'd almost convinced himself to be done with her.

She gave him a wide smile. "Excellent. Because I could very much use a friend like you right now."

His heart tripped over itself as it rushed to every possible erroneous conclusion. "Whatever for?"

"Why to select a new target, of course. I know you stay as current on gossip as I do. If we combine our knowledge, we'll find me the perfect candidate. I'm running out of time, you know."

He didn't know what to say. What could he say? He pulled his plate back to him and took a bite of toast to give his mouth something to do. It tasted like sandpaper.

"Well?" She took a sip of her drink.

"Eversly," he mumbled.

She blinked. "The viscount?"

"You are friendly with each other, he is well liked, and his purse is not likely to run out on you." He would also be extremely difficult to drag to the altar. Eversly wasn't showing any interest in settling down anytime soon.

Georgina could probably do it though.

And suddenly, Colin didn't think he could stomach staying around to watch it. He pushed away from the table. "My apologies, but I've just remembered another engagement this morning. Please convey my good-byes to your brother."

Her eyes blinked slowly in obvious surprise. "Of course."

He bowed and left the house.

And then he left town.

Ryland accepted Colin's presence without question, even when he spent the first two days at Marshington Abbey sitting in the library or staring out the window of his bedchamber. Ryland and Miranda had left him alone, though the occasional food tray was delivered.

Colin appreciated the silence, even though he knew the duchess was probably driving Ryland mad discussing the possible reasons for Colin's unannounced arrival.

What was he going to do now? He supposed he could return to London, go on as he had been, but it felt flat somehow. He'd amassed an enormous sum of money over the years. Maintaining his existing investments would allow him to keep his family beyond comfortable should disaster strike or his father give in to another foolish, greedy impulse.

He'd lost the motivation that had pushed him so hard these past five years. Or was it that once he'd decided to take the position in Glasgow he'd begun to think of his life differently? He'd pictured a family of his own, a sense of purpose, the ability to grow something besides his bank account.

If the idea of doing these things with Erika Finley at his side was only moderately interesting, he blamed it on not being near the girl. If she were as wonderful as she sounded in his mother's letters, his regard of her would grow with proximity.

Maybe.

Not that it mattered now, since he'd sent Hugh to manage the shipping company.

There were a few things of which he was certain. He couldn't go back to London and watch Georgina work her charms on the elusive Lord Eversly. He also couldn't go back to Scotland without a reason. What if his family rejected him? Left him standing on the doorstep the same way his father left him on the London docks when Colin refused to turn over the portion of the company he'd won?

He still had ties in the War Office. Maybe he should consider their offer to employ him instead of just rubbing shoulders with him every once in a while. He'd have to keep it a secret from Ryland. The duke had threatened to shoot Colin himself if he took the Office up on their offer.

Movement outside caught his attention, and he pressed closer to the window. A large coach was coming down the drive. He hadn't known Ryland was expecting company, though that was probably due to his chosen solitude rather than his host's secrecy.

The coach's crest became visible as the conveyance pulled up to the house. Colin groaned the moment before the door was opened and the Hawthorne siblings spilled out of it. Georgina's hair glinted as she turned her face up to the sun. Her smile was wide as she said something to her brothers that made them laugh.

Moments later Miranda was running down the front steps to wrap her arms around her brother. Ryland followed her at a more sedate pace. After shaking the men's hands, he looked up at Colin's window, a half smile on his face.

Ryland was obviously done with Colin's silence.

Chapter 27

She'd been skeptical when Griffith suggested they all take a few days at Marshington Abbey, but Georgina was surprised at how much easier she was already finding it to breathe. The balls, dinners, card parties, and trips to the theatre had grown tiresome over the past week. Even before Lord Ashcombe had left town, the pleasure had dwindled from the activities.

Perhaps because she had never taken the time to find the pleasure in them in the first place. She'd enjoyed her successes, the evidence that she was achieving her goal, but she'd never taken the time to let herself enjoy an event for what it was. The thought brought a heavy sense of guilt and failure with it.

As Miranda wrapped her arms around Georgina, though, she felt as if the hug was squeezing away the problems, lifting the weight from her chest.

She'd missed her sister. More than she'd expected to.

"Come in, come in. Perhaps more in attendance will coax our other guest to show his face at dinner tonight." Miranda hooked her arm though Griffith's as they all made their way inside.

Trent paused in the act of brushing dust from his coat. "Other guest? You're entertaining?"

Miranda snorted. "Hardly. Colin's done little more than—"

"Price will see to everyone's luggage. I think tea has been set out in the drawing room." Ryland interrupted his wife, making everyone look at him with varying degrees of surprise. He continued as if he hadn't done anything unusual. "At least half the rooms are still buried in a decade of dust, but we've aired out the best bedchambers for your use."

"There is quite a bit of house." Miranda looked at her husband sideways but didn't try to return to the conversation he'd cut short.

Georgina wished they would. She'd wondered where Colin had disappeared to, even as she told herself not to care. He'd been gone for more than a week, stayed in Town for a day, and then left again. Most people didn't even know he'd returned, if they'd noticed his absence in the first place.

Not many of the ladies she talked with even knew who he was. She'd mentioned him once a day or two ago and everyone had looked at her strangely before moving on to discuss the daring dress Lady Yensworth had worn that evening.

And now he was here.

She wasn't sure how she felt about that.

The drawing room looked a good deal better than it had when they swooped in to rescue Miranda several weeks ago. The furniture still looked a little worn, but at least it was clean and welcoming. The tea smelled wonderful, but the idea of sitting made her shudder. "Please don't stand on ceremony, gentlemen. I have the desire to take a turn about the room and stretch my legs."

Georgina wandered over to the fireplace, admiring the exquisitely carved mantel. The scrolls and flutings didn't make any sort of recognizable pattern, but they were all the more lovely for their seeming chaos.

Ryland joined her, pressing a cup of tea into her hand and softly asking, "How does your Season go?"

She accepted the drink with caution. What was this man up to? She'd tried to avoid him since learning of his covert activities. If Lord Ashcombe could become suspicious of her, a trained spy would strip her secrets bare. "Things couldn't be better, Your Grace."

"We're family. Feel free to call me Ryland. Or Marsh, as your brother does." Ryland sipped at his own cup of tea. "We've seen several betrothals in the paper."

"Yes." What else could she say? He knew she was not betrothed. Even she would not keep that information from family.

Even she? What did she mean by that?

Perhaps that you've lost a bit of yourself in your pursuit of the perfect husband?

She turned to Ryland. "I doubt you'll see my name anytime soon."

His eyebrows lifted. "Truly? I thought you'd been seen frequently with Lord Ashcombe. Has he no intention of making an offer?"

"That would be quite difficult, Your Grace, as he is no longer in Town." She paused. "Of which I'm fairly certain you are aware." Georgina glanced over her shoulder to see if anyone was concerned about their quiet conversation. All of her siblings were engrossed in their own discussions, not paying her a bit of attention.

He grinned. "Oh, I'm aware. He hied off to Cheshire to take care of things when his manager found a better position. I've tried to hire the man away myself before. He didn't take the job."

Not trade up to a duke for employment? "Whyever not?"

"He was raised on the coast, you know. Said the only way he'd move his family was if it got him back to the water. I'm sure he's very happy in Glasgow." Ryland toasted her with his cup and then walked away to engage Griffith in a discussion.

With everything in her she was quite certain that the conversation had not been happenstance. Ryland did not do anything without a reason. Which meant the conversation about Ashcombe's manager was more than idle information.

She was supposed to get something out of it.

But what? Ryland had relayed very few facts that she wasn't already aware of, which must mean she had missed something she should have known, something he expected her to be able to put together.

The rest of her family rumbled on, but she ignored them, choosing to think over everything Ryland had said, word for word.

The door opened, but Georgina ignored it.

Until Colin's voice cut through her musings, scattering her thoughts from her head. She turned around, trying not to make too much of the burning need to see him. The sun angled through the window, catching his hair and making it look redder than normal. His hair was mussed, as if he'd been running his hands through it or standing against the wind on the deck of one of his ships.

His ships.

Glasgow.

Colin was from Glasgow. His family was in shipping. And most importantly, he had never thought she should marry Ashcombe. The shock of a dawning revelation added a coldness to her voice she'd never heard before. "Good evening, Mr. McCrae."

His gaze met hers across the room. "Lady Georgina."

Her family looked back and forth between them, but Georgina ignored them. If Colin had purposely ruined her last chance at safety, she would never forgive him. "You've been traveling quite a bit lately. Where have you been going?"

His eyes narrowed a bit before his gaze slid to Griffith. "I was checking on some things at Riverton's estate."

Her fingers grew chilled, sending ice trickling through her veins to her heart. "Oh? Which one?"

He looked tired as he pulled his gaze back to hers. "Crestwood."

Crestwood. In Cheshire. The coincidences were too much to ignore. Colin McCrae had overstepped the bounds of any sort of friendship he could have considered them to have. Knowing why she needed to marry, knowing that she was counting on an offer from the earl, knowing her predicament, he had still taken it upon himself to remove her best prospect for a successful marriage from her vicinity.

She would never forgive him.

Her family stretched between them, their heads still turning back and forth to watch them both, their jaws slack, as if they couldn't be bothered with the effort to shut them.

Colin straightened his shoulders and faced her scrutiny. He looked concerned but not regretful. She wanted to toss the remaining tea in his face. But she wouldn't give her family the satisfaction of a scene.

"I find myself tired from the journey." She turned to her sister. "Might I be shown to my room, please?"

Miranda rose, still looking from her to Colin with a questioning glance. "Of course."

Georgina refused to look at Colin as she left the room, but her gaze fell on Ryland as she turned away. His face was blank of expression, and she couldn't help but wonder how he'd known and why he'd told her. Or rather given her the nudge to figure it out herself.

All the questions were making her head hurt, and she found her desire to retire was real after all.

Sleep wouldn't come.

She lay on the bed until her body began to ache from the tension. A cold supper tray sat on the desk. Miranda had sent it up nearly an hour ago, and Georgina had allowed the maid to leave it even though she had no desire to eat. She'd had even less desire for company. Even Harriette had been sent from the room, although she'd refused to go any farther than the cot in the dressing room.

Georgina didn't really care where her friend slept so long as she wasn't in the room to question Georgina.

Unable to stay in bed any longer, Georgina grabbed a piece of cheese from the tray and nibbled it while she paced the room.

What had Colin been thinking?

I wanted to save you.

She scoffed. Even the imaginary Colin was impertinent and overbearing. So what if he thought he was saving her? Why then? If he had the means to remove Lord Ashcombe from her sphere, why wait? Why not take care of things when she first declared her interest in the earl? Colin had been very aware that she'd set her cap for Lord Ashcombe despite her family's objections.

The thought quaked her, sending her tripping across the floor until she wrapped her arms around a bedpost.

Her family had objected. All of them. Not even Mother had been happy when the earl came to visit. How could Georgina not have seen that? How could she not have cared? Was she so absorbed by her fear of discovery that she'd thrown aside her family's good opinion?

She hadn't meant to. A tear rolled down her cheek. When had she shut them out? Had it happened slowly, as her shortcoming became more and more difficult to hide? Or had it happened when she and Harriette sat up one night, concocting a plan to secure her place at the top of society, placing her above reproach or suspicion? Perhaps it had been when her plan started to fall apart. Had she panicked and shut them out then?

Whenever it was didn't matter. The question was, was it too late to change it?

And did she want to?

The fact was, if she let them into her life, if she stopped pushing them away, it would be nearly impossible to protect herself.

You don't have to protect yourself. You're safe.

No. No, she wasn't. Colin was wrong. She didn't know what he was made of that allowed him to accept that the written word was her enemy, but she couldn't believe that everyone had that. Perhaps it was because he'd had to work for what he had. He appreciated the effort her deception had required. Most people didn't think like that. She'd seen what everyone, her own sister included, had thought of Lavinia. And there was nothing Lavinia couldn't actually do.

At best, they would pity her. More likely they'd see her as a failure. How could they not?

But maybe they didn't need to know. Maybe she could just re-establish her relationships with them. Maybe here in the privacy of Marshington Abbey she could let down her guard a bit. Forget about appearances and be herself, get to know her siblings again. Let them get to know her.

And if she slipped up and they discovered? It wouldn't be the end of the world. Besides, she hadn't messed up in so long. . . .

A vision, a memory of Lord Ashcombe holding the note out to her, asking her why she hadn't read it, flashed through her mind. Him lying about what it said, tricking her.

Georgina dropped the last two bites of cheese back on the tray, suddenly afraid what little she'd eaten was about to make another appearance.

He knew. Or at least suspected. He knew.

That's why Colin had done it now. It had to be.

She threw open the door and ran into the corridor, ignoring the fact that she was in a dressing gown and high-necked night rail. She needed to see him. Needed to know if she was right.

Needed to know if he had been more of a friend than she could ever imagine. She stumbled to a halt as she realized how quiet and dark the house was. She must have lain in bed longer than she realized.

It could wait until morning, then.

She returned to her room, wondering if her conclusion was true or if she was trying to come up with a reason because she wanted Colin to be sincere and trustworthy. To be nice.

Think about what you know about me, Georgina. This thing with Ashcombe is not all there is.

Sleep nudged at her as she crawled back into bed. She slept in fits, interspersed with memories of Colin McCrae. Yes, he'd helped her save Jane, but he'd also teased her mercilessly in front of her brother. He'd uncovered her darkest secret. But then he'd kept it to himself. There were times he'd prodded her to reveal it, but never in public. Never where it would shame or ruin her.

Did that make him a good sort of fellow or not?

By the time the sun edged over her windowsill, she was more than ready to welcome a new day. Between fits of slumber, she'd argued with herself and the Colin in her head over whether or not the man was likeable.

Like me or not. You know I'm honorable.

That was true. If Colin had indeed been the one to ruin any chance of marrying Lord Ashcombe in the near future, he'd done it with the best of intentions.

But in the light of day, she knew that it didn't matter. His actions, honorable though they may be, had left her with no options. None that would save her. She had failed. All of the work, memorizing passages of books and knowing everything about everyone so she would never be at a disadvantage—it had all been for nothing.

Harriette's sacrifice had been for nothing.

The sun peeped around the edge of the curtain, slashing across the room to light up the clock on the mantel. Harriette would arrive soon. She would bring hot chocolate.

But it wouldn't be enough.

Georgina wasn't sure she had the strength to start over.

Chapter 28

Colin stopped his horse in front of the stable and considered sending the beast barreling over the countryside again. His morning ride had cleared his head—or so he'd thought before he returned to find a blond vision in white strolling through the back gardens of Marshington Abbey.

"May I take your horse, sir?"

Colin glanced at the groom, waiting with his hand hooked in the horse's bridle. So much for escaping again. Not that another excursion would be fair to the animal.

With a nod to the groom and a final pat on the horse's neck, Colin dismounted and walked away. He rounded a stack of wood being used in the revamping of the stable area. Ryland and Miranda had truly taken hold of the Abbey, doing their best to make up for the years of neglect. Everywhere he turned there was evidence of renewal.

He crossed the wide expanse of lawn, his eyes never leaving the figure in white. Should he explain? She should know that her secret was vulnerable, that he'd only bought her a window of time. But he didn't know how to say it, didn't know how to make her understand why.

The gravel crunched under his boots as he entered the garden path. Unless she'd become afflicted with deafness as well, she knew he was there.

Yet she didn't turn. She sat on a bench, her pencil flying over her sketchbook, transferring the pink-and-purple plant in front of her to shades of white, black, and grey.

Colin started to walk past her as if they were nothing but dancers passing each other on the ballroom floor. But as the aroma of lemons blended with the floral fragrances in the garden, he found his feet refused to move.

Curiosity, that burning desire to know everything and figure everyone out, dug its claws into his mind and refused to let go. Where was his undying patience? The skill he'd used to wait out more than one unsure situation?

"What are you doing here?" he asked.

She peeked at him over her shoulder, one delicate eyebrow winging upward while her green eyes widened and one side of her lips curved upward. The perfect blend of coy and innocent. Was there any situation she had not prepared a persona for?

"I'm drawing."

He grunted. "Why that one?"

"I beg your pardon?" She looked up, a hint of real confusion in her face.

It was enough to spur him on. Even as he told himself not to care, he clung to the idea that he could break through her façade, even if only temporarily. "Why choose to draw that plant?" He pointed to a bush of brilliant white roses. Clean, elegant. Like her. "Why not those?"

She frowned at the two plants. "This one has more interesting lines."

He watched her draw. Perhaps it would be easier to speak to the back of her head. "He knows."

Her hand paused. "I thought as much."

"He was going to threaten Riverton, reveal your secret unless Crestwood became part of your dowry."

Her pencil moved once more, adding shadow beneath a bloom.

It seemed to rise from the page until Colin was sure he could pluck the bloom and tuck it into her hair.

"You're very good."

She was quiet for so long he thought he'd been dismissed. Whatever had possessed him to think a conversation could work? Whatever sort of friendship they'd been building, he'd crushed it when he drove her suitor away, the man she pinned her hopes of salvation on.

"Thank you."

The whispered comment stopped him mid-turn. His back was to her, but he knew she still sketched, the scratch of the pencil blending with the call of distant birds. "You're welcome."

"For everything."

Colin's breath hissed between his teeth. What was she saying? He started to turn back toward her.

"No, don't turn around." The words tumbled from her mouth in a rush.

He froze once more. Would he ever make the correct move where this woman was concerned?

"Did it cost you much?"

Spearing his hands into his hair, he tried to dispel his frustration. What was the fool woman talking about now? "What?"

"Getting the man to move to Glasgow. Did it cost you much?"

Had it cost him much? He swallowed, remembering Erika standing on the docks, the wind plucking her red hair out of its braid and toying with the strands like a child with a handful of ribbons. It was a picture many a painter would have loved to capture. She could have been his wife.

He thought of his mother and sister, waiting to see if this job would bring him home. Would they be angry that he'd given it away?

Yes, it had cost him. But it was his sacrifice to make, not her guilt to bear. "The enticement of the coast was enough for him to take a job I knew of. I might have added a bonus to hasten his departure."

There was silence for a while. Should he turn back toward her? Continue on to the house?

"I wanted to be angry at you, was angry at you for a long time last night."

Colin swallowed. "What changed?"

"I was reminded that even when I don't like you much, you've never shown yourself to be lacking in honor. You at least try to do the right thing."

He couldn't bear it anymore and turned to find her looking over her shoulder at him. Her green eyes were soft, and a little smile played at the corner of her lips, as if a fond memory were dancing on the fringes of her mind.

He couldn't help but smile back. "Who told you such a thing?"

She blinked up at him. "You did."

"I . . . but I haven't spoken to you in days."

Her laugh, colored by a self-deprecating nervousness, washed over him. He loved it when she was real. When her actions were real, her emotions uncovered. "You're in my head. Didn't you know that?"

"I'm in your head." His tone was flat, even to his own ears. What on earth was she talking about?

"Oh, yes. Quite firmly. I've tried to kick you out." She held up a hand, counting off the ways she'd tried to dispose of him. "Thrown you out of windows, locked you in the closet. Even imagined stabbing you with a fork once or twice, but you keep coming back. I've grown used to it."

"To me."

"Yes."

"You imagine that you're talking to me."

She cut her eyes in exasperation before turning back to her drawing. "Yes. Though I have to say the you in my head is never quite this slow."

He needed a seat. Or a bed. Perhaps he would simply lie down in the grass. "You're telling me that when you think through things, you pretend you're talking me?"

She sighed. "Yes."

A few moments passed, and he got over the shock of the idea. "How accurate is he?"

The pencil scratching stopped. "I beg your pardon?"

"Does he actually speak like me?" Colin eased onto the bench next to her, curiosity blooming out of his shock. He'd never been the voice of someone's conscience before. At least not someone else's conscience.

"Let's test it, shall we?" She angled her body toward his until their knees were touching on the bench. "I've realized that in the past few years I've grown distant from my family."

She lifted her eyebrows at him. Was he supposed to respond? Just tell her what he thought she should do?

"Well . . . I think you have a great opportunity to renew that relationship here. You're safe at the Abbey with no one but family. You wouldn't have to try to protect yourself. You know I think you should tell them."

He braced himself for the ire that usually came his way when he mentioned revealing her struggle.

Instead, she smiled at him and leaned forward to pluck a flower from the bush. "Very good."

The bud twirled in her fingers as she spun the stem and ran her thumb along the edges of the petals. "I'll be ruined, tossed aside like Lavinia, if my secret comes out."

Colin shook his head. "By some, perhaps, but Lavinia possesses neither your rank nor your position. You've enough poise and family support to weather the repercussions well enough."

That was true to an extent. She would be relegated to the edges of society, and every poetry reading or impromptu play would renew the cutting remarks of those who wished her harm or found pleasure in the dismay of others.

"Hmmm. Until someone had a poetry reading or wanted to put on a play and the cutting remarks started again."

Her words were so very close to his own thoughts it was scary.

She fiddled with the petals, easing the flower open. "What do you think of Harriette?"

"She must be brilliant." Truly she had to be to aid Georgina as much as she did. "You should make the woman your housekeeper or something. Her talents must go further than a mere lady's maid."

"The merits of the newspaper?"

That was something she'd pretended to talk to him about? "A good source of information on a large variety of things, but nothing beats discovering the information yourself. Especially about society."

"The war."

"I hope we win it."

"My morning mug of chocolate?"

What went on in that head of hers? "I don't quite understand it. Coffee is more invigorating, and tea is more soothing."

"The fact that I dread going in to church every Sunday because I fear God will strike me down for daring to show my face after He clearly marked me as someone who is less than worthy."

Air hissed through Colin's teeth. She didn't think that. She couldn't think that. "You can't be serious."

She handed him the flower. Colin took it without thinking. "Yes. I believe the little man in my head is fairly accurate at guessing what you will say. Though I did expect a bit more scoffing at my morning chocolate."

The polite smile, the shell he hated so very much, slid over her face. "Did you have a nice ride?"

Did he have a nice ride? The fool woman kicked him like an irate horse with the fact that she thought God hated her and she wanted to talk about his ride? He forced the words out from his muddled brain. "It was quite pleasant."

"Excellent. I was thinking earlier about your suggestion of Eversly. If I'm going to consider a viscount, I think Cottingsworth might be a better choice. I had begun to wonder with Ashcombe if his popularity would last once he was no longer one of the most eligible bachelors of the *ton*. I fear the same of Eversly."

Colin's brain hurt from the sudden shift in demeanor, the altered conversation from unpardonably personal to the absurd bordering on inappropriate. She was returning to her practiced persona.

What happened to the girl who mere moments ago was lamenting that she had grown away from her family? That she wanted to take her time here at the Abbey to let her guard down? The girl who'd revealed such a stunning misconception of God?

Even considering the fact that the topic of conversation was very personal, there was little of her in it beyond the superficial. Colin knew he could mention anything about one of the men in question and she would reply with facts about their worth as a suitor. Nothing would scratch below the surface appearance of a young girl obsessed with achieving a good marriage.

Never mind the fact that a marriage based on such a thing would crush what little of her soul remained unscathed by her own efforts to pound it into submission.

Nothing was worth this turmoil. When he saw Georgina, the real Georgina, he was very much afraid that he liked her. Possibly more than he should. To see her gain the light of day only to be shoved back into her perfect cage was killing him.

He looked from the flower in his hand to the drawing on her pad. They were the same flower, but only one was real. The fake one looked real. So real that he would probably imagine the softness of the petals if he were to reach out and stroke the paper. But it was colorless. A mere image of the real thing. It wouldn't spin in his hand, taking on new life with every angle. It wouldn't have the aroma or texture of the real thing.

But it also wouldn't break. Considering the bloom in his hand, he took one bright petal between his fingers and broke it. A sharp, stinging waft of sour, hot odor hit his nose from the crushed petal. If he did the same to the drawing, it would do nothing but mar the paper.

The drawing was beautiful, requiring a skill that few possessed. But he much preferred the bloom in his hand, even with the damaged petal.

He reached over and tucked the bloom into Georgina's hair. "I believe your sister is in the upstairs parlor. Perhaps now would be a good time to try your new habits."

She pressed the sketchbook to her chest. "Yes. I suppose so."

Her body remained on the bench for several moments until he couldn't stand it anymore. He couldn't deal with the colorless, flat Georgina, not when he knew the vibrant and real one existed.

He pushed up from the bench and began walking along the path toward the house. "I'll see you at dinner."

Ryland wouldn't let him get by with skipping another meal now that there was company in the house. So, yes, he would see her at dinner, but he'd avoid her as much as possible the rest of the time. And as soon as he figured out somewhere to go, he'd leave.

He cast one more look at her before he went into the house, her slumped shoulders urging him to retrace his steps back to her side.

Who was he fooling? He wasn't leaving this house until she did. She was quickly becoming his weakness. The thing he'd rashly sacrifice for in order to save. He still didn't know, might never know, what his father had been trying to save when he put his company up as a bid that long ago night. But if his motivation was anything like what Colin felt when he looked at Georgina, it was a wonder Colin didn't own the entire company.

"I would like to stay."

Five heads swiveled in her direction, each portraying varying degrees of surprise. They'd been here four days. A ridiculously short trip by most standards, but long enough to provide a bit of a respite from the busyness of London. Griffith and Trent were making plans to return to Town in the morning. They had assumed Georgina would be going with them.

But she didn't want to.

"Stay?" Griffith leaned forward, looking her up and down as if to ensure himself of her good health.

"Yes. I would like to stay." She turned to Miranda. "With your approval, of course."

Miranda's mouth gaped a bit. Her teeth snapped together as she exchanged looks with Marshington. "Of course. We were planning a trip to Town in a couple of weeks. It would be no trouble to take you back then." She fiddled with her skirt. "Assuming you wish to stay that long."

Two more weeks away from London, away from parties and balls.

Away from potential husbands.

Away from failure.

"Two weeks sounds perfect."

Air suddenly seemed like a very precious commodity. Her heart tripped over itself in its rush to beat faster. She clasped her fingers together in an effort to hide their sudden shaking.

She was taking two weeks away from the goal that had driven everything she'd done for the past three years.

Because the voice in her head had told her she needed to.

Obviously, she was going insane.

Her siblings looked from her to each other, their heads snapping back and forth fast enough to do themselves damage. Georgina shifted in her seat to glance toward her right, where Colin and Marshington were sitting in a matched set of tufted club chairs. Marshington was watching Colin with raised eyebrows. But Colin was staring directly at her.

What was he thinking?

Even the little man in her head shrugged.

"That's decided, then." Griffith rubbed his hands together. "Trent and I will depart first thing in the morning."

Conversation moved on, but Georgina sat quietly in her seat, happy to let the words float past her. The past four days had been difficult. She'd tried on more than one occasion to speak to Colin, but he'd immersed himself in Marshington's reconstruction plans and, other than mealtime, was nowhere to be found.

She was rather surprised he hadn't made excuses to miss this evening gathering in the drawing room. Perhaps he'd only attended because he thought she would be leaving.

Things hadn't been going much better with her siblings. After years of perfecting the art of keeping her distance, attempts to be less guarded were falling victim to instinct. Before she could stop herself, she'd cut down every friendly overture they'd made. Frustration had birthed more than one set of tears in the past few days. Harriette had taken to visiting the laundry every day just to keep Georgina in clean handkerchiefs.

Perhaps, if she initiated the conversation, she wouldn't reject her family out of habit.

"Have you plans for this next week, Miranda?" Georgina winced as she blurted out the question. She hadn't the slightest idea what the rest of the group had been talking about, but she knew she'd interrupted them. "When you're finished, of course."

No one in London would believe her in possession of masterful social skills at the moment.

Miranda's smile was tentative, her expression guarded. "I had plans to visit with all the tenants before we went back to Town."

That sounded like a supremely dull way to spend a day, but Georgina would need to do that herself one day. Besides, she'd always done well with initial introductions. It was the relationships that followed she didn't do as well with. "Excellent. May I join you?"

Once more, five stunned faces turned her direction.

"I should learn how to do things such as that. Whomever I marry will surely have estates and tenants."

Unless you marry me.

Georgina nearly fell out of her chair. Her imaginary Colin hadn't said much since she'd talked to the real Colin in the garden—and then he decided to speak up and say something like that? Marry Colin? What was she thinking? Sometimes she didn't even like the man.

Yes, you do. That rush in your blood when you match wits isn't anger—it's excitement.

If she didn't know better, she'd think the little man in her head was truly a different person. She couldn't be coming up with those thoughts on her own.

"Of course." Miranda's voice reminded Georgina she had a real conversation going on. "I usually gather a selection of foodstuffs or other necessities to take with me."

"Do we shop for them? I'm excellent at shopping." Though unless the tenants wanted their hams trimmed in lace and wearing a spruced-up bonnet, none of her shopping skills were going to be particularly helpful.

"We'll shop tomorrow, then." The look on Miranda's face was one Georgina couldn't remember seeing before. A bit befuddled, a touch of happiness, and perhaps a little relief? Whatever made up the emotions and thoughts swirling across her sister's face, one thing was clear—Miranda was looking at Georgina as if she'd never met her.

And maybe she hadn't.

Because Georgina was beginning to wonder if she'd played a part for so long that she'd forgotten who she really was. Or if she'd ever even known.

Chapter 29

One week later Georgina didn't feel any closer to her goal. She'd visited tenants and embarrassed Miranda thoroughly because she'd had no idea how to interact with them. She'd spent her life studying aristocrats and gentry. She could observe a dinner party for five minutes and then move through the room with utter grace and to her complete advantage.

Not so in an encounter with a farmer's wife. After the third cottage, Miranda asked if Georgina wouldn't be more comfortable waiting in the wagon.

It wasn't much better back at the house. Harriette hadn't packed all of Georgina's art supplies, thinking a sketchbook and pencils would be sufficient for the trip. And it would have been if she had gone home when planned. But without her supplies, Georgina found herself more than a little bored at the country house. Particularly since Miranda enjoyed spending the late afternoon in the library.

After-dinner entertainment frequently involved reading to the group, which Georgina actually enjoyed, until they offered her a turn with the book. She turned down the offer in a way that effectively ended the evening each time. And each time she saw a sad look cross Colin's face. Did he expect her to blurt it out in a public setting? Confessions were for intimate gatherings in bedchambers or private parlors. Not drawing rooms.

Only there wasn't anyone in this drawing room except her sister, her brother-in-law, and a bothersome man who she wasn't sure what to call but who already knew her secret anyway. It didn't get much more intimate than that.

And yet, she couldn't. Last night she'd turned her nose up at the book and stomped from the room, even though she desperately wanted to know what happened next in the story. She'd have to see if Harriette could sneak it up to the room later.

Her time at the Abbey was supposed to be healing, but instead she was nothing but exasperated. She never saw Colin except at meals and the occasional evening gathering. The entire city of London and she couldn't stop stumbling across him, but now that they were in the same house, she couldn't bump into him even when she tried.

And she had tried. She didn't realize how much she missed his voice until she heard him read during the evenings.

She supposed things with Miranda weren't all bad. They had spent a great deal of time poring over upholstery samples. Bonding time to be sure, but nothing more than a superficial discussion on the merits of brocade or wool.

Georgina was an utter failure.

No, you're not.

Yes, I am. And she didn't know what to do next. She was desperately afraid that she was on the verge of finding herself alone in the world, her only friend a maid she paid exorbitant sums of money to in order to ensure she stayed by Georgina's side.

Who wanted to live like that?

Not her. And it scared her. Because if she didn't want the life she was living, what was the alternative? Not to live it?

She began avoiding balconies. And her family. And even Harriette. She started walking in the woods instead of by the lake because the thoughts in her head terrified her.

For the first time in three years she considered what would come after the wedding. What would happen once she found the perfect man and married him in spite of her problem? How would she live? How would they live? There wasn't a man alive who wouldn't come to resent the fact that she could do nothing useful or helpful and that she hadn't let him know before the wedding.

She couldn't save herself by doing what she'd always done. It was going to take something new, something so out of character she couldn't even come up with it on her own.

So she asked the man in her head.

And somehow she found herself in the library. A room she'd been in more in the past week than the rest of her life combined, but never by herself.

The room must have been a small chapel in the building's previous life as an abbey. She understood now why Miranda had decorated the room in such light, subdued colors.

It was transformed by the afternoon sun.

Soaring stained-glass windows splashed jewels of colored light on every surface. Green, red, and purple streaked across the bookcases, while blue and orange swirled over a plump sofa.

In the middle of the room a Bible sat open on an ornate stand, bathed in a circle of golden yellow. Behind it rose another window, the shards of colored glass blending into a fractured picture of a beautiful sunrise.

She crossed the floor in slow steps, watching the brilliant colors creep across her white skirt. Deep green flowed into purple and then red. It felt as foreign as the walls of books surrounding her.

This was an unbelievably cork-brained idea. It was a book, like every other book in this room, and all it was going to do was make her feel alone and despondent. Who cared if the rest of her family believed it held the secret to incredible power and peace? It was written in a book, so it wasn't meant for her.

God wasn't meant for her.

But she was just desperate enough to beg Him to give her a chance.

She stopped at the edge of the yellow circle. The shadowed line created by the leading in the window formed a wall she couldn't break through. What would she do if this didn't work?

Miranda put a great deal of stock in the Bible. She refused to start her day without reading it. Griffith had spent his entire life claiming to never make a decision without looking at it. All Georgina knew, though, was what the bishop read each week before he droned on about how horrible people were. Georgina was well aware that God found her wanting. She didn't need a church to tell her that.

She could see the book now, the pages open, far enough away that the sea of black ink would be indistinct to anyone. It made her a bit bolder, knowing that from where she was right then, no one had access to the words in that book.

Colin seemed to think those words were the secret to everything, though. Yesterday he and Ryland had been bent over the thick book, talking intently about some decision. They'd walked away, confident they'd come to the right conclusion.

If this book could do that, she had to try.

For the first time in memory, she prayed for a miracle.

Her toes peeped out from beneath her skirt, glowing blue in the filtered sunlight. She edged her foot forward. The white she thought so bright and special looked bland as it crossed from the light to the shadow.

Easing the next foot forward into the yellow brought the brilliance back.

Another five tiny steps brought her to the stand. Yellow light made the book glow. A thick ribbon poked out between sections of pages in the back. A river of black swirled across the page, the letters blurring into a blob even more indiscernible than normal.

It was proven, then. God considered her damaged. Unworthy. He wouldn't even allow her to read the book He'd gifted to the others.

A tear slid down her cheek and splashed onto the edge of stand.

Tears. She swiped at her eyes, a glimmer of hope sparking once more. The extra blur was caused by tears.

She looked toward the ceiling and blinked until the wetness left her eyes. Two deep breaths and she was ready to try again.

A large E caught her eye, but the word was long and she couldn't tell if it was complicated or she couldn't see the right letters. Moving on, she picked a place on the facing page. The letters shifted and jumped, blurring together. She squinted and worked one small area at a time. It seemed to take hours but a few words finally managed to come through.

All is vanity.

It was certainly turning out that way in her life. Everything she'd done, all the plans she'd made had brought her nothing. Everything had failed. Could this book tell her why?

A quick tug pulled the ribbon from the back of the book. She turned it sideways, laying the smooth edge along the words. Her breathing deepened as a few more letters slid into a semblance of order.

Another edge. She needed another edge.

She reached behind her and yanked at the knot of her sash, tearing at the ribbon until it finally fell free. Smoothing it across the page in front of her, she slid it down until only a single stream of letters marched across the page.

Memories of her governess's tired sighs and condescending explanations threatened to bring tears of frustration to the forefront again. But she also remembered Harriette's gentle encouragement as they tried time and again to find a way to keep the words where they belonged. Her friend had cheered with every word Georgina managed to read, even when it took half an hour and left her with a headache that sent her to bed for the rest of the day.

Georgina swallowed hard and pushed back her shoulders. She wasn't five years old anymore. She could do this.

He that loveth silver shall not be satisfied with silver; nor he that loveth abundance with increase . . .

314

Her back ached from the amount of time spent hunched over the bookstand, but she wasn't about to move. She struggled through the sentence, going back over the words twice until she was able to make the sentence flow in her head. Well, she wasn't after money. Not directly.

Aren't you though?

A sigh brushed through her lips as she brought one hand up to rub at the dull pain swelling behind her left ear. Yes, she wanted wealth and prestige and everything that came with it. But what she'd read did beg the question of what would be enough. Would she be satisfied if she weren't the reigning patroness of Almack's? How much popularity was required for her to feel safe?

She flipped the page and set her ribbons in another section, curious if everything in the book was like that line. She didn't remember the words being so admonishing when they were read on Sunday.

For oftentimes also thine own heart knoweth that thou thyself likewise hast cursed others.

Georgina swallowed. The dull ache spread across the back of her head and down her neck. It was true. She had belittled and used others for her own gain. But if this book did nothing but point out everything she did wrong, where was the hope? Reading it was agonizingly slow, though somewhat easier than the last book she'd tried. The ticking of the tall clock in the corner marked the long minutes.

With nowhere else to turn, she pressed on.

And I find more bitter than death the woman, whose heart is snares and nets . . .

No. No, there had to be something good in here, something to make the effort worth it. Heart pounding, head aching, she flipped the page back again, wincing at the small rip her panicked, trembling hands created.

They also that come after shall not rejoice in him. Surely this also is vanity and vexation of spirit.

A stabbing pain that had nothing to do with the act of reading and everything to do with the words themselves shot through her body. Was that her fate? No matter what she did, would the approval she thought would protect her fade and falter? If this book was right, if they all believed what it said . . .

"Georgina?"

She wrapped her fingers around the edge of the stand, twisting to look at Colin over her shoulder. "Is this what you think?"

He entered the room slowly. "What?"

"Do you think this is true?" She wanted him to say no, willed him to say it. Because if he told her it wasn't true, she'd believe him. Colin never lied to her. There was no one else she could say that about, not even her family.

His throat jerked as he swallowed and he rubbed a hand along the back of his neck, but his eyes remained locked with hers. "Yes."

A laugh stumbled and jerked from her chest as she broke the connection and looked back at the book. "You haven't even read it."

"If it's in that book, I believe it."

He finished crossing the room and stood behind her, his heat surrounding her, but it went no deeper than her own skin. She had failed. Somehow this man had come to mean everything to her. His high opinion the one she craved more than any other.

Perhaps because he saw the truth and found her worth saving. But apparently not worthy enough. "This is what you think of me, then."

His hand covered her left on the bookstand, and his right arm wrapped around her. The black of his sleeve cut through the yellow light as he shifted her ribbons out of the way. His breath stirred her hair as he read the passage over her shoulder. "I've never approved of your ambitions, Georgina. And I've never kept that a secret from you, even when I probably should have."

Anger sparked in her gut, and she grabbed at it, hanging on

for dear life. Anything was better than this helplessness. "Oh, no you don't."

She whirled, her head bumping his chin and sending them both dancing sideways in an attempt to regain their balance. His strong hand wrapped around her arm, anchoring her upright even as he scrambled for his own footing. "What on earth?" he mumbled.

The tang of salt met her tongue as she licked her lips. When had she started crying again? "You don't get to claim your precious honesty right now. How can you say you've been honest with me?" She pointed to the Bible. "God thinks I'm worthless. That my life is nothing but . . . but . . . dismal futility. Vanity of vanities and vexation of spirit. And you've pushed me. You went on and on about truth."

"Georgina, I—"

"And I believed you." She swiped a hand over her eyes. "But all along you felt the same way He does." A painful hiccup sliced through her chest. "Do you love God? Griffith says he loves God more than anything. He says things like you say, about honesty and justice and kindness. So I have to know, Colin, do you love God like that?"

He swallowed. She watched the movement of his throat as if she could see the words before he said them, could brace herself for the implications. "Yes, I do. More than anything. Sometimes I don't do—"

A sobbing laugh born of despair cut him off. "I can't compete with that. I thought I could be different, that I could change and you would like me. But I can't compete with God for your affection."

His eyes widened, and his hand relaxed its grip on her arm.

"You . . ." His voice was dry and croaky. He coughed, clearing his throat. "You want my affections?"

Years of hiding her frustrations kept Georgina's groan locked in her throat, and she managed to slow her tears to a trickle. That was what he got from her speech? That she'd developed a *tendre* for him? "Is that all you heard?"

He shook his head, still looking as if she'd rammed him in the stomach with her art easel. "I assure you I shall address the rest of it in a moment. But I want this settled first."

Her lips pressed together. She considered pushing past him and leaving the room. All the books were starting to close in, mocking her with their very existence. But he'd recovered enough to grip both her arms now.

His might could keep her in the room, standing inches away and smelling the exciting blend of leather and soap, but he couldn't make her speak.

"Georgina, do you want my affection?" He took a deep breath, his chest expanding until the buttons on his waistcoat pulled. "Because I would sincerely like to earn yours."

Her gaze flew to his face, searching every nuance for the truth of his statement.

His breath sighed across her face moments before his lips brushed against hers. She'd never been kissed before, had always been too busy thinking and planning to get caught up in the moment.

She wasn't thinking now.

Warm hands slid up her arms to her neck as his lips returned, pressing a bit firmer this time. She brought her arms up, gripping handfuls of his coat, pressing her fists to his sides, afraid he'd leave before she was ready.

His lips slid from hers like a shadow, leaving the ghost of their taste and the tingling memory of pleasure. He touched his forehead to hers.

She looked up to meet his eyes but found them closed. The lashes looked more red than light brown when she was this close. It was a funny thing to fixate on, but she treasured the knowledge that she was one of the very few, if not the only one, who knew that about him.

His eyes flicked open and caught her staring. "You look good in green."

She glanced down at her skirts to see them bathed in a patch of green light. A giggle broke free as she brought her eyes back to his. "You look good," she whispered, "always."

There was no telling how long they stood there, drinking in each other's souls, sharing the same breath. It felt like forever, but she nearly protested when he started to pull away.

His hands slid to either side of her face, thumbs curving in to rub away the last of her tears. "Come here," he whispered.

Even as she told herself not to, she let him lead her back to the book. His arm lay across the back of her shoulders while his hand rubbed up and down her arm, drifting from sleeve to arm and back again. Each brush of his hand against her skin sent warmth to her toes.

He slid her ribbons the rest of the way off the book and started to read.

Chapter 30

Thoughts of God should be the only thing in his mind. A soul hung in the balance here, after all. Something told him that if Georgina walked away from God this time, she wouldn't turn back.

And then where would he be?

He shouldn't have kissed her. He'd told himself he wouldn't, that Lady Georgina Hawthorne wasn't for him. But the moment he'd seen her fighting, struggling to make out the passage in the Bible, he'd been lost. That kind of determination commanded his respect, his admiration.

Everything he knew about her went through his mind. She'd been as crafty, resourceful, and diligent as the best businessman he'd ever worked with. He had no defenses left. So it was either help God draw her to himself or walk away, because Colin had seen what happened when a man and wife wanted different things in life. He couldn't see himself spending that life with anyone who didn't share his faith, his views, his guiding principles.

No matter how much he cared for her.

"'There is no new thing under the sun,'" he read aloud. Ecclesiastes. Of all the books, why did it have to be Ecclesiastes? Difficult for even the devout to take in.

Georgina's shoulders trembled against his arm. He felt her shaking against his side. How long had she been in here? Standing before the Bible, facing her greatest fear?

He retrieved one of the discarded ribbons to mark his place in the Bible and scooped the book from the stand. With his arm firm around her shoulders, he led them to one of the sofas.

The book fell open on his lap, the words of John staring up at him. He wished he could read from there, give her something easier to understand, something where the hope was considerably more obvious. But he couldn't leave her thinking that a part of the Bible said she was ridiculous and worthless. She would always wonder.

Georgina stayed under his arm, pressed to his side. She pulled her feet up onto the sofa and curled them under her skirt.

Distracted by the image and the sensations running along his side, Colin fumbled to turn the pages back to where he'd been reading. And he read. He read until his voice started to crack and he prayed for stamina. God provided, though Colin almost choked on the rush of saliva that filled his mouth to wet his tongue.

"'Let us hear the conclusion of the whole matter,'" Colin read, thankful they were reaching the end of the book, but wondering if Georgina would be able to find meaning in it, praying she would see the point.

"Fear God, and keep his commandments: for this is the whole duty of man. For God shall bring every work in judgment, with every secret thing, whether it be good, or whether it be evil."

Georgina sat up, putting at least half a foot between their bodies. Relief and regret warred in Colin's heart.

"That's it, isn't it?" Her eyes were wide, her voice touched with awe.

He lifted his brow in inquiry but didn't say anything. He was afraid to say anything.

"That's why you do things the way you do them. Why Griffith is so determined to do things a certain way, even when it's family. Even though he's a duke. Because no matter what we do, be it good or ill, it goes away and only God is left. And fearing God, following God is the whole duty of man. The only thing that remains."

A sob choked out of her, dampening the flame of hope that was flickering in his gut at her understanding.

She took a shaky breath. "Which means everything I've done is folly just as He says. Everything."

She was seeking God. That could be enough, couldn't it? It was going to have to be, because Colin didn't think he could stay away from her any longer. He was drowning in the need to offer comfort, to tell her how wonderful she was without all the masks and machinations.

"I have to go." Georgina sprang to her feet. "I have to think."

She fled the room, a flurry of white bursting through the colored pattern that stretched along the floor.

Colin watched the door for a long time. What he was looking for, he didn't know. Georgina had spent the last thirteen years scheming and planning to achieve a single goal. To have that goal called into question would take time to acclimate to.

If she ever did.

He shouldn't have kissed her. It wasn't his first kiss. He'd given in to the turmoil of emotions and kissed Erika on that dock in Glasgow five years ago. She'd kissed him back in an effort to convince him to stay, begging him not to board the ship. Kissing Georgina had been different. In truth, the two events shouldn't even share the same name.

What would he do if she came downstairs tomorrow, still determined to make the best social match in order to protect herself and her reputation? Because there was no way he'd ever be that man. He clung to the edge of society by his fingernails. Marrying him would be a step down from spinsterhood.

The solid weight of the Bible in his lap drew his attention.

He flipped the pages to Romans and settled in for the evening.

Georgina wasn't at breakfast the next morning. Not that she'd shown up for the morning meal any other day since coming to the country, but part of Colin had hoped to see her as a sign that things had changed overnight.

He lingered in the breakfast room knowing he was being foolish. Eventually he pushed away from the table and went in search of Ryland. Whether for advice or distraction Colin didn't know, but he couldn't bear to be alone with his thoughts anymore, and if he didn't do something soon, he'd track Georgina down wherever she was hiding.

The duke was stacking boards near a half-finished paddock fence behind the stable. Worn boots, patched wool trousers, and white lawn shirt open at the throat made the man look as far from the aristocracy as possible.

Colin raised his eyebrows as Ryland dropped three more white-painted boards on the pile. "Feeling nostalgic?"

Ryland had worked more than one menial job in his years as a spy. It was probably hard to accept an idle life after living on the edge of danger for so long.

"Physical labor can help clear the mind." Ryland tapped his head with one finger.

"Have something serious you need to think through?" Colin leaned against one of the completed sections of fence.

"Not me." Ryland scooped a hammer from the ground beside the pile of wood. A gentle toss sent it arcing in Colin's direction. He scrambled to grab it before it connected with his midsection. "You."

There was no denying that Colin's brain was working hard and going nowhere, like trying to row up a fast-moving stream. If swinging a hammer would help straighten things out, he was more than willing to pound a few nails.

He draped his coat over the fence rail and jerked the knot out of his cravat. Hefting a board from the pile, he walked to the end of the completed sections. "I've never built a fence before."

"I've seen the ship you helped build. I think I can trust you with my paddock." Ryland hauled another board and a bucket of nails.

Fortunately the support posts had already been placed, leaving nothing for Colin and Ryland but the mindless setting of boards and hammering of nails.

They put up three sections of crossbeams in silence, and then, "One of my horses went on an interesting journey recently."

Colin slid another board into the notch on the support post. What amazing patience the man had that he could wait two weeks before bringing up Colin's trip to Cheshire. Colin had been beginning to wonder if Ryland even knew he'd borrowed the horse. "Thank you for that. I had urgent business to attend that couldn't be delayed."

Ryland handed Colin a nail. "Yes, I know. In Cheshire."

Colin placed the nail against the wood and tapped it in enough to hold its place.

"Interesting how Ashcombe also had to hie off to Cheshire, isn't it?"

Colin missed the nail entirely, banging his hand into the fence post and sending his hammer flying through the air.

Leaving his hand on the post for support, Colin turned to glare at Ryland. "What are you implying?"

"That Hugh Carson is a fine manager." Ryland picked up the hammer and held it toward Colin. "I've tried to hire him away from Ashcombe myself."

Colin took the hammer and pounded the nail in with a satisfying thud. His friend was too perceptive by half. How had he known about the position in Glasgow? "Your network is reaching far these days."

He shrugged. "I like to know what's going on in the country."

The sentence lacked a note of finality, so Colin looked to Ryland's face, trying to find the unsaid meaning.

Ryland didn't leave him searching long. "And in my own home."

Colin sighed. "Let me guess, the stained-glass shepherd is in your employ as well? Or perhaps that atrocious statue of Socrates told you."

The grin that crossed Ryland's face was boyish in its note of victory.

With a groan, Colin hung his head in shame. He'd fallen for a simple trick he often employed himself. Ryland had known nothing. He'd simply gone fishing and Colin had taken the bait.

Ryland lifted another board. "I've a staff of former spies, Colin. Did you really think they wouldn't tell me when you and she spent upwards of an hour alone in the library? I must admit I'm surprised she'd step foot in the library of her own volition. She's never shown much affinity for the written word."

Colin focused on the nail. He wasn't about to let that secret slip. It was possible Ryland had figured it out on his own. He had spent months hiding out among the family's staff last year. Unless he said the words directly, though, Colin would assume the other man knew nothing. No matter how much he wanted Georgina to share her secret with her family, it was still her secret.

"Will you be considering me her closest male relative, or should we send word to Griffith?"

Colin hit the nail so hard it bent sideways, burrowing uselessly into the wood.

Ryland shot a questioning glance between the nail and Colin.

As if he could talk marriage right now. He wasn't even sure Georgina ever planned to speak to him again. Colin grunted. "Even the most conservative Englishman reads."

"Reads."

"That is what normal people tend to do in a library, is it not?"

"I haven't a clue what normal people do." Ryland whacked his own nail into the board. "But you'll never convince me Georgina was in that room for a book."

Colin normally delighted in the rare occasion that Ryland was wrong about something. In this case, it was too dangerous to crow over his misconception. Georgina had been in the library for the very specific purpose of finding a book. A specific book. But he couldn't tell his friend that. "Let's just build a fence, shall we?"

One strike of his hammer set the nail, and another sent it to its new home in the fence. At least someone was going to benefit from his frustration.

Harriette crossed her arms over her chest and tapped her foot on the floor. "Should I pull out a dress for dinner, or will the effort be wasted as it was this morning and this afternoon?"

Georgina winced at the derision in her friend's voice. Harriette had been uncommonly patient with Georgina as she roamed the room in her gown and wrapper all day. She'd said nothing when Georgina rang for a tray for breakfast and again for luncheon.

She wasn't going to be quiet much longer. If Georgina didn't tell her about the library soon, Harriette was going to start prying.

"Perhaps we should simply ring for a dinner tray. Is there really any point to dressing this late in the day?" She'd deliberately stayed in her nightclothes so she wouldn't give in to the urge to leave her room and find Colin.

"Only if you want Lady Miranda delivering the tray herself to see what the matter is."

Georgina frowned. Harriette was right. Then again, she usually was. "I'll go down to dinner."

Her agreement didn't mean she was happy about it though. She took her time dressing and swept into the drawing room at the latest acceptable moment, calling on every acting skill she'd developed.

"You've decided to grace us with your presence, I see." Miranda crossed the room to kiss Georgina on the cheek. It was so much better than the pecks on the head they used to give her. Was there anything more condescending than a kiss on the head?

Marshington patted her on the head. "Sleep well?"

Georgina considered growling.

Colin sipped his drink across the room, watching her with a million questions in his eyes. Questions she wasn't prepared to answer, no matter how much time she'd spent thinking today.

Everything churned around in her brain until she didn't know which way was up anymore. Three times today she'd been sure she knew what she wanted to do, but she'd changed her mind before she could do more than remove her wrapper to change dresses.

"Dinner is served, Your Grace."

Praise God for good timing. Georgina headed for the door, wondering at the ease with which she'd thanked God. Her whole life she'd avoided giving Him too much credit for the things that happened in her life, afraid the blessings would be overshadowed by the overwhelming judgments, punishments she'd somehow earned as an infant.

She still wasn't convinced He wanted anything to do with her. He could just as easily have been saving Colin from an awkward conversation with the timely dinner announcement.

"Good evening." Colin offered his arm to escort her in to dinner, his look still seeking, more open and hopeful than she'd seen him in a long time.

Blood rushed through her ears, and her fingers turned cold. What if she failed him?

She gave him her most practiced, perfect smile, determined to make it through dinner.

The mask that fell over his face cut her to the bone. She'd forgotten that he knew about her practiced motions, her careful movements. And he disapproved of them all.

Thankfully, eating would keep them busy for the duration of dinner. The other three could have whatever conversation they wished. She would eat enough to avoid questions about her health and then excuse herself for the evening.

"Georgina, have you seen the library in the afternoon? The sun through the stained glass is quite breathtaking." Marshington wasn't looking at her as he slid his soup spoon into his mouth, but she felt him staring at her anyway.

A glance around the table revealed that only Colin's eyes were trained on her.

"Yes," Georgina blurted. "I had the chance to see it yesterday. It's truly wonderful what the right sun does to the room."

Miranda blinked at her. "You were in the library?"

"Er . . . yes." Georgina stuffed an uncouth amount of soup into her mouth. The problem with soup was it required the diner to do little more than swallow. As a delaying tactic it was sadly lacking.

"I can suggest some books if you'd like. Several of my favorites are in the collection here." Miranda looked nearly giddy with the idea of taking Georgina on a literary tour.

The idea made her stomach clench. She set her spoon aside. "That won't be necessary. I found what I was looking for."

Colin looked up. "You did?"

She should have chosen her words more carefully. Now he thought. . . . What did he think? Did he think she was referring to the kiss? The Bible? The closeness they'd shared on the couch as he read?

For that matter, what was she referring to when she said she'd gotten what she needed? It was hard to say that Colin was thinking the wrong thing when in a way Georgina had been looking for all of those things.

She just hadn't known it. As the soup was cleared, Georgina looked into Colin's eyes. Suddenly everything seemed so simple. It was clear that Colin didn't find her lacking in anything. He was probably right that her family would still love her if they knew. And the fact of the matter was that God had made her the way she was. He'd given her this imperfection, this problem.

Didn't that mean He would accept her as she was? If all that was left at the end of time was God and what He willed, didn't that mean her shortcoming wasn't folly? That it didn't make her unwanted?

She looked around the table at the curious faces. How long had the table been silent? How long had she been reflecting? "Yes," she said looking at her sister, then Marshington, and finally settling on Colin. "Yes, I think I found exactly what I was looking for."

Chapter 31

Colin's suggestion of a card game after dinner had seemed inspired to Georgina at the time. After all, one wasn't supposed to talk much while playing cards. But with her mind elsewhere, it wasn't long before the men were winning by enough points to make continuing the game laughable.

"Let's do a reading." Miranda tapped her hands repeatedly on the edge of the table, excitement nearly rolling off her. "I was reading the most marvelous book today, and there was a passage that begged to be reenacted."

She trotted across the room to pick up a slim volume from the seat by the window. "It's the perfect number of parts, though we'll have to pass the book back and forth, as I only have the one copy."

Georgina turned to find Colin staring at her. He was waiting to see what she would do. Never would there be a better moment. She could tell Miranda the truth and end the charade now.

A movement to her right caught her eye and she saw Marshington sit back in his chair, switching his attention from her to Colin and back again. Somehow he knew there was a silent conversation going on.

You can tell her.

Georgina tried to shove Little Colin into a mental closet. This was her decision, not his.

I know. I just want you to make the right one.

She looked up into the real Colin's eyes.

It's safe. I'm here.

Somehow she knew it wasn't the imaginary Colin that time, but the real one. He was asking her to trust. To give them a chance. To believe there was something more to life than the vain pursuit of wealth and popularity.

Miranda brought the book back to the table and laid it open on the surface. "Here, Georgina, you can do the part of Isabel."

And in that moment she knew she couldn't do it.

"What's the point of doing a reading when there isn't an audience?" The derision dripping from Georgina's voice almost made her cringe. She couldn't look at Colin, didn't dare.

Miranda blinked. "We'll be our own audience. It really is a splendid scene, even if you haven't read the rest of the book."

It was so tempting. To break the chain and tell them all.

Marshington leaned over to look at the book. "That does look amusing."

Georgina's own glance at the book brought her crashing into reality. It didn't look amusing to her. It didn't look like anything to her. The refinement of her station, where accomplished women were to be well-read and perform plays and spend their evenings doing literature readings, and she couldn't even make out the part she was supposed to play.

"It doesn't look like Isabel has many lines," Colin said.

I'll help you. We'll do it together. Little Colin held her mental hand, interpreting the underlying meaning of Colin's words.

She could do it now, could create a circle of people with whom she didn't have to be on guard. Yesterday afternoon in the library had been so freeing. To be with someone and not keep any secrets, to be herself, even if all she'd done was sit and listen.

Well. That wasn't all she'd done.

*It can be like that every day. You don't have to tell the world—
just tell your family. They'll protect you.*

"It looks foolish." Georgina choked on the words even as they
spilled from her mouth. She couldn't do it. She couldn't tell them.
It was too scary. The *what if* was too strong.

What if they called her simple?

What if they didn't understand?

What if they told her she just wasn't trying hard enough?

What if she was wrong? What if God didn't accept her with
the shortcoming He'd given her? What if that was the very reason
He'd given it to her? And while wealth and status may be folly,
they were better than nothing.

What if God didn't replace wealth and status with something
else if she let go?

She'd have nothing. If Colin was wrong and her family offered
her nothing but pity . . . then she would have nothing.

She waited for Little Colin to say something. To tell her she
was wrong. To say the words to give her assurance and courage.

But Little Colin was more than silent. He was gone.

Her eyes flew to her left, looking at the real Colin. He was
looking quietly down at his fingernails.

She'd lost him. Her secret remained intact but at the expense of
his friendship. There would be no more passionate kisses, no more
cuddled readings. It wasn't fair for him to hang their relationship
on this. Wasn't it enough that he knew?

He rose from the table. "Since the reading is not going to happen, I think I'll retire early. Good evening."

As his footsteps echoed down the corridor, an ache settled in
Georgina's stomach. If she'd managed to protect everything, why
did it suddenly feel as if she'd lost it all?

Colin didn't sleep. He packed his bag and then lay on his bed
staring at the ceiling until dawn peeked in through his uncovered
window.

He was waiting in the breakfast room, dressed in traveling clothes, when Ryland entered, dressing gown thrown over his trousers and white lawn shirt.

Ryland's blink of surprise told Colin how shocked his friend was to find him up and about. "Going somewhere?"

Colin drummed his fingers on the table, praying he wasn't making a rash decision for emotional reasons. He'd prayed while he stared at the ceiling in his bedchamber, and this decision had brought him the closest he'd come to peace in a long time.

Ryland sat at the table, waiting in silence for Colin to speak.

With a deep breath, Colin made his decision final. "I'm going home."

If Colin expected Ryland to display shock or surprise at the statement, he was doomed to disappointment.

"I have to say it's about time." Ryland busied himself fixing a cup of tea.

Colin took his turn sitting back in stunned silence. "About time?"

"How long has it been? Five years? Six?"

"Five." Colin grunted. Five very long years. He narrowed his eyes at Ryland. "You're one to talk. You avoided your family for nearly a decade."

"Quite rightly, as it turns out. My aunt tried to kill me when I came back." Ryland nodded at the footman who delivered a plate piled high with eggs, toast, and a hash Colin knew was particularly delicious. He'd already had two servings himself.

Ryland pointed his fork in Colin's direction. "Your father is unlikely to attempt murder."

No, he leaned toward attempted ruin.

Not that he could ruin Colin anymore. Or even the rest of the family. Colin had seen to that.

Colin sat forward, turning so that one arm lay across the table and he could look Ryland straight in the eye. "You think it a good idea for me to return home? You think things have changed?"

"Doubtful." Ryland took a bite of hash and chewed slowly.

Colin slumped into his chair. It was doubtful anything had changed. Though Colin owned part of Celestial Shipping, he'd limited his involvement in the business. His father's life would be running similar to how it always had, just without the complication of a son suggesting new ventures, practices, and customers.

Ryland swallowed and took a sip of tea. "But you have."

Colin's brows drew together. "Me?"

"You don't need Celestial Shipping."

Colin sat back confused. "What do you mean?"

"If you were to stop working right now, never open another crop report, cash out your investments, and set yourself up to live off a bank account somewhere . . . would you run out of money?"

"Only if I lived very foolishly." Colin took his fork and pushed around the remnants of his own breakfast.

"Precisely. When we met, you were a boy trying to save the family business." He shrugged. "Now you're a man." He took another sip of tea.

Colin smirked. Ryland's flair for the dramatic was certainly growing. "I'm but a year younger than you. Are you implying that you were still a boy when we met?"

The duke lifted an arrogant brow. "I'd been spying on Napoleon for four years by that point. One grows up quickly in that sort of life. The fact remains that you no longer need Celestial Shipping."

Ryland fell silent as the truth of that statement hit Colin in the heart. He didn't need Celestial Shipping, not the way his father did or even the way his mother and sister did.

What he needed was his family.

Georgina watched from her window as Colin got into one of Ryland's traveling coaches. That was it, then. She'd known it was, had come to the realization that he was right somewhere around two in the morning. He couldn't be with her while her secret held such power over her. It would always be between them, and he would grow to resent it if he didn't already.

Harriette entered with a breakfast tray but stopped when she saw Georgina standing by the window. "My lady?"

"Good morning, Harriette."

The maid set the tray on a table. "The papers have come from London."

A stack of papers took up half of the tray. For years Georgina and Harriette had read every bit of those papers, analyzing everyone mentioned to find the most advantageous connections. It had gotten her nowhere. "I've a different plan this morning."

Harriette's eyes widened as she stopped, one hand extended toward the top paper. "A different plan?"

Georgina reached under her pillow and pulled out the large Bible she'd snuck to the library to get in the dark hours before the sun rose. "Yes. A different plan."

"You want me to read you the Bible?"

Georgina didn't blame Harriette for her confusion. Church and everything in it had never been Georgina's favorite subject.

"No." Georgina dropped the book onto the writing desk, where she'd already arranged two straight-back chairs. "I want you to help me read it."

The ribbon draped from the book at the place she'd chosen to start reading. She'd flipped through everything this morning, not trying to read anything, but simply getting a feel for the pages, the weight of the book, the idea of reading it.

Harriette's thin arms wrapped around Georgina as she flipped the book open at the ribbon.

"James?" Harriette asked, looking over Georgina's shoulder at the book.

Georgina wiped her suddenly sweaty palms down her skirts. "It seems to be a short book."

"James it is, then."

The two women sat, hunching over the book in a way they hadn't in a long time. For years after Harriette joined her, Georgina had continued to try to learn to read. Once they'd begun to plan her marriage, though, those efforts had fallen by the wayside.

Harriette helped Georgina arrange the ribbons, blocking off as many words as possible.

Georgina took a deep breath, but Harriette's hand on her arm stopped her from looking at the book.

"Should we . . . I don't know, pray first?" Harriette had never seemed to think much of God either. That she looked as unsure of their morning plans as Georgina did gave her a bit of confidence.

"Why not?" Georgina asked. But the *why not* proved to be that neither one of them knew what to say. The bishop's prayers always seemed long and elaborate. Georgina couldn't think of anything other than, "Please help me read this. And please don't hate me."

So she left it at that and bent over the book.

Thirty minutes later, Georgina pushed the book aside. Her head was beginning to pulse with pain, and she didn't want it to get bad enough to send her to bed. She wasn't ready to abandon the book though. "You'll have to read for a while, Harriette."

So the maid read. More than once they stopped to discuss what a passage could possibly mean. Several times Harriette offered to find someone to help them, but Georgina refused.

"All of my life," she said, "I've been listening to people talk about what God means, what the Bible says. I think I always thought of Him as their God when they said those things because they didn't match what I had experienced."

Georgina ran a hand over the page in front of her. They'd finished James and flipped to 1 John. "I think, if this is going to mean anything, He's going to have to become my God. If He wants me to . . . to change, then He's going to have to speak to me himself."

Harriette looked at the book. She reached out a hand and wrapped her fingers around Georgina's before she continued reading.

There was something fascinating about the rhythm of writing, at least when someone else was doing it. Dip the quill, write a line, dip the quill, write a line. The quiet *scritch* of Miranda's quill against paper broke the silence of the morning, accompanied only by Georgina's unsteady breathing. Envy at the easy way Miranda wrote her thoughts threatened to send Georgina retreating back to her room. Miranda was a constant letter writer, maintaining correspondence with numerous friends and family members. She'd never understood why Georgina didn't do the same.

Perhaps it was time to explain. What did she really have to lose? Colin was gone. She'd hoped he would return, that he'd simply been going to the village to get something for Ryland or Miranda, but after two days passed, she'd admitted the truth.

She'd lost him. Regardless of that breathtaking kiss in the library, he'd refused to be with her if she refused to be herself.

Not that she blamed him. The more she thought about what she'd become, what she'd tried to become, the less she liked it herself. The more she and Harriette had read, and they had read a lot in the past two days, the more she realized how wrong her thinking had been.

Even if Georgina returned to London, she'd never see the Season the same way again. Her calculated hunt for a husband was dead. Even the idea left her feeling hollow and tired.

Georgina cleared her throat.

Miranda jerked her head up and looked at Georgina with surprise. "Oh, good. You're feeling better."

Georgina and Harriette had spent so much time in her room reading the past few days that the household had come to the conclusion that she was sick. She hadn't corrected them.

"May I talk to you?" Georgina shifted her weight from foot to foot. Nothing was going to make this any easier.

After a moment of dumbfounded silence, Miranda waved Georgina into the room and moved toward the little grouping of chairs near the window.

Georgina stopped two steps from the chairs. She wanted to maintain a ready escape path in case this conversation went poorly. "I can't read."

"You can't what?"

"Read. Or write. I've never been able to."

"Never been . . . I don't . . ."

Georgina had no idea how long they would have stayed there, Miranda gaping like a fish and Georgina biting her lip and shifting her weight, praying—yes, praying—that the sweat rolling down her back wasn't visible through her dress. The stalemate was broken by Ryland's sudden entrance.

"Darling, I—Oh." He looked back and forth between them. "What's going on?"

"I can't read." Georgina blinked in surprise. That had been considerably easier to say the second time.

"Hmmm." Ryland leaned one shoulder against the wall. "Well, that explains a great deal."

Miranda looked at her husband. "What?"

"Harriette, I assume, does your correspondence, then?" Ryland guided Georgina to a chair before settling into one himself. Miranda continued to look stunned, her gaze flitting from one face to another.

"Yes." Georgina looked at her hands, clasped in her lap, wishing the chair would swallow her and remove her from Ryland's steady contemplation. Had she really thought she wanted to marry this man? He'd have unnerved her in a matter of days. How did Miranda stand it?

"If you ever want a job, I'll recommend you both to the War Office without qualm. I had no idea."

Miranda sprang to life. "You'll do no such thing. My sister isn't going to wallow through the muddy fields of France plucking secrets from the air." She stuck her nose in the air. "White is much too visible."

A laugh sputtered against Georgina's lips.

Ryland scoffed. "Nonsense. I wouldn't waste her in a muddy field. She is much too skilled at working a ballroom. I'd place her directly in Napoleon's court. He'd never know what hit him."

Georgina let the laugh roll free, looking from Ryland to Miranda and not finding a modicum of censure in their eyes. A considerable amount of curiosity, but not a lick of disdain.

It was true what she and Harriette had read in Philippians that morning, that there was much to be gained when she let go of everything and trusted in the Lord. One could even gain back a family.

Chapter 32

Colin's first stop was the only place he felt reasonably certain he would be welcome. Hugh Carson had been delighted to see him again, full of thanks that was topped only by Alastair's exuberant gratitude. Either the man had never actually wanted Colin to take the job or Hugh was working out so well all disappointment had been forgiven.

It didn't matter much to Colin which was true. He was simply thankful that he hadn't taken the position. Now that he was here, he knew it wouldn't have been right.

While his lungs welcomed the sting of salted air drifting off the River Clyde and the idea of investing his time and energy into a single thing was still appealing, he soon discovered that Ryland was right. Colin had changed. He didn't want this life anymore.

He took a deep breath, easing a bit of the tightness in his chest. While he didn't want a life of shipping and constant travel, he was definitely going to have to spend more time at the coast. The crisp air felt wonderful.

"You know," Alastair said from the open doorway to the shipping office, "Erika is at home still. We'd love to have you for dinner while you're in town."

Colin tried and failed to recall a clear mental image of Erika's red hair and blue eyes, but he couldn't. The only visions he had were blond-haired, green-eyed, and capable of ripping his heart to shreds. "That's very gracious, sir. I'm not sure of my plans yet."

It was still possible his father would run him out of town before sunset.

Alastair clapped Colin on the shoulder. "Let me know. The invitation is open."

"Thank you, sir." Colin nodded and waved before hailing a hack to take him across town.

It didn't take as long as he would have liked.

He had the driver drop him off a few streets away. He wasn't quite ready to face them yet, to find out just what awaited him.

Not that anyone was waiting for him. He hadn't sent word, wanting to maintain the option to change his mind.

Glasgow was bustling, crawling with people patronizing the businesses he remembered as well as several new establishments. By and large, though, the city looked as he remembered it.

So did the large house just off the center of town.

The same could not be said for the woman darting out of the house with a scream. Colin braced himself, not sure what to expect. Was she in danger? Was someone chasing her?

And then she was upon him, throwing herself into his chest and wrapping her arms around his neck. Her red-gold curls smothered him, but he didn't care. It had been so long. Too long.

He felt a drop hit his cheek and trail down into his cravat. No doubt it was a tear but it was impossible to say whose it was, because Colin's eyes were wet and his sister's teary hiccups filled his ear. He tightened his arms and shifted until he could look over her shoulder at the older version of his sister standing in the doorway.

His mother wasn't bothering to hide the tears streaming down her own cheeks, but she came no farther than the doorway.

Time had found his mother, just as it had found the town and himself. She was recognizable, easily identified as the woman who'd raised and loved him, but now, seeing her through the eyes of a grown man, he saw the burden she carried. In part because of him.

The missing years crashed down on him like a wave in a storm.

His sister finally released his neck but only moved her clasp to his hand to drag him down the walkway and into the house.

Colin went willingly, too numb to resist her, even if he'd wanted to. He had missed so much. The letters had not been enough.

Mother smiled through the tears as she reached her hands up to cup his cheeks. "My boy. I knew you would come home. You needed only to have the idea planted in your head."

What was she saying? Colin's eyes narrowed as his brain wiped away his emotional stupor. "You told Alastair to write the letter."

His mother shrugged, and in that moment Colin saw himself in her. He remembered all the times he'd seen his mother nudge his father in a particular direction, using tactics Colin himself now employed. He wouldn't be surprised to learn that his family hadn't been in as much danger as he thought all those years ago. Mother probably had a small fortune tucked away in an old teapot somewhere.

"Where is Jaim—" He cleared his throat. "Where is Father?" Colin couldn't wait anymore. He wanted his family whole, he wanted to put the past where it belonged. He'd been so adamant about Georgina sharing herself with her family, but he hadn't realized he'd done the same thing, pretending he didn't need these people, that the tenuous connection they maintained was enough.

"I'm here."

The rough voice drew Colin's attention. His father looked much as he had in Colin's drawing room, but with an extra air of wariness about him. Had the old man done as much thinking as Colin had since their visit?

Their family had never been like the Hawthornes—close-knit, affectionate, sharing—but they had loved in their own quiet, respectful way. Colin was realizing there were good things to both. If Georgina had been raised in a more practical family, would she have felt free to share her struggles? If Colin had been in a closer family, would they have been able to talk things out before now?

Speculating wouldn't change anything, so Colin shoved the thoughts aside. The important thing was that this was his family, and he wasn't going to let them suffer anymore.

Father straightened his shoulders. "You didn't take the job."

Colin shook his head. "No."

Jaime McCrae took a step into the room and then stopped, looking unsure of how to proceed. When he'd left London, he and Colin had opened the door to reconciliation—someday—but the old man probably thought Colin was here to slam that door shut again.

Colin stepped forward and pulled a sheaf of papers from his jacket pocket. He'd stopped in London for them—had almost decided to stay there, but God wouldn't let him rest. These papers had driven too much of a wedge between him and his father. Even as he left London to head for Scotland, he hadn't known what he intended to do when he got here, but now he did. And he knew it was right.

"Here." He shoved the papers toward his father.

The air of wariness grew as the old seaman stepped forward. He'd spent enough years in business that it took him little more than a glance to realize what the papers were. Colin hoped his father took them for the peace offering they were meant to be. He'd had a week's worth of traveling to think about things. He'd spent miles of road in prayer and he'd come to one conclusion.

Ryland was right.

Colin didn't need Celestial Shipping. For his entire adulthood, the business had been the thing that stood between him and his father. Colin would be forever grateful that he'd been there that day to save the business, but now he knew his relationship with his father was so much more important.

"You've signed over your share." His father's eyes widened, looking dumbfounded as he read the papers.

"Yes." Part of him wanted to make a comment cautioning his father not to gamble away any more of it. But the truth was, if a five-year separation from his son hadn't taught him that lesson, an admonishment from that son wouldn't do it either.

Besides, somewhere between Kent and Glasgow, Colin had realized something. He'd forgiven his father.

"I'm sorry." The sentence tumbled from both men's lips at the same time.

His mother's laughter filled the room as she wrapped an arm around each man. "Yes, yes, we're all dismal, fallible creatures, but we're family, yes?"

Colin grinned at his mother and then his father. "Yes."

"Then we have a party! Your sister's stepping out in society this year, you know. It's about time her big brother came to scare away the no-good ruffians."

"You go ahead, Teagan." Father looked from the papers to Colin again. "We'll be along shortly."

Mother looked as if she wanted to protest, but she and Bronwyn went farther into the house, both throwing smiles over their shoulders as they went.

Colin faced his father, waiting for him to speak, knowing the next move had to come from him.

"I'm proud of you." The gruff voice was almost a whisper. "You've become a better man than I ever will be, and that's as it should be. Each generation should stand taller than the last. My only regret is that I had so little to do with it."

Colin slung his arm around his father's shoulder, wondering when they'd gotten to be the same height. His father had always seemed so much larger in Colin's memory. He couldn't stomach the idea of the strong man breaking himself for the sake of his son, so Colin steered them both in the direction his mother had gone.

"I don't regret my years in London, Da. And nothing can change what happened. I think I understand what drove you to it, if not the particulars. A good friend recently reminded me that all the answers are in the Bible, and I think this is definitely a case of God using an evil to create good."

"So we move on, then?"

Colin nodded. "We move on. Tell me what you've decided to do with the Caribbean routes."

Georgina blinked, trying to bring the world into focus. In his typical fashion, Griffith had tried to fix Georgina's problem for her as soon as he'd learned of it. That his solution was a pair of spectacles that made everything blurrier was beside the point.

She was wearing the spectacles to make him happy. Eventually she would tell him that they were useless, but for now, she'd wear them as a symbol that her family loved her even though she was strange.

"I think the t-tulips were an inspired choice. Very unique." Lavinia ran a finger along the soft petals of one of the nearby flower arrangements.

"Thank you for coming early to help with the final touches." Georgina linked an arm with her friend. One of the first things she'd done when they returned to London was add a few names to the guest list for her ball. Lavinia and her aunt were at the top of the new list, and Lavinia had even agreed to come over early to help calm Georgina's nerves.

She'd sent Colin an invitation as well. A second invitation, actually, since his name had been part of the original list. No one in the family had heard from him though, and Georgina had asked. Frequently. It was part of her new commitment to have no barriers with them. For the most part it was working, though she still shocked them on occasion when she didn't turn into a brat of the highest order when someone suggested an activity.

"This is a nice way to end my t-time in t-town." Lavinia hugged Georgina's arm.

Georgina nudged the spectacles down her nose so she could better see her friend. "Lavinia, why are you marrying Mr. Dixon?"

Lavinia tilted her head to the side, giving serious consideration to the question. Georgina liked that. She liked that Lavinia looked past her first instinct to make sure it was true. Georgina was trying her best to cultivate a similar habit. "I think I'll like it. I d-didn't realize how much unt-til I was here in London."

"Truly?"

Lavinia nodded. "He stays in the village mostly. And he'll let me help with the b-business. I'll be happy and useful."

Which was more than Georgina could bring to a marriage. "I can't read."

Good gracious. Where had that come from? At this rate she'd be telling all of London by midnight. Her family had agreed there was no need to tell the world about her issue. No one discussed all their maladies with the public anyway. But Georgina had wanted Lavinia to know. Perhaps as a sign that she truly valued the other girl's friendship.

"You c-c-can't?" Surprise made Lavinia's stutter stronger.

Georgina shook her head. "Letters don't make sense to me."

Lavinia shrugged. "Me either."

The girls giggled at the idea that one couldn't read and one couldn't speak. What a pair they made. Lavinia pulled Georgina around the ballroom one more time. "Let's take a last look at everything b-before it fills with p-people."

And fill it did.

Georgina's two weeks in the country with Miranda hadn't seemed to dim her popularity any. And if some people were surprised by her spectacles or Lavinia's presence, they chose not to say anything. At least not in Georgina's hearing. She'd considered taking them off for the evening. Most women did. But the spectacles reminded her that things were different now. This was her first significant social outing since reconnecting with her family, and she would risk the strange looks if it meant she didn't fall back into old habits.

The music was soft and flowing, and as far as she was concerned, the food a good bit better than most other balls. Georgina was having a spectacular time.

Until a familiar brown head was bowing before her, asking for a dance.

Ashcombe had returned.

Georgina took his hand, hoping she wouldn't stumble through the dance with her blurry vision. She peeked over the tops of the spectacles to see the earl giving her odd looks as they worked through the quadrille. What was he going to say? She almost wished they were waltzing so they could speak more freely. Would he shout her secret for everyone to hear?

"Spectacles."

Georgina blinked. Half a song of silence and the word he finally spoke was *spectacles*?

"Yes," she said. "They're new."

He lapsed back into silence as they finished the dance. Georgina had never been so happy to curtsy in her life.

"Pardon, my lady, but this is for you."

Georgina looked at the folded parchment on the servant's silver tray. This could not be happening. Not in front of the earl, who was suddenly looking at her with narrowed eyes.

"Thank you." She choked out the sentence as she took the paper. Her fingers were trembling as she opened it.

And then she laughed.

Because the paper held no letters save the large looping *L* in the corner to show that the note was from Lavinia. Instead, the girl had drawn pictures. Very bad pictures. Assuming the stick with a triangle on the bottom and a swirl of loops on the top was supposed to be Georgina, Lavinia wanted to see her on the terrace.

She refolded the note and smiled up at the earl. "If you'll excuse me, Lavinia has need of me on the terrace."

Lord Ashcombe's eyes widened. "You invited her?"

"She is my friend and is perfectly respectable."

"But I forbade it."

Georgina straightened her shoulders, wishing Little Colin would deign to revisit her mind for just a moment of encouragement, even though she knew her mental prayer would be much more productive. "My lord, you haven't the right to forbid me anything. Nor will you."

He wasn't happy. Georgina could see his displeasure even through the spectacles.

"The terrace, you say?"

Georgina nodded and led the way across the room. *Dear God, please let Lavinia be there.*

She was, though her wide smile drooped a bit when she saw the earl escorting Georgina out.

"My lord." Lavinia dropped into a curtsy.

Lord Ashcombe looked stunned. Then angry. "Spectacles." He spat the word at Georgina as if she'd tricked him on purpose.

She touched the rims and pulled out her coyest smile. She'd been trying not to use her practiced smiles much these days, but there were occasions that called for it. And allowing the meanest person she'd ever met to believe he'd been wrong about her was the perfect occasion in her mind. If he wanted to believe she hadn't been able to read his note because she didn't have spectacles, she wasn't going to correct him.

"Thank you for the escort, Lord Ashcombe." She smiled sweetly at him and almost asked if he intended to visit soon, but it was best to leave well enough alone.

As the earl stomped away, Georgina hugged Lavinia to her and thanked God for brothers who couldn't keep themselves from helping.

Glasgow's social whirl was nothing compared to London's, and Colin wasn't sure which he preferred. There was something to be said for being openly welcomed. He didn't fade into the fringes here. Instead he danced, played cards, and speared his sister's suitors with icy stares he'd learned from Ryland.

It was one of the things he'd enjoyed most over the three weeks with his family. Though they had their fair share of awkward moments, they soon learned how to be a family again—an even better family than they were before. Colin enjoyed Glasgow, spending time with his family, renewing old friendships, and reacquainting himself with the Scotland he'd loved growing up.

But he didn't think he could stay there. He tried to ignore the fact that he missed the challenge of London, of staying one step ahead of things. He kept checking the paper, reading the marriage announcements with more interest than normal. Her name never appeared, and he wasn't sure if he was relieved or not. Could he return before she married? Should he? He was afraid that if he saw her again, touched her again, he'd forget that she needed more. He'd promise to shield her secret forever and it would slowly eat away at their happiness.

Assuming she even wanted him anymore.

He sat in the breakfast room, watching a bird fly from tree to tree. These were the hardest times, when there was no one demanding his attention. He missed Georgina so much it hurt. More than one lady had made it clear that he could start a family here in Glasgow, but he couldn't do it. Any woman he courted would be found lacking when she didn't possess the intelligence, wit, and nerve to make the rest of the world do her bidding.

Who would have guessed he'd want a woman as manipulative as his mother. As himself.

"A letter has arrived for you, sir."

Colin thanked the butler and turned the letter over with interest. He recognized Miranda's loopy handwriting and panic choked him. Was Georgina safe? Had something happened?

Was she getting married?

He tore at the seal.

As he flattened the paper and read the first words, he felt dizzy. He blinked twice and read them again.

> *My dearest Colin,*
>
> *I don't know how to tell you this. Miranda is writing this for me. I hope that tells you something. She's a bit slow about it and keeps telling me what to say. (I am not the one being slow—she is! She should just tell you what she wants to say.—M)*
>
> *Harriette could get this done much faster, but I thought having Miranda write it would mean more to you. That we spent time in prayer before writing it might mean even more.*

Colin dropped the paper and rubbed his hands hard over his face. They came away wet.

> *There is a time to keep silent, and a time to speak. Perhaps I am speaking too late, but I have to try. You were right about Miranda. She still doesn't understand, but she's trying. (I can't believe you kept this secret!—M)*

Here the handwriting changed from Miranda's familiar loops to a more precise, slanted hand.

I am having Harriette finish this letter. Miranda would not stop putting her own thoughts on the page.

Then the writing changed back to Miranda's. A smile stretched across Colin's face.

Miranda has promised to be good. We shall see if that remains true.

I miss you, Colin. I am delivering this letter myself in the hopes—

Colin stopped and reread the last sentence. The letter went on for another half a page, but he couldn't move on as the implications of that sentence sank in and the breath hardened in his lungs.

She was delivering it herself.

Which meant . . .

Colin jumped from his seat, knocking the chair to the floor with a crash, but he didn't care. He was out the door and down the stairs before he was even sure he'd started breathing again. His chest was heaving as he pushed open the drawing-room door.

There she stood.

In the middle of the drawing room, with her lower lip caught in her straight, white teeth. The confidence she so often wore like a suit of armor was gone.

And she was wearing green.

Georgina pinched her lip between her teeth, hoping the sharp sting would keep her patient, remind her to give him time. He didn't know what all she'd been through the past few weeks. It would take him a while to catch up.

Silence stretched and still he stood in the door, breathing like a man who'd just run a foot race across London instead of one who'd simply run down the stairs.

So she waited.

His breathing returned to normal but still he said nothing.

Still she waited.

Her own breathing started to pick up as panic set in. What if she was too late? Why hadn't she sent a letter right away? She'd needed those weeks. Needed them to rebuild her relationship with her family, to have Harriette read more about the sacrifice of Jesus and how it let God be *her* God, not just the higher being spoken about in church.

Without the need to hide constantly, she was discovering more about herself as well. It had seemed important at the time, but had it cost her a chance with Colin?

"You look good in green." His words were low and scratchy, but they were the most beautiful music she could have imagined.

"So I've heard." She plucked at the skirt. "It's Miranda's."

His eyebrows rose at her comment, and he stepped fully into the room. The tight band squeezing her chest relaxed and blessed air rushed in.

"I told Miranda."

"So I read." Colin crossed the room until he stood just far enough away that she couldn't reach him. His hair was mussed. It was so strange to see him looking anything but perfectly polished. She liked it.

She wished she had the courage to bridge the gap and run her fingers through it, to straighten the wave that had fallen across his forehead, but her resolve had gotten stretched a bit thin the past couple of weeks, and her courage was failing. "I'm sorry, Colin. You were right. I should have listened to you earlier."

His eyes closed for a moment before opening again and staring straight into her gaze. "Is that why you're here? I don't want apologies and gratitude, Georgina."

Georgina's knees trembled beneath her borrowed skirt. She squeezed enough breath through her tightening throat to whisper, "What do you want?"

"You."

"I was afraid you'd changed your mind."

Colin swallowed and eased another step forward. "I'll never be more than a gentleman."

"I'll never be able to read."

He smiled. "I'll never go back to working for my father."

"I'll never tell all of England my secret."

"I'll never protect you without your knowledge again."

The absurdity of the conversation made Georgina smile. It might not seem romantic to anyone else, but she heard the honest caring behind every negative promise. "I'll never hide myself from you."

"I'll never stop loving you."

Georgina sucked air between her teeth. "Me neither."

Colin's hands reached out to cup her cheeks. He took a final step to close the gap, until their breaths mingled and she could see the flecks of light brown in his blue eyes. "Lady Georgina Hawthorne, I love you. Do you think you could be happy splitting your life between London and Glasgow? I find I have a great need to spend more time here."

She tilted her head, pretending to be deep in thought. "Have they a decent modiste here? I find I have a great need to replace my entire wardrobe."

Colin laughed and wrapped her more firmly in his embrace. "Will you do me the greatest honor of my life and marry me?"

"I will." Georgina went up on tiptoe and pressed her lips to his. Her arms reached around his middle, thrilling at the warmth of his body. This man was nothing she'd been looking for, but he'd known everything she needed.

He took her for a walk then, introducing her to the city of his childhood. The unfamiliar sounds and smells were exciting to her because here, with Colin, she was going to get a fresh start with people who wouldn't know her as anything other than the woman God had meant for her to be.

Epilogue

Colin couldn't stop watching his wife across the room. She was smiling and laughing with the ladies of Glasgow, and none of it was forced. Well, no more forced than your average society matron. Two years of wedded bliss and she still made his heart flutter.

A few minutes later he was appreciating the sway of her rose silk skirts as she made her way back to him. She stood on tiptoe to whisper in his ear. "The Earl of Kennelwhite is unhappy with his current shipping arrangements."

Colin looked at her in surprise. "And how do you know that?"

The false innocence stamped across her face nearly made him burst out in laughter. "Because his wife is tired of coming to Glasgow."

Colin lifted a brow. Considering the earl was from the Highlands, the wife's distaste for the journey was not entirely uncalled for.

"And"—Georgina drew the word out—"she is especially tired of hearing about ships and warehouses."

Colin grinned. "We shall have to tell my father to call upon the earl tomorrow."

"Are you truly not going to involve yourself? Even though we're spending several months a year up here?"

They'd decided to split their time equally between Glasgow, London, and Crestwood, with which Griffith had surprised them all by adding to Georgina's dowry. Colin found he enjoyed managing the estate almost as much as he'd enjoyed handling investments. He'd cut back considerably on that front, not bothering with anyone's finances outside the family. It was almost more of a hobby now, though a lucrative one. He occasionally advised Lavinia and Mr. Dixon, though they didn't need much help. With Lavinia at his side, Mr. Dixon was on his way to becoming one of the wealthiest gentlemen in his district.

Harriette was certainly enjoying her role as Crestwood's housekeeper. She still did most of Georgina's writing, but Colin had taken over the reading duties, and after a few months of adjustment, Margery had turned out to be a fine lady's maid.

With one arm wrapped around his wife's shoulders, Colin steered them toward the door. "I am truly not going to get involved. Father and I are getting along well now. We talk business but only in a casual sense. When he asks for my input, I give it, but other times I hold my tongue. I no longer find I have to be right all the time."

"How very mature of you." She looked around the front hall. "Are we leaving?"

"Yes. As much as I enjoy watching you gather information for me, I find I'd rather spend the rest of the evening alone."

Her eyes narrowed at him. "You knew I was getting tired."

"Yes."

She turned so he could help her with her cloak. "I thought we'd agreed you wouldn't protect me without my consent."

"I'm not protecting you." He leaned in to whisper in her ear. "I'm protecting our child."

Her gasp was, for once, not feigned or exaggerated for effect. "How did you know?"

He laughed. "Darling, it doesn't take a genius to do the math or realize you spend your mornings in rather close proximity to the chamber pot."

"How indelicate of you to say."

He handed her into the carriage and climbed in after her, pulling her close to his side as he settled on the seat. They sat like that, her head resting beneath his chin as they drove to the small terrace house they kept in town.

As they prepared for bed, Colin thumbed through a stack of letters he'd missed earlier in the day. "Darling, you've a letter from Jane."

Georgina smiled as she brushed through her hair. "And?"

"She met a man."

Georgina groaned. "I think that harrowing tale can wait until morning."

They chatted about everything and nothing as they finished preparing for bed. Once snuggled beneath the covers, Colin pulled her close and lifted the large book from the bedside table. "What shall we read tonight?"

Georgina's eyes drifted shut on a sigh. "The part where Jesus tells them to let the little children come to him. I find myself quite preoccupied with such a visual."

Colin chuckled as he turned to Mark and began to read.

Acknowledgments

I know you've finished the book, but don't stop reading now, because this is the place I get to thank all the people who made this book possible, whether they're living, dead, fictional, or something other than an actual person.

My first gratitude will always go to God, for allowing me the opportunity to do what I love and share it with you. He has also blessed me with the most gracious and supportive family imaginable. To the Hubs and the Blessings, I couldn't do it without you, even though I frequently kick you out of the room.

Next, I must acknowledge Scrivener for allowing me to write a novel entirely out of order and for allowing me to keep some semblance of sanity while working on the parts that overlap *A Noble Masquerade*. If you are a writer, I don't recommend doing that. Ever. Unless it makes an incredible story like this one. Then, of course, you do it, because the chances of keeping a hold of your sanity through the entire book-writing process are slim anyway.

To my most amazing beta readers, Alana, Amanda, and Jacob, thank you for your honesty and your feedback and your willingness to provide both in a ridiculously short time frame. I'd like to take this opportunity to promise that I'll never cut it that close to the wire again, but we all know I'd be lying, so I'll just say thank you and you're awesome.

Much appreciation goes to Dr. Pringle Morgan, James Hinshelwood, and the many other scientists and ophthalmologists who started the ball rolling on the examination of dyslexia in the late nineteenth century. Though acknowledgment didn't come until many years after Georgina would have dealt with the issue, treatment and options have come a long way since then. I applaud the many of you walking this difficult path today. May you have all the support and encouragement you need to live life to the fullest despite an additional obstacle.

Mark Hall and Kristena Tunstall, my deepest appreciation to you for taking the time and opening up about how dyslexia has affected so much more than just your ability to read. Your openness about the mental, emotional, and spiritual impacts of dyslexia helped me make Georgina real. I can't thank you enough for that, because I know it wasn't easy or convenient for either of you.

Huge thanks to the many teachers, such as Dianna Shuford, who shared tips with me on ways they've helped their students over the years, so that I could give Georgina an authentic bag of tricks. If you see a teacher today, give them a hug. These men and women do incredible work and care so much for their students. Thank you for taking the time to share some of those experiences with me.

When it comes to writing the actual book, I have to send some thanks to Laurie Alice Eakes for helping me brainstorm my way out of a panic attack when I realized Colin couldn't be an American. War of 1812 and all that. Scottish turned out to be much better anyway. (Insert a shout of agreement from all Scottish people here.)

Karen, Raela, and the rest of the Bethany House team deserve a huge plate of cookies. Which I would send, except they'd probably end up as a big box of crumbs if I packed them myself, and I'm too cheap to buy anything from one of those gourmet cookie-delivery services. (If a reader runs one of these and would be willing to cut me a deal on sending this incredible team some treats, let me know!) Hugs to the cover art team for continuing to make me such gorgeous, eye-catching covers. Y'all make me look good.

Speaking of making me look good, check out the incredible new headshot for which I can thank my unbelievably talented cousin. Thanks, Brett, for marrying such a sweet lady. And if you're getting married in Alabama, look into using Rebecca Long Photography because she's amazing and I'm not at all biased on the subject.

Of course, none of this would be possible if it weren't for you, the readers, because a story can't do anything unless it's heard. Thank you for joining me on this adventure.

Lastly, I want to thank Georgina. Telling her story has been a life-changing journey for me. Getting to know her, seeing the similarities in myself, and growing along with her was so much more than I expected it to be when I started this series. I hope you've fallen in love with her and Colin as much as I have. While there's a part of me that knows they aren't real, there's also a part of me that has to thank them for letting me be the one to tell their story.

Also participating in the inspiration for this book, Rob Long.

Kristi Ann Hunter graduated from Georgia Tech with a degree in computer science but always knew she wanted to write. Kristi is an RWA Golden Heart contest winner, an ACFW Genesis contest winner, and a Georgia Romance Writers Maggie Award for Excellence winner. She lives with her husband and three children in Georgia. Find her online at www.kristiannhunter.com.

If you enjoyed *An Elegant Façade*, you may also like...

Lady Miranda Hawthorne secretly longs to be bold. But she is mortified when her brother's new valet mistakenly mails her private thoughts to a duke she's never met—until he responds. As she sorts out her feelings for two men, she uncovers secrets that will put more than her heart at risk.

A Noble Masquerade by Kristi Ann Hunter
HAWTHORNE HOUSE, kristiannhunter.com

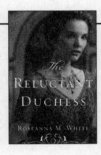

After a shocking attack, Rowena Kinnaird is desperate to escape her family and her ex-fiancé. She finds an unexpected protector in the Duke of Nottingham, but will she ever be able to trust him—let alone fall in love—when his custody of the Fire Eyes jewels endangers her once more?

The Reluctant Duchess by Roseanna M. White
LADIES OF THE MANOR, roseannamwhite.com

When disaster ruins Charlotte Ward's attempt to restart a London acting career, her estranged daughter Rosalind moves her to a quiet village where she can recover privately. There, Rosalind gets a second chance at romance, and mother and daughter reconnect—until Charlotte's troubles catch up to her.

A Haven on Orchard Lane by Lawana Blackwell

More Fiction From Bethany House

After the man she loves abruptly sails for Italy, Sophie Dupont's future is in jeopardy. Wesley left her in dire straits, and she has nowhere to turn—until Captain Stephen Overtree comes looking for his wayward brother. He offers her a solution, but can it truly be that simple?

The Painter's Daughter by Julie Klassen
julieklassen.com

At Irish Meadows horse farm, two sisters struggle to reconcile their dreams with their father's demanding marriage expectations. Brianna longs to attend college, while Colleen is happy to marry, as long as the man meets *her* standards. Will they find the courage to follow their hearts?

Irish Meadows by Susan Anne Mason
COURAGE TO DREAM #1
susanannemason.com

In Scotland's Shetland Islands, a clan patriarch has died, and a dispute over the inheritance has frozen an entire community's assets. When a letter from the estate's solicitor finds American Loni Ford, she is stunned. Orphaned as a child, Loni has always wanted a link to her roots. She sets out on a journey of discovery, but is this dream too good to be true?

The Inheritance by Michael Phillips
SECRETS OF THE SHETLANDS #1